In the Shadow of Evil

Center Point
Large Print

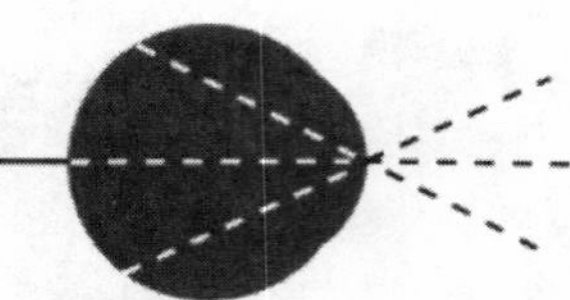

In the Shadow of Evil

ROBIN CAROLL

CENTER POINT PUBLISHING
THORNDIKE, MAINE

This Center Point Large Print edition
is published in the year 2011 by arrangement with
B&H Publishing Group.

The text of this Large Print edition is unabridged.
In other aspects, this book may vary from the original edition.
Printed in the United States of America on permanent paper.
Set in 16-point Times New Roman type.

ISBN: 978-1-61173-054-8

Library of Congress Cataloging-in-Publication Data

Caroll, Robin.
In the shadow of evil / Robin Caroll.
p. cm.
ISBN 978-1-61173-054-8 (lib. bdg. : alk. paper)
1. Police—Fiction. 2. Homicide investigation—Fiction.
3. Construction industry—Fiction. 4. Louisiana—Fiction.
5. Large type books. I. Title.
PS3603.A7673I52 2011
813′.6—dc22

2011005385

For Trace

Because we've been friends
of the heart forever . . .
You love me in spite of
knowing all my faults . . .
You're my harshest critic and
my loudest cheerleader . . .
And you're still the best
partner in crime I've ever had.

ACKNOWLEDGMENTS

I'M ALWAYS SO BLOWN away by the amazing team of talented and hardworking people who come together on my books to bring the project to publication. Everyone I've been blessed to work with at B&H Publishing inspire me with their gifts. My most heartfelt thanks to the entire group—sales-team members, marketing, art department, media, and administrators, but especially those I'm honored to work with closely: Karen Ball, not only the editorial driving force behind the Pure Enjoyment line, but also a woman with a heart for God who inspires me; Julie Gwinn, marketing guru extraordinaire who has such vision and energy that it simply amazes me . . . and humbles me; Jeff Godby, über talented art designer who takes the essence of what my book is about and brings it to living color on the book cover; Greg Pope, the whiz whose talent brings me to tears to see his interpretation of my story in the design of my book trailers; Haverly Robbe, phenomenal promotions and marketing assistant who works tirelessly behind the scenes on the fiction line to ensure we authors get first-class treatment; and Kim Stanford, managing editor, Product Development, whose hard work ensures my book is in stellar condition prior to going to print, and that's just a part of what she does. For everyone at B&H, thank you for being part of my publishing "family." I truly appreciate each and every one of you extending your talents and skills on my behalf.

My very wise mentor once told me that a book is nothing more than words on a page until someone reads it and interacts with the characters and story. I'm beyond blessed to have the honor of working with genius editor Julee Schwarzburg, who does just that—steps into my characters to make them richer, the plot better . . . all with grace and talent. Thank you so much for all your hard work and sharing your wisdom with me to make my book the best it can be.

Colossal thanks to Pam Hillman, who gave me the story idea for this book and sat on the phone with me for hours brainstorming it. Not only a visionary plotter and talented writer in your own right, you're also a dear friend. Special thanks to Cara Putman for helping me when I hit the wall in the plot and to Cheryl Wyatt for talking me through some seriously rough patches. And thanks to Rachel Hauck, for talking me through the idea of the final twist in the book. It ROCKS and I wouldn't have even gone there had Rach not made such stellar suggestions.

I owe a huge amount of gratitude to several medical professionals who answered my complicated and detailed questions to make my plot work: neighbor extraordinaire and host (with his wife Malinda) of awesome Halloween parties, Dr. Skipper Bertrand; author and fellow ACFW member, Dr. Richard Mabry; talented writer and fellow ACFW member, Dr. Ronda Wells; and staff members of the CDC. No way could I have written the medical plot intricacies without your help. Thank you for sharing your knowledge with me.

So many law enforcement professionals put their lives on the line each and every day. I hope I portrayed their dedication and bravery in this story. Enormous thanks to Mike Byrne, commander, Criminal Investigation Division, Calcasieu Parish Sheriff's Office, who not only answered my many, many off-the-wall questions regarding titles, procedures, and policies, but also provided me with a virtual map of the office. Thank you so much for taking the time to never tire of responding to my inquiries.

Special thanks to certain NARI (National Association of Remodeling Industry) staff who answered my random questions regarding the CotY Awards: Gwen Biasi, Mary Harris, Tracy Wright, and Nikki Golden. To learn more about NARI and the CotY Awards, visit their Web site at www.nari.org.

My most sincere thanks to my critique partners: Ronie Kendig, Dineen Miller, Sara Mills, and Heather Diane Tipton. With this novel, I greatly appreciated the quick turnarounds of the chapters and your amazing insight. I love y'all and am so thankful to have you in my life, not only as my CPs, but dear friends as well.

I owe a huge thanks to my mentor and friend Colleen Coble, who never fails to encourage me every single time we talk and e-mail. Love you!

Special thanks to fellow authors who allowed me to vent, celebrate, and/or scream: Margaret Daley, Jim Rubart, and Camy Tang.

Huge thanks to one of the most respected agents in the industry, my agent, Steve Laube. You always know the right thing to say, even if I don't want to hear it but need to.

Every author needs first readers who point out inconsistencies and pose the questions that need to be asked. Special thanks to mine: Lisa Burroughs, Krystina Harden, and Tracey Justice.

Enormous gratitude to my extended family whose support and encouragement keeps me going on the hard days: Mom and Papa, BB and Robert, Bek and Krys, Bubba and Lisa, Brandon, Rachel, Johnny and Elizabeth, Shawn, Julie and Dan, Shannon, Meghan, Scotty and Jan, and Bob and Linda. And especially to my Aunt Millicent, my "biggest fan."

My most heartfelt thanks to my girls: Emily Carol, Remington Case, and Isabella Co-Ceaux. Without you three, my life would not be complete. I love you so much.

To the newest blessing in my life, grandson Benton Alexander—your smile lights up my life. Gran loves you.

To my husband and soul mate, Case. Every day, you give me a reason to get up and do what I do. I couldn't chase my dreams without your love, support, and encouragement. And your awesome input and suggestions. I love and adore you.

Finally, all glory to my Lord and Savior, Jesus Christ. *I can do all things through Him who gives me strength.*

In the Shadow of Evil

“There is no dark place, no deep shadow,
where evildoers can hide.”

JOB 34:22

PROLOGUE

Eighteen Years Ago

WHAT A NIGHT!

Maddox turned into the residential area and glanced at the digital display on the car's dash—12:28. *Great, late for curfew.* He smiled. Being late was worth it when he'd had a hot date with Julie Cordon. Man, the girl was something else. Beautiful, sexy, and funny. Just being with her made him feel special. Made him forget lots of things, including time.

He was seventeen and shouldn't have a curfew anyway. A senior in high school and he had to be home by midnight? All his pop's doing.

Tyson Bishop . . . Mr. Air Force man, determined to force the entire family to live by rules and regulations.

But his dad was over foreign soil right now, jumping out of perfectly good airplanes. His mom understood better, wasn't quite the stickler about curfews like his dad. Good thing too. Maddox was almost thirty minutes late tonight. Pop would blow his top and ground him for at least a month. Probably take away his car. But not Mom. She'd just caution him to pay closer attention to the time. Launch into the whole spiel about responsibility and accountability. He could recite it from memory.

Maddox whipped into the driveway and pressed the garage-door opener. The light from the kitchen door spilled into the garage. Mom would be up . . . waiting. He should've called.

But being around Julie was like being caught in a time warp. Even the car's interior held her smell. Light, flowery . . . teasing and tempting.

He killed the engine and jogged up the steps, slipping his charming smile into place. His mom had never been able to stay mad or disappointed when he flashed his dimples at her. He'd promise to mow the grass tomorrow before Pop got home, and she'd forget all about his tardiness.

He shut the garage door behind him and entered the kitchen. "Mom? I'm home." The hint of roast lingered in the air.

The house was as silent as a tomb.

Odd. She would normally be on her feet to meet him.

He passed the kitchen's butcher-block island and continued into the living room. A soft light filled the space beside her reading chair, but no sign of her.

"Mom?"

Maddox backtracked to the kitchen. Maybe she was in the downstairs bathroom.

"Hello?" His voice rose an octave as his pulse

hammered. The bathroom door was wide open, the room dark.

Where was she?

His steps faltered as he pressed into the kitchen again. The back door stood open, the glass pane closest to the knob—shattered. His heart jumped into his throat.

"Mom!"

Using the agility that had garnered him the wide receiver position on the varsity football team, Maddox flew down the hall toward his parents' bedroom. He pushed open the door with shaking hands.

His mother lay sprawled on the floor, a pool of blood staining the carpet around her. A knife stuck from her heart, her face pale against the dark red spilling from her chest. A metallic odor permeated the room.

What? He blinked repeatedly, his mind not processing what his eyes saw. Then . . . he did. And nearly vomited.

He raced to her side and lifted her head into his lap. "Mom." Tears backed up in his eyes as he smoothed her hair.

"Mad-dy," she croaked.

He grabbed the phone from the nightstand, the base landing on the floor with a resounding thud. He grabbed the receiver and punched in 9-1-1.

"Hang on, Mom. I'm calling for help." Every nerve in his body stood at high alert.

"Too. Late." Her face grimaced into a snarl-smile. A gurgling sound seeped from between her lips. Her body went slack in his arms.

"9-1-1, what is the nature of your emergency?"

"My mother. She's been stabbed."

ONE

"It is possible to provide security against other ills, but as far as death is concerned, we men live in a city without walls."
—EPICURUS

THE WICKED DRUG HELD him hostage in its merciless grip. Crack turned his eyes red and wild, his face stark. He brandished the knife, stabbing the air in jerky motions. Jittery.

Dangerous.

Layla stood still as the stone wall beside her sister, Alana, her attention never shifting from the young man who ranted and paced the gazebo, a mere twenty feet in front of them. Where were Ralph and Cody? Shouldn't they have arrived to contain him by now?

"Gavin, just calm down." Alana's voice hitched.

"Y'all are the ones excited." His eyes darted back and forth between Alana and Layla like he was watching a tennis match. "I need space, dude."

The January wind came across the lake and cut through the grounds of Second Chances retreat. Layla shivered in her hoodie. All the recent rains that had brought a screeching halt to Layla's business left the ground saturated and put a dampness in the cutting wind.

Alana glanced over her shoulder, then took a slow step toward Gavin.

Layla grabbed Alana's arm, holding her in place. What was her sister thinking? With Alana's slight build, blonde hair cut in a short pixie, and big, blue eyes, she looked more like Tinker Bell than someone equipped to handle a drug-induced, deranged kid wielding a hunting knife.

Alana shook off Layla's grip, then inched toward the gazebo. "Gavin, look at me. Look at me." Her voice barely wavered.

His stare snagged on her face.

"I'm calm. Only Layla's with me. We're calm."

"Stop boxing me in." His gaze flitted back and forth again. "Just back off. Leave me alone." He waved the knife with a jumpy hand.

Layla moved beside her sister. No way would she allow Alana to get within striking distance of this hyped-up, armed kid. No telling what could happen with the drug in control. *Lord, please watch over her. Us. Send Cody and Ralph quickly.*

But Alana moved away from Layla. "Gavin, no

one's trapping you. I'm trying to help. You know that."

"Right." He snorted and teetered backward. "Just go away."

From the corner of her eye, Layla caught a shadow of a figure. Cody crept to the gazebo. Ralph crouched behind him, a syringe in his hand.

Alana froze. "Okay. Okay." She took a step back and moved alongside Layla.

He stopped pacing and glared at them. The leeriness came through loud and clear in his body language. He pointed the knife in Alana's direction.

Layla wrapped her hand around Alana's. She tugged her sister back a foot, then another, and another—never turning away from the strung-out kid.

Still glaring and holding the knife, he inched to the stairs.

The interns lunged from the shadows as he stepped. Grabbing Gavin in a choke hold, Cody restrained him while Ralph slipped the needle into Gavin's arm and lowered the plunger on the syringe. The kid bucked and thrashed, then went limp in Cody's arms. The knife clattered to the wood floor of the gazebo.

Layla remembered to breathe. *Thank You, Lord.*

Alana dropped her hand and approached the gazebo. "Thanks, guys." She squatted beside

Gavin. Her hand didn't tremble as she stroked the hair off his forehead. "He was doing so well. Five weeks . . . all gone now." She shook her head. "What a waste."

Cody and Ralph hoisted him between them. "We'll take care of him, Ms. Alana." They shuffled along the stone path across the retreat grounds, heading to the main cabin.

Alana stood and popped her hands on her slight hips. Her brow furrowed as she sighed. "I'll have to call his probation officer. He won't take this lightly."

Once again Alana would carry all the world's burdens on her own shoulders. Layla met Alana's intense expression and concentrated on keeping her tone neutral. "Hey, it's not your fault he chose to get high." She nudged her sister. "You can't be responsible for someone else's bad decisions."

Alana lifted her chin. "No, but I'm going to find out where he got the crack. He hasn't left the grounds except to work. I'm going to the big house to check his schedule." She marched away, her steps punctuating her irritation, just as she'd done since her teens.

Layla smiled at her sister's retreating back and followed at a slower pace. The big house. She'd never get used to calling the home her family had once shared *the big house,* even though she had signed the house and property over to her sister three years ago. It was no longer a family residence but the main office of Second Chances. Oh, Alana still lived in the second-floor loft, but the downstairs was now the retreat's community kitchen, dining, and living room.

Retreat. How about a drug rehabilitation center? That's what Second Chances really was. Set along the bayou in Eternal Springs, Louisiana, it had cabins instead of cells and therapy sessions called group sharing. But it was rehab all the same.

Layla trudged behind her sister, stuffing her hands into the front pocket of the hoodie. The wind whistled through the cypress trees and swayed the Spanish moss. A hint of fishy odor drifted over the vast acreage.

A shiver stuttered down Layla's spine.

She paused, staring across the bayou. While she couldn't detect any movement out of the ordinary, she couldn't stop the feeling that someone watched her.

She shook her head and continued behind Alana. Gavin's behavior must've spooked her more than she'd thought. But she couldn't have ignored Alana's panicked call if she'd wanted. Somebody had to look out for Alana, and since their father's passing and their mother's move into the hospital, the responsibility fell to Layla. Sure, Cameron was in the picture now as Alana's fiancé, but still . . .

When Layla found her sister, Alana was in the office, perusing a spreadsheet sprawled over the desk.

"He didn't even have a weekend privilege." Alana stabbed her fingers through her hair. "So he had to have gotten the crack here." No mistaking her distress at the possibility of drugs being on the retreat's property. It defied everything the retreat stood for.

What Alana stood for.

Layla perched on the edge of the desk. "Has he worked any? Maybe he had someone bring him the drug on-site." She hated the thought of someone having drugs on any construction site as much as Alana hated the possibility that drugs were at Second Chances.

Crossing her arms over her chest, Alana stared out the window. "How could he have contacted anyone? He hasn't been given phone privileges. He only received his last work assignment on Monday."

Four days ago.

If he didn't have privileges last weekend, only got his work assignment on Monday afternoon and it was now Friday, then by process of elimination, he had to have gotten the crack on a construction site. It'd been raining for the last three weeks, so all sites were concentrating on indoor projects.

Layla shifted to scan the work assignments. "He was with Bob every day this week?"

"Yep. Gavin wanted to learn plumbing as his trade."

Splinters! Bob? No way. Bob Johnson was one of the best plumbers in the parish. He was Layla's favorite, by far. She used him more than the other three local plumbers combined. To think there was a chance that drugs would be on one of his jobs . . .

"Where's Bob been working this week?"

Alana's brows bunched as she read. "The Thompson repairs."

Old Ike Thompson had allowed his nineteen-year-old son to live in his rental house. Big mistake. When the kid left two weeks ago, the house had been trashed. Holes in the Sheetrock. Burned places in the floor. Plumbing destroyed. And that was just the bottom floor. A sad situation for Ike but an opportunity for Alana.

"You know, Gavin could've found some drugs at the site. Ike's kid was into partying hard, so he might've left some drugs behind. Gavin might have stumbled upon them."

"Maybe. But in my experience, users don't normally leave a stash behind when they split."

"But it's not beyond the realm of possibility. I mean, Ike's kid snuck out of town in the middle of the night. For whatever reason, he left in a hurry. Maybe he was too rushed to get everything."

Alana chewed her bottom lip. "Could be."

"Look," Layla slipped off the desk, "I'll run by Bob's on my way home. Talk with him and see what he says about Gavin."

"I'd appreciate that. It would be best to have as much information as I can before I call his probation officer. I'll call Fred in." Fred was Alana's assistant director. Sweet man who adored Alana.

Layla dug into her jeans pocket for her truck keys. "I'll run there now and talk to Bob."

"Call me as soon as you can." Alana touched Layla's arm. "Thanks. I just can't believe this happened."

"It'll be okay." Layla could only pray that was true.

THIS MEETING WAS GOING to end badly. Not so much for him, but for Dennis.

Dennis just didn't know it. Yet.

Night stole over Eternal Springs, Louisiana. The January wind gusted, whistling around the house. A heavy mist cloaked the parish, a remnant of the gully washers they'd received over the last several weeks.

He leaned against the interior wall of the house and lit a cigarette. Just completed two months ago, the Hope-for-Homes house would welcome its new owners in a matter of weeks. He had to move fast to destroy the evidence and keep his name clear. Although no one suspected him of anything less than stellar quality, he couldn't take the chance. Not with what he had riding on his reputation.

But Dennis had to be taken care of first.

"You shouldn't smoke in here. The smell lingers." Dennis cracked open the front door. The security light at the end of the cul-de-sac spilled into the room. "Someone will know somebody was here that wasn't supposed to be."

He cut Dennis off by tossing the cigarette in the front yard. "There. Happy now?"

Dennis shot him a hard stare in the dim lantern light. "Hardly."

He sighed and quietly moved to the bar, standing in front of the shelf holding the gun he'd placed there before Dennis arrived. The gun he'd stolen from Dennis's car two days ago. The shadows would work in his favor. "What's your problem now, LeJeune?"

"You know what my problem is. You're trying to cut me out."

"How do you figure?" Just how much did Dennis know?

"I know you've put in bids with the casinos."

Dennis knew more than he had thought. Who had Dennis told? "I have."

"And you have an inside source somewhere because word on the street is that you'll get the job."

"So?"

"So?" Dennis crossed to the other side of the bar, resting his bony palms against the finished granite. "You're not including me."

"How did you hear all this?"

Dennis scraped a thin hand over his face. "That's not important. What matters is you're trying to go solo."

"The boats don't use local inspectors. They bring in their own. Federals." He casually lifted a shoulder. "I don't need you on this one."

Dennis's eyes narrowed as he stroked his shaggy mustache. "After all I've done for you—"

"That you've been paid well for. Let's not pretend you've done anything out of the goodness of your heart. It's always been about the money."

"Same with you."

He spread his hands through the air. "I've made no other claims."

"But the boats are big deals. Really big. We're talking a lot of money to be made. You didn't think I'd let you cut me out, did you?"

Laughing, he lowered his hand to rest on the butt of the gun. "You have nothing to do with this deal."

"What about the others?"

"What others?"

Dennis snorted. "Don't think I haven't noticed what you've been doing these last eight or nine months."

Maybe the old inspector was onto more than just the casino deals. "What's that, LeJeune?"

"All these buildings we fudged on . . . some freaky accidents have happened to them." Dennis's thinning gray hair flew as he shook his head.

He swallowed. "I don't control Mother Nature. A lot of our homes were lost in the hurricanes. A lot of the offices."

"What about the fires? Three, over the last six months. Tell me you didn't burn those down to hide the evidence."

He sucked in air, struggling to keep his composure. Everything he'd fought so hard to achieve could be lost because of this . . . this moron. "Who else have you told about our agreement?"

"No one." Dennis paused, his jaw popping as he ground his teeth. "Yet. We have a nice setup going here."

They did. But he had to go legitimate to get the casino boats deal. They'd check him out thoroughly. He couldn't take a chance on any link between him and certain buildings. He had no other choice but to destroy them.

Like this house.

He sighed. "Bottom line, what do you want?"

"I want my cut, just like always."

"But you aren't going to inspect the boats. No one will find a single problem. Why should I give you a percentage for doing nothing?"

"Because that will keep my mouth closed." Dennis crossed his arms over his chest and cocked out his hip. "About the past. I kept records too you know."

And there it was—the threat. The bluff.

He couldn't allow that. He couldn't allow Dennis to be a loose end.

Dennis had just sealed his own fate.

"Just cut me in on this deal, and we'll go on with business as usual." Dennis shifted and shoved his hand into the pocket of his coat.

He gripped the loaded gun and whipped it from the shelf in one fluid motion. He pointed the barrel at Dennis's chest. Didn't even take a breath before pulling the trigger.

Crack!

A muzzle flash barely registered before Dennis took two steps backward. He staggered. Swayed. His eyes widened for a split second before Dennis slumped. His limp body didn't move once it hit the floor.

He let out the breath he'd been holding. He leveled the gun, shot Dennis in the head just for good measure, then wiped down the gun. Using the corner of a rag, he dropped the gun beside Dennis.

He moved to the garage and retrieved the gallons of gasoline he'd stowed there earlier. Now to kill two birds with one stone, so to speak.

Disposing of the body to remove all evidence and burning down the house with the substandard materials.

Fate couldn't have given him a better gift.

TWO

"If there is no struggle, there is no progress."
—FREDERICK DOUGLASS

HONK! HONK!

Maddox grabbed his badge and gun off the table and headed out into the darkness of night. A dusting of rain covered him as he ducked to the road. He swallowed a yawn and slipped in the passenger seat of the unmarked cruiser.

"Already missing your beauty sleep?" His partner, Houston Wallace, popped gum while steering the car down the street. Even in the wee hours, his partner looked the same as when they'd clocked out at five. Even right down to the untucked, wild Hawaiian-print shirt and stained coat. His thinning, salt-and-pepper hair was kept short, which did nothing to mask the receding hairline. At five foot eleven, Houston was a couple of inches short of Maddox's height. A fact Maddox never let him forget.

"It's three in the morning. Of course I'm missing my sleep." He cocked his gaze to his partner. "Man, being on call bites."

"If you make commander, you won't have to take these early calls." Houston popped his gum again and turned the car onto I-210. "A homicide. Practically right in our backyard."

Maddox's gut tightened. He wanted to make commander, could taste it. A *real* rank, as his father would say. Houston had turned down the promotion a year ago. The new commander was making noise about running for sheriff in one of the little bayou towns in the parish. If the slot opened . . . "Yeah, we'll see."

"It could happen." Houston popped his gum again. "Dispatcher said they'd found a gunshot vic."

"Yeah, that's what he told me too."

Maddox looked down into the mouth of the west fork of the Calcasieu River as they topped the bridge. So high up . . . He forced himself to release the fists he'd balled his hands into and pinched his eyes shut.

Eternity passed. Slowly.

"We're off the bridge."

He opened his eyes. Even though Houston had never teased him about his fear, the heat crept up the back of Maddox's neck. He glanced out the window. They now sped along LA378 into Westlake. "Outside city limits, huh?"

"Yeah. Local FD called dispatch." Houston slowed as they crept off Miller Avenue, leaving the small town in the rearview mirror. "Address is in rural Eternal Springs. Help me look for the road."

"Fire department called it in, huh?" Maddox grabbed latex gloves and a couple of evidence bags from the crime-scene kit and shoved them into his pocket while Houston rattled off the street name. Murky darkness cloaked the area, leaving visibility next to nil. Even as versed as his partner and he were in the parish, Maddox had never heard of the street. Must be a private drive.

Sure enough, Houston slammed on the brakes and took a hard right onto a gravel road that drew them closer to the river.

Flashing lights atop fire trucks welcomed them to the crime scene. Smoke mixed with the falling mist, filling the bayou area. Exterior half walls, charred and smoldering, stood under the bright rigged lights of the fire trucks. No roof remained on the building. Some interior walls had held, but mostly the site was unrecognizable as a house.

The haze shrouded them as they picked their way over stretched fire hoses toward two uniformed officers hovering by what was once the main entrance to the home, talking with the fire chief. The oldest uniform looked up at their approach. "Detectives?"

Houston nodded. "Wallace and Bishop." He hitched the shoulder strap to the crime-scene bag higher and held out his hand.

The older man shook it. “I’m Assistant Chief Rex Carson and this is Officer Thibodeaux.”

“Whatcha got?” Maddox rested his hand on the butt of his gun. A natural position for him after six years of wearing the gold badge for the Calcasieu Parish sheriff’s office.

The fire chief interrupted. “Found a body in the living room when we got the fire contained. Thought maybe it was smoke inhalation, then we saw the big hole in the remains of the chest and found a charred handgun beside the body.”

Sounded like homicide to Maddox. Adrenaline leaned him in closer to the fireman. This was what he lived for. Cases just like this. One dead body and a whole lot of questions. “The owner of the house?”

Carson shook his head. “Owner hasn’t moved in yet.”

“Any ID on the body?” Houston asked.

“Once we figured it was a murder, we didn’t want to touch the body.” The fire chief removed his hat, smoothed down his dark hair, then plopped the headgear back down. “Prelim looks like it was arson, which makes sense if someone shot somebody, then wanted to destroy the evidence.”

Carson picked up the details. “As soon as we confirmed it looked like a homicide, we called Chief Samuels who made the decision to call you.”

Maddox remembered Chief Ethan Samuels

from the homicides he'd assisted Officer Lincoln Vailes with several months ago. "Anybody have a clue who the vic is?"

Thibodeaux finally spoke. "No, sir."

Hopefully the rain wouldn't destroy any crucial evidence. Well, what the fire hadn't obliterated. "Okay, we'll take it from here." Maddox glanced at the loafers he'd slipped on. They'd be ruined as soon as he entered the scene.

Houston chuckled and almost choked on his gum.

Maddox took in his partner's dirty sneakers with a grimace. "Would serve you right to choke to death."

Laughing louder, Houston followed the chief into the charred remains of what was once a house. Maddox trailed at a slower rate, pulling on latex gloves as he walked. If he took care with where he stepped, maybe he could salvage the shoes from being a total loss.

But as soon as he saw the sprawled body, all other thoughts fled. He circled the body, committing every detail to memory, as Houston whipped out his notebook and began scribbling.

Both men squatted. Maddox cocked his head to study the charred handgun from a better angle. "Revolver. Smith & Wesson?"

"Or Taurus."

Maddox glanced at Carson who'd come in behind them. "Coroner been called?"

"On his way."

Houston withdrew the digital camera from the crime-scene kit and took shots. He shifted, getting pictures of the body and crime scene from every angle.

Leaving the body, Maddox turned back to the front yard. He scanned the ground around the entry and walkway. Even with the soggy terrain, they wouldn't be able to gather any footprint casts—too many firemen had tracked over the area. Somebody knew what he was doing.

Headlights cut through the mist and smoke still wisping in the dark. The coroner's wagon sloshed into the dirt driveway.

Maddox moved from the threshold. A spot of white against the red mud beside the walkway caught his attention. He squatted, inspecting the area. A cigarette butt, barely smoked, sat pressed into the mud. He withdrew an evidence bag from his coat pocket, bagged and tagged the butt before shoving it into his pocket, then stepped forward to greet K. C. Casteel.

The fifty-something coroner made his way to Maddox, his assistant on his heels. "Hey, Bishop. How's it going?" He jabbed glasses up the bridge of his nose.

"Got new specs, huh, Doc?"

Casteel shot him a wary look. "Doctor said I need them now." He grunted and toed a rock. "Don't know why. I can see just fine without 'em."

Maddox stifled a grin. "It's hard getting old, ain't it?"

"Speak for yourself." He narrowed his eyes for a moment, then grinned. "So, where's your body?"

Leading the way, Maddox filled Casteel in on what they knew. As soon as they approached the body, the coroner and his assistant slipped on their gloves and began inspecting. "Definitely a gunshot wound to the chest." Casteel turned the skull. "And in the head."

Maddox bent over his shoulder. "I missed that." But now that Casteel had pointed it out, Maddox could clearly see it.

"Don't surprise me," Casteel muttered.

"Can you give us an estimate of time of death?" Houston asked.

The coroner straightened and shook his head. "Burned like that? Not even a guess right now. I'll see what I can uncover once I get Mr. Doe here back to my slab."

Carson grinned at him. "How are you likin' your updated digs?" Months ago funding had come through for the coroner's office to get a total overhaul. While the renovations were conducted, the coroner had to temporarily move to the only area facility that had an adequate setup—Eternal Springs. Just two weeks ago Casteel and his crew were able to return to their updated space in Lake Charles.

"Lovin' it. Got all the newest equipment."

"How long before you'll be able to get to our vic?" Maddox asked.

Casteel pushed his slipping glasses higher up his nose. "I'll get on him Monday."

Maddox nodded. "I'd appreciate that."

The coroner and his assistant began their process of removing the body. Maddox turned back to Houston. "Find anything else?"

Houston shook his head. "Just the gun. You?"

Maddox pulled the evidence bag from his pocket and waved it. "Found this out front."

"Cigarette butt?"

Maddox shrugged and slipped the bag into the scene kit Houston carried. "Might be nothing but could be something."

"Never know at this stage in the investigation."

And that's just what they'd walked into—a full-blown investigation. Maddox's curiosity kicked into gear.

Maybe this was just what he needed to get in line for the commander position.

SHE'D WON THE REGIONAL award!

Layla's hand holding the letter trembled. After everything—her hard work . . . clawing her way to the top despite the men's attitudes toward her—finally, she was up for national recognition. The one that would show the world that she was a great contractor, just as her father had been.

Contractor of the Year. Even on a regional level, it was an honor. But a national win would mean so much more.

At least to her.

She swallowed back the emotion and glanced around her kitchen. All of her father's skills passed down to her, which she'd used to design her house. Her home. She smiled at the plaque hanging over the breakfast bar. Scripture of 1 Corinthians 1:9, her father's favorite.

> "God, who has called you into fellowship with his Son Jesus Christ our Lord, is faithful."

God was faithful. She'd gotten recognition for her ability. True joy she hadn't felt since before her father had died filled her chest until she thought it'd burst.

"Layla?" The front door slammed. "Where are you?"

Moving from the kitchen counter, Layla called out to her sister. "In here." She rushed to meet Alana in the foyer, waving the letter. "Guess what!"

Her sister's frown deepened. "What?"

Layla laughed and handed the letter to Alana. "Read for yourself." She twirled around on the hardwoods, dancing in the light flooding through the panes in the front door. Even the rain had disappeared, making the day all the more celebratory. "It came in the mail yesterday, but after meeting with Bob and then calling you, I didn't even check the mail, so I opened it this morning. I can't believe it!"

Alana's eyes widened and moisture pooled. "Oh my. You've won. Congratulations. You deserve it." She grabbed Layla in a hug and squeezed.

"It's the regional, but that means I'm under consideration for a national. Can you believe it?"

"I'm so happy for you. This is wonderful." Alana laid the letter on the entry table and hugged her again. "Daddy would be so proud." Her voice cracked.

Layla's eyes filled with tears and her throat clogged. Only her sister knew exactly how much this meant to her. Sure, recipients of the CotY awards got great promotion out of the contest. Got new clients because of the recognition. But Layla wanted it for a different reason.

To honor her father's memory.

She hugged Alana again, then lifted the letter. It still felt so surreal. "I think I'm going to get it framed."

"I don't blame you." Alana laughed, but it didn't carry her usual chipper tone.

Something wasn't right.

Layla glanced at the clock—8:10—then studied her sister. "So, why'd you come by this morning? It's a bit early for you to be away from the center."

"You haven't heard?" The frown marred her sister's delicate features again. "Fred called me first thing this morning."

"Heard what?"

"Apparently not." Alana moved to the living room. She flipped throw pillows from the couch and recliner. "Where's your remote?"

Layla grabbed the remote from the top of the television and handed it to her sister. "What's going on?"

Alana turned on the TV, set it to the local news channel, then upped the volume. "Hang on, they'll be running it again in a minute. They've been covering it all morning." She glanced at Layla and shook her head. "How can you not watch the news?"

"Doesn't interest me. Anything really important, I hear from you." She smiled, but her sister didn't return the gesture.

Must be serious if Alana was in a sour mood on the wings of the award notification.

"Here it is." Alana perched on the arm of the couch.

Layla sunk to the recliner while the reporter stood in front of a burned house. Her mind stuttered and her heart caught as the news fed her more information. Nausea rose, searing the back of her throat. "Hope for Homes? *Our* house?"

Alana flipped off the television and nodded. "Burned. And they found a body inside."

"But the owners haven't moved in yet."

"Right."

So whose body was inside?

THREE

"High achievement always takes place in the framework of high expectation."
—CHARLES KETTERING

HE STARED AT THE caller ID. That was quick.

Maddox flipped open his cell and leaned back in the tattered chair of his desk at the Criminal Investigations Division. "Hey, sweetie."

"Don't *sweetie* me, Maddox Bishop." Megan's voice didn't carry a trace of irritation. "This is gonna cost you."

He grinned as he pictured Megan's blonde hair, blue eyes, and pouty lips. "I know, I know. Supper at a five-star restaurant of your choosing."

"It *is* a Saturday, you know. Maybe I should make you spring for a movie too." Her flirting came across the phone line as thick as her Southern drawl.

He chuckled. "If you're good, I might even buy you a nightcap."

"Oh, Bishop, you *know* I'm good."

Maybe it'd been a mistake to call Megan. After all, he'd stopped seeing her when she crossed that line . . . when she'd gotten that look in her eyes. The look that said she wanted more. Of the relationship. Of him. He could never let that happen. Not with Megan.

Not with anyone.

"What'd you find out?" He fought to keep the sternness out of his words.

She laughed, full and throaty. "You always were good at evasion."

"Megan . . ."

"Stop sweating, Bishop. I'm not holding out for a ring or anything. I got all the details you wanted. And more."

He heard the hurt in her voice but forgot all about the sweating of his palms as he grabbed a pen and sat forward, hovering over a legal pad. "Ready."

"I think it'd be easier to fax it. Your number still the same?"

"Yeah." Why wouldn't she just tell him who owned the house? "What's up?"

"This one's complicated. You'll see. I'm shooting it to you now."

The fax machine in the space he shared with Houston hummed to life.

"It's coming through." He spun to face the office machine.

"Good. I'm outta here. Believe it or not, I have

better things to do with my Saturday than come into the office to do you a favor."

The first page dropped into the slot.

"Thanks, Megan. I really appreciate this."

"Yeah, yeah. Like I haven't heard that before. You still owe me. I won't let you slip out of it."

"I'll call you as soon as I get a breather on the case."

"Bye, Bishop."

He shut the cell and reached for the three pages the fax already spit out. His stomach tightened as he scanned, then read the information. The crime scene had been a Hope for Homes? That made no sense. Who would want to burn down a charity house?

He grabbed the rest of the pages and read faster than his mind could process the information. Recipient of the home was to be one Sally Caldwell, single mother of four children all under the age of eight. Worked as a waitress at the local diner. Nothing about her indicated any criminal history. But Maddox would definitely interview her today.

His cell phone chirped, causing him to spin the chair. He flipped open the phone. "Bishop."

"Hey, Maddox. How ya doing?"

Maddox smiled at the usual greeting of "Uncle" George Vella. "Hey, yourself. What's up?"

"I'm heading to the woods this evening for a

hunt in the morning. Wondered if you wanted to tag along."

Oh, man . . . what he wouldn't give to go. He hadn't been able to bag a buck all season. And hunting with George was always a good time. "Camping out?"

"Yeah. Near Scotty's place. You interested?"

Maddox glanced at the fax sitting in front of him. Wasn't like he could get much done on a weekend anyway.

"Maddox?" Something in George's voice . . . a hesitation . . . a question . . .

"Who all's going?"

"Just a couple of us old-timers. And you, I hope."

Maddox ground out a sigh. "Is Pop going?"

"Well, Tyson ain't said for sure yet."

Shaking his head, Maddox worked to keep his temper in check. Wasn't George's fault—he was such a peacemaker that he only wanted the rift between father and son to be mended. But he couldn't understand. George could never grasp the enormity of blame Tyson had dumped on Maddox. Even though *Pop* was the one to blame.

"Come on, Maddox. It'll be fun."

Fun? With Tyson involved? Not hardly. The man never missed an opportunity to harp on Maddox and every fault he ever had. "I can't. Had a homicide land in my lap early this morning."

"It's the weekend."

Maddox forced a chuckle. "Yeah, tell that to the murderers. They don't exactly take nights and weekends off."

"And you're positioning yourself for the promotion."

This time Maddox's chuckle was sincere. "There's always that."

"I understand, but I'll miss you."

And he'd miss hanging out with George. Maddox swallowed. "We'll do it another time."

"Hunting season's almost over."

"Maybe next weekend?"

"I'll call you."

"Good luck, George. Get a twelve-point for me."

George laughed and then the line went dead. Maddox shut the phone and shoved it into his belt clip. He ignored the unnamed emotion rising in his chest as he turned his attention back to the fax.

He flipped to the next page. Construction on the house had been completed two months ago. By—he turned the page to find the information he sought—Taylor Construction. Maddox lifted his pen and jotted himself a note to pull records on the company.

He finished reading the pages. Still didn't understand why Megan thought this was complicated and felt he needed to see this himself. Made no sense.

And then he saw the last line of the notes.

> Contractor utilized licensed professionals who employed Second Chances residents on the work-release program.

He didn't know what Second Chances was, but he sure didn't like the sound of *work-release* program.

Obviously Megan had known what it was. He opened his cell and dialed her number. It rang twice before going to voice mail. Maddox shut the phone without leaving a message.

Footsteps in the hall drew his attention.

Houston ambled into their shared space and plopped onto the edge of the desk. "Thought I'd find you here."

Maddox leaned back and propped his feet up on his desk. "Question is, what're *you* doing here?"

"Boys are headed to the hunting lease with their buddies, and Margie's pulling a double shift at the hospital."

Maddox laughed. "And she left you a honey-do list you don't wanna do?"

Houston had the decency to blush. "Hey, I'm here to work the case. Can't you show a little appreciation?"

"Something going on at the hospital?" Houston's wife was an RN.

"Margie said there's a baby they admitted last night she's all worried about. Respiratory stuff.

Doesn't know if the kid's gonna make it."

"That's sad." Little kids made him nervous—they were a commitment to a woman. One woman. Maddox handed his partner the papers on the property. "Check out the background on the house. It was one of the Hope for Homes."

"Ouch." Houston scanned the pages as he swung his foot back and forth. When he was finished, he set the stack of papers on Maddox's desk. "Dare I ask where you got this?"

"I have a friend in the courthouse."

"Who was willing to go in on a Saturday morning to look this up for you?" Houston slipped a piece of gum between his lips.

Heat raced up the back of his neck. "A good friend."

Houston wasn't fooled. "A female friend?"

Why did his partner constantly bring up or insinuate about Maddox's lack of desire to find a nice lady and settle down? If only he could tell Houston he'd never, ever, allow a woman to steal his heart and let himself be weakened. Not again. Not after what happened to his mother.

Talk about the pathway to destruction.

But Maddox had learned long ago how to distract his partner. "Hey, why don't you head home and get the laundry done for Margie?"

"Touché." Houston stood, popping his gum. "Why don't we go visit Ms. Caldwell instead?"

Maddox shoved to his feet as well and reached for his coat from the back of his chair. "We haven't left yet?"

LAYLA SHUCKED OFF HER coat, grabbed files from the wooden cabinet, and spread them over her desk.

Bright sunlight, a shock after weeks of nothing but rain, burst through the windows of Taylor Construction. The wind whistled outside the brick building. Most construction companies officed up in double-wides or prefabs but not Layla. Her father had taught her that a craftsman's home and office was his best advertising. So when she'd opened her own business, she made sure she built an office building her father would be proud of.

"Could we turn up the heat a little?" Alana shivered. "It's freezing in here."

Sighing, Layla flipped on the heat on the thermostat. "It's Saturday. Not like we're normally in here on a weekend. Not in this season anyway." She spun back to the desk and knocked over a montage picture frame in her haste. It clattered to the tile floor.

Alana retrieved it, glancing at the photos. "Acrylic instead of glass, smart idea." She tapped her fingernails on the frame. "You know, you really should update these pictures. You still have ones with Randy in here."

Oh, splinters. Layla stilled. She couldn't explain that she'd deliberately left those pictures in the montage. To remind her that no matter how handsome and genuine someone appeared, he always had an ulterior motive. She couldn't let herself lose focus of what was important.

Ever.

She took the frame from Alana, shoved it in the top right drawer, then hunched over the desk, scanning the papers.

All the files, contracts, and details of the Hope-for-Homes project.

"I didn't mean to upset you," Alana whispered.

"You didn't." She wasn't upset. Well, not really. It was more like she'd recognized the loss of ever getting a happily ever after in the love department. She was more grieving than upset.

"I'm really proud of you for staying with the competitive dancing after . . . well, after you and Randy split up."

Layla smiled, belying the pain. "I enjoy it. Even more without him." She chuckled. "I like having partners who are interested in good moves on the floor without the romantic entanglement."

But sometimes, late at night when Layla was alone, she did think about men and romance. About being alone.

"You know, you really ought to let me fix you up. There's this coworker of Cameron's—"

"No." A geeky software creator nerd? Cameron was great and all, really loved Alana and was good to her, but that just wasn't Layla's cup of tea. No, thanks.

"Well, if you change your mind . . ."

"You'll be the first person to know." Layla winked at her sister, then went back to the stack of files. What kind of man was her cup of tea? She'd thought it was Randy—tall, dark, and handsome. But look how that'd turned out. Now she just didn't know. She wanted someone who appreciated her as a woman. Someone who made her feel safe. Someone who made her feel loved and accepted for who she was.

"I don't know what you're looking for." Alana flipped through the electrician's contract.

Layla breathed a sigh, not wanting to dredge up old wounds right now. "I want to know every single person who worked on the project. Every electrician, plumber, construction worker."

"Why?"

Was her sister really that naive? Layla denied the sigh struggling to escape. "Because someone knew that house was empty. He knew it was complete but hadn't been moved into yet. And the first place to look is the workers. They knew the schedule better than anyone."

Alana handed her the electrician's paperwork. "Isn't this a job for the police?"

"Maybe." Layla set the pages on the pile with

the others, then grabbed the listing of every independent she'd hired for the project.

"Then why aren't you letting them do this?"

Layla made eye contact with her, allowing Alana to see the despair and desperation she felt. "Because *this* is the project I just won the CotY regional award for. And I was site foreman for the job." And if there was a link between the incident and someone she'd contracted, she could lose. Worse, her reputation would be damaged beyond repair.

"Oh, Layla, I'm sorry. I didn't realize—"

"You couldn't have." Layla blew her bangs off her forehead. "Now you see why I need to check everything." She ran her finger down the list of independents.

Electrician: Denny Keys. Carpenters: J. B. Carpentry. Supplier: Y Building Supplies. Plumber . . . Bob Johnson.

Layla's gut clenched, and she snatched Bob's contract. *Please, no. Don't let it be.* But her niggling fear was there in black and white.

Bob had utilized three people from Second Chances.

Coincidence? She didn't believe in them. But Gavin hadn't been at the retreat yet. Still, what were the odds?

"What?" Alana studied her.

"Bob was the contracted plumber."

"So?"

"He used three people from the retreat."

Confusion then understanding then worry crossed over her sister's face. "You like Bob. Trust him. You talked to him yesterday. You said he was outraged at the prospect of drugs being on his site." Alana smoothed down her hair.

"I did. And he was. Someone could be involved in drugs without his knowledge." Layla touched her sister's arm. "You know how addicts hide things."

"There are signs. Physical deterioration. Loss of—"

"I know." Didn't they both know it all too well? Too intimately? How her sister could stand to be around addicts all day after what they'd lived through was beyond her.

"I'm just saying surely someone would have noticed a change."

"Maybe. Unless he didn't know them well."

Alana's eyes narrowed. "Just because three of mine were used, doesn't mean they're involved."

"I didn't say that, Al—"

"Anybody could be involved. You know this program works. You've supported it. Fred and I make sure the psychiatrist says they're ready to work before we consider letting them enter the work-release program."

"I do support it." Layla shook her head. "There might not even be any connection between Bob and whatever crew he used and the murder. I'm just trying to be proactive. Knowledge is power."

"By insinuating the retreat's residents could be involved?" Alana crossed her arms over her chest. "And don't quote *Dadaisms* to me."

"I'm not saying that. Not even implying it. I'm just trying to get a handle on everything."

"It's not even your job."

Layla swallowed hard, forcing herself not to react to her sister's hostility. It was only the fear talking. "I know. But the police will ask, and we'll already have the information prepared."

Alana cocked her head but her stare pierced Layla. "And you need to know."

"I do." She held her breath as her sister chewed her bottom lip.

Finally, Alana sighed. "I do too. If someone from the retreat is even remotely involved, I need to know. If I'm not careful, I could lose funding." She shook her head. "If it's proven the retreat is involved, it could even close me down."

Layla nodded. "So we need to do everything we can to find out the truth. To protect both of us."

FOUR

"A man of courage is also full of faith."
—MARCUS TULLIUS CICERO

ONLY ONE LEFT. JUST one.

He slammed the folder shut. He'd shredded Dennis's files as he took care of the evidence trail. He'd come so far in the past nine months . . . covering up every single lead that could come back to him. Nothing that would draw the attention of the authorities. Nothing that would link them so anyone would get suspicious.

And now he just had one building that could be tracked back to him. But that one was a doozy. He'd have to finesse his way through the last one.

What would be the best way to get rid of it? Not another burning. Couldn't do that right on the heels of this morning.

But with the bids under review and the casino jobs about to be awarded, he'd have to accelerate his schedule.

His phone rang, jarring him from his thoughts. "Hello."

"You're late with my check. Again." Andrea's voice grated against his ear. "I'm sick of this. Don't make me take you back to court. I will, you know."

Yeah, he knew all about his ex-wife's fascination with the legal system. "Sorry, Andy. I'll get the check in the mail Monday."

"I've told you not to call me that."

Right. After their divorce had become final, she'd decided to go by her full name. Not the pet name he'd given her back when they were dating. How easily someone could change.

Like warping from a sweet girl with the softest eyes into a greedy, image-freak woman. Heartless.

"I'd better have it by Wednesday or I'm calling my attorney."

When had her voice turned into a whine? "I'll mail it Monday, just like I said. I don't have control over the postal service."

"Then maybe you should have mailed it sooner. Like when it was actually due."

How could he have loved her so much once? Had he really been that blind?

"And the kids won't be able to spend the weekend with you."

He curled his free hand into a fist. "But it's my weekend," he ground out between clenched teeth.

"Deena and Ellie have a slumber party. They've been looking forward to it for weeks now."

"Then why didn't you offer to switch off with me this weekend?"

“Don’t be difficult. They really want to go. Would you begrudge them that just to get back at me?”

She never understood. He loved his kids . . . wanted to spend time with them. He never wanted to be an absentee father. “Okay. Then it’ll just be Eddie and me. We can go hunting or have a guy’s night.” That sounded good. It’d been a long time since he and his son hung out alone together.

Andrea sighed into the phone. “He has a date.”

“A date?” His son was dating? Wasn’t that something he should’ve been told? “He’s only fifteen. He can’t even drive yet.”

“I’m taking his date and him to the school dance.”

Over his dead body. She’d embarrass Eddie. “I’ll take them.” If Eddie was dating, it was time for him to have *that* conversation with his son.

“He asked *me* to drive them.”

“I’ll be happy to do it.” But he knew she would keep this from him if she could. “If the girls are at a slumber party and I take Eddie, then you’ll still have the weekend free for you.” Hadn’t she complained about his long hours at work, whining that she had no time for herself? She’d griped at him to make more money, then hollered at him for never being home. No pleasing the woman.

"This is important to Eddie. I'm fine with taking him." She sighed again, a long, heavy sigh. "You can get them all weekend after next. No sense messing up *our* schedule."

Typical Andrea, keeping their kids' important things from him.

"I'd rather have them my weekend. Not wanting to mess up *our* schedule and all."

"Don't get smart with me. Technically, you're so far behind on child support I really shouldn't even let you see the kids until you're current."

She held all the cards. What else was new?

But maybe . . . once he got the big bucks from the casino job, he'd hire a top-notch lawyer and take Andrea back to court. Get that absurd child support amount lowered. Or better yet, get joint custody and do away with this every-other-weekend gig.

"The check had better be here by Wednesday. And it'd better not bounce again." She didn't bother to say good-bye before hanging up.

One time. Only once did his check bounce, but she wouldn't let him forget it. Typical Andrea, always focusing on the negative.

He replaced the receiver to its base. The folder sitting on his desk mocked him.

He had one more building to take care of, then it was smooth sailing. He'd be in the clear. He'd have the money to put Andrea in her place. Maybe he'd go for full custody. See how she liked being told when and where she could see the kids.

Still annoyed and disappointed, he glanced at the calendar. Next weekend would actually be perfect to take care of this last detail. He had no plans because he'd expected to have the kids. Everyone in his circle thought he'd have the kids too. Could work in his favor.

He slammed the folder closed. Yes, indeed, fate seemed to smile at destiny and shine on him.

"MAN, *THIS* IS WHERE she's living?" Maddox stared at the government-subsidized temporary housing unit. The shotgun-style house looked to be in desperate need of repair. Paint peeling, loose boards, and tape covering breaks in the window.

Houston shut off the unmarked cruiser's engine. "This is where records show Ms. Sally Caldwell and her kids living for the time being."

"No wonder she got approved for Hope for Homes." Maddox opened the door and stood on the cracked sidewalk.

Maddox fell into step beside Houston and made his way up the rickety stairs. The handrail wobbled under his grip. The place should be condemned.

Houston took a breath, then rapped on the front door. The splintered wood vibrated in the hinges.

Shuffling sounded from the other side of the

hollow door. “Who is it?” a hesitant female asked.

“Sheriff’s department. We need to speak to Sally Caldwell.”

A dead bolt clicked, then the door creaked open. A woman’s face peered in the crack. “I’m Sally Caldwell. Can I see a badge, please?”

While Houston pulled his out, Maddox inventoried every detail about her appearance. Probably stood about five foot even. Couldn’t tell about her build because she used the door as a shield. Wrinkles had etched deep into her face, belying the fact that he knew she was only twenty-six years old. Her eyes were the color of warm chocolate, at least two shades darker than her creamy cocoa skin tone.

She narrowed her eyes to study Houston’s badge, then opened the door, stepped over the threshold, and shut the door behind her. “What’s this about?” She hugged herself.

Against the chill . . . or them?

Houston’s smile seeped into his voice. “We understand you’re set to move into a new Hope-for-Homes site soon.”

She nodded. “In thirteen days.” When she smiled, a mouthful of snow white teeth flashed in the midday sun. “We’re excited. The kids made a countdown calendar.”

Something in Maddox’s chest tightened. Poor woman. Didn’t know yet that her kids’ and her dreams had burned to the ground early this morning. He cleared his throat. “Ms. Caldwell, we’re sorry to have to tell you, but there was a fire at the site this morning.”

Her expressive eyes widened. “What happened? Was there much damage?”

Houston laid a hand on her shoulder. “I’m sorry, Ms. Caldwell. The house is a total loss.”

Tears pooled in her eyes. She sucked in air and grabbed the doorjamb. “All our work . . .”

Maddox glanced back to the cruiser. He’d never been able to handle a crying woman. Suspects he could take—their tears were normally as false as their statements. But a woman crying in pain . . . he didn’t know how to process that.

“I’m so sorry.” Houston was so much better at handling women. Probably learned a lot from being married for nearly three decades.

She sniffed. “What happened?”

Maddox met her painful stare. “Arson.”

She blinked rapidly, seeming to take in the information. Then her chin jutted out and she made eye contact again. “Well, praise God we hadn’t already moved in or we’d have lost everything.”

Was she kidding? She’d just been told her new house had been burned down—deliberately—and she was praising God? She couldn’t be serious. These religious nuts had no sense at all.

“Was anyone hurt?”

His partner caught his eye before focusing back on her. "Actually, Ms. Caldwell, there was a body found in the house."

Her tears returned. "Oh, dear Lord, someone died in the fire? Who?"

"That's what we're trying to find out." Maddox waited until she faced him again before he continued. "Do you have any idea who might've been in the house?" No sense giving her too many details. As sweet as she seemed, she could still be involved. It was, after all, her house.

And she knew it was vacant at the moment. A perfect setting for murder.

She shook her head, fingers pressed to her mouth.

Houston leaned in closer and withdrew his notebook from his pocket. "You can't think of anyone who would be in the house?"

"Not a single soul. We'd finished almost everything. The only one who was still going by and doing little things was the electrician, because he wanted to change out the dimmer switch in the living room to match the wallpaper better."

"We?" Maddox cocked his head.

Ms. Caldwell nodded. "Part of the deal with Hope for Homes is the new owners have to work a certain number of hours. I was there nearly every day."

"And this electrician . . . he's the only one you know of who still had business at the property?"

Houston scribbled in his notebook.

"Maybe Layla. She kept a careful watch on every stage of the house's progress."

"Layla?" Houston hovered his pencil over the page.

"Layla Taylor, the contractor."

Maddox almost shook his head. A woman contractor? And with a name like Layla? Brought up images of blonde and flighty.

"Or maybe her sister."

Now Maddox was thoroughly confused. "Her sister? Why would the contractor's sister be at the house?"

"Because some of the workers were from Second Chances."

The work-release group. But it still didn't correlate. "I don't understand what that has to do with being the contractor's sister or being at the house."

Sally smiled. "Because Layla's sister, Alana, oversees Second Chances. Could be she went by to check on the workers or something."

"Was that common? I mean, for this Alana to drop by the site?"

"No. I only met her once. She came by the house to talk with her sister about something."

He'd just bet. Sounded fishy. Maddox clenched his jaw. These sisters, Alana and Layla, were about to get a visit.

And they'd better be prepared with some answers.

• • •

THE TINKLING OF THE bell over the main entrance to Second Chances drew Alana and Layla's attention.

Alana sighed. "Let me go see who that is. If it's Gavin's probation officer . . ."

Layla allowed a smile to creep to her face since Alana had already left the room. Her sister's determination always amused her. She shook her head, then lifted the paper again, studying it. Fred had pulled all the information for Alana and her, and now they were knee deep in reviewing it.

The three men Bob had used on the Hope-for-Homes site were Darren Watkins, Sam Roberson, and Kenny Lindsay. All three had been into at least their twelfth week at Second Chances, and all hadn't had a single incident since entering the retreat. Only one had a previous history of violence—Darren. He'd physically abused his girlfriend before his arrest. Beating two men with a baseball bat during a mugging had landed him four months' incarceration prior to giving him the opportunity to attend Second Chances.

Did Darren have any connection to the site?

Layla opened her mouth to ask Alana, then realized her sister had never returned. No probation officer would've shown up on a Saturday afternoon. Maybe Fred had come back. Layla shoved the chair back from the desk and stood. If Alana had gotten sidetracked with something minor about the retreat when this was so important, Layla just might scream.

She walked down the short hall to the front area. Voices reached her before she rounded the corner. Male voices that didn't sound too friendly.

Layla fisted her hands stiffly and strode into the room.

Alana stood on the welcome rug, worrying her bottom lip. Clearly uncomfortable. The hair on the back of Layla's neck jumped to full attention as she took in the two men looking down at her sister.

One man had to be pushing fifty, with thin gray hair. He wore an outlandish print shirt over well-worn khaki slacks. The other man was taller and younger, probably closer to Layla's own age of twenty-nine. He had dark, dark brown hair worn in a crew cut. His shoulders were wide enough for him to play for the Louisiana State University Tigers, and he looked like he was solid muscle in the jeans and long-sleeved pullover he wore very well.

"Alana?"

Her sister and the two men simultaneously faced her.

She continued her approach, taking in both men's silent appraisal of her. She squared her shoulders and moved beside her sister. "What's up?"

Alana licked her bottom lip. "These are

Detectives Wallace and Bishop. Gentlemen, this is my sister, Layla."

So the police didn't waste any time.

The older man extended his hand. "Detective Houston Wallace, Ms. . . ."

She shook his hand. "Layla Taylor."

She turned to the younger man, then trapped her gasp before it escaped her throat. He had the truest blue eyes, framed by the darkest, longest lashes she'd ever seen on a man. But it was the expressiveness of them that snatched her breath and held it hostage.

Suspicion hung in the blue irises with rings of accusation surrounding.

He said nothing, just stood there, staring at her with a stare so penetrating, the urge to squirm nearly strangled her. Tall and dark-haired . . . just like Randy. Layla swallowed, refusing to see any further similarities.

Detective Wallace cleared his throat. "That's my partner, Maddox Bishop."

"Maddox?"

He narrowed those blue eyes at her.

Had she asked his name aloud? She pinched her lips together. She hadn't meant to speak. It was just that his name was so unusual.

"Yeah, my name's Maddox. Why?" His voice was as masculine as his appearance.

"It's nice. Odd. I like it." Oh, splinters! She stammered like a kid.

He kept his eyes narrowed. "Layla, huh? Sounds like a song."

Heat spread across her face. "Like I haven't heard that before."

"So," his partner interrupted, "your sister was just telling us about Second Chances. Sounds like this is a really good program."

Funny, she didn't believe him. But she also didn't look away from Maddox. The unspoken line had been drawn. No way would she break eye contact first. Childish? Perhaps. But she wouldn't drop her gaze.

Silence hung heavy over the room, as tangible and cold as the wind whipping outside.

"Layla, they're here about the Hope-for-Homes house that burned down."

"I figured," she replied, still not dropping her stare.

"Is there a place we can sit down and talk?"

"Certainly, Detective Wallace. Let's go to the reception room. It's this way." Alana's voice cracked, but her footfalls moved toward the hall.

His two steps squeaked behind Alana's, then he halted. "Bishop?"

Maddox lifted a single brow at her before he turned to his partner. "Yeah. Coming." He moved alongside Detective Wallace. Together, they followed Alana.

Layla swallowed. Hard. She hauled in a deep breath, then released it slowly before trailing them. So much had been in Maddox's glare. Distrust . . . accusation . . . loathing. All unwarranted, but his scrutiny had unnerved her just the same.

Yet she hadn't looked away first. At least she'd won that unspoken challenge.

But what would she lose now?

FIVE

"The best way out is always through."
—ROBERT FROST

SHE WASN'T *REALLY* STRIKINGLY attractive. Not dainty and petite like her sister—more lean and toned and athletically built. But something about Layla Taylor definitely grabbed his interest. Didn't really surprise him. He found most ladies interested him in some form or fashion.

And Layla Taylor was hot. At least to him.

Maddox sat in the chair opposite Houston, with the two sisters sharing a couch between his partner and him. Easier for them to observe the facial expressions of the sisters.

"You have no idea why someone would have been in the house?" Houston asked.

"No." Layla flipped her shoulder-length dirty blonde hair over her shoulder. As she did, a whiff of a spicy scent teased Maddox's nostrils.

He liked women. Lots of women. While Layla Taylor definitely appealed to him, she was different. It was as if just being in the room with her hit him in the gut or something. He didn't like it. Made him feel weak. Reminded him of Julie. He wouldn't go there again. Last time he'd allowed himself to be wrapped up in a woman, his mother had died. He no longer let himself be distracted by any woman. He inhaled slowly and focused on her sister. "Do you?"

Alana's eyes widened. "Of course not."

"Why would she know anything? She wasn't ever on the site." Layla's hands were balled on her lap.

A defensive gesture. Maddox's instinct rose. Why was she so defensive? He kept his face neutral as he dared to meet her eyes.

Huge mistake. An exotic green color, her eyes tilted up in the outer corners. They snatched Maddox's attention no matter how hard he fought to ignore them. Especially now, when something flickered in them, making them appear to glimmer under the afternoon sunlight stealing in through the windows.

"Our records indicate that some of the workers on the site were staying here," Houston said.

Alana licked her lips. "Yes, that's correct. The work-release program has been very successful for the Second Chances' residents. After they complete their initial sessions and the therapist believes they're ready to start the process of returning to society, we pair them up with tradesmen. It's kind of an apprenticeship program."

"How long has this working program been in effect?" Houston held a pencil over his notebook.

Alana shrugged. "We started it a year after we opened. So for about two years now."

Maddox leaned forward. "Any problems?"

She licked her lips again—a definite nervous gesture. "One or two, but nothing major."

"Every program has glitches. Especially in the beginning," Layla interjected.

Maddox forced his eyebrow to stay in place and concentrated on Alana. "What kind of problems?"

"One of the residents stole tools from some carpenters." Alana smoothed her palms over her jeans. "Of course, we recovered most of them."

"And what they didn't, Alana reimbursed the carpenters." Layla's facial features tightened.

"I see." Houston looked up from his note taking. "What else?"

"The only other incident was when a person reverted back to his addictive ways." Alana stared at the worn rug under the coffee table.

What wasn't she saying? Maddox inched to the edge of the chair. "So, you found someone using drugs again?"

"Not exactly." Alana lifted her gaze. "He got high, stole my truck, and left. He caused an accident." Big tears shimmered in her eyes.

Not again. Two crying women in one day?

She sniffed. "He hit a lady and her daughter. Both died."

Layla wrapped an arm around her sister's shoulder and threw daggers at Maddox with her glare. "None of which is your fault."

"I know."

"Bet that one's still doing time," Houston mumbled.

Layla snapped her gaze to him. "No, he committed suicide when he sobered up and realized what he'd done."

Houston cleared his throat. "If I'm understanding correctly, Second Chances has been in operation for three years, right?"

Alana nodded. "Yes. I hired the assistant director, Fred Daly, two years ago. Approved by the federal board who oversees rehab programs such as Second Chances."

"And in that time, you've only had two incidents?"

"Yes."

"Not a bad record." Houston swallowed loudly, which meant he'd finally gotten rid of his gum. "No other problems or issues?"

The sisters glanced at each other. Maddox could almost hear a conversation happening between them. Certainly there were other issues. They just didn't want to talk about them.

He straightened. "Ladies, we're investigating a murder. We need all the information you can give us."

The nudge Layla gave her sister would've been unnoticeable had Maddox not been scrutinizing their body language.

"Ms. Taylor?"

Alana lifted her gaze to meet Maddox's. Her eyes were as blue as her sister's were green. But they didn't captivate his attention. A little gasp slipped through her bow-shaped lips.

He gentled his tone. "Is there anything else you can think of that might possibly be relevant? Even if you don't think it's important?"

She cut her gaze to her sister, then back to him. "We had a bit of an episode yesterday."

This was like pulling wisdom teeth without Novocain. He leaned forward, inviting her to share. "What kind of incident?"

"One of the newer residents backslid a little. He got high and had to be restrained."

Houston looked up from his notepad. "His name?"

"Gavin Benoit. But he can't be involved because he was secure inside our facility after we found him."

"When was this?" Houston asked.

Alana glanced at her sister again. "About one or one thirty."

Layla nodded.

Houston continued to scribble notes.

"Where'd he get the drugs?" Maddox asked.

Both ladies' reactions screamed out to him. Alana's, panicked and fearful—Layla's, hostile and accusing.

Interesting. He pressed on. "Did you find the drugs?"

Alana shook her head. "We searched his room and found nothing. I've opened a full investigation into the incident."

"He was never on the Hope-for-Homes site." Layla spoke with resolve.

Why was she so defensive? Just protective of her sister, or was she hiding something? She certainly wouldn't volunteer anything. But maybe he just hadn't asked the right question yet. "So, he had no connection to any of the construction crews?"

Layla's mouth tightened into a straight line. Score!

"He did some, but as Layla said, not on the Hope-for-Homes site." Alana crossed her legs at the ankle.

Houston stood and slipped the pencil behind his ear. "We'll need all his information, if you don't mind, along with the list of everyone here who worked on the Hope-for-Homes house."

"Sure." Alana stood as well.

Maddox and Layla rose slowly, cautiously, as they eyed one another.

"I'll just go get the information from my office. I'll be right back." Alana walked out of the room and down the hall.

Houston turned to Layla. "We'll also need to come by your office and discuss the house itself. How about Monday around eight?"

"That's fine."

Maddox continued to study her. She shifted her weight from one foot to the other and tossed him scathing looks. He swallowed a smile. This was the part of the job he loved—knowing someone hid something and making them extremely nervous until he found out what it was. He could always uncover secrets, no matter how deeply hidden.

He'd find out what Layla Taylor's was.

Soon.

A NEW YEAR . . . a new beginning. New opportunities to do what's right instead of being right.

For two weeks Pastor Chaney had used the same theme for his sermons. Not that Layla didn't enjoy them—she did—but she'd be glad when January drifted into February and Pastor would find a new focus.

Then again, maybe not. February's theme was normally centered on love and relationships. Two issues that didn't necessarily go hand in hand, and ones she definitely didn't want to contemplate too deeply.

She'd failed at both. Miserably.

Alana nudged her forward. The congregation filled the aisle, pushing toward the double mahogany doors to shake Pastor Chaney's hand. The church remodeling had been concluded three months ago, and Layla was still proud of the end result. Everyone said the church looked amazing.

All the bodies caused the temperature of the sanctuary of Eternal Springs Christian Church to rise above a comfortable level. Layla couldn't wait for the January chill to cool her.

She smiled at ladies who gave her curt nods, all too aware that several of the older generation thought her daft for her chosen profession. She smiled wider as Ms. Ethel Thomas grabbed her arm.

"You performing this week, Layla dear?"

"Yes, ma'am."

"You'll do beautifully." Ms. Ethel was so loving. Encouraging. And she'd helped out with Alana after their mother had been admitted to the nursing home.

"Thank you." Layla gave the woman a hug.

Ms. Ethel nodded, then gripped her walker with both hands and made it down the aisle.

Layla followed. Finally she and Alana made it to the narthex.

"Beautiful morning, isn't it, ladies?" Pastor took Layla's hand but included her sister in his smile.

"Very much so." Layla nodded. Maybe with the clearing of the weather, Taylor Construction would get more work. She withdrew her hand and took a step away.

"Heard about that body found in your burned house." His words stopped her. "Just tragic."

Layla squared her shoulders. "It is a tragedy."

"Have the police identified the body yet?"

"Not that I'm aware of." She hitched her purse strap higher on her shoulder. She hated the thing, wouldn't carry one even to church if Alana wasn't so insistent.

Pastor clucked his tongue and shook his head. "Heard some of the residents at Second Chances might be involved." He looked over Layla's shoulder as one of the church elders touched the back of his hand.

Layla turned slightly, just enough to catch the paleness of her sister's face. "I don't think the police believe that. At least not that they've indicated to us."

"Well, I'm praying for a quick resolution." He laid a hand on Alana's shoulder.

"Thank you," Alana whispered. "Good sermon."

"Pastor," the elder interrupted, "both bathrooms have sprung leaks."

"Again?" Pastor sighed, then smiled at Layla and Alana. "Please excuse me."

Layla took hold of her sister's hand and pulled her out into the sunny but crisp morning. "How about a late brunch at the diner?"

Alana frowned as they spilled into the parking lot with the rest of the congregation. "I'm going to see Mom today. Why don't you come with me?"

Little shards of old wounds sliced down Layla's spine. "I don't think so."

"Layla, come on. Don't you think it's time?"

That one thing twisted her emotions into tight knots, and she couldn't make her sister understand. "I'm not ready." Did they always have to have the exact same conversation whenever their mother was brought up?

Alana worried her bottom lip and stopped between their vehicles. "You always say that. It's been years. Time to move on. A new year and all that."

If only Layla could. But the bitterness . . . the resentment . . . wouldn't let her. "Not yet." And she didn't know if she ever could.

She didn't know if she wanted to.

"Scripture tells us to forgive, you know." Alana dug in her purse for her keys.

"Don't start quoting Scripture to me, Al. I'm well aware of what the Bible says." She knew she sounded like a petulant child, but Layla didn't care. She was sick and tired of having the same point drilled into her head, over and over again.

Alana held her keys and stared into Layla's face. "Then why won't you visit Mom with me? Dad forgave her. I've forgiven her. It's only eating at you because you won't."

"I can't." The words nearly strangled her. "We've been over this. I just can't."

Alana tilted her head, held Layla's stare for a long moment, then let out a heavy sigh. "One day you'll have to come to terms with Mom and the past. You won't be able to move forward until you do."

Maybe . . . maybe not. She seemed to be just fine without coming to terms with anything. Unless Alana brought her up, Layla never even thought about their mother. What did that say about her as a person?

"Besides, I have to practice this afternoon." She needed to change the subject. "Uh, have you heard from Cameron? When is he supposed to be back in town?"

"Tomorrow." Alana leaned in and planted a soft kiss on Layla's cheek. "I'll call you tonight."

Layla nodded and watched her sister slip into her Jeep and pull out of the church parking lot. She gave a little wave before getting behind the wheel of her truck.

Alana was too good, unlike Layla. She could

forgive their mother for her abuse . . . her neglect . . . ripping their family apart. But Layla couldn't. Not when Roseanna Taylor had made the choice to destroy herself and her family. Layla could remember everything—Alana's memories were jaded.

Shielding her sister, Layla had stepped in where their mother failed, striving to never let Alana endure the neglect they'd suffered as children. And the pain and humiliation Layla had experienced as a teenager.

No, she wouldn't walk down that path again. Not today. Not now.

Layla started her truck and steered onto the street, heading toward the diner. She was accustomed to eating alone, having been considered an odd bird by so many and left to her own ways, so she didn't mind.

It took her two loops of the diner's lot to find an available parking space. Good thing she was alone—less waiting time. The aroma of onions, grease, and spices enveloped her in a welcoming embrace as soon as she entered. She moved past the sets of two- and threesomes waiting, found a free seat at the bar, plopped down, then shrugged out of her coat.

Seconds later the waitress came by with a pot of coffee. "Morning, Layla. Want a hit of java?"

"Thanks." She smiled at the pretty brunette who filled her cup, then laid a menu in front of her.

The waitress jerked her head to the vacant seat beside her. "Alana coming?"

"Not today." Layla forced a smile. She didn't like being at odds with her sister, but she doubted they'd ever see eye to eye on the issue of their mother.

"I'll be back in a minute to take your order."

Layla nodded and lifted her coffee. The robust odor wafted under her nose. She closed her eyes and inhaled deeply. Warmth seeped deep into her bones.

The vinyl seat of the stool beside her creaked.

"It tastes as good as it smells," a masculine voice boomed.

She opened her eyes to meet the stare of Eternal Springs police officer Lincoln Vailes. She smiled. "Hey, Lincoln." She peered over his shoulder. "Where's Jade?"

He nodded at the waitress before he turned back to Layla. "She had to head home right after church. A group of ladies are having some type of get-together at her place, and she wanted to finish tidying up. I'm just here to pick up the gumbo she called in."

Layla chuckled and took a sip of her coffee. "There is that. Tell her I said hello."

"Will do." The smile shifted off his kindly face. "Saw the report about that building and the body."

She set the cup back on its saucer. "Two

detectives from the parish office came by to talk to Alana and me about that." She traced the lip of the cup with her finger. "Didn't like them much."

"Why not?"

"One of them was a real jerk. The other one, older, was nice enough. But that Maddox one was a jerk."

Lincoln's laugh startled her. "Maddox Bishop?"

"Yeah. Do you know him?"

"Worked with him on Jade's case, actually. He's a good guy, Layla."

She tried to stop the snort but couldn't.

"Seriously. He's rough around the edges and can be a bit stubborn, but he's a good detective. Interested in getting to the truth."

She hated that Lincoln gave him a glowing recommendation. Lincoln Vailes was as honest as the day was long, and if he said someone was a good man, then he must be. But she couldn't stop thinking about Maddox's penetrating stare.

Like he could see right into her very soul. Could he see her fears? Her insecurities? The reaction he caused?

The waitress slid a bag across the counter to Lincoln. "Jade already paid when she placed the order, so you're good to go."

"Thanks." Lincoln stood and smiled at Layla one last time. "Yeah, Maddox can be ornery and stubborn, but give him a chance."

"I will." She lifted her cup at him in salute. "Don't forget to give my best to Jade."

He nodded and wove through the diner and out the door.

Layla took another sip of her coffee. Maddox Bishop was a good cop, huh? Well, if Lincoln said so, she'd give him the benefit of the doubt.

For now.

SIX

"There is nothing more uncommon than common sense."
—FRANK LLOYD WRIGHT

CLOUDS HUNG LOW OVER Monday morning like a wool afghan on a summer night. Stifling. Suffocating.

Layla jerked the truck into her parking space at Taylor Construction. Of all days to oversleep . . . She killed the engine and grabbed her travel cup of coffee and attaché case. She stepped to the ground and sunk an inch in mud. Gritting her teeth, she trudged up the stairs. She balanced the travel mug and case with one arm while unlocking the door.

An engine roared behind her.

She spun, dropping not only the mug and attaché, but also her keys. Hot coffee splashed up and dotted her jeans. So much for its claims of being spill proof. She narrowed her eyes at the men getting out of the car now parked beside her truck.

Should have known. Maddox Bishop and his partner. Just her luck.

The older detective—the *good* cop—rushed up the stairs. "Sorry for startling you. Here, let me help." He bent to gather her mug and keys.

She grabbed her case and straightened. "Thank you, Detective . . ."

He smiled with the kindest eyes. "Wallace. Detective Houston Wallace."

"Thank you, Detective Wallace." She took the keys from him and unlocked the door, then waved him inside. "Come on in." She glanced over her shoulder to find Maddox leaning against the bottom of the stair railing. "You too."

He quirked a single brow at her, but she refused to allow him to put her on edge. Not today. She'd remember what Lincoln said. Maddox was a good cop, interested in getting to the truth. And that's what she wanted.

As quickly as possible.

She stomped her muddy boots on the welcome mat. Not that it did any good. The reddish goop stayed adhered. Well, the good detectives could think what they wanted. She wouldn't track mud all over her hardwood. Layla kicked off her boots and let them fall beside the front door before moving to the reception desk where she set her case and mug.

Detective Wallace glanced at his own shoes, then at Layla's boots.

She smiled. "Yours are fine. I stepped right into a puddle."

He chuckled and swiped his feet on the mat. "With all the rain we've had, it's a mess most everywhere."

Maddox filled the doorway. Not just physically, but the mere presence of him in the room pressed against her.

She swallowed and backed against the reception desk. Heat fanned the nape of her neck most uncomfortably. Made no sense at all. She was a grown woman, a business owner in a male-dominated field—she could ignore the stupid stirrings in her gut.

"So, how can I help you gentlemen?" Layla forced her voice not to wobble.

"We need a list of all the workers you contracted to work on the Hope-for-Homes site."

Maddox's voice unnerved her more than she was willing to admit. "Of course." She sat behind the desk and wiggled the mouse, waking the computer. She'd created a file yesterday with all the pertinent job information. Anything to make *this* visit as short as humanly possible.

Maddox lowered himself to perch on the edge of the reception desk. The heating unit kicked on, blowing a hint of his cologne her way. Just enough for her to detect. Just enough to distract her.

Layla accessed the file and set it to print. The sooner she gave them the information they needed, the sooner they'd leave.

And she could return to being a full-functioning adult.

"Have you met Ms. Caldwell? The lady who was supposed to move into the house?" Maddox asked.

"Yes." She chanced looking him in the eye. Well, the world didn't spontaneously combust, but she felt affected just the same. "Hope for Homes lets the new homeowner be involved in the interior completion."

"What'd you think of her? Ms. Caldwell."

"I think she's a strong, resilient, nice lady." She crossed her arms over her chest. Where was he going with this? "Her kids are well behaved and respectful. She's had a hard life but is doing the best she can for herself and her kids." Layla stood. "Why?"

"Just wondering what your impression was." Maddox lumbered to his feet, towering over her.

"Let me get you that printout." She turned and headed down the hall to her office. For once she was glad she'd purchased only one printer for the office and networked all the computers to it.

Gave her an excuse to get away from Maddox. Get a little space to clear her head.

Splinters! The man muddled her mind.

She snatched the papers from the printer, took a deep breath, then returned to the main office. Layla handed the pages to Detective Wallace. "Here's all the information on everyone involved in the Hope-for-Homes site. I included most of the independents' phone numbers for you as well."

"Thank you. This is very helpful." Detective Wallace scanned the pages she'd given him.

Maddox glanced around the office. Just what was he looking for? She took a seat behind the reception desk, putting distance between the detectives and herself.

"Nice office," Maddox mumbled under his breath.

"Thank you. I designed it myself." She couldn't stop the pride from filling her voice, but she didn't really try. She'd worked hard to get to her current point in her career and she was proud of herself.

He looked out the window. "Not too busy today?"

"As Detective Wallace pointed out earlier, with all the rain we've had lately, everything's a mess." She smiled. "Hard to erect buildings when we can't lay a foundation."

He slumped to one of the chairs facing the

desk. “Guess so. Must be bad for business. All the rain, I mean.”

She shrugged. “Nature of the industry. Always slow in the beginning of the year, then we get swamped early spring to late fall.”

“So, that’s pretty much normal?”

What was he trying to ask? “Yes.”

“Says you were the site foreman on the job.” Detective Wallace lifted his eyes from the papers.

“That’s correct.”

“Is that common practice?” Detective Wallace took the other seat in front of the desk. “For the contractor to also act as the site foreman?”

“It depends.”

“On?” Maddox’s stare pinned her to the chair and made her want to fidget.

She forced herself to remain calm. “A number of things. In this particular instance, because it was a Hope for Homes—a charity—we didn’t want the extra expense of a site foreman.”

“Do you act as foreman on the majority of your jobs?”

“No.”

“But this one you did?” Detective Wallace asked.

“Yes. As I said, because we didn’t want the extra expense.” The way they kept badgering her . . . made her sweat, and she’d done nothing wrong. She’d saved the project a good chunk of money. "A lot of contractors often act as site foremen on their jobs."

"How many? How often?" Maddox's questions came as rapid-fire as nails from her air gun. His cynicism annoyed her.

"I don't know." Her hackles rose. "You'd have to ask around."

"How about on yours?"

"I don't know, exactly. I'd have to pull records." What was their deal? She'd saved a charity project money. What was the crime? It wasn't like it was a shady business practice or anything.

"Just give us a ballpark. Ten percent? Twenty? Fifty?" Maddox's arms were crossed tight over his chest.

She swallowed. Hard. "If I had to guess, I'd say maybe fifteen to twenty percent."

Detective Wallace scribbled in a little spiral notebook. "So, it's fair to say that it's not all that common. In your particular business."

"Fifteen to twenty percent isn't rare, Detective."

"Oh, of course not." Detective Wallace smiled, but this time she didn't see the kindness in his eyes.

She stood. "If that's all, I have to get some work done."

Both men took the cue and stood. Maddox glanced out the window again, then smirked at her. “Yeah, I can see that.” The men exited without further conversation.

She fisted her hands stiffly at her sides. In her profession she’d been exposed to the worst sexists in the state. Men who thought women should stay at home, preferably barefoot and pregnant. Construction workers were awful—viewing women as objects, not people. She’d had her fill of them.

And Maddox Bishop came across as bad as a male chauvinist, as she’d seen in a long time. He reminded her of Randy.

The phone rang, pulling her from her thoughts. She grabbed the receiver. “Hello.”

“Layla, you okay?” Alana’s voice was laced with concern.

She steeled her emotions. “Yeah. What’s up?”

“I’m on my way to the hospital.”

Layla’s heart and stomach collided as she gripped the phone tighter. “What’s wrong?”

“It’s Ms. Ethel.”

Layla let out a slow breath. Her sister should’ve known better than to scare her like that. “What’s wrong with her? We just saw her at church yesterday.”

“She got really sick last night. Had trouble breathing. Couldn’t stop her nosebleeds. They admitted her from the ER.”

“I’ll definitely be praying for her. What do they think she has?”

“They don’t know. They’re running tests, but she’s not doing so well. I’m going to see her this afternoon. Do you want to go with me, Layla?”

“It’s that bad?”

“If she doesn’t improve, they’re talking about putting her in ICU. They have her on oxygen, but her levels are dropping fast.”

“Yeah, I want to go. But can’t until later.”

“I’ll swing by and pick you up around four.”

“Okay.” Layla hung up the phone and ran her teeth over her bottom lip. Sweet Ms. Ethel. Kind. Gentle.

At her desk Layla bowed her head and lifted Ms. Ethel up before the throne.

“HAVE SOME INFO ON your John Doe.” K. C. Casteel’s voice came through loud and clear over the connection.

Maddox shoved the receiver between his chin and shoulder and grabbed a pen and paper from the mess on his desk. “Shoot.”

“Fifty-five to sixty-year-old Caucasian male. Approximately five-feet-ten inches tall. Slight frame. Probably weighed around 150 pounds.”

Maddox finished scribbling the information and tapped the pen against the desk. “Cause of death?”

“A .357 bullet to the chest. Slug retrieved. Secondary gunshot wound to the head was delivered postmortem. That slug was also retrieved. Embedded in Mr. Doe's skull."

What? "Shooter nails the guy in the head after he was already dead?"

"Guess someone wanted to make sure he wouldn't recover."

People were crazy. Maddox knew that, of course, but the level of violence some sickos took never ceased to make him shake his head.

"Time of death is between eleven thirty and midnight on Friday," the coroner continued.

Maddox scribbled faster.

"Talked to the police chief. Arson department determined regular gasoline was the accelerant used to start the fire. I concur that the body was soaked in it prior to burning."

"Someone shot the guy in the chest, then in the head to make sure he doesn't get up, then soaks him in gas and sets the house on fire?"

"Those are the facts, Detective."

They were dealing with one sick puppy. Maddox dropped his pen to the desk. "Anything else?"

"Nothing of remark. I'll send you a copy of my report this afternoon."

"Thanks, K. C., I appreciate you getting to this so quickly."

"Yeah, well, you can owe me a venison backstrap."

Maddox laughed. "As soon as I get a buck,

you'll have it." He hung up the phone, then gave Houston the details.

"Let's search missing persons to see who matches John Doe's description." Houston plopped behind his desk in the shared space and opened a search on his computer.

"I don't recall any new postings of missing persons, though."

"It's a start." Houston's fingers flew over the keyboard as he entered the information on John Doe into the state's missing persons' database.

"I suppose." Maddox flipped through the case notes. "Hey, ballistics is back. Revolver at the scene was a Smith & Wesson. Forensics will test to see if it's a match to the recovered slugs."

"I'm betting it's 100 percent. Any hits on the serial number?"

"Shaved off, but forensics is working on it to try to pull it off anyhow." Maddox turned the page to the notes Houston had typed up earlier. The ones from their visit with Layla Taylor this morning. "What was your impression of Layla?"

Houston hit the ENTER button, then met Maddox's glance over their desks. "I think we make her nervous." He shrugged. "Could be just because she was talking to police. Makes some people jumpy."

"Could be she knows something." Maddox leaned back in his chair.

"I'm more interested in her sister's Second

Chances. Known druggies working on people's houses? What's up with that?"

"I sure wouldn't want them anywhere near my place."

"Me either. Makes me wonder if home owners are even told the druggies are on their property."

"I'll check into that." Maddox lifted his pen and scribbled a note. "Still, strikes me as too fishy about Layla being the foreman on the job. And the contractor."

"We could do a little checking into the sisters' backgrounds."

Maddox scrawled another note on his page. "I think I will. Did you notice the pictures Layla had on the desk?"

"No. Something I should be aware of?"

"Just a little out of character, I think."

"How's that?"

"There was a picture of her with some guy. She was wearing one of those long dresses, and they were dancing."

Houston chuckled. "Ain't nothing wrong with dancing, Bishop. You do your fair share of belt-buckle shining."

"Yeah, but it's odd. She's a contractor. A builder. Works in a man's world. But she gets all gussied up in a long dress and dances?" He shook his head. "Just seems odd. She's like a contradiction. I think she's hiding something. I can feel it."

"Maybe, but my gut doesn't think so."

"Your gut's too busy thinking about your next meal."

Houston chuckled and rubbed what his wife dubbed his beer gut. "You got a point with that, partner?"

Before Maddox could reply, Houston's computer beeped. "Okay, let's see what we've got." He turned back to the monitor. "Just two hits."

"Give 'em to me."

Tapping filled the cubicle as Houston accessed the database. "First one is a Milton Ward. Retired oilfield worker. Reported missing by his son two weeks ago." He squinted at the screen. "Just outside Orleans Parish."

Maddox laughed as he made notes of the information. "Might help if you actually wore your glasses."

"Shut up." Houston leaned closer to the monitor. "Second one is Dennis LeJeune. Reported missing by his wife Friday." He leaned back in his chair and stared at Maddox. "Guess what Mr. Dennis LeJeune does for a living?"

They'd been partners long enough for Maddox to know that look. Houston had found a connection. "What?"

"He's a building inspector." Houston snatched a sticky note and scribbled. "Got the home address. Lives just outside Sulphur."

Maddox shoved to his feet and grabbed his coat. "We haven't left yet?"

SEVEN

"A man should look for what is,
and not for what he thinks should be."
—ALBERT EINSTEIN

"LAYLA? MS. LAYLA TAYLOR?"

She turned around at the woman's voice. A young woman hustled across the parking lot after her. Layla waited, shifting her bag with her take-out lunch to a more comfortable position, and took in the woman's appearance: short, auburn hair, a little on the heavyset side, smiling mouth too big for her round face. Layla didn't recognize her.

"Hi." She stood before Layla, catching her breath before extending her hand. "I'm Krissy Morgan with *The American Press*."

What did the Lake Charles newspaper want with her? "Yes?"

"First off, congratulations on winning the CotY regional award. That's quite an accomplishment."

Layla's smile widened automatically. "Thank you. I'm honored by the award." The exposure was already starting? Awesome.

"And I understand this means you're up for a national CotY as well?"

"Yes. The national winners will be announced at the NARI gala in the spring."

"If you have a moment, I'd love to talk with you a bit. Get a comment from you on the story we'll be running tomorrow."

Layla's heart shot into her stomach. This was more than awesome. This could really put her business over the top. She tightened her grip on her bag. Who cared if her shrimp po'boy got cold? Or if she froze, for that matter? "Of course."

Krissy waved her toward a park bench in the Eternal Springs courtyard. The wind gusted, nearly stealing Layla's breath. She set her sack on the bench beside her and tried to gather her thoughts. It'd be awful to sound like an idiot in her quote. That would do her business no good.

Sitting beside her, Krissy pulled out a notebook and a small digital recorder. "Do you mind?"

"Of course not." She sure didn't want to be misquoted. Layla curled her hands in her lap, then splayed her fingers loosely over her legs. She hoped she didn't look uncomfortable or nervous. *Lord, I could really use a little peace right now.*

"How do you feel about having been awarded a regional CotY award?"

Layla inhaled slowly. "So many wonderful contractors entered. I'm honored just to be in their company." That sounded good, right? She sounded intelligent, knowledgeable, and she'd plugged the organization that put on the awards.

She let out a breath. This wasn't as difficult as she'd imagined.

"Sounds exciting."

"It is." Layla nodded. "It's the highlight event of the year for every contractor I know."

"Let's move on, shall we?" Krissy smiled, but it was more like a bared-teeth grimace of one competitor to another before a big bout.

Splinters of apprehension darted through Layla. "O-kay."

"The project you won the award for . . . isn't it a Hope-for-Homes house?"

Those splinters sprouted into full two-by-fours. Layla licked her lips and wiped her palms against her jeans. "Y-yes."

"Wasn't it, in fact, the house that burned down late Friday night?"

How could she get away without making a scene?

"Ms. Taylor, wasn't it the house that burned down late Friday night?" Krissy held the recorder closer to Layla.

"Y-yes."

"How do you feel about that?"

Was this woman for real? How was she supposed to answer something like that?

The recorder pushed almost in her face. "Ms. Taylor?"

Layla's mouth felt stuffed with cotton. "Horrible, of course. I hate that any building burns, but especially a house. Someone's home." She needed to get away from this woman . . . fast.

"Wasn't a body in the house when it burned, Ms. Taylor?"

This was going from bad to worse. Enough was enough. Layla struggled to her feet, gripping her bag like a vise. "I couldn't say."

Krissy stood in a flash. "Come on, Ms. Taylor, you know a body was in that house. A house that you built. Do you know who it was?"

"N-no. You'd have to ask the police for that information." Layla glanced across the courtyard, her heart beating double-time. "If you'll excuse me, I have to get back to work." She turned toward her truck.

"One last question, Ms. Taylor. Do you think someone burned the house you built to make a statement of some sort to you personally?"

Layla froze, then spun around to face the meddlesome reporter who held the recorder out like a shield. "What?"

Krissy closed the distance between them. "Do you think someone burned down that house to send you a message? Maybe someone was jealous of your award and wanted to make sure you didn't win on a national level?"

This woman was unbelievable. Layla glared. "No comment, Ms. Morgan." She turned and marched across the courtyard to her truck. Not hesitating once inside the cab, she started the engine and peeled out of the parking lot. Her heartbeat pounded in her head.

The nerve of the woman. Stupid reporter.

Layla gripped the steering wheel tighter to stop her hands from trembling. How dare the woman waylay her like that? Acting all sweet and congratulatory before slamming her. Flattering her to get her off guard, then knocking her to her knees.

Plain and simple, she'd been ambushed.

How would the story in tomorrow's paper read?

Pushing aside the worry, Layla went back to the office and finished her estimates and bids. All too soon a honk sounded outside.

Layla glanced at the clock. Four already? She shut down the computer, grabbed her coat and attaché, and stomped out the door, making sure she locked Taylor Construction behind her. A blast of warm air hit her in the face as she slipped into the passenger seat of her sister's Jeep. "Sorry. I lost track of time."

"I just called the hospital." Alana put the Jeep in reverse and eased out of the muddy parking area.

"How's Ms. Ethel?"

"Not so good. I talked to her grandson. He said they're discussing moving her to ICU right now."

"What did he say the doctors think it is?"

"That's what's so frustrating. The doctors don't have any idea. Her nosebleeds keep coming back. She can hardly breathe. She's wheezing, and none of the test results show anything."

"I just can't imagine."

Alana turned the car toward Lake Charles. "Me either. Her grandson says he's really scared. The doctors are baffled so they don't know what to do for her except give her oxygen."

"We'll just keep praying." But Layla knew that might not be enough to save their dear friend.

"THIS IS MR. LEJEUNE?" Maddox pointed at one of the framed photographs on the mantel. A man bowling.

Mary LeJeune twisted in her seat on the tattered recliner. "Yes. That was taken just a few months ago." She sniffled and lifted her teacup, slurping as she took a sip.

Maddox returned to his seat beside Houston on the couch. He'd done his usual inspection of the living room and found nothing of interest. No dust lined the ceiling fan blades. The LeJeunes collected thimbles from around the world and displayed them. Only photographs of the two of them—no smiling baby photos to indicate children or grandchildren.

"And the last time you saw your husband was Friday?" Houston asked around the wad of gum in his cheek.

"Yes." The teacup rattled against the saucer. "He left for work around seven, same as always."

"Did you talk to your husband during the workday on Friday?"

"Why, no. Why would I? We never really talk on the phone. Unless I need him to pick up something from the store on his way home. But that's rare. I keep my groceries stocked, you know."

"What time did Mr. LeJeune normally get home from work?" Maddox interjected.

"Four forty-seven on the dot. Like clockwork." She glanced at the clock over the mantel. "Right about now." Tears filled her time-faded eyes.

"All the time? Even in traffic?" Maddox couldn't believe someone's life was so predictable.

Mrs. LeJeune bobbed her head, the gray tendrils that had escaped from her bun scraped against her leathered face. "No matter what, he pulls into the carport at four forty-seven every day, the same time for the past ten years."

She took another sip of her tea. "Friday night was just like normal. He came home right on time, we had supper, then he changed into his bowling shirt and headed to the alley at six thirty. Same routine he's had for years."

"Ma'am, has your husband been acting strangely or said anything odd recently?" Houston asked.

"Like what?"

"Odd phone calls. Unusual visits." Houston shrugged. "Strange messages."

"No, nothing like that."

"Does he talk to you about work?" Maddox remembered to keep talk in the present tense.

"Not at all. Dennis is real good about keeping his work on a professional level. He doesn't believe in telling tales outside of school. He would never share information like that. His work is confidential."

They were getting nowhere fast. Maddox took a breath and changed directions. "Does your husband own any guns, Mrs. LeJeune?"

"He has rifles and shotguns for hunting."

"And handguns? Revolvers?"

Mrs. LeJeune patted her bun. "Land sakes, no. Why would he have a gun like that?"

"No reason, ma'am." Maddox stood. They wouldn't get anything more useful out of her. Just wasting their time.

Houston stood as well. "As I said, ma'am, we can't positively identify the body we found just yet. We'll have the coroner send for your husband's dental records for consideration."

Mrs. LeJeune wobbled to her feet. "I'm sure it's my Dennis. He wouldn't break his routine unless someone had stopped him." Her voice cracked.

Maddox joined Houston at the door. "We'll let

you know something just as soon as we can, Mrs. LeJeune. Thank you again for your time."

They'd barely shut the car doors and Maddox started the engine before they both began talking at once.

"You first," Houston said as Maddox turned back onto a main road.

"Dennis is our John Doe." Maddox gripped the steering wheel tighter. "I feel it."

"Same here."

"We need to—"

Houston's cell phone interrupted Maddox. Houston glanced at the caller ID. "It's Margie." He flipped open the phone. "Hey, honey."

From the corner of his eye, Maddox took in the tightening of his partner's jaw.

"Oh, honey, I'm so sorry." A long silence on Houston's part, then he continued. "That is horrible. I love you." Houston closed his cell and glanced at Maddox.

"Everything okay?"

"That baby Margie was all worried about?"

"Yeah?"

"The baby died."

"From what?"

"Margie says it's baffled the doctors. Family's calling for an autopsy."

"Man, that's rough."

"Yeah. Margie's pretty tore up over it. Baby was only a month old."

Maddox shook his head. Instances just like this proved his point that there was no big, loving God. No way would anything with a heart let a baby die.

Houston ran a hand over his face. "Anyway . . . you were saying?"

"Right." Maddox pulled to a stop at a red light and regrouped his thoughts. "We need to find out if LeJeune was the building inspector who approved that Hope for Homes."

"Yep. That'd be a connection. A good start. I'll see if Dennis LeJeune had a Smith & Wesson registered." Houston nodded as the light turned green. "I'll get our status updates to the commander."

"Man, that'd be cold. Shot with your own gun."

"It happens."

Maddox shook his head. His mother had been murdered with a knife from her own kitchen. "I know," he whispered.

ONE MORE.

He stared at the building, letting his imagination wander. How was he supposed to destroy it?

After burning the Hope-for-Homes house, setting another building on fire wasn't an option. Too bad Hurricane Francis hadn't wiped it out as it had so many others.

A tree stood off to the side of the main building. If lightning were to hit that tree . . . it *could* fall right in the middle of the building. With a little help, it could definitely hit the main structure and call for a total replacement. That would be like an act of God. Very ironic.

He narrowed his eyes. A bayou ran behind it.

Which could play well in his favor.

What if the bayou got dammed just a little up from the curve, causing the water to back up and flood the area? The building sat not two hundred yards from the bank. With the hoopla over drainage issues, no one would think twice about the flooding being anything other than a natural occurrence. And with all the rain the area had gotten recently . . .

His palms slicked with sweat. He had to protect himself. Had to remove every threat so he could get the casino deal. Get his kids. Get out of debt. Start over in life, no matter how old he was.

Focus, that's what he had to do. He'd already eliminated all the other buildings. Had killed Dennis to keep him quiet. Now he was so close to reaching his goals. His dreams. The desires of his heart.

And he deserved it all.

He let out a long breath and started his car. He'd do what needed to be done. He wouldn't back down now.

He was in—all or nothing.

EIGHT

"Ignorance is preferable to error."
—THOMAS JEFFERSON

THUNDER RATTLED THE WINDOWS. Layla shoved the pillow over her head. Maybe if she was still enough, got it quiet enough in the room, she could fall back asleep.

Another roll of thunder shook the walls just as the phone rang.

She threw the pillow across the room and glared at the clock at her bedside. Five twenty-one. Who in her right mind was awake at such an hour? Certainly shouldn't be her. Maybe it was all a bad dream. She groaned and rolled onto her stomach, burying her face in the mattress.

Just thirty more minutes, God. That's all I'm asking.

The phone rang again.

So much for going back to sleep. Layla flipped over and reached for the receiver. "Hello."

"Good morning. Were you asleep?" Alana's voice grated against Layla's sleepy nerves.

"It's not even five thirty—what do you think?" Thunder boomed outside.

"Sorry. I forgot to check the time before I dialed."

Layla yawned and pushed to sitting with her

back against the headboard. She laid her head against the leather and closed her eyes. "Question is, why are you up and calling me so early?"

"I take it you haven't seen the paper yet?"

"I haven't seen anything other than the clock." And then she remembered. Krissy Morgan. Ambush. Layla sighed and rubbed a hand down her face. "How bad is it?"

"You know there's an article about you?"

"Yeah. A reporter accosted me yesterday." She yawned again before telling her sister the details.

"It's pretty bad."

Layla opened her eyes and drew her knees to her chest. "Read it to me." She rested her chin on her knees. Lightning flashed, filling the room with light before plunging it back into darkness.

"Um, it's kinda long."

Her heart slammed against her ribs. "It's more than just a little filler article?"

"Layla, it's half a page."

She swallowed the groan. "How bad?"

"Well . . ."

"Just tell me."

"They talk about your award, launch right into the house burning and a body being inside, insinuate that maybe this was all done against you personally, and end with posing the question of will this disqualify you from being eligible to win a national CotY."

This time she didn't even try to stop it—she let out a loud groan.

"And the reporter closes with stating that even if you aren't disqualified, this certainly should kill any chances you have of winning the national."

And the surprises just kept coming.

Lightning flickered, followed by a ripple of thunder.

"They won't disqualify you, will they?"

Layla licked her lips. "I don't know." Surely they wouldn't . . . Could they take away the regional award? A weight sat in her stomach like lead.

"But the house burned after you'd completed it. There's got to be consideration for something like this happening, right?" The panic in Alana's voice came through loud and clear.

"I'm sure it's all fine. Krissy Morgan just wrote it with that slant to get attention." Probably trying to make a name for herself and using Layla to do it. The nerve.

"Can you find out?"

Layla smiled. "It's gonna be okay. If there's a problem, NARI will contact me. Don't sweat it."

"Well . . . if you say so."

Layla jumped on the opportunity to change the subject. "What time is Cameron supposed to get back?"

"He hopes to return in time for supper. We won't miss your performance tonight."

"I know you're anxious to see him."

"You have no idea." A chirping sounded in the background. "Oh, that's him calling on my cell now."

"Bye." Layla hung up the phone, then rested her head against the cold leather. Problem was, she did have an idea how Alana felt about Cameron.

She had felt that way about Randy.

Or thought she had.

Layla pushed back down to a prone position and laid her forearm over her forehead. *God, this day has* got *to get better. Please.*

She dozed until thunder shook her awake again. Lightning split the darkness.

She shoved out of bed and staggered to the bathroom. No way would she waste good anger and aggravation by getting depressed.

After thirty minutes of hot water pelting down on her and singing at the top of her lungs, she dressed, feeling much better. The storm continued to rage outside, but she'd choose to ignore it.

The phone rang just as she pulled on her socks. Probably Alana calling her back. Layla fell across the bed, took in the time—7:52—and grabbed the receiver before it rang again. "I'm fine, really."

"Layla?" The masculine voice sent her to her feet.

"Sorry, thought you were someone else. Yes, this is Layla. Who is this?"

"Detective Maddox Bishop."

Oh, joy and rapture. "Yes, Detective, what can I do for you?"

"We'd like you to come down to the sheriff's office this morning. To answer a few questions." He let that sink in for a minute. "We can come pick you up if that'd be more convenient."

A veiled threat? Agree to come in, or we'll come and get you? "No, I can drive myself. What time?"

"How about nine?"

"Fine."

"See you then. Just ask for me or Detective Wallace."

She let the phone fall back to its cradle and sank to the bed. Thunder growled outside her window. Today just wasn't her day.

"BALLISTICS CAME BACK." HOUSTON grinned across the desks at Maddox.

"Hey, don't keep me in suspense."

"Slugs taken from our John Doe match the Smith & Wesson found at the scene."

Maddox leaned back in his chair. "Big surprise."

"Forensics can't pull the serial number. Too much damage."

"What about registrations to Dennis LeJeune?"

"His wife was right—only rifles and shotguns had been registered to him. Not a single handgun. So that's a dead end."

"Unless it was an illegal and he's been hiding it from his wife."

Houston shrugged. "Then we'll never know."

Maddox glanced over the random pieces of paper covering his desk. "Dental records?"

"Delivered late yesterday afternoon. Casteel says he'll call us today as soon as he knows one way or the other."

"Guess we just wait now."

"We did get the reports back on the Taylor sisters."

Maddox wove his fingers together and supported the back of his head in his hands. "Do tell."

"Alana Taylor, twenty-five, has a bachelor's in psychology. Father died about nine years ago. Mother's mentally ill and lives in Westneath Nursing Home." Houston flipped a page. "She was right about when she opened Second Chances, but what she didn't volunteer is that the land it sits on was once the family home."

"She got the house and land?"

"Her sister and her. Layla signed it over to her a few years ago."

Maddox dropped his hands to his desk and sat

up straight. “She gave her sister the family real estate to use for the rehab program?”

“Looks that way.” Houston turned to another page. “According to federal records, everything about Second Chances is on the up-and-up. Files the right paperwork on time. Only has licensed employees. Properly accounts for all federal funds.”

“So, the program is clean?”

“Looks that way. She and her sister are members of Eternal Springs Christian Church.”

Great. Religious women. Maddox suppressed his moan.

“Oh, and she’s engaged.”

“Really? I didn’t notice a ring.”

“Well”—Houston tossed the stack of papers across the desk—“according to this report, she’s been engaged to Cameron Stone for four months.”

Name didn’t ring any bells. “Should I know who he is?”

“Some computer genius type. Writes software programs. Works in Lake Charles.”

“Like Bill Gates? Is Stone rich?”

“Not really. Makes about ninety grand a year.”

Maddox scrubbed his face with his hand. “Interesting.”

“Yeah.” Houston reached for another stack of papers. “Now, about Layla. Twenty-nine years old, licensed contractor. Opened her own business five years ago.”

"Yet she signed over the family real estate to her sister."

"Her father apparently left her some land on the bayou just outside of Eternal Springs. She built a house there just before she opened Taylor Construction."

"She lives out in the bayou alone?"

"It would appear." Houston flipped to the next sheet. "Better Business Bureau has no open complaints on her. She's a member of several of the local business-owner organizations. Has a good reputation in the industry, which is really saying something since she's a woman in such a male-dominated field."

"I'd say."

"But she followed in her father's footsteps. He was a contractor, worked for various locals over the years."

"He never hung out his own shingle?"

"Nope." Houston rubbed his chin. "As I recall hearing around town, Layla worked summers with her dad back when she was in high school." He glanced at the report again. "Must've gone straight into the business after she graduated. All her licenses and registrations are up to date and current."

"You said their dad died about nine years ago . . . from what?"

Houston shuffled the papers. "Massive heart attack."

"Ouch."

"Yeah. And their mom was admitted to Westneath about a year or so after that."

"Tough break for the girls." Maddox didn't want to feel empathy for them. They were suspects, after all. But with his own past, he couldn't help it.

"Reports show Alana goes every week to visit the mother."

"And Layla?"

"This is not verified, of course, but records don't reflect she's *ever* been to see the mother."

That didn't add up. Maddox crossed his arms over his chest. "What's the report on the mother? Dementia? Alzheimer's?"

"Report doesn't say."

"Maybe we should find out. Could be important."

"Yeah." Houston scribbled on a sticky note.

"Is Layla engaged as well?" Just asking the question left a bitter taste on his tongue. Why should he care about her love life? She was nothing more than a suspect . . . a person of interest in his case.

"Not that this report states."

Relief spread through Maddox.

"However, she was linked to one Randy Dean for several months last year."

Maddox didn't like the sting of jealousy stirring in his gut. "Who's he?"

"An electrician. Specializes in those high-dollar alarm system installations. Does volunteer firefighting."

"But they aren't linked anymore?"

"Nope. Report says they broke up about six months ago."

Again, relief filled Maddox. Stupid, betraying emotions.

"But there is something interesting about Layla."

There were a lot of things Maddox found interesting about her, but he wouldn't volunteer that to Houston. "What's that?"

"Guess what her hobby appears to be?"

"Sharpshooting?"

Houston chuckled. "So far out in left field you've made it into right."

"What?"

"Ballroom dancing."

Ballroom danc—The picture of her in a long dress in another man's arms drifted across his memory. Ballroom dancing surely was a contradiction to a building contractor.

Yet . . . it fit her too. He wouldn't have thought that except for the picture. She'd looked graceful and totally feminine.

And beautiful.

Maddox's stomach tightened. "Well, that is interesting," he said with a dry mouth.

"I thought so. She performs with a group called

Flows of Grace. Six couples formed together to compete and perform around the state." Houston set the stack of papers on the desk. "And that's all I have, folks."

Maddox made a note of the group's name. "Not much to go on."

"No. What do you make of the article?"

Maddox lifted the paper turned to the local interest section. "I don't see how someone would be so jealous over her getting an award that they'd kill someone and burn down the house she entered."

The intercom buzzed before the receptionist's voice filled their cubicle. "Wallace and Bishop? There's a Ms. Taylor here to see you."

Houston stood and straightened his shirt. "We've seen people murdered with a lot less motive."

Maddox set down the newspaper as he stood. "Let's go find out what Layla has to say."

NINE

"Be faithful in small things because it is in them that your strength lies."
—MOTHER TERESA

"MS. TAYLOR?" THE RECEPTIONIST called out.

Layla stood. The receptionist motioned toward the door where Detective Wallace waited. A buzz sounded, then the click of a security lock disengaging.

He smiled at her. "Thank you for coming in on such a nasty day." His wild-print shirt was untucked, his slacks already wrinkled.

"Did I have a choice?" She pressed her lips together tightly. So much for her speech to herself to keep her attitude in check. "Sorry," she mumbled.

Detective Wallace cleared his throat. "Okay. Right this way." He led her through an open hall. Phones rang. Voices muffled. The stench of burned coffee hovered. Their footsteps were stifled by the brownish carpet.

She followed him through a large room broken apart by workstation cubicles with six-foot walls, creating individual enclosed work areas. Into another hall they went. The reek of old coffee grew stronger. The tan walls closed around her, reminding her of the hours spent hiding in her bedroom as a teen. Hiding from her ranting mother. Layla shuddered.

Detective Wallace waved her into a room outfitted with a long table. Maddox sat on one side, standing as she entered. "Good morning."

Remembering her admonishment to keep her tongue in check, she nodded. "Morning."

Maddox gestured for her to take a seat on the other side of the table. She crossed the room, pulled out the chair, and dropped onto the hard, cold metal. The sooner she answered their stupid questions, the sooner they could get to really working the case.

Almost against her will, her gaze traveled over to Maddox. In contrast to his partner, Maddox was neatly dressed in khakis and a pullover. She just about missed the telling dark shadows under his eyes but registered them as his gaze met hers.

Unease pressed against her chest.

"Can we get you some water? Coffee?" Detective Wallace asked.

"No, thank you." Just get on with it so I can get out of here.

Detective Wallace closed the door and took a seat beside his partner. Maddox tapped a pen against a legal pad. "We have a few questions for you."

Obviously, or she wouldn't be here. "What can I help you with?" She concentrated on the top button of Detective Wallace's obnoxious shirt.

"I'm sure you've seen today's *American Press* . . ." Maddox looked over papers beneath his legal pad.

"Actually, no, I haven't."

Maddox's head jerked up. "You haven't?"

"No." Just answer their questions. Don't elaborate.

"Did you speak with a . . ." Maddox flipped papers. "A Krissy Morgan?"

"Yes. Yesterday." Oops. Just yes or no.

Silence fell over the table. Tension so palpable it took on a life force of its own. Layla went back to staring at Detective Wallace's button.

Maddox sighed. "So you know about her possible theory that someone burned down the house because of you."

"I—yes." She gripped her hands together in her lap under the table.

Maddox tapped his fingers on the table. Annoyingly so.

She chanced looking at him again.

Fire flickered in those true-blue eyes of his. "Well, what do you think about that?"

Letting out a slow breath, she struggled to keep her anger in check. "I think she's nuts. The only ones who care about the CotYs are contractors, and I don't know a single one who'd burn down *any* building. Period."

Detective Wallace scribbled on a legal pad, then set down the pen. "Have you had anyone make threats, even in jest, against you? Anyone with an ax to grind against your business?"

"No."

"What about someone personally?" Maddox jumped in.

"Excuse me?"

He set his elbows on the table. "A boyfriend? An ex?"

Randy was the only guy she'd really dated. He probably didn't even know what a CotY was. "No boyfriends—past or current."

"Someone who might want to see you fail?"

Now that list could be long and distinguished. Many, many men didn't think women belonged in the construction industry. But someone who would go to such extremes? "Not that I'm aware of." Not exactly a simple no, but it was the best she could do.

"Any competitors who'd like to steal some of your business?" Detective Wallace asked.

"Not that I can think of."

The frustration coming off the two of them slammed against her. She couldn't help it. She couldn't help them. They needed to realize they were barking up the wrong tree. That stupid Krissy Morgan . . .

"Who is Dennis LeJeune?" Maddox asked.

That snapped her attention to him. "An inspector."

"Was he the inspector on the Hope-for-Homes site?"

Where was this going? "Y-yes."

"So, you know him?"

"Of course. I know all the inspectors. So does every other contractor in the parish." She couldn't imagine *not* knowing the inspectors. It was almost part of her job.

"Is he a friend?"

She shrugged. "He's a business associate."

"What's your impression of him?"

Her impression? Of Dennis? Layla licked her lips. "Well, he's been an inspector for years. He's tough . . . by the book. A real stickler. He's well respected in the industry."

"A stickler?"

"Doesn't let anyone get away with anything." She'd veered far off her yes or no answers.

Maddox leaned forward, resting his elbows on the table again. "And you know this from personal experience?"

Oh, as if. "No. Like I said, he has a reputation because of his toughness."

"Where were you between eleven thirty and midnight on Friday?"

They thought she was a suspect! Her stomach balled into a tight knot.

"Ms. Taylor?" Maddox pierced her with his eyes.

Splinters! Think. Friday . . . Friday . . . And then she remembered. "I was at the home of Jeffery Davis." She and Jeffery had been practicing while his wife cheered them on.

Detective Wallace's pencil scraped against the paper.

A knock sounded against the door. Detective Wallace stood and cracked the door, whispering to the person in the hall. Layla felt Maddox's hot stare. She avoided eye contact, studying the nicks in the table.

"Well, thank you for coming in, Ms. Taylor. That's all the questions we have for now." Detective Wallace opened the door all the way.

She glanced up, catching a silent exchange between the two men.

Whatever.

She stood and pushed her chair back under the table.

Detective Wallace motioned her into the hall. "Let me walk you out."

Maddox said nothing.

She shook Detective Wallace's offered hand at the door to the reception area.

"Again, we really appreciate you coming in on such short notice."

"Happy to help." Well, that wasn't the whole truth, but she *had* shown up. Only to find they thought she was a suspect.

He gave her a final nod, then hurried out of sight.

She ducked out into the downpour, rushing to her truck. Somehow she was left feeling like they wouldn't really get to the bottom of this anytime soon. Not if they thought she had anything to do with this.

Thanks to Krissy Morgan's stupid article, Layla's name and reputation would be tarnished until the truth came out. No one would want to hire her for fear something might happen to his project.

Maybe she'd do a little investigating herself. She knew the people in the business better than the detectives, that much was certain. Maybe she could just ask around. Get her ear to the ground. See what she could find out.

She smiled as she started her truck, imagining what Maddox's expression would look like if she solved the case.

When she solved it.

"CASTEEL CALLED. POSITIVE ID of John Doe." Houston hurried down the corridor, returning to their cubicle.

"Dennis LeJeune?" Maddox paused in front of his desk.

"Give the man a gold star."

Maddox sat opposite his partner. "We need to trace Dennis's steps those last few days."

"Yep." Houston's fingers flew over his keyboard. "Am requesting the records of all the buildings he inspected over the last twelve months."

"Wonder how many of them were built by Ms. Taylor?"

Houston paused in his typing and met Maddox's stare. "She bugs you, doesn't she?"

Maddox made a *pffffing* sound. "She's a person of interest in this case."

"Oh, you definitely find her interesting, don't you?" Houston crossed his arms over his chest and grinned.

Maddox wadded up a scrap of paper and tossed it across the desk. It hit Houston before falling to the floor. "Puh-leeze. Give it a rest."

Houston cocked his head and chuckled. "She's really gotten under your skin."

"Man, I think those bright shirts have damaged your brain. Why must you wear things like that?" Maddox sneered but heat had already crept across the back of his neck.

"This shirt was a gift, I'll have you know."

"Margie has better taste than that." Maddox snorted. "Well, then again, she did marry you."

Houston laughed. "The boys got it for me."

"They should have better taste," Maddox mumbled. But at least the subject of his interest in Layla had been dropped.

"Did you hear about the upcoming memo?"

"What?"

Houston's face was somber. "The commander'll be sending a memo around next week. About the *future of the department*."

Maddox's stomach squeezed. "Think he's gonna announce he's running for sheriff?"

"Don't know." Houston clapped Maddox's back. "Don't sweat it. You're a shoo-in if he does."

Maddox nodded, but any words were caught in his chest.

"Anyway," Houston continued, "we already got confirmation back from the bowling alley. Workers remember seeing LeJeune there, but his team left around ten. By all counts, he should've been home before ten thirty."

"That's interesting. What about others there? Anybody see him leave with someone?"

"According to all reports the uniforms got, LeJeune was seen getting into his car alone about ten to ten fifteen. Nobody saw him after that."

That was no help. Maddox reached for the papers filling his in-box. Memo, tossed on the desk. Softball team-forming flyer, wadded up and thrown in trash. Memo, tossed on desk. Reports.

He stopped flipping and began reading. That familiar stirring churned in his gut. "Hey, Houston. Got the report back on those three druggies from Second Chances who worked at the site."

"Yeah?"

"First one, Sam Roberson."

Houston swiveled in his chair. "Whoa! Sam Roberson, the dentist?"

"No, his son. Sam Junior."

"Ah. Heard something about his boy getting into some trouble over in Orleans Parish."

"Apparently it was drugs." Maddox continued reading. "Shows the judge released him from the program two months ago. Now he works full time at J. B. Carpentry."

Houston scribbled in his notebook. "We'll visit him."

"He was released right about the same time the house was completed." Maddox turned the page. "Next up is Darren Watkins."

"Don't think I know him."

"Name should be familiar. Kid's got quite the rap sheet."

"Really?"

"Two counts of assault. Five counts of drunk and disorderly. One count of possession, but that was when he was a minor so the details are scrubbed. Three counts of domestic assault."

Houston scratched his head. "And a judge gave him rehab?"

"After a four-month stint at the parish jail."

Houston pushed his pen across his notebook. "Where is he now?"

"Still at Second Chances. Papers here say the judge hasn't released him from the program yet."

"We'll talk to him today."

"Along with Alana Taylor." Maddox leaned back in his chair. "Wonder why she didn't mention him when we talked to her before?"

"Maybe he's been a model patient in rehab?"

Maddox snorted and grabbed the papers. "Right. And I'm the Queen of Sheba."

"Who's the third candidate in our lineup today?"

Maddox smiled. "Kenny Lindsay. No previous record. Judge released him from the program almost three months ago."

"Where is he?"

"Last report shows he left town. Went back to the Baton Rouge area." Maddox shoved the papers into the file. "And that's the hits for today."

"Why don't we start with talking to Mrs. LeJeune, then interview Sam, then run by Second Chances and talk with the Watkins character?"

Maddox stood. "We haven't left yet?"

TEN

"Enemies are so stimulating."
—KATHARINE HEPBURN

DARK AND DISMAL. SEEMED the weather mimicked the sentiments of her heart on this January afternoon. Even though it was Tuesday, it felt like Monday all over again.

Even Alana had called with bad news. Fred had traced the drugs Gavin used back to the Ike

Thompson site. One of the crew remembered a stranger talking with Gavin off to the side. Now Gavin's probation officer had pulled him from the program. Alana was beside herself.

Layla rested her chin in her hands, staring at the computer screen with Taylor Construction's schedule. She'd received umpteen calls this morning—all asking or commenting about that stupid newspaper article. But the calls that worried her most were the ones from clients. Two had already called and delayed their upcoming remodeling projects. If a couple more did the same, her business could be in for some rough months.

She couldn't blame them, really. If they believed what that nervy Krissy Morgan implied in the article, Layla's doing any work for them could put their project in danger of being destroyed. Who wanted to take that risk?

Understanding that didn't make it any easier to accept.

Do what needed to be done. Wasn't that her motto?

Layla lifted the phone and dialed the number. She would call every independent she'd contracted on the Hope-for-Homes site. There had to be an answer somewhere. She just had to find it.

"J. B. Carpentry."

"May I speak with Jonas, please?"

"Hang on."

Layla glanced at her notes while she waited on hold. She knew every name on the list—knew these people personally—and just couldn't believe any of them would burn a home.

"Jonas Baxter."

"Hey, Jonas. It's Layla." She smiled and leaned back in her chair.

"Hi, Layla. Sorry to read that article about you in the paper. Nasty business."

She let the smile slip away. "It is. Listen, I wanted to ask you about that project."

"Yeah?"

"Do you remember anything odd about the job?"

"The Hope-for-Homes house?"

"Yeah." She lifted her pen and chewed on the end.

"What exactly are you thinking of?"

"Nothing in particular. Just wondering if you remembered anybody hanging around the site who didn't belong or something like that."

"No. I'm sorry."

"Do you have a list of your crew who worked there?"

"Of course."

"I know you had one Second Chancer."

"Yeah. Sam Roberson."

"What do you remember about him? Was he a good worker?" Sam had also worked for Bob

Johnson on some days. Was he flipping interests to get onto sites?

Jonas laughed. “I hope so. I hired him on full time after he was released from the program.”

Alana would be pleased to hear that. “No problems with him, then?”

“Not a one. He’s one of my best workers.”

“Thanks, Jonas. I appreciate it.” She replaced the receiver and made a note. At least she could cross one name off her list. If Sam Roberson had gone even slightly over the line, Jonas would’ve yanked him back faster than a flooding in a hurricane. He sure wouldn’t have hired him.

Layla glanced back over the list. She’d save the call to Bob for last. Going to the next number, she lifted the receiver again and dialed.

“Denny Keys Electric.” The older woman’s forced chipper tone grated against Layla’s nerves.

“Denny, please.”

“May I ask who’s calling?”

“Layla Taylor.”

“Hi, Layla. You haven’t heard?”

She sat forward, hunched over the desk with every muscle tensed. “Heard what?”

“Denny had surgery two weeks ago. Had his hip replaced. He’s still in the physical-therapy unit.”

Two weeks ago. Definitely couldn’t be involved with the burning. “No, I didn’t know. I’ll have to send him a card. Thanks.”

"Anything I can help you with, hon?"

"No. Just give Denny my best when you talk to him." Layla replaced the receiver and crossed another name off the list.

Progress, although she hadn't learned anything useful for her situation. She didn't even really know what she hoped to find out. Something. Anything.

The phone rang, startling her. "Hello."

"How's it going?" Alana sounded awful, even compared to her tone earlier that morning.

Layla swallowed the sigh and forced her voice to come out upbeat. "Making some calls. What's up?"

"I just heard Ms. Ethel passed away."

Words wouldn't form. Layla's heart tripped.

Alana sniffled. "Her grandson says she slipped into a coma and just stopped breathing."

Tears welled in her eyes, blurring her vision. "I-I can't believe it."

"I know." Alana sniffed again. "I called Pastor Chaney. He's headed to the hospital now. It's awful."

"I don't know what to say."

"There's nothing to say. I just wanted you to know."

"Thanks."

"Cameron and I are still planning on going to your performance tonight."

"You don't have to."

"I want to."

"Well, considering Ms. Ethel . . ."

Alana let out a little laugh. "She'd be the first one to tell you the show must go on."

Layla smiled as the woman's face danced across her mind. "Yeah, she would."

"She loved watching you dance, Layla."

The ache in her chest tightened. "I know."

"Well"—Alana cleared her throat—"we'll see you tonight. Seven, right?"

"Right. Thanks." She hung up the phone, a large hole already forming in her heart. She'd miss Ms. Ethel. More than she missed her mother.

No. She wouldn't go there now. Layla forced herself to shove aside the grief. She knew all too well she'd take it back out and deal with it later. When she was in the privacy of her house.

Layla glanced at the clock. She had time for another call or two. She lifted the phone and dialed the next number.

"Y Building Supplies, how may I direct your call?"

"Ed Young, please."

"May I tell him who's calling?"

"Layla Taylor."

"One moment, please."

Music flooded against her ear. She tapped her pen to the beat of the easy-listening tune. This was probably a waste of time. Ed had been the supplier her father used most often. He'd been so supportive when Kevin Taylor had died. Encouraging to Layla when she started her own company. She never had to prove herself worthy of his business.

Not like some of the independents she'd had to convince.

"Well, hello, Layla." Ed's booming voice vibrated over the line.

Layla smiled. "Hi, Ed. How're you?"

"Fine. Fine. How's business?"

"You know. Slow season."

"What can I do for you?"

"I need to pick your brain about the Hope-for-Homes project we concluded a few months ago. You were the supplier on it."

"I remember."

"Do you recall anything odd about the job?"

"Odd?"

"Yeah." She lifted her pen and chewed on the end again. "Like if you remember anybody hanging around the site who didn't belong or something like that."

"No. I'm sorry." Ed paused. "Then again, we only delivered the materials and dropped them off."

"That's what I figured." She sighed. "Just had to ask."

"Why? What's going on?"

"Did you see the article on me in today's paper?"

"I haven't read the paper yet. What's the deal?"

She wrapped the cord around her finger. "Long story short, that house was burned down and they found a body in it."

"Oh, dear. I hadn't realized."

"Yeah. So I'm just trying to figure it out."

"Aren't the police investigating?"

She snorted and let the cord go. It sprung off her finger and hit the desk. "I don't think they're doing a good job of it."

"So, you are?" Ed's voice deepened. "Layla, you need to let the police do their job."

"I know. It's just frustrating."

Ed chuckled. "That's why I'm considering retiring at the end of the year. Get out of this crazy business."

"You aren't serious?"

"Not really, but I have thought about it."

"You're too good to retire." She smiled. "Besides, you're my favorite supplier."

He laughed again. "And you're one of my favorite contractors."

A buzzing sound came over the line.

"But now I've got another call."

"No problem. Thanks, Ed. It was great talking with you."

"You too. And I'll think about it tonight. If any memory pops up, I'll let you know."

"Thanks." She placed the receiver back in its cradle.

Another dead end. They were all long shots. What did she think she'd find out?

She glanced at the clock. Four fifty. She'd have to call Bob on his cell. With a sigh, she lifted the phone and dialed the number.

"This is Bob." He answered on the second ring.

"Hey, Bob. It's Layla Taylor."

"Yeah?"

"Do you remember the Hope-for-Homes house?"

"Of course. Do you think drugs were there too?"

She couldn't really blame him for being defensive. Days ago she'd questioned him about drugs on his sites. Even though she'd been as diplomatic as possible, nobody liked the inference.

"Not that I'm aware of. I was just wondering if you remember anything odd or strange about the site."

"You were the foreman."

"I know. But maybe something I didn't see. Like strange visitors to the site when I wasn't there."

"Like a drug dealer? I know you think that's what happened on Thompson's site."

She sighed, sorry she'd ever talked to him. "No. Just someone who didn't belong."

"I can't think of anybody. I didn't see anything out of the ordinary."

Another dead end. And she'd irritated Bob

even more. He'd probably never do any plumbing work for her again. "Well, thanks anyway. You have a good evening."

"Why do you want to know?" He interrupted her dismissal.

"Well, the police are supposedly asking around. Trying to find out about the house burning and the body inside."

"So, why are you calling me? Did you tell them you thought someone was using drugs on one of my sites?"

"No, no. Nothing like that." Even though that's what Fred and Alana had determined. She bit her bottom lip. Why *was* she calling? What did she hope to find out? "I'm just trying to look into it. The police don't know any of us."

"You think one of us in the industry is responsible?"

"It would make sense, don't you think?"

"No."

"Then what do you think?"

"I don't know, Layla. I let the police do their job."

The chastisement stung. "Well, thanks anyway, Bob." She hung up the phone, letting her hand rest on the number pad as she thought.

She'd called all the independents she'd contracted and didn't learn a single thing. Except that Bob would never work for her again.

Right now she had to head home and get ready. She had a performance to give.

She'd give the best performance of her life tonight and may just have to do the same to save her business.

"THAT WENT BETTER THAN I thought." Houston started the car and pulled out of the LeJeune's driveway.

Maddox swallowed. "Always hard to tell someone her loved one is dead, though." Worse was witnessing a loved one dying right in front of them. He'd never forget the image of his mother dying on her bedroom floor. The memory was emblazoned upon his brain forever.

Houston glanced at the clock on the dashboard light. "I'm going to interview Fred Daly, Second Chances' assistant director and the good doctors there. Want to tag along?"

"I have plans tonight."

Popping his gum, Houston took his attention off the road for a moment to look at him. "Do tell?"

Heat fingered out across Maddox's shoulders and neck. "Yeah. I promised a certain lady supper in exchange for her help. She called it in today."

"Anyone special?" Houston concentrated on the road again.

"No. Definitely not." Maddox could've bit his tongue. He didn't mean to sound so sharp and callous.

"I see."

And by Houston's tone, Maddox knew he was

about to get yet another lecture on the joys of a committed relationship. He wasn't in the mood, so he would cut off the spiel before Houston could start. "And I'm kinda working."

Houston grunted. "How's that?"

"Well, after supper, I'm taking the lady to a performance."

"A performance?" Houston steered the car into the sheriff's department parking lot. "How is that considered working?"

"It's a *Flows of Grace* performance."

Houston turned off the engine and twisted to stare at Maddox. "That rings a bell."

"It should." Maddox smiled. "It's the dancing group Layla Taylor belongs to. I already checked . . . she's scheduled to dance tonight."

"Think that's smart? Just to show up like that?"

"It's a public performance." Maddox reached for the door handle. "She probably won't even notice me in the audience."

Houston opened his door and got out of the car. He spit his gum into the trash can beside the parking lot. "And if she does?"

"So what?" Maddox slammed the door shut.

"She could take your presence there as harassment."

Maddox chuckled as he dug his keys out of his pocket. "Puh-leeze. Harassment? By attending a public performance? That's not harassment by anybody's standards."

"Stalking?" Houston stopped beside Maddox's truck.

Maddox frowned. "You're reaching now."

"I don't think it's a good idea."

"She won't even know I'm there. I promise."

"So, why are you going?"

"She's a person of interest in the case. I'm just trying to get a handle on her."

Houston grinned. "Yeah, you're trying to get a handle on her all right."

Maddox pointed at him. "Don't forget Uncle George invited us both over for lunch tomorrow. Fried backstrap. Noon."

"I'm in."

"See you tomorrow." Maddox slipped behind the wheel of his truck. He couldn't explain why he wanted to see Layla Taylor perform her ballroom dancing. He just did.

And he sure couldn't explain why he was taking Megan Goins with him. That could truly be an incident waiting to happen. But he'd needed an excuse to be there, and what better one than to be on a date.

Just in case Layla did see him.

Maddox started the engine and backed out of his parking space. A fleeting thought slashed across his mind. Would Layla get jealous if she saw him out with Megan?

Why did he even wonder?

ELEVEN

"A thing of beauty is a joy forever:
its loveliness increases; it will never
pass into nothingness."
—JOHN KEATS

NERVES GNAWED HER STOMACH.

Layla let out the breath she'd been holding and flexed her fingers. She and Jeffery were up next. An American Viennese waltz—a one, two, three count. Performing to "Waltz for the Moon." Tempo of 177 beats per minute. Natural turn. Reverse turn. Closed changes forward. Closed changes back. Beautiful and elegant. She should be able to do this dance in her sleep.

She checked her dress a final time. The off-the-shoulder black Lycra dress clung to her like a second skin. The two sections of horizontal lace as well as the lace long sleeves itched against her dry skin. Layla kicked out the flaring bottom skirt. Perfectly hemmed, it didn't catch on her four-inch rhinestone-encrusted heels.

"You look amazing and we'll do fine. Stop fidgeting," Jeffery whispered in her ear.

She turned to smile up at him. "Easy for you to say. You don't have to worry about your dress getting caught in your shoes."

He chuckled, deep and reassuring. "Thank

goodness." He ran a hand over his slicked-back hair. "How do I look?"

"Handsome as always." Handsome, he was. Tall, dark-haired, and as lithe as a cat.

And very much married to the love of his life.

He smiled. "My bride said to tell you she likes your hair that way."

Layla's hands automatically went to smooth her hair. She normally wore it up in a bun, but tonight she'd left it down, taming it into large waves reminiscent of the fifties. "Tell her thanks."

"You tell her after we dance."

His wife refused to dance but loved watching Jeffery glide across the floor. She never missed a performance. Layla thought her the sweetest thing. "I will."

The last bridge of Chester and Buffy's fox-trot began.

Layla exhaled slowly but smiled at Jeffery. She wiped her palms on the towel by the stage entrance. In a minute the announcer would introduce them.

A door slammed behind her. She shifted to see around Jeffery.

And almost threw up.

Looking more dashing and dangerous than ought to be legal, Randy Dean slipped backstage. He wore black slacks and a red silk shirt. He gripped a rose in his hand.

Layla remembered to shut her mouth. "What is he doing here?" she ground out between clenched teeth.

"I don't know, but by his outfit, I'd say he's come to dance the tango."

Oh, she *was* going to be sick.

Natalie Combs flitted to Randy, her long, black hair wound up into a French twist. "I thought you were going to stand me up." She kissed the air beside his face.

Every muscle in Layla's body tensed. The hair on the back of her neck stood at attention. And every word of her last argument with Randy flooded her.

> *"Well, maybe I'd be interested in something more permanent if you were more feminine," Randy sneered.*
>
> *Layla's back stiffened. "Excuse me? More feminine?"*
>
> *"You're a joke, Lay. All the guys laugh at you behind your back. No one takes you seriously as a contractor."*
>
> *She couldn't have been more hurt if he'd slapped her.*
>
> *"Why don't you stop trying to live up to Daddy's expectations?"*
>
> *The urge to vomit nearly gagged her. She fisted her hands at her sides. "And do what, pray tell?"*

"Act like a lady. Be more like Natalie."

Red flashed before her eyes. She'd heard all the rumors . . . and ignored them. Never even asked him about them.

Maybe she should have. "Natalie's so great, is she?"

"She knows how to be a lady. Be feminine. Knows how to keep a man interested." His words held the hidden meanings that ripped her heart from her chest.

So the rumors were definitely true. Her body went numb. "If she's such a lady, why are you here with me? Why aren't you chasing after Ms. Feminine herself?"

Randy's face contorted with anger. "Maybe I should be. Beats wasting my time with you—a boy wannabe."

Defiance lifted her chin. "There's nothing stopping you from leaving."

He grabbed his jacket. "Consider me gone."

Layla hadn't heard from him in six months. Six months! She'd been told he'd moved out of town. Natalie had never said anything during rehearsals.

Now he was back. His eyes met hers in the dim backstage lighting.

Her world tilted on its axis.

Chester and Buffy whizzed by. The emcee announced the waltz and introduced Layla and Jeffery.

She couldn't move.

Jeffery grabbed her by the shoulders and spun her to face him, away from Randy's debilitating gaze. "Ignore him. Concentrate. You can do this." He led her two steps toward the stage entrance.

She nearly tripped over her feet.

He steadied her. "Layla, look at me. Layla!"

She swallowed and met his stare.

"You can do this. Just follow my lead. Listen to the music. The beat. The tempo. Count it out in your head. One, two, three."

She nodded numbly.

"Layla!"

She shivered.

"Don't give him the satisfaction of making you mess up. Put him out of your head and concentrate on me. Look into my eyes—nowhere else, just in my eyes."

She focused on the bridge of his nose and nodded.

"Okay." He let out a breath and took her hand, shaking them loosely. "Let's do this. Remember, keep your focus on me."

Oh, Lord, help me.

SHE WAS STUNNING.

Maddox swallowed back his surprise. Layla

Taylor was attractive in her own way, but tonight . . . in that dress with her hair looking all silky . . . she stole his breath.

Her body moved as one with her partner's. Her eyes never left his face.

A claw of jealousy raked across Maddox's chest. He shifted in his seat.

"They're good," Megan whispered.

Maddox struggled to remember Layla was a person of interest in the case. He forced his arm draped across the back of Megan's chair not to tense. He lifted his glass from the linen-covered table and took a sip, not even tasting the sweetness of the sparkling cider.

Layla and her partner floated above the dance floor. Her dress swooshed through the air at her ankles. Her posture was picture perfect.

They rounded the dance floor closest to Maddox, and he noticed her expression. Eyes glazed over. Brow wrinkled in concentration. Neck stiff.

Something wasn't right.

Maybe that was her normal dancing posture, but Maddox didn't think so. The set of her jaw. Her unsmiling face.

Yep, something was definitely off.

He glanced over to the other side of the dance floor where he'd spied her sister earlier. Still seated and holding hands with the man Maddox could only assume was her fiancé, Alana

Taylor's eyes followed every step of her sister's.

The worry lining her face told Maddox he was right. Alana saw it too.

With a final, elaborate dip, the song ended. Layla and her partner stood in the center of the floor, took a bow to each side, then eased off stage. Across the dance floor Alana stood. She kissed her fiancé, leaned over to whisper in his ear, then turned toward the side exit.

The emcee held the microphone. "And to close out this evening's performance, we welcome back Randy Dean dancing the tango with Natalie Combs."

Alana stopped in her tracks, gaping at the stage.

Maddox followed her stare to the man taking a starting position. The dancer popped a rose between his teeth and straightened his spine. Maddox glanced to Alana. She'd back-stepped to her table and sunk into her chair. Her eyes were wide. Her face pale.

Looking at the couple on stage, taking their first steps as the music started, Maddox blinked several times. What was he missing?

His heart thudded hard against his rib cage. *Randy Dean*. The guy Layla had been involved with.

Maddox studied the man moving across the stage. Tall. Dark hair. Was he handsome? Maddox sneaked a peek at Megan. Her eyes were wide . . . her mouth slightly parted. Yeah, she found Randy Dean attractive.

Another bite of jealousy burned in Maddox's gut.

The emcee had said "we welcome back Randy Dean," indicating he'd been gone. The look on Layla's and Alana's faces said neither knew he'd be making a return appearance tonight.

Could it have something to do with the case?

Maddox took another sip of his sparkling cider. Where had Randy been? Why was he back? Odd coincidence that he'd returned right after a home Layla built had burned down. Where was Randy on Friday night between eleven thirty and midnight?

Was there bad blood between the two of them? Enough that Randy would do something to hurt her business, like that reporter had insinuated? Maybe jealousy wasn't the motive but revenge?

Tomorrow he'd find out everything he could on Randy Dean.

WHY WAS LAYLA GETTING mixed up in the investigation?

He didn't want to hurt her—hadn't wanted to hurt anyone, but Dennis had pushed him. Had given him no choice.

But Layla?

Why couldn't she just leave the sleuthing to the cops? They wouldn't be able to piece anything together. But Layla? Well . . . there was a good chance she'd see the connection. Especially if she started looking at past records.

Records!

He needed to destroy her records, then she wouldn't put the puzzle together. And it would give her something else to concentrate on. The police could do their minor investigating, but they would eventually file the case away. Another crime would take its place.

Tonight. He'd destroy her records tonight.

By tomorrow Layla Taylor would forget completely about playing Nancy Drew.

TWELVE

"And, after all, what is a lie?
'Tis but the truth in a masquerade."
—ALEXANDER POPE

THE NERVE OF HIM! Coming back. Dancing with Natalie. Jeering at her with his stare.

Layla slammed the door to her truck and marched up the stairs to her cabin. Forgetting she hadn't wanted to take the time to change clothes, she stepped too hard and her heel caught in the space between the boards and broke off. She pitched forward and fell hard on her hands and knees. Her anger and frustration gave way to pain.

Hot tears slipped down her cheeks. After she'd left the performance, she had driven for hours, letting her anger and embarrassment go with the miles. But now . . . She curled into the fetal position on her cold front porch. For once she let her emotions overtake her. *Why, God? Why let him come back? Not that I care about him, but . . . God, why?*

The phone ringing inside the cabin snagged her attention. Who would be calling at this hour? Had to be an emergency. Or Alana calling to check on her, probably worried sick. With a slow exhale, she pushed to standing, wiped her scraped hands on her now-snagged dress, unlocked the front door, then hobbled inside as fast as possible. Stupid broken heel.

The fourth ring echoed off the walls.

"Hello." She leaned against the kitchen counter and kicked off her shoes.

"Layla Taylor?"

"Yes." Her hose were ruined. Her knees bloodied and scraped. And now burning. She snatched a towel from the bar, wet it, and dabbed at her knees.

"This is Homestead Security."

She dropped the towel and forgot all about her painful knees. "Yes?"

"We received an alarm notice from your business system. We tried to contact the location for the password but received no response."

"No one should be in the office."

"Yes, ma'am. Police have been dispatched."

Her blood ran colder than the dropping temperature outside. "T-thank you for letting me know."

"Yes, ma'am. We'll report back after we hear from the police whether it was an actual break-in or not."

Layla's heart started beating again. "So you're not certain there was a break-in."

"No, ma'am. As per procedure, we contacted your secondary number for notification."

"Thank you again." She dropped the phone back to its base and turned to rush out.

Her hosed feet slipped on the hardwood and she fell again. She slapped her hands on the floor. *God, what is going on? Why is this happening to me? Please let the office be okay.*

Only the throbbing of her knees answered her.

Using the kitchen metal trash can for support, she pulled herself to standing. She walked down the hallway to her bedroom. At a much slower pace. After a quick change into jeans, sweatshirt, and sneakers, Layla grabbed her keys and headed back into the blistery wind.

She continued to pray on her drive to Taylor Construction. Her heart hammered into her throat. What if someone had read that stupid article in the paper and got ideas? What if someone had broken into the office and set it on fire, like the Hope-for-Homes site? She pressed harder on the accelerator.

Whipping onto the street that the office was on, Layla let out a little sigh. No flames licked the predawn skyline. No firefighters fought a blaze.

There was, however, an Eternal Springs police cruiser in the driveway. The strobing lights sent her heart back into double speed as she parked in front of the front door and jumped out of the truck.

A uniformed officer met her at the door. "Hold it right there, ma'am. Who are you?"

"Layla Taylor. This is my office." She took in the broken window in the front. *Lord, no. Don't let this be something awful.*

In a moment another officer joined them. "Ms. Taylor, I'm Assistant Chief Rex Carson and this is Officer Thibodeaux."

"What happened?"

"Looks like someone broke in."

A mountain moved into her gut.

"We think they were looking for something."

"Can I go in?"

Carson shook his head. "This is a crime scene, ma'am. We've called in detectives from the sheriff's office to send over a unit to dust for prints and collect any evidence."

She swallowed against an arid mouth. "How long will that take? I need to know what's missing."

"Ma'am, I'm sure the detectives will want to talk with you, and I imagine they'll want you to walk through with them." Carson nodded toward the cruiser. "You're welcome to sit in the car where it's warm until they get here."

She chewed her bottom lip. This couldn't be happening. "I'll wait in my truck."

A chill that had nothing to do with the January weather crept over her as she climbed into the cab of her vehicle. Her teeth chattered as she gripped her hands tightly together in her lap and hunched over. *Why, God, why? Why this? Why now . . . when everything was starting to go right?*

Her knees began to throb, but she ignored the pain, choosing to stare at her office. Two officers stood in the doorway. Guarding it? Had they run someone off? She hadn't even thought to ask. She glanced at the cruiser with its lights still flashing. No one sat in the backseat. Obviously they didn't catch whoever had broken in.

Why would someone break into the office? She didn't keep money in there ever. There was nothing of extreme value, not even tools. She kept her tools in her truck or at the house. There was nothing of worth to anyone in the office, so why break in?

To hurt her, like that stupid article had suggested? Who would do such a thing?

Layla rested her forehead against the steering

wheel. Exhaustion weighted down every muscle in her body. It was all too much. First, Randy coming back. She'd closed that part of her life off for good. Or so she thought. But his return flared the hurt and anger she'd buried deep inside. She felt raw.

And now this break-in.

A car engine hummed. She jerked up her head in time to catch an unmarked cruiser sloshing into the space beside her truck. She recognized the driver. And groaned. *Seriously, God?* Could her luck get any worse?

Maddox exited the car. His features were lost in the darkness but not his hulking presence. Detective Wallace stepped in front of the vehicle, its headlights shining on his wild Hawaiian-print shirt. He climbed the stairs and spoke with the officers in the doorway.

She eased open the truck door.

Maddox stood waiting against his car, his arms crossed over his chest, as she joined him. "Good morning, Ms. Taylor."

Something about his casual demeanor set her off. "There's nothing good about it, Detective Bishop."

"True." He pushed off the vehicle and dropped his arms.

"I thought you handled violent crimes or something."

"I do. But when Taylor Construction popped up

on the radar, the detective recognized the name as involved in our case, so he called us."

"Involved in your case? How, exactly—?" She shook her head, remembering he thought of her as a suspect. "You know what? Never mind. I don't care. Whatever." She glanced at the doorway. One of the officers and Detective Wallace had disappeared into the office. "Can I go inside now?"

Maddox looked over his shoulder, then back at her. "In just a minute. Houston's taking some photographs of the scene without any contamination."

Contamination? She bit her lip and nodded.

"Can you think of any reason someone would want to break in?"

"No. I don't keep cash or equipment in there."

"Any idea who'd break in? Maybe just to hurt you or your business?"

"None." She worked the clumps of mud with the toe of her sneaker. "I know that article might have given somebody ideas, but I can't think of anyone."

"What about someone who wanted revenge on you?"

She snapped her gaze to meet his. "Revenge for what?"

He shrugged. "Maybe a relationship gone bad?"

"N—" She closed her mouth. Randy was back

in town. By the scowl he'd thrown at her earlier, he hated her. Although she couldn't imagine why—he'd been the one who'd left her. And she remembered her conversation with Bob Johnson. He hadn't exactly been friendly. Honestly, he'd been quite bitter.

But that didn't mean either man was involved.

"Layla?"

It wouldn't be fair to name the men without proof of some sort. "No."

Maddox's jaw tightened. "I see."

Detective Wallace emerged from the office. "Layla, you ready to walk through?"

She nodded, then tossed Maddox a final glance before she headed into her office.

Lord, don't let the damage be bad. Please.

THE CHANGE IN LAYLA . . . Maddox shook his head. Gone was the picture-perfect posture. The grace. The intensity in her demeanor.

As he followed her and Houston on the walk-through, all he noticed was the dejection. The brokenness. It was heartbreaking.

No. She was just a person of interest in one of his cases.

But she was now also a victim.

There had to be a connection.

"So, is anything missing?" Houston asked.

"My computers. I had one here in the reception area. Y'all saw it the other day. And one in my office." Her voice was without emotion as she stepped over upturned plants and scattered papers.

"The printer in your office is still there."

She shook her head. "Looks like all they took were the computers and my records." Her voice cracked. Her shoulders slumped. "And trashed the place."

Everything in Maddox wanted to go and hold her. Comfort her.

What? Where did *that* come from? He was a cop. She was a victim of robbery. He had no business thinking about holding or comforting her.

But despite all logic and reasoning, his arms ached to do just that.

Houston made notes, then laid a hand on Layla's forearm.

Her head popped up.

"That's all you can do for now. We have a unit coming that will dust for prints and try to recover any evidence."

Her eyes were glazed over. "Can't I start cleaning up? This is my business."

Houston shook his head. "Not until our unit finishes gathering evidence."

She sagged. Again, Maddox wanted to hold her. He needed to get a grip on himself. Maybe he was coming down with a cold or something.

He'd never been one to be attracted to weaker

women. Houston said he used that as an excuse. But Layla Taylor wasn't weak. She was strong. To see her downtrodden because of something that'd happened to her beyond her control . . . well, it made his gut stir in a strange way.

One he wasn't sure he liked.

"Okay. When will that be?" She jutted out her chin as she spoke to Houston. Regaining her stance.

Good for her. A fighter. Not one to roll over and play dead when the bad stuff hit.

"Several hours. Why don't I call you when they're done?" Houston closed his notebook and stuffed it into his back pocket.

"Fine." She turned for the door.

"Layla?" Maddox called out, surprising himself.

She looked over her shoulder at him, the question in her eyes.

"We'll find out who did this."

She hesitated, then gave him a curt nod before leaving.

Houston cleared his throat.

"What?" Maddox asked.

His partner lifted his brows. "Since when do you make promises to find a B&E perp?"

Heat shot up his neck and across his face. "This is connected to our case, and you know it."

Houston laughed. "Yeah, I think so too. But

making such a vow?" He continued to chuckle, which annoyed Maddox.

Only because he suspected his partner was on to something: the truth about how he was beginning to feel about Layla Taylor.

"My interviews with Fred Daly and the doctors turned up nothing."

Maddox turned back to his partner. "Odd that someone breaks in and only steals two computers and paperwork, wouldn't you say?"

"Sounds like someone's either looking for something specific or trying to destroy something."

"Because there's a link between LeJeune's murder, the Hope-for-Homes burning, and Taylor Construction."

Maddox nodded, letting his mind wander to come up with viable scenarios. "We already know who all worked on the site. Why destroy records now, if that's what they were after?"

Houston moved down the stairs and leaned on the cruiser. "Maybe the perp didn't know we already had that information."

"Maybe." But it didn't fly with Maddox. "We need to do a background check on Randy Dean. He's someone Layla was involved with who left town but has returned. Recently."

Houston's cell phone went off. He glanced at the caller ID. "Margie." He flipped open the phone. "What's wrong?"

Maddox tried not to stare, but his partner's face paled and he stared at Maddox. "Okay. I'll let him know." Houston closed the phone and shoved it back into his belt clip.

"What?"

"It's your dad."

THIRTEEN

"The value of a man should be
seen in what he gives and not
in what he is able to receive."
—ALBERT EINSTEIN

HE'D KEPT HIS SECRET safe.

Although he hadn't wanted to hurt Layla, he'd destroyed everything. Her records . . . her documents . . . even her personal notes.

The act gave him a measure of comfort. He'd protected himself and his family. Now the police could try to reconstruct all the information, but they wouldn't see the connection. They wouldn't figure it out. No one could.

Except Layla Taylor.

And maybe the break-in would be enough to keep her busy. Keep her from digging. She was the one person who could assemble the details and have it make sense. But if she had other things keeping her occupied . . .

He liked her. Admired her. Respected her.

Appreciated that she was a good contractor and a good businesswoman.

But if he had to, he'd take more drastic measures. His own future depended on Layla not figuring it out. Not seeing the connection.

He'd play it by ear. See what she did. Maybe she'd confide in him a little about the investigation. That'd be nice—knowing where the police were in the case.

It might come down to him having to act further. Do something else to get Layla to lay off the searching. Not for the money, even though that's what he stood to gain. But his own preservation. And a future with his kids.

He would do everything he could to avoid hurting Layla. She'd always been nice to him. Treated him with respect.

Her father had been inspiring. Honorable. A good, good man.

If need be, he'd send Layla another message. But not hurt her. That would only be a last resort.

Feeling better about the situation and himself, he dumped Layla's computers into the bayou. The dark water bubbled as the machines sank, welcoming them to their new home. They'd never be found, but even if they were, he'd beaten them with a baseball bat earlier. No way could anybody retrieve anything off of them. Not even the FBI tech geeks.

For now, he was safe.

• • •

MADDOX GROUND HIS TEETH as Houston pulled the cruiser into the parking lot outside the emergency entrance to the hospital. The information pounded against his sanity. His father had come into the ER with chest pains but refused to let anyone call Maddox.

Stubborn, ornery man.

Thank goodness Margie had been working. Otherwise Pop could drop dead and Maddox would be none the wiser.

"I'll go back to Taylor Construction until the crime-scene unit is done. Call in the request for the report on Randy Dean, then I'll be back." Houston paused. "Unless you'd like me to go in with you."

"No. Thanks." Maddox curbed his emotions as the automatic doors whooshed open. Bypassing the waiting room, he stopped at the triage desk and flashed his badge. "Tyson Bishop?"

"Exam room 4," the nurse responded without hesitation, pointing in that direction.

Funny how a badge eliminated the need for explanation.

He headed down the hallway, noting the numbers outside the doors. The overpowering odor of disinfectant burned his nostrils. His soles squeaked on the waxed-to-a-shine floors.

Maddox paused outside room 4. He hauled in a

deep breath, then exhaled slowly. The door eased open with a gentle push.

His father's stare locked on to him as soon as he crossed the threshold. Pale, with wires coming off his chest and arm attached to machines, Pop looked sick. "I told them not to call you." He glared at Margie.

She paid him no attention, nodding to Maddox. "We're waiting on the cardiologist to get here."

"I can tell him what I want," Pop all but growled. "What about my privacy?"

Margie rolled her eyes. "I'll be back to check on him." She patted the covers over Tyson's feet, then left.

Alone in the room with his father, Maddox felt like the air had been vacuumed out. He pulled the guest chair next to the examining bed and slumped into it. "So, want to tell me what's going on, Pop?"

"Nothing. They're making a fuss over nothing." His father stared at the ceiling.

"Well, why don't you just humor me anyway?"

Pop locked his stare on Maddox. "Don't you have murderers or rapists to catch? Something more important than sitting here with me over a case of indigestion?"

Maddox leaned forward, resting his elbows on his knees and forcing the anger he felt from his voice. "Not at the moment."

Silence prevailed, save for the beeps and burps

from the machines attached to his father. The room was chilly, almost too sterile. Gave the sensation of isolation. "Tell me what's going on." How could his father be so . . . so . . . frustratingly pompous? The man would rather die than tell his son how he felt. That old, familiar resentment rose in the back of Maddox's throat, burning.

"I ate too much chili." Pop yanked Maddox from his thoughts. "I was practicing for the church's chili cook-off this weekend and got it a little too hot. Ate too much is all."

Something else that annoyed Maddox. In the past few months, his father had started attending church. A *church,* of all things. No telling what was up with that. Pop had casually mentioned going to church but never explained. Maddox hadn't asked. He still wouldn't.

"If you thought it was just indigestion, why'd you come to the hospital?"

"Wasn't my choice. George brought me here. The traitor."

"George is here?" Why hadn't George called him?

"I suppose. They wouldn't let him back here. I told him to go home." Pop narrowed his eyes. "How'd you get them to let you?"

Maddox flashed a sheepish grin. "I badged the triage nurse."

Pop gave a hearty roar of laughter, then

grabbed his chest. His laughter turned to moans. The machine's beeping increased.

Maddox jumped from the chair, knocking it against the wall with a clang. "Pop?" He reached for his father's hand.

The door flew open, Margie and another nurse, a flash of motion as they went to his father.

"What's happening?" Maddox's pulse thrummed through his veins as he was pushed away from his father.

Margie didn't look at him. "Maddox, you need to go to the waiting room. Now."

Pop's face contorted with pain.

"But—"

"Now." Her tone left no room for argument. "We need the space. I'll come talk to you in just a minute."

Knowing she was right but hating it, Maddox stepped from the room. He couldn't make himself move away though. Not until another nurse all but knocked him over.

With his heart in his toes, Maddox trudged down the hallway to the waiting room.

George was on his feet in a moment. "Maddox. What's going on?"

"Pop." Maddox dropped to a tattered chair and ran a hand over the stubble of his face. "He was laughing, then . . . I don't know. The machine went crazy. He grabbed his chest like he was in pain. The nurses came in and kicked me out."

"That's how he was at the house." George sat in the chair beside him and placed a hand on Maddox's shoulder. "Argued with me not to bring him in. Until the pain got the better of him."

Maddox lifted his head. "Why didn't you call me?"

"He asked me not to. And if it was just indigestion like Tyson swore, I didn't want to worry you."

"You should've called," Maddox mumbled.

"I was going to as soon as someone updated me with news."

The waiting room reeked of burned coffee. Even worse than at the office at the end of a shift. That stench mixed with the disinfectant smell turned Maddox's stomach. He glanced at the clock on the wall—5:20. Had he really been here so long?

He pressed his fingers against his forehead, mashing. What if Pop was having a heart attack? What if he was bad sick? What if—?

"It's going to be okay, son." As always, George was a rock. "No matter what, Tyson's a strong old bird. He'll get through this."

Words caught in Maddox's throat. Pop was strong. But a heart attack . . .

"What can I do for you?"

Maddox lifted his head and stared at George. Over the years he'd noticed his honorary uncle mellowing and changing. He'd always chalked it up to advancing in age. But now . . . well, he appreciated George more than ever.

Margie burst into the waiting room.

George and Maddox bolted to their feet. Maddox met her across the floor. "How is he?"

"Maddox, I'm really sorry—"

TRYING TO SLEEP WAS futile.

Layla punched her pillow and stared at the dawn peeking through her curtains. The sky brightened as the rising sun's rays illuminated the clouds.

Why hadn't Maddox or Detective Wallace called yet? What was taking so long processing the crime scene . . . her office?

She had so much to do. Clean up the mess in the office. Order new computers. Call her insurance company to file a claim. All her responsibility. The burden was almost suffocating. She wasn't even sure where to begin. She needed to make a to-do list. That would help her sort things out. Give her a plan of some sort.

She sat up against the headboard and turned on the bedside lamp. After a few seconds, her eyes adjusted to the light. She glanced at the clock—5:20. Too early to call Alana with the bad news, although she'd have to do that first thing. Her sister would be furious if she heard about the break-in from anybody other than Layla.

She opened the nightstand drawer for a pen and paper. Her fingers grazed against bonded leather. Her Bible.

With a pounding heart, she pulled out the Bible and held it close to her chest. The weight and weathered pages seemed to hug her. Sometimes she forgot to go to God first. She forgot she didn't have to be strong and in charge all the time. She didn't have to bear the burdens alone. She closed her eyes, praying and allowing herself to be comforted.

A few hours later found her showered, dressed, and sipping coffee in her kitchen in front of the bay windows. The sun had risen over the tree line, casting prisms of light over the bayou. A curtain of Spanish moss draped off a cypress tree swayed in the morning breeze. A new day. A new beginning.

Layla smiled to herself as she finished her java. Maybe Pastor Chaney's messages were especially for her, had she been paying better attention. Perhaps she should've appreciated his sermons a bit more.

Her phone rang, startling her so that she nearly spilled coffee down the front of her shirt. She set down the mug and grabbed the cordless from the kitchen base. "Hello."

"I'm sorry to call you so early, but something terrible is going on." Alana sounded distraught.

So she'd heard. Now Layla would have to reassure her. "It's okay. They didn't get anything but the computers and my records. No big deal. The computers were insured, and I have copies of everything here."

Alana's breathing sounded faster over the connection. "What are you talking about?"

"The break-in?"

"What break-in?"

Oh. She hadn't heard. Keeping the details as minimal as possible, Layla filled in her sister on the incident at Taylor Construction.

"Layla, this is awful."

"No, really. It's okay." And Layla knew it would be. The initial shock had worn off, and she was fine. Ready to keep moving forward. This was nothing but a minor break in her stride. But Alana wouldn't grasp that. Not yet. She was still stunned. "So, if you weren't talking about the break-in, what did you mean about something terrible going on?"

"It's Mr. James. Ms. Betty had to call for an ambulance to take him to the hospital."

James Page's image slammed against Layla's mind. The sweet older man who drove the church van and helped with janitorial duties. The one who always had a smile for everyone. "What happened to him?"

"It's scary." Alana's words spilled out so fast, they almost fell on top of one another. "His symptoms are almost the same as Ms. Ethel's. Trouble breathing. His nose started bleeding and he couldn't get it to stop." She paused. "I'm really worried. Ms. Ethel and now Mr. James. And the EMTs didn't have a clue what was wrong with him."

Two people of the community having the exact same symptoms . . . getting sick within days of each other. Especially the nosebleeds. Those weren't all that common. What was happening?

Alana continued, her voice warbling with emotion. "I would go to the hospital to sit with Ms. Betty, but Gavin's probation officer is on his way out, and both Fred and I have to be at this follow-up meeting. His doctor's already on his way over, so I can't just blow it off."

This could work out. Layla turned and leaned against the granite kitchen counter. "I haven't been cleared to go back to the office yet, so I'll go up to the hospital to be with Ms. Betty." James's wife was a sweet lady who baked cakes and made casseroles for the church shut-ins and sick. She'd been very good to Layla and Alana over the years. "I don't want her to be alone."

Alana breathed heavily over the phone. "Are you sure? I mean, I know you've been hit with a lot right now. Randy coming back, that break-in . . ."

"I'm fine. This will give me something to do

until I can get back to work. Keep my mind occupied."

"Really?"

"I'm positive."

"That's great. Thanks. Listen, I have to run. Gotta meet with Fred before the probation officer gets here. Call me later and let me know what the doctors find out about Mr. James."

"I will." Layla hung up the phone and stared back out across the bayou. The landscape was eerily beautiful. Quiet. Serene, even. The breeze rippled the water. Bare branches dipped low. Dried grasses bent in the wind.

So misleading with what was happening to their little community.

What was happening with the people of Eternal Springs?

FOURTEEN

"Good actions give strength to ourselves
and inspire good actions in others."
—PLATO

MADDOX'S HEART CLENCHED, THEN plummeted to his toes. He crumbled to the chair in the waiting room. George squeezed his shoulder.

"No, no! It's not your father. Oh, mercy, I just realized how that sounded. I'm so sorry for my insensitivity." Margie moved closer, her face red.

"I was apologizing for being so rude when I asked you to leave the examining room."

Nausea still roiled in his gut. "When you said you were sorry, I thought—"

"I apologize." She shook her head. "Let me start again. Your father's EKG shows he was having a minor heart attack earlier. The cardiologist is with him now. He'll be out to speak with you as soon as he's completed his exam."

George cleared his throat. "Thank you."

Margie grabbed Maddox's hands. "Again, I'm sorry for the way I burst in here. I must be losing my touch in bedside manner."

"Don't worry about it. As long as Pop's okay." Still alive, anyway.

A siren wailed just outside the door, followed by the screeching of tires.

Nodding, Margie released her hold on Maddox. "I'll let the cardiologist know you're waiting." Her shoes squeaked against the floor as she rushed to the entrance where EMTs unloaded an elderly man on a stretcher from the ambulance.

George sighed heavily into the empty waiting room. "For a minute there . . ."

"Yeah. Me too." Maddox ran a hand over his face. Every bit of energy he had drained from his body as his muscles relaxed. He leaned back in the chair. "I don't mind telling you, when that pain hit Pops . . ."

"I know, son. I know." George clapped his back, then straightened. "It was the same way at the house. I wanted to call an ambulance, but Tyson wouldn't hear of it. He didn't even want me to bring him in." He gave a humorless chuckle. "Good thing I ignored him as usual."

"It scared me, Uncle George. Bad." He couldn't admit that to anyone but George, who knew, understood, and loved him despite a weakness.

"Me too."

An elderly woman wearing a robe over a pair of pajamas was escorted in and sat before the desk. She kept glancing down the hallway where the examining rooms were. Her shoulders hunched as she sobbed silently.

"Son, this is why I keep telling you to talk to your dad." George's wrinkled face scrunched even tighter. "Rebuild your relationship."

"Rebuild? We never had a relationship. You know he was never around when I was a kid. And then . . . well, he blames me for what happened." Raw pain seared his gut. Just like it always did.

"He doesn't really blame you."

Maddox snorted.

George shook his head. "Maybe at one time he thought he did. But it's in the past. He's had time to grieve and heal. And he's going to church now. Got religion and all that."

God again. Where was He when someone

broke into their house and attacked his mother? Just where was *God* when Mom lay on the floor dying in his arms?

"Tyson loves you, Maddox. Always has. But he's stubborn too. Doesn't know how to reach out to you. Let this be the bridge that brings you two together."

Maddox bent over, staring at the floor, and rested his elbows on his knees. Why did he have to be the one to make the gesture? What made Pop more excusable? Pop was his father, for pity's sakes. Shouldn't *he* be the one reaching out to Maddox?

The elderly woman shuffled into the waiting room. Her housecoat flapped as she slowly lowered herself into a chair. She rested her arthritically gnarled hands holding a tissue in her lap. Her head stayed bowed, but Maddox could see her lips moving.

George lowered his voice. "You know all too well that life's too short, son. Don't let something happen without at least trying to mend this rift. This should be a wake-up call. To both of you."

Yeah, but what about—Maddox jerked upright and stared at George. "Is there something about Pop's condition you aren't telling me?"

"No, nothing like that. At least, not that I know about. Tyson hasn't said a word to me about anything." George stretched out his legs and crossed his ankles. "It's just that human life is so fragile. It can be gone in the blink of an eye. Don't let things go unsaid when you could just as easily say something. That's all I'm sayin'."

Like he didn't know about the fragility of life? He glanced at the elderly lady across the waiting room. Her lips were no longer moving, but her head was still lowered. She looked so . . . alone.

George nudged him. "Just consider what I'm telling you, okay?"

"Yeah. I'll consider it."

"That's my boy." George slapped Maddox's leg and nodded toward the coffee station in the corner of the room. "Think that's safe to drink?"

Maddox followed his glance. About two inches sat in the pot. Black sludge. "I wouldn't advise it. Probably puts a lot of people *in* the hospital."

George chuckled and hefted to his feet. "I'm going to hunt down something that won't rip up my stomach. Want a cup?"

"Sure." Not that he'd be able to drink anything, much less coffee, but he understood some people's need to do something instead of just waiting to hear what might be bad news. "Lots of sugar."

George grinned. "I know. Just like your mom drank it." He headed toward the main entrance of the hospital.

Maddox's muscles tensed involuntarily at the mention of his mother—the way she'd been alive. His memories of her had dimmed so much over the years. For a long time he could close his eyes and almost feel her around him. Catch a whiff of her distinct smell. Hear her whispering voice.

But not in a long time. It was hard for him to even conjure up her living face without looking at a photo. The image of how she looked as life left her was burned upon his memory forever.

And that scorched his heart with guilt and shame.

He stood and paced. This wasn't about his mother. This was about Pop. He glanced at the hallway. No sign of Margie or a doctor. What was taking so long? Shouldn't the cardiologist have come out and updated him by now?

The elderly lady looked up and offered him a half smile.

He smiled back.

"My husband's back there too. The nurse said she'd have a doctor come out to talk to me when he could."

"I'm waiting on the cardiologist to tell me about my dad." Why was he telling this to a perfect stranger? Must be the exhaustion and stress. He was a cop. Knew better than to offer information.

"What's your father's name?"

"Tyson." His voice cracked. He cleared his throat. "Tyson Bishop." He sat back in his chair.

She smiled again. "I'll be praying for him."

God again.

He forced a smile for her, swallowing back his rant. Her husband was sick—she didn't need him to unload his anger on her. He balled his hands and stood again. Pacing helped keep him focused. Moving. Anything besides just waiting.

A man in scrubs and a white coat appeared from the hallway. "Mr. Bishop?"

Maddox nodded and hurried to meet him.

"I'm the cardiologist on staff."

"How's my father?"

"He's suffered a minor heart attack. EKG reflects he's probably had several small attacks."

"He never said anything." Maddox's heart tightened. How could Pop have kept this to himself?

"It's possible he wasn't aware. That's fairly common."

"Oh." Maybe he shouldn't jump to conclusions.

"His heart has sustained some damage. We won't know the extent until we run some more tests. I'm admitting him now, mainly for observation."

"Okay." Damage. Tests. Admitting.

"As soon as we get him transferred, a nurse will notify you."

"Can I see him?"

"Once he's in his room you can." The doctor offered his hand. "A nurse will come for you."

"Thank you."

The doctor left as quickly and quietly as he had appeared.

Maddox ambled toward the main entrance. He needed to find George and tell him what the doctor said.

Damage. Tests. Admitting.

His body began to shake.

FOR ONCE, LUCK WAS on her side. Unbelievable, especially for a Wednesday. Layla found a parking space just outside the hospital's emergency room entrance. She grabbed her scarf and wound it around her neck before securing her truck and heading into the automatic glass double doors. Early morning wind pushed against her, blowing her bangs into her eyes. Maybe she should've taken the time to pull her hair up.

She paused inside the entryway. Where would Ms. Betty be? Back in the room with Mr. James? Would they let Layla go back there?

A nurse behind a desk glanced at her. "May I help you?"

Layla approached. "I'm looking for a lady whose husband was brought in by ambulance. Last name of Page."

The nurse typed the name into her computer. "Mr. Page is still being evaluated. Anyone with him should be in the waiting room around the corner." She pointed to her left.

“Thank you.” Layla shivered against the chill of the room and turned the corner. She immediately spied Ms. Betty alone in the stark white waiting room. The poor thing was in her pajamas and robe.

Layla quickly crossed the space and sat beside the elderly lady. “Hey, Ms. Betty. How’re you holding up?”

“Oh, Layla. You’re such a dear to come.” Her face lit up like the morning’s dawn after a weeklong storm.

“I came as soon as Alana called me. Have you heard anything about Mr. James?”

“Not yet. They haven’t been out to talk to me yet.” She smiled again. “I’ve just been praying.”

“I have too.” Layla shucked out of her coat and wrapped it around Ms. Betty’s shoulders. She glanced over the room. Why didn’t they put blankets out here for people during the winter? Or at least turn up the heat?

“Thank you, dear.” She snuggled into the warm folds of the soft cashmere.

“Alana said he was having trouble breathing?”

Ms. Betty nodded. “He was fine last evening. Went by the church to look at the pipes for Pastor. James got home around four. We had supper at five, just like we always do, then watched the telly. We turned in just after the news. Same as always.”

Layla patted her hands. The woman’s hands

were like ice. Layla unwound her scarf and laid it over Ms. Betty's lap.

"Thank you." She bunched the scarf around her palms before continuing. "His wheezing woke me up. I couldn't get him to talk to me. To open his eyes. And then I noticed the blood on his face."

"Blood?"

"His nose was bleeding." Ms. Betty pressed a shredded tissue against her nose. "I went and got him a handkerchief, and he finally woke up. But he couldn't talk. Couldn't catch his breath."

The poor woman must have been frightened out of her mind. Layla ached for both of them.

"We couldn't get his nose to stop bleeding either. We tried toilet paper. Rags. Pinching. It wouldn't stop, and his wheezing got worse. He couldn't breathe sitting on the side of the bed. So I called 911."

She wrapped an arm around the still-shivering woman.

"The medics said they didn't know what was wrong with him. Kept asking me if he was on breathing medicine. Asked if he had asthma. I told them James didn't have any of the like. He's healthy as a horse." She sniffed. "At least he was."

Sudden onset of symptoms just like Ms. Ethel's. Ice ran through Layla's veins. There was no way this was a coincidence. Something was happening to the people of Eternal Springs, and it wasn't good.

"They put him on oxygen at the house and loaded him up. I had to follow in my car because they said they didn't have room for me."

Someone's shoes squeaked on the floor in an adjacent hallway. The sound skidded down Layla's spine like a malfunctioning power drill. She shivered.

"I filled out all their paperwork, and now I wait."

Men's whispered voices were muffled around the corner.

"I'll stay with you." Layla's eyes filled with tears as she squeezed Ms. Betty's shoulders. "Would you like me to pray with you?"

Shoes screeched right in front of her.

"What are you doing here?"

FIFTEEN

"All life is an experiment. The more experiments you make the better."
—RALPH WALDO EMERSON

LAYLA LOOKED UP AT his question. Her breath caught.

She removed her arm from around Ms. Betty and stood. "Maddox." She barely breathed his name. "I'm sitting with my friend while her husband is being checked out. What're you doing here?"

"My father." His voice cracked.

Her stomach tightened, remembering what it felt like to sit in the emergency room waiting area anticipating news of her father. She laid a hand on his arm. The touch sent her stomach into a downward spiral. "What's wrong with your father?"

"His heart."

Just like her father. Tears welled in her eyes at the memory. "I'm sorry. How is he?"

"They're admitting him."

"I've been praying for him," Ms. Betty announced.

Layla smiled at her friend, then looked back at him. "I'll pray for him as well."

She remembered the feelings she had when she'd been waiting—fear, pain, grief. Her heart went out to Maddox. "Do they think it's a heart attack?"

He nodded.

She tightened her grip on his arm, willing comfort to seep into him. "I'm so sorry, Maddox." She hated not to be able to say anything other than offer apologies. They'd always felt weak when people said they were sorry about her father.

An older man appeared at his shoulder. "Maddox?"

Maddox cleared his throat. "Layla Taylor, this is George Vella. Uncle George, Layla Taylor."

She removed her hand from his arm to shake hands with George. Maddox had called him uncle. Were they related? She couldn't detect a resemblance, but the man's smile was heartfelt.

"This is my dear friend Betty Page." She gestured to Ms. Betty.

Maddox bent to shake her hand, then George did.

George straightened and shot Maddox a look with tons of questions in his eyes. "How do you know Ms. Taylor?"

Even Layla didn't miss the implication. Heat flamed in her cheeks.

"A case Houston and I are working."

"Ah. I see." But it was clear he'd have more questions later for Maddox.

She was glad she wouldn't have to undergo the man's interrogation. He'd give Maddox a run for his money, she'd bet, but she hoped he'd be gentle. Waiting to hear news about your father when he'd had a heart attack was unbearable.

Layla knew. She'd been there. Done that. And the hole in her heart would never heal.

A doctor turned off the hallway into the waiting room. "Ms. Page?"

Layla helped Ms. Betty to stand, her own nerves bunching. "If you'll excuse us."

Lord, please don't let Mr. James die. Not like Ms. Ethel.

• • •

MADDOX SAT DOWN. GEORGE did as well, then twisted to face him. “So, what’s the story with Ms. Taylor?”

“She’s a person of interest in Houston’s and my case.” The response rolled automatically off his tongue. But if he was honest, he’d have to admit Layla undid the places he’d worked hard to keep hidden. How could a woman he barely knew have that kind of effect on him?

“Right.” George lifted that single brow again.

“And she’s also a recent victim of breaking and entering. Her office was trashed. Computers stolen.”

“You don’t handle break-ins.”

“I do when the vic is involved in my murder case.”

“Murder case.” George scratched at his thinning hair. “As a possible witness or a different kind of involvement?”

“Not sure yet.” Maddox glanced over to where Layla kept her arm around Mrs. Page. “We’re working on it.”

“Working on something else as well?”

Maddox dragged his attention from Layla to George. “What do you mean?”

“I see the way she looks at you and the way you look at her. Something’s there between you two. Under the surface but there.”

Maddox shook his head. “It’s your imagination, old man.” He gave George a friendly nudge.

"I'm serious, son. Don't let the opportunity pass you by. Trust me, as one speaking from experience, I can tell you that regret is a hard pill to take every day for the rest of your life."

Maddox had never heard anything about George's love life. Funny thing—he'd loved George all his life but never wondered about aspects of George's private life outside of how they related to him. Even as a man, Maddox had never asked. He knew the basics of George's hobbies: hunting, fishing, and wood carving. He knew some of George's darkest secrets: He was a recovering alcoholic but had been dry for almost ten years, as well as once having a very hot temper. But he'd never heard George talk about a lady. Ever.

George's eyes filled with remorse. "Take it from me, son . . . you don't want to let the opportunity to find love pass you by because you're too stubborn or stupid."

"You let love pass you by?"

"I didn't tell someone I loved her. Until it was too late." Moisture pooled in George's eyes.

That really caused Maddox to start. He hadn't seen George cry since his mother's funeral. "I didn't know."

George pawed at his reddening face and dropped his head. "Well, I want you to learn from my mistake. I've regretted not telling her I loved her as soon as I felt it."

"If you don't mind my asking . . . what happened?"

Lifting his head, George stared at the stark white wall across the room. "She ended up falling in love with someone else. Got married. Had kids."

Man, that had to hurt. "That bites."

George nodded. "I accepted it and moved on." He slapped his leg. "Enough of my regrets. Just remember what I said. Life and love are precious and rarely do you get a second chance. Grab the opportunities when you can. At least you won't live the rest of your life with what-ifs."

The doctor left. Layla turned Mrs. Page around and helped her to the ladies' room.

"Don't forget," George whispered.

Layla returned to her seat and kept her gaze glued to the restroom door. "They're admitting him to ICU."

"ICU?"

Layla nodded and leaned forward, lowering her tone. "They don't know what's causing his breathing to be so labored or his nosebleeds. This is the second elderly friend who's come into the hospital in the past two days with these symptoms."

"Has your other friend been diagnosed? Maybe it's the same thing."

"I'm sure it is. But my other friend died." Layla shook her head.

Died? Same symptoms. Both elderly. The detective in Maddox jumped to full attention. Maybe he should talk to Margie about Mr. Page.

LAYLA CHECKED HER TEXT message and nodded to Ms. Betty. "Jade's here to run you home to get into some clothes while they're moving Mr. James. The doctor said it'd take them the better part of an hour, so you have plenty of time. I'll wait here." Layla couldn't stand to not do anything. While she couldn't do anything for Mr. James, she could make this as easy as possible on Ms. Betty.

Especially if Mr. James . . . No, she wouldn't even think it. *God, please. Not Mr. James too.* Losing him would kill Ms. Betty.

"Are you sure you don't mind staying, honey?"

"Of course. You take my coat. I'll be fine. I'll wait right here."

Ms. Betty stood and let Layla help her slip on the coat. She loosely wound the scarf around Ms. Betty's sagging neck.

"You're such a dear. I'll be back in a flash." Ms. Betty shuffled toward the exit.

"Where's she going?" Maddox moved to the seat next to her.

"Jade Laurent is here to drive Ms. Betty home to get some decent clothes." Layla's gaze followed Ms. Betty out the automatic doors. "Bless her heart, she didn't even bother to get dressed before she followed the ambulance here."

"So tell me more about these mysterious symptoms."

His tone caused her to jerk her gaze to Maddox's face. Why was he prying? Did he really care, or was he digging for something?

His face reflected genuine interest. His uncle's did as well.

Maybe they needed something to keep their minds off of Maddox's father. She could understand that—she had. She'd give him the benefit of the doubt. After all, he could be facing heartbreak. If she could help, even in some small way . . .

"It's strange. Ms. Ethel came in with shortness of breath. Well, she could hardly breathe. And her nose wouldn't stop bleeding." Chills skittered down her spine, and she rubbed her arms. "From what Ms. Betty says, Mr. James's symptoms are the same."

"Was she younger?"

Layla didn't really know. Not for sure. But there couldn't be too much of a difference. "Maybe by a few years. Not more than five."

"Do they live at the same nursing home or apartment maybe?"

"No. Ms. Ethel lived at her apartment. Mr. James and Ms. Betty have their house."

"In Eternal Springs?"

"Yes."

"Guess they don't work at the same place?"

She chuckled. At least he was trying to make a connection. And his mind was off his father for the moment. "Nope. Mr. James drives a van and does light janitorial work. Ms. Ethel is retired."

He rubbed his chin covered with black stubble. "How do you know both of them?"

"We go to the same church."

He sat forward to the edge of his chair. "Both of them?"

She nodded, her pulse jumping. Was this the connection?

"What church?"

"Eternal Springs Christian Church."

George Vella gasped.

Maddox twisted and looked at his uncle. "What?"

"That's the church your father recently started attending."

Layla's heart hiccupped.

"Why would Pop go there?"

George shrugged. "Close enough to Westlake. He met a couple of people who attended that invited him. He likes it."

Maddox turned back to Layla. "Do you know my father?"

"Who is he?"

"Tyson. Tyson Bishop."

His image flitted across her memory. She

locked stares with Maddox. How could she not have noticed the resemblance before? "I met him a month or so ago at a covered dinner. Very nice man."

The muscle in Maddox's jaw flinched.

As the realization hit, trembles shuddered through her. She leaned forward and grabbed Maddox's hand. "Are they sure it's his heart? Is he having breathing problems? A nosebleed?"

Maddox looked to his uncle.

"No nosebleed and he was breathing fine," George said.

So that wasn't the connection. Disappointment fanned but she pushed it down. Then she realized she was still holding Maddox's hand. She jerked hers back into her lap. Heat spread across her face.

George cleared his throat and stood. "I'm going to find something cold to drink." He threw Maddox a look she couldn't understand. Apparently Maddox did because he shifted and the tips of his ears turned red as George headed to the hospital's main entrance.

"It was a good thought. About the church connection." Maddox smiled, as if he'd read her mind. "Good detective instincts."

The heat moved all the way to her feet. "I just feel so helpless."

The smile slid off his face. "I know what you mean."

"You? Big, bad detective?" She grinned.

"Yeah, me." He spread his hands, then jabbed his fingers through his hair. "I can't do anything for Pop."

"You can pray."

He finally made eye contact again. "Well, that's not really my thing."

"Really?" Every nerve in her body tingled. "Why not?"

"I don't buy into the whole God-is-a-loving-God deal."

She struggled not to let the shock show on her face. "Why not?"

"Why not? What kind of question is that? Why not?" He ran his fingers through his hair again. "Why do you buy it?"

Oh, Lord, help me out with the right words. I don't want to offend, but I must share my faith. "Because I believe what Scripture teaches."

"The Bible?"

"Yes."

"One hundred percent?"

"Yes." The certainty in her heart pounded.

"Even when your friend died?"

She clenched her sweating palms together in her lap. *Lord, guide my tongue.* "Yes. I might not understand why things—bad things—happen, but I believe that God loves us all and won't leave us alone during a tragedy."

He snorted and rolled his eyes.

Her heart ached for him more than Mr. James. To be so lost . . .

A nurse squeaked into the waiting room. Maddox was on his feet in an instant. "Margie?"

"He's fine. We've got him moved up to the cardiac ward. You can see him now. I'll take you up."

Maddox turned back to Layla. "I hope your friend's okay."

"Thanks. I'll be praying for your father."

He paused, as if wanting to say something but wasn't sure what. Then he gave a nod and followed the nurse.

Layla let out a long breath and then bent her head to pray. For Mr. James. For Ms. Betty.

And for Maddox Bishop's salvation.

SIXTEEN

"Our life is made by the death of others."
—LEONARDO DA VINCI

"MADDOX." HOUSTON WHISPERED AS he gave Maddox a slight nudge.

Bolting upright in the chair, Maddox automatically reached for his gun. "What?" Houston knew better than to sneak up on a sleeping cop wearing a firearm.

"Shh. Keep it down. You'll wake your dad."

Maddox glanced at the hospital bed. Pop

snored softly while the machines attached to him continued their monotonous beeping. The oxygen tank gave off a slight hum. Pop had a little color back to his face. He looked . . . peaceful.

"Come on." Houston tiptoed to the door and stepped into the hallway. Maddox followed.

"Margie says your dad's doing good."

"Yeah. That's what the cardiologist says." Exhaustion tugged at Maddox, enticing him back to sleep. He yawned.

"You look beat. Why don't I take you home so you can sleep a bit?"

"I'm fine." Maddox glanced at his watch. Two in the afternoon already? He'd barely closed his eyes once Pop was settled. They'd given Pop something to relax him that had knocked him out. Maddox had just wanted to rest for a bit until George returned. "What's the latest on the case?"

"Unit finished at Taylor Construction. They don't think they recovered anything useful, but they'll still process it."

"No prints?" Man, he really needed a strong cup of coffee. Maybe the hospital cafeteria would have some.

"Tech says looks like glove smudges."

"Somebody was smart."

"Or just careful." Houston shrugged. "You plan to break into a business, steal records, and trash the place, you probably think to wear gloves."

"Yeah." Maddox yawned again. The fogginess hovered in his brain.

"Come on." Houston grabbed his arm and led him to the elevators.

"Where're we going?"

"To find coffee. Black. Hot. And as strong as we can get."

They'd been partners way too long when Houston started reading his mind. But Maddox was desperate enough for java that he followed Houston into the elevator. "So, they think they got nothing at the site?"

"Didn't even get any fibers. They got zilch."

The elevator dinged and they followed the signs to the cafeteria. Maddox picked up the aroma of java, and his mouth practically watered. And then the enticing scent of fried chicken wafted to him. His stomach growled.

Houston laughed. "Maybe you should eat something too." He patted his own stomach. "I think I should join you. Make sure you take care of yourself."

Maddox shook his head. "Sacrificing for a friend. How nice of you." He chuckled under his breath as he headed to the line serving the fried chicken.

The line moved quickly and they soon sat alone at a table for four. Maddox took a large gulp of coffee. It nearly scalded his throat, but it certainly woke him up. Didn't taste too bad either.

"Now," Houston said between bites, "I'll call Layla and let her know she's clear to go back into Taylor Construction."

"Think we ought to request a couple of drive-bys for the next few days?"

"Already talked with the chief of police. He'll have officers drive by a couple of times each night. Just to monitor the place."

Maddox swallowed the chicken. It smelled better than it tasted, but beggars couldn't be choosy. "Good. What else?"

"Thought maybe if you were interested, we'd head over to Second Chances and talk with Darren Watkins. And Alana." Houston took a sip of sweet tea. "Or if you'd rather stay here, I can go alone."

Margie had told him the medicine they'd given Pop would keep him asleep most of the day and into the night. Seemed silly to sit here just to watch him sleep. But what if something happened? What if he had another heart attack?

"I can go by myself. No biggie." Houston swiped his mouth with the napkin.

"No. I'll go with you. Pop's sleeping and will be for some time. Besides, George said he'd be back this afternoon. He'll let me know if anything changes."

"Then let's get to it."

Maddox stood and lifted his tray. "We haven't left yet?"

Thirty minutes later Maddox sat beside Houston as they pulled in front of Second Chances retreat. He'd called George and explained he was leaving. George assured him that he was on his way up to the hospital to sit with Pop. Maddox made sure the nurses had his cell phone number . . . just in case.

"What did Layla say when you called and told her she could get into her office?" Maddox hadn't been able to stop thinking about her. Not as a subject in a case, but as a person. A woman. With soft, caring eyes and a gentle tone.

"I think I woke her up." Houston parked and turned off the engine. "She sounded as groggy as you did when I caught you sleeping in your dad's room."

"Dozing. I was dozing."

Houston opened the car door. "Yeah, whatever. You were snoring almost as loud as your dad."

"You're delusional." Maddox shut the car door and reached the front entrance to Second Chances before Houston. "And slow."

"Right." Houston slipped into the door Maddox had opened and rushed to the desk.

"May I help you?" a perky redhead asked.

Maddox pulled out his badge and flashed it to the lady. "We need to speak with Darren Watkins, please."

The redhead's eyes widened and her jaw dropped an inch. She swallowed, her eyes nearly bugging out of her head. “I-I . . .” She pressed a button on the phone system. “Just a moment, please.”

Maddox faced Houston and lifted a shoulder.

“Officer?”

Maddox turned back to the redhead. “Yes?”

“It’ll be just a moment. If you’ll have a seat.” She waved toward the little grouping of three chairs by the door.

He nodded but took only a couple of steps away from the reception desk. Finally he was awake. Ready to work. Ready to solve the case.

“Detectives.”

Both spun at Alana’s voice. Her shoes made *tap-tap-tapping* sounds against the floor as she crossed to them. “May I help you?”

Maddox tightened his jaw and glared at the redhead. Had he been unclear in asking for Darren Watkins?

“Ms. Taylor. Nice to see you again.” Houston smiled and shook her hand. “We need to speak to Darren Watkins.”

“May I ask what this is in regards to?”

As if she didn’t know. Maddox crossed his arms over his chest. “An ongoing murder investigation.”

“I see.” She straightened and gave a slight nod to the redhead. “He’ll be here in just a moment.”

Fielding questions? What’d she have to hide? Or was she protecting someone?

Maddox dropped his hands to his sides. "Well, while we're waiting, why don't you tell us where you were between eleven thirty and midnight on Friday?"

Her expression went slack. "E-excuse me?"

"Friday night. Between eleven thirty and midnight. Where were you?" He stepped closer, deliberately invading her personal space.

"I-I was at home."

"Alone?" He leaned forward.

She took a step back. "Y-yes. Alone."

"Can anyone verify that?"

"I-I talked to my fiancé around that time." She blinked several times. "Yes. Cameron was in California at a software conference. He called me when he got back from supper. That was about nine thirty, West Coast time, so about eleven thirty here." She swallowed. Hard.

"We'll verify that with your phone records."

She raised her chin and met Maddox's stare. "Feel free."

"Alana?"

All three shifted to see the young man straggling out of the hall. "You wanted to see me?"

"Darren, these detectives are here to see you." Her voice was so soft, almost like Layla's.

Maddox gave himself a mental shake. He wasn't going down that path. He had a job to do. "Mr. Watkins, we need to speak with you." He glanced at Alana, then back to Watkins. “Privately.”

“You can use the conference room.” Alana didn’t back down an inch. In that moment he spied a glimpse of Layla in her.

“Thank you.” Houston motioned in the direction of the room they’d met in before with Alana and Layla. “This way.”

Maddox gave Alana one last glance before following his partner and Watkins. Her face was pale. Her eyes wide. She was definitely worried about their talk with Watkins.

And Maddox intended to find out why.

SUCH A MESS.

Layla emptied the vacuum for the third time. It was unreal how much dirt she’d missed when resetting the potted plants throughout the reception area. The rug in the entryway would have to be professionally cleaned.

There. Done. She put the cleaner back in the closet and turned to the reception desk. It looked so bare without the computer. Scratches covered the top of the desk where whoever had stolen her computer scraped it against the soft wood.

She propped open the front door despite the cold. The office smelled . . . violated. And in a way, she could relate. Someone had broken into *her* office. Destroyed *her* belongings. Damaged *her* property.

There was no other way to describe how she felt except violated.

Layla glanced over the office area. The insurance adjuster had come as soon as she'd called. After his note taking and picture snapping, he helped her tape up the broken window the burglar had broken to gain access to the office. She'd have to replace the pane. Something else for her to do this afternoon.

The copier had been flipped over. No telling how much that would cost to repair if it was broken.

She swallowed, denying the tears. All her records, gone. Thank the good Lord she had copies at home, but it would take time to duplicate them all. And file them. Although the mess was now gone, the remaining tasks before her seemed too much. Too daunting.

Slumping onto the edge of the desk, she glanced at the rolling chair sitting lopsided. It would have to be replaced. The wheels had been damaged. The protective pad under the desk had been slashed and would need replacing as well.

Why would someone do this to her? It was senseless.

And it infuriated her.

She stood and headed to her personal office to retrieve the trash bag she'd filled. Whoever did this broke the filing cabinet in her office as well.

It'd been locked, so the burglar smashed the wood cabinet. Splinters were imbedded in the carpet behind her desk. She'd have to remember not to go shoeless for a while.

She let out a sigh and grabbed the trash bag and went back to the main room. Three other trash bags had been filled from the front room. Although she'd slept for several hours, she was beyond fatigued. The image of her warm, comfortable bed beckoned to her.

After opening the back door, she lifted the bag toward the Dumpster. Wind lifted her hair. She shivered and hurried to collect the next bag. As she did, something white caught her eye on the steps.

Slowly, she leaned over the object. A cigarette butt.

No one she employed smoked. It was one of her rules. Smoking and construction didn't mesh.

Could the culprit have left this? Maybe there was DNA or something on it.

Her pulse raced. This could be a clue.

She finished throwing out the trash bags, then raced back inside. She needed to call Maddox.

Layla stopped before she grabbed the phone. Maddox's father was in the hospital. His mind was wrapped up in that. She shouldn't bother him.

What about Detective Wallace? He'd been the one to walk through the office with her. He'd been the one to call and tell her she could go in and start cleaning up. She worried her bottom lip. Maybe she should just call Lincoln Vailes and tell him. If he thought it was important, he could call the detectives.

Yet Detective Wallace had told her to call if she found anything else missing.

Layla let out a sigh and reached for the phone. No dial tone. She checked to make sure it was plugged in. It was. Apparently, something else she'd have to replace. She grabbed her cell from her purse and flipped it open. She'd call Detective Wallace as he'd instructed.

But in the back of her mind, she began to form a list of everyone she knew who smoked.

SEVENTEEN

"We are all pencils in the hand of God."
—MOTHER TERESA

TWITCHING EYE . . . jostling foot—nervous markers.

Maddox continued to observe Watkins's body language, watching for the telling signs.

Watkins crossed his arms over his chest and leaned back in the chair in the conference room. "What can I do for you?"

Houston sat directly across from Watkins, notebook open and pen at the ready. "We understand you work with Bob Johnson, as a sort of work-release apprentice."

"I did on a couple of jobs. So?"

Ah, the belligerence. Maddox kept his mouth closed and his face neutral. He and Houston had played this type of interrogation many times. He knew his part.

"Was one of those jobs the Hope-for-Homes site?"

"Yeah. Maybe."

"Maybe?" Houston leaned forward and tapped his pen against the notebook. "Yes or no."

"Yeah."

"How did you get along with everyone on the site?"

Watkins sniffed and shrugged. "Okay, I guess."

Maddox hadn't missed the sniff. Cocaine or crystal meth had probably been Watkins's drug of choice. Could make someone erratic. Unpredictable. Especially if he already had a history of violence.

"Anybody there you didn't like or who didn't like you?"

"Dude, this isn't high school." Watkins wore his sneer like an ill-fitting suit jacket. Almost as telling as his attitude.

Houston set down his pen, popped his knuckles, then lifted the pen again. A stalling tactic to give Watkins time to think. To stew. To worry.

By the way the kid bounced his knee, Maddox would say the man was cooked.

"Were there any problems on-site? Arguments? Disagreements?" Houston blinked slowly at Watkins.

Maddox swallowed his smile. His partner was an ace at his job.

"No."

"So, everyone got along well?"

"Like one big happy family." Watkins uncrossed his arms and chewed on his thumb's cuticle.

"I see." Houston snuck a glance at Maddox.

They had Watkins on edge . . . panicky. Good.

"What did you think of Dennis LeJeune?" Houston tossed the question out so quickly a Southeastern Conference running back would be jealous.

"Who?"

"Dennis LeJeune. The building inspector on the site. What did you think of him?"

"The old guy?" Watkins shrugged. "Didn't talk to him much."

Maddox kept his expression neutral even though adrenaline spurted through his veins. How did a plumber's apprentice know who the building inspector was?

"Who did talk to him?"

"Ms. Layla. Bob. Mr. Keys. Mr. Baxter."

"What did they talk about?"

Watkins scowled at Houston. “Like I know? Dude, I was the grunt. Nobody talked to me about anything important.”

“What did they talk to you about?”

“Just telling me what to do.” He gave a condescending glare. “And Bob telling me how to do it.”

“What do you think of Bob Johnson?”

“He was my boss.”

“But not anymore?” Relentless, Houston never missed a beat. His questions came rapid fire.

“No.”

“Why not?”

“We finished the job.”

“But that’s been some time ago. Surely Mr. Johnson has had other jobs since then.”

“I guess.”

“But you haven’t been invited back to work with him?”

Watkins narrowed his eyes. “Apparently not.”

“I see.” Houston staged another long pause and cut a glance at Maddox.

Game time. He was up.

Maddox stood and paced until he was right behind Houston. He narrowed his eyes and stared at Watkins. “Where were you Friday night between eleven thirty and midnight?”

“Dude, Ms. Alana locks the main doors at ten sharp. No one leaves or comes in without her knowing.”

"That doesn't tell me where you were between eleven thirty and midnight on Friday."

"I was here."

"Where, here?"

"At the retreat, man."

Retreat? That's what they called this place? "Where in particular?"

"My room."

"Doing what?" Maddox could be just as relentless as Houston.

"Sleeping." But Watkins shifted and his gaze dropped and went to the left.

Lying.

Maddox gave a deep snort and cocked his head. He'd been told the combination was quite intimidating. "On a Friday night?" He leaned forward, resting his palms on the table. "Let's try that question again, why don't we?"

"Dude, I was in my room. Sleeping." Again his gaze went down and to the left.

Maddox pushed off the table and rounded it, hovering over Watkins. "Now, why don't I believe you, Darren?"

Watkins's foot bounced, causing his knee to hop like a Mexican jumping bean. "I don't know, dude."

"Why are you so nervous?" Maddox stood straight, letting his height intimidate.

"I'm not nervous."

"Really? Then why are you biting your nails and being so jittery?"

"I want a cigarette, dude. Having a nic-fit."

Maddox backed off. "Smoking's a nasty habit."

"Yeah, but it's better than snorting. It's legal."

"It is that." Maddox returned to his chair and met Houston's glance. Switch off, take two.

Houston tapped his pen against the notebook. "Is there anyone who can verify you were in your room Friday night?"

"No. Like I said, I was sleeping." Again the markers of deception.

Maddox locked looks with Houston. They weren't going to get any more from the kid. He was lying but wasn't going to come clean. At least not yet.

Closing his notebook, Houston stood. "Well, we thank you for your time, Mr. Watkins."

His bouncing stopped. "I can go now?"

"Sure." Maddox stood and waved at the open door.

Watkins wasted no time scrambling out of the chair and from the room.

"Let's ask Alana for any documentation she has for entering and exiting on Friday night." Houston pocketed his notebook.

Maddox could just imagine how willing she'd be to give them those details. She was hiding something. Or covering for someone. She'd probably make them get a warrant for the records.

Oh man, happy day. Let the fun begin.

• • •

"SORRY I'M LATE." ED Young walked into Taylor Construction. "Had a last-minute glitch with an order."

Layla smiled at her friend. "No worries. I just finished prepping the window."

The late afternoon sun spilled into the area from the open door. A cold breeze pushed through the office.

He glanced around the office. "Doesn't look too bad."

"I've been cleaning for hours."

"Sorry." He shook his head. "Do the police have any idea why someone would do this? Any clue *who?*"

"Not that they've told me." She reached for her gloves. "I'm still going to try to figure things out."

"Layla, you need to be careful. Apparently someone doesn't like you looking into things."

"I know." She tugged the gloves over her hands. "Let's get the glass unloaded so I can get it installed."

"You need me to help you install?" Ed led the way to his truck.

"Nope. I can do this in my sleep."

Together they unloaded the glass and moved it inside the office. Layla walked him back out to his truck. "Thanks again for delivering this for me on such short notice."

"When's the alarm company going to come out and wire the window?"

She glanced at her watch. "In about forty-five minutes. Guess I'd better get busy installing, huh?"

He patted her shoulder. "I'll see you later. Take care, Layla."

Nodding, she grabbed her tool belt. As always, touching the smooth, worn leather sent memories skittering over her. It'd been her father's tool belt. Every memory she had of him included him wearing the belt. It was the one specific thing she valued most.

It took her less than thirty minutes to install the glass. She'd just finished cleaning it with mineral spirits when a car sounded out front. Must be the alarm company. Early for once.

Layla put away her tools and went to the door to meet them.

Alana stepped over the threshold first. "What is that awful smell?" Her upturned nose scrunched.

Laughing, Layla shook her head. "Mineral spirits. Or it could be the caulk. Both reek."

"It's disgusting. Doesn't it make you light-headed?"

"No. That's why the door's open." Layla perched on the edge of the reception desk. "What're you doing here?"

Alana tossed her purse on the desk. "I'm just so mad. Frustrated. Ugh. I could just scream."

"What's wrong?" If she'd gotten into a fight with Cameron, Layla would be no help. As the big sister, she should be able to dispense advice, but in the love department . . .

"That Detective Bishop. The man's infuriating."

"Maddox?"

Alana's eyebrows shot up. "Since when do you call him by his first name?"

"I-I . . . what's he done to get you all riled up?"

"He and his partner came by the retreat this afternoon to talk with Darren Watkins. While I understand they're trying to be thorough, they don't have to be obnoxious."

Layla sighed as her sister paced. "What did he do?"

"He actually asked me where I was on Friday night. From eleven thirty to midnight. Like I'm a suspect or something."

"He's just doing his job. They have to get everyone's alibis."

"Mine? Like I'm involved in that murder or burning down the house?"

"It's nothing personal. They asked me the same thing." And she remembered how angry it had made her. But at least they were following up. Investigating.

"He's a jerk."

Layla rubbed her palms on her jeans. "Cut him a little slack. His dad's in the hospital. Heart attack."

"How do you know that?" Alana narrowed her eyes.

"He was in the waiting room when I was there with Ms. Betty." Layla pushed off the desk. "He's worried about his father. You know how that feels."

"Doesn't excuse him for being a jerk."

"Well, I wasn't the nicest person when we were worried about Dad." Her throat tightened at the words, at the memory.

Alana dropped her scrutiny. "Yeah. I remember."

Layla pushed down the emotions that threatened to explode. "I'm just saying to give him a little extra allowance."

"I will."

And Layla vowed she would as well. Even if he did keep her off balance just by being in the same room with her.

EIGHTEEN

"Old friends pass away, new friends appear.
It is just like the days. An old day passes,
a new day arrives. The important thing
is to make it meaningful: a meaningful
friend—or a meaningful day."
—DALAI LAMA

THE SUN'S RAYS STOLE around the faded curtains and danced into Tyson Bishop's hospital room.

Maddox stood and stretched. The padded chair had become uncomfortable around three this morning. Now his neck felt like a jackhammer had plowed at it all night. Thursday morning. Would this week never end?

He checked the clock. George would be here soon. Maddox would run home, take a shower, then meet Houston at the station.

"You still here?" Pop yawned.

"Of course." He moved to the bed beside his father. "Are you in any pain? Can I get you anything?"

"A little peace and quiet. You snore."

Maddox chuckled. "Hi, pot, meet kettle."

"I don't snore."

"Sure, Pop. How're you feeling?"

"Tired of being poked and prodded."

If his surly disposition was any indication, Pop must be feeling better. “George said the doctor would make rounds about ten or so.”

“Yeah.” Pop leaned forward, twisting his arm behind him and grabbing the top pillow with the tips of his fingers.

“Let me help.” Maddox took hold of the pillow and fluffed it before easing it behind the small of his father’s back.

“I can fix my own pillows.”

There was the winning attitude of his father’s. Made Maddox feel all warm and fuzzy inside. “I was just trying to help.”

“Don’t need help.”

Maddox swallowed hard. Same old Pop. Same old argument.

He crossed the room and opened the curtains.

Pop snarled. “Did I ask you to blind me?”

“I thought maybe you’d—”

“You thought? That’s your problem. You always think too late.” Pop turned his head toward the door.

Maddox’s muscles tensed and his gut balled. He would not get into the same argument yet again. Not here. Not while his father had suffered a heart attack. He’d ignore the jabs. The low blows. He’d be the bigger man.

He snapped the curtains shut and returned to the uncomfortable chair. Maybe if he just sat silently, his father would change the subject.

Pop stared at him. Brows lowered, chin set. He sighed. "Maddox, we need to talk. About the night your mom was killed."

Nope, he wasn't going to let it drop. Maddox's mouth went dry. "No, let's not. We know how it will all end." With him being blamed.

"I know you think I blame you."

Where was George? Maddox stood and went to the bedside. He lifted the insulated cup on his father's tray. "Why don't I go get you some ice?"

"I don't want any ice! You need to listen to me, Maddox. The night your mother was murdered—"

Maddox set the cup down on the tray with a thud. "I know. I know. I was late for curfew and it's my fault she was killed. If I'd been on time, she'd still be alive. I know all that."

Pop held up his hand. "Listen—"

Maddox shook his head. "No, I've heard it from you so much over the years that it's a scar against my soul." He backed to the foot of the bed, guilt curling his hands into fists.

"That's just it. You need to understand something—"

The emotion erupted in Maddox—burning from his gut, into his chest, searing his throat and coating his tongue. "I've understood you've blamed me for her death from the beginning. But here's something you need to consider, *Pop*."

He bent over his father's feet, glowering. "Where were *you* when she was murdered? You were out defending our country when you should've been home, defending your wife. She died in my arms while you were more worried about your precious military career." Maddox strode to the door. He glanced over his shoulder at his father's pale face. "Live with that."

He pushed from the room, gulping in air as he leaned against the wall in the hallway. His heartbeat thudded in his head. His entire body shook. He fisted, then relaxed his hands. He inhaled . . . held the breath until his lungs burned, then exhaled slowly. And again.

The overpowering smell of disinfectant nearly made him gag.

"Hey, son. How's Tyson?" George appeared out of nowhere.

"Same as always—meaner than a snake." He ground out the words from between clenched teeth.

George gripped his shoulder. "What's wrong?"

Maddox shook his head. "He'll never let it go, Uncle George."

"What're you talking about?"

"Mom's murder. He'll always blame me. And let me know what a failure I am. How I'm basically responsible for her death."

"Oh, son, that's not so."

Maddox snorted. "Really? That's what Pop

thinks. What he's always thought. Never lets an opportunity to remind me slip by him either."

"He said something?"

"Are you not hearing me?" Maddox stared at George. "He wanted to talk about the night she was killed. Again. I tried not to let him bait me. Tried to change the subject. But he'd have none of it. He's itching for a fight."

"He's just distraught. Upset over being in the hospital and letting off steam. I know for a fact that it's not your fault about Abigail. And Tyson knows it too."

"Whatever, man." Maddox pushed off the wall. "I've got to get home and get showered. I have a job to do."

George grabbed his arm. "Maddox, don't go off half-cocked. It's probably the pain medication he's on that's making him so ornery."

"I don't know how you've managed to stay his friend all these years. You're a good man, Uncle George." He jutted his chin toward his father's door. "Better than him."

"Don't say that."

"It's true. He was never around when I was a kid and then Mom got killed. He's blamed me for that from the beginning. It's his own guilt talking because he knows he should've spent more time at home. With Mom and me. But he was too fixated on his almighty career. It always came first."

"You've got a jaded memory, Maddox."

He jerked his arm free from George's hold. "I don't think so. I'll call you later."

Storming to the elevator did nothing to quench his desire to hit something. Hard. Really hard.

Maddox punched the button and paced while he waited. Always blamed. It was always his error. *All* his burden.

He stepped into the elevator, and the doors slid shut with a *ding*.

Alone, with his eyes closed, the one familiar question clawed against his soul . . .

Was his mother's murder his fault?

ANOTHER DAY, ANOTHER DOLLAR. That's what her father had always said. Layla missed him more than she could've ever imagined. His quick wit. His warm smile. The pride in his eyes when she talked with him.

Brring!

Layla jumped. The new phone system was louder than the old one. It would take some getting used to. She grabbed the receiver before it could ring again. "Taylor Construction."

"Layla? It's Pastor Chaney."

She smiled. "Hi, Pastor. How're you?"

"Not so good, actually. That's why I'm calling."

Uh-oh. What now? "What can I do for you?"

"It's the plumbing at the church. We can't seem

to get our issue fixed. I was wondering if you could recommend someone."

She hesitated. Bob Johnson was the best plumber she knew, hands down, but with the circumstances as of late . . .

"I know it's an imposition, and I normally wouldn't ask, but we're getting desperate. James Page was working on it, but—"

"I know. I was at the hospital with Ms. Betty and him yesterday."

"She told me that last night when I visited. It was very nice of you. James isn't looking very good. The doctors still can't find what's causing his symptoms. They're still running tests."

"I'm praying for him."

"We all are." Pastor waited a beat. "But we've got to get this plumbing fixed."

It wasn't fair not to recommend Bob. He was fair and would do a good job. And there was no proof he'd done anything unethical or wrong. "Bob Johnson. He's the plumber I contracted when we did the renovations last year."

"Layla, I don't want to speak out of turn, but Bob's been by. Twice. He can't figure it out."

If Bob couldn't figure out a plumbing problem . . . "What's going on?"

"From what Bob says, the copper pipes and tubing keep getting corroded. He's replaced them twice."

Since the renovation less than a year ago? That

made no sense. "He doesn't know why they keep corroding?"

"Says he hasn't a clue. It's baffled him, and it's frustrating to the deacons. The pipes get corroded, then they blow. We have to keep cleaning up the mess. Both times Bob's replaced them, we've thought the issue was resolved. Then it happens again."

That was odd. Very odd. "Tell you what, I'll head over to the church and have a look. Maybe I can figure something out."

"Thanks, Layla. I really appreciate it."

"No problem. See you soon." She hung up the phone and rubbed her bottom lip.

What could be causing the pipes and tubing to corrode?

Differences aside, this was business. With only a moment's hesitation, she lifted the phone and dialed Bob's cell.

"This is Bob."

"Hi, Bob. It's Layla."

A pregnant silence filled the connection. Had he hung up?

"What do you need?" His voice was gruff.

"Look, Bob, I'm sorry if you felt like I was accusing you before. I'm just trying to figure out what's going on."

Another space of silence.

"You heard who the body was, I suppose." Bob had softened his tone.

"No. Who?"

"Dennis LeJeune. I heard this morning."

The stickler inspector? Why would somebody have killed him and put his body in the house? "That's awful." It explained why Maddox had questioned her about him.

"I know." He inhaled sharply. "I'm sorry I was so rude to you. It's just I would never allow drugs on my sites. Ever." He blew against the phone.

She'd jumped to conclusions and hurt someone. A friend. "I know that, Bob. I'm sorry. It's just that nothing makes sense."

"Do the police have any leads?"

"Not that they've told me about. You heard my place got broken into and trashed?"

"Yeah. Sorry to hear that." He inhaled again.

"It's more annoying than anything else. It won't be over until I figure everything out."

He exhaled against the phone. "So, you're still poking around?"

"I don't have a choice." She slumped in her chair. "Maybe that newspaper reporter is right and someone's trying to send me a message."

"Don't listen to that woman's rantings. She's just trying to make a name for herself and is using you to do it."

"Maybe." She straightened and wrapped the cord around her finger. "Listen, the reason I'm calling is about the pipes at the church."

"That's something I can't figure out." Again, a sharp intake came over the line.

"Is it possible the pipes and tubing you installed were bad from the factory?"

"I thought of that. We pulled the batch records. I've used the same copper from that batch in other buildings, and we haven't had a single report of a problem. It's just in the church."

"What could cause them to corrode? And so quickly?"

"I wish I knew. It's got me baffled." Another quick intake.

Her too. If Bob couldn't figure it out, she surely couldn't. But she'd given her word to Pastor. "I'm going to run by there and see if I notice anything odd."

"Good luck. Let me know if you find something."

"I will. And thanks, Bob." She unwound the cord from her finger and hung up the phone. Was Bob having breathing problems? With his audible breathing over the phone—Wait a minute. Did Bob smoke?

She grabbed her tool belt and truck keys from her desk, then headed out the front door. It seemed like lately nothing but confusion and trouble resided in Eternal Springs.

NINETEEN

"In a moment of decision the best thing
you can do is the right thing.
The worst thing you can do is nothing."
—THEODORE ROOSEVELT

"HOW'S YOUR DAD?" HOUSTON asked as soon as Maddox slipped into the passenger's seat.

"Same as always." Mean and unforgiving.

His partner cut his eyes to Maddox before looking back at the road. "You're surly this morning. Didn't get enough rest?"

"Man, I slept in a chair in Pop's hospital room. Of course I didn't get enough rest." He took a sip of the now-cold coffee he'd picked up on his way into the office. "And Pop's downright cantankerous this morning. Rude."

Houston chuckled and braked for a red light. "Morning grumpiness must run in the family."

Maddox's blood ran cold, and his muscles tensed. "I'm *nothing* like him."

His partner gave him a hard stare. "Why don't you tell me how you really feel?" He inched the car through the intersection and turned.

"Sorry. Didn't mean to bite your head off." But how could he explain? He and his father were like oil and water—they didn't mix at all.

"What's bugging you?"

There it was in a nutshell—the million-dollar question. "He still blames me for Mom's murder." It hurt to speak the words, but it was time to get it all out on the table.

"You were a kid, Maddox. He can't blame you."

"He can and he does. Trust me on this."

Houston checked the street sign, then made a quick left. "And this came up this morning? At the hospital?"

"Yep. Pop wanted to talk about the night she was killed. Again." The tightening in his chest increased. "As if anything had changed." Maddox slapped the dashboard with the side of his fist. "If only they'd caught her murderer. Maybe we could understand."

"Sounds like y'all need to heal."

"Never knowing what really happened, not knowing why . . . I don't think Pop can ever let it go."

"I think that applies to you too, partner."

Maddox stared at Houston as he pulled into the parking lot at J. B. Carpentry. "How do you figure?"

Houston turned off the ignition and shifted to face him. "Isn't that the reason you became a cop? To give people justice?"

Heat stormed across his face. "No. I wanted to be a cop. Plain and simple."

Houston waggled his brows. "And why is that?"

"I dunno. Just did." The heat kicked up a notch.

"Maybe you should ask yourself when you decided to become a cop. Then you can figure out why. I'm betting it has to do with your mom's case never being solved."

"What are you, a shrink?"

Houston shrugged and opened his car door. "Just done a little more living than you." He stepped from the cruiser. "Think about it. Later. Right now, we have a suspect to interview."

Maddox followed his partner into the carpenter's office. He'd never really thought about why he wanted to be a cop. He swallowed the lump in the back of his throat. Could guilt have pushed him into his profession?

A cute brunette sitting behind a counter smiled as they entered. "Good morning. How can we help you?"

"We need to see Sam Roberson, please." Houston flashed his detective's badge.

The girl didn't seem fazed. She lifted the intercom and paged Sam over the loudspeakers. "You're in luck," she said as she hung up the phone, "the crews haven't left for their jobs this morning yet."

"Thank you." Maddox smiled at the girl. He and Houston took a few steps away from the desk, moving off to the side of the entrance. Houston slipped a piece of gum into his mouth.

Heavy footsteps rushed into the area. "Hey,

Pam. Whatcha need? We're about to head out."

The girl waved toward Maddox and Houston. "Those two cops want to talk to you."

The young man's face went whiter than white.

Houston took a step toward him. "Sam Roberson?"

"Y-Yes."

Houston nodded at the front doors. "May we speak to you privately, please?" His badge glimmered on his waist.

Sam pushed open the doors and waited for Maddox and Houston. "What's this about?"

"We understand you were at Second Chances recently." Houston flipped open his notebook, popping his gum.

"Yeah. But I've been released." The kid shifted his weight from one foot to the other.

"We know that." Houston rocked back on his heels. "We understand you were part of the work-release program, working with J. B. Carpentry."

"I was, then Mr. Baxter said I was such a good worker that he hired me on after Second Chances." The defiance screamed from his squared shoulders and widened stance.

"And you worked on the Hope-for-Homes site that burned down last week?"

"Yeah." The kid's eyes narrowed. "I worked directly under Mr. Baxter. I was never alone at the site or anything. I had nothing to do with it burning."

A little defensive? "We didn't say you did." Maddox shifted, moving a couple of inches closer to Sam. "But since you brought it up, why don't you tell us where you were Friday night from eleven thirty until midnight?"

His face turned chalk white. "I was out on a date."

"Who were you on the date with?" Houston asked.

"Pam." Sam nodded toward the front door. "The receptionist."

Really? She'd shown no interest that police wanted to talk to a guy she was dating. Very odd. Maddox cocked out his hip, the one his gun sat on. "Where did y'all go?"

"We ate dinner at Copeland's."

"And then?"

His face reddened. "Then we hung out at her place for a while. Watched some stupid chick flick. I left a little after midnight." Sam glanced into the glass doors. "Look, is there anything else? My crew's gonna leave any minute now, and if I'm not in the truck, I'll get left. That's a day I'll be docked."

"Sure. You can go." Houston nodded.

Sam made fast tracks around the side of the building.

"Let's go question the receptionist. Verify his alibi." Houston pocketed his notebook and reached for the door.

"Why don't you do that? I'd like to talk to Mr. Baxter. See if he has anything to share."

"Good idea."

Maddox followed Houston back into the office. He asked to speak to the owner. Pam didn't page the man. Instead she called him on the phone, nodded, then directed Maddox to Mr. Baxter's office.

The indoor-outdoor carpet in the hallway to Mr. Baxter's office was matted down, almost bare in places. Maddox knocked on the door.

"Come in."

Maddox inched open the door, stepped inside, then closed it behind him.

"I'm Jonas Baxter. How can I help you?" He extended his hand.

Maddox shook it, noticing the calluses that scraped against his palm as the man nearly crushed his hand. Mr. Baxter was a hulk of a man—almost equal to Maddox's six-one stature—and had wide shoulders. Everything about him told that he was a man who did manual labor for a living.

"Thanks for agreeing to see me, Mr. Baxter."

"I figured you'd be by." He gestured to the chair in front of his desk. "Have a seat." He plopped down into his own chair. The leather creaked out affectionately, like a glove's perfect fit.

Now wasn't that odd? Maddox sat. "Why's that?"

"After Layla Taylor called me, I figured the police would be coming round."

Layla—"She called you? When? Why?"

Mr. Baxter chuckled. "She called me the other day and asked what I remembered about the Hope-for-Homes site. If I could recall any strangers on the site or anything amiss."

She was interfering in a homicide investigation. *His* investigation! "I see. And did you? Remember anything out of the ordinary on the site?"

"Like I told Layla, I don't. Nothing strikes my memory as anything other than ordinary."

"I see. And you hired Sam Roberson after he participated in the Second Chances work-release program?"

"I did. He's a good worker." Mr. Baxter crossed his arms over his chest. "And his father's my dentist."

A backdoor brother-in-law arrangement?

"Before you start thinking something's going on, let me assure you. I would never hire someone I didn't trust or know would do a good job. When J. B. Carpentry sends crews, it's my name and reputation on the line."

"Speaking of that, what is your experience with Taylor Construction?"

"Layla?" Mr. Baxter smiled. "She's a good contractor. Honest. Reliable. Good as her old man was." He tented his hands over his desk.

"She had to work twice as hard to prove herself, even though she was just as good as any of the guys. And she's done that. I'm proud of her."

"You knew her father?"

"Of course. This is a small community and an even smaller industry in this area."

"What was he like?" Not that this line of questioning had anything to do with his investigation, but he couldn't resist.

Mr. Baxter leaned back in his chair. It squeaked in response. "Kevin Taylor? Hard-working. Honest. A good man. Layla takes after him in a lot of ways." He shook his head. "Almost killed her when he dropped dead of a heart attack. That girl hero-worshipped her father, but the feeling was mutual."

Made sense of her being so nice and accommodating to him at the hospital. What would it be like to have a father who loved you and who you looked up to? Maddox couldn't fathom.

He focused on the case at hand. "Just one more question, Mr. Baxter. Where were you on Friday night between eleven thirty and midnight?"

"THANKS AGAIN FOR COMING over, Layla." Pastor Chaney met her in the foyer. "I didn't know where else to turn. This has about got us beat."

"I talked to Bob Johnson this morning. He

can't figure it out." She smiled at the kindly man who'd presided over her father's funeral so eloquently. The man who'd counseled Alana and tried to counsel Layla when their mother overdosed. He was such a good man. "Let's go look at the pipes."

Pastor led the way to the bathrooms off the narthex. "I've made sure no one is in either one." He pushed open the door to the men's room.

Layla stepped inside and nearly gagged. The stench of rotten eggs almost reversed the coffee she'd ingested this morning. She covered her nose. "What *is* that smell?"

"I have no idea. We've cleaned in here with everything—bleach, pine cleaner, even specialty odor-fighting cleansers." He coughed, wheezing. "We mask it on Sundays with air fresheners all the time."

"I've heard men's rooms stink, but this is ridiculous." She tried to smile, but the smell turned her stomach.

Pastor grinned and reached for a can of air freshener. He sprayed it generously. "It's the same in the ladies' room." He set it back on the counter with another rattling cough.

The air freshener made her eyes water, but it was better than the horrible reeking. "I'll see what I can find out." She knelt before the sinks. The beautiful tile floor she'd secured at a 40 percent discount was covered in old towels. The yellow-painted Sheetrock covering the pipes had been removed, revealing the inner plumbing.

Sure enough, the copper piping was corroded. The insulation that had surrounded the space had been removed.

"We had to tear it down when the leaks came back. This is twice we've had to replace the Sheetrock, paint, and insulation."

She slipped on her gloves, grabbed the pipe, and inspected it. Totally corroded. She sat back on her heels, surveying the area. What would cause the pipes to corrode so quickly?

Worrying her bottom lip, she processed everything she knew about plumbing. Nothing made sense. Bob said this was the second set of pipes installed. The renovation wasn't even a year old. The shipment of pipes weren't faulty. This didn't add up.

"Oh my goodness." Pastor ripped paper towels from the dispenser. Blood gushed from his nose.

Layla was on her feet in a flash. "Pastor, are you okay?"

He coughed and couldn't catch his breath. The blood kept flowing from his nose.

She helped him sit and grabbed more paper towels.

His coughing and wheezing increased, and his face turned red. The rattle in his chest echoed off the tile walls.

Layla's heart clenched. "Pastor?" She grabbed his arm.

He slumped forward.

She jerked just in time to save his head from cracking against the floor. "Pastor!" She eased him to a lying position on his side.

His breathing was slow . . . shallow.

She reached for her cell from her hip. She flipped it open and dialed 9-1-1. Her hands trembled as she waited for the call to connect.

Bleeding nose. Difficulty breathing. Coughing and wheezing. Losing consciousness.

Just like Ms. Ethel and Mr. James.

Dear Lord, what's happening?

TWENTY

"Beyond a doubt truth bears the same relation to falsehood as light to darkness."
—LEONARDO DA VINCI

LAYLA TAYLOR WAS A thorn in his side.

She wouldn't stop asking questions. Couldn't just let the police do their job—wouldn't stop looking into matters. Didn't she realize the danger she'd put herself in?

He lifted his glass and finished off his drink. The bourbon warmed all the way to his stomach.

Think. He had to come up with something.

Anything to distract Layla from continuing her investigation.

Her records were destroyed, so he didn't have to worry about the proof. Breaking into her office and trashing the place hadn't dissuaded her. If only it were spring, when construction business was booming. But this was the slow season. Gave her plenty of time to play Nancy Drew.

Maybe she needed a message. Something that would make her realize she needed to concentrate her efforts elsewhere.

Layla Taylor's Achilles' heel was her sister. No doubt about that. But he'd forever remember Alana toothless and in pigtails. He couldn't harm her.

But he could hurt something Alana cared about deeply, which made Layla care about it. Would that be enough?

He lifted the bottle and poured himself another shot of the cheap liquor. One day . . . one day, he'd be able to afford the top-shelf stuff. That day was in sight.

If he could just get Layla Taylor to mind her own business.

He downed the soft amber liquor. Yes, hitting what Alana cared about most would send a message to Layla. He just needed to figure out how to pull it off.

All his careful planning could go up in smoke

soon. Rumor had it the riverboat casinos would begin their final eliminations on their rebuilding projects next week. He'd have to act fast.

And if this didn't stop Layla . . . well, he'd have no other choice.

"THAT WAS ANOTHER DEAD end." Houston plopped into his chair in Maddox's and his cubicle.

Maddox slumped into his own seat. "We're missing something." He lifted reports from his in-box and scanned them. "Great. Initial forensic analysis on the break-in at Layla's netted us nothing. Since it's a business, too many outside factors played into the retrieved samples." He tossed the report to his file. "Wordy way of saying they got zilch."

Houston reviewed his case notes. "There's nothing about Dennis LeJeune that stands out. Background check came back clean. Nothing to indicate someone would want to kill him."

"What about his friends?"

"Nothing. The man only had bowling buddies from what we can uncover. He didn't go to church. Didn't hunt. Didn't fish. Didn't do anything but work and come home to be alone with his wife, and bowl occasionally."

What a boring life. But then it occurred to Maddox that he hadn't been hunting or fishing in months. He sure didn't go to church. All he did was work and go home. He didn't even have someone to go home to. "Which means that his murder had to be related in some way to his work as a building inspector."

Houston nodded. "I haven't missed the irony of his grave being a site he inspected. Who wanted to send such a message?"

"And the overkill of the crime. Shooting him in the head when he was already dead. That's anger."

"Or revenge." Houston tossed a stack of papers on Maddox's desk. "Got the report back on Randy Dean. Clean."

Maddox reached for the papers and scanned. Layla's ex didn't have a record, no outstanding warrants—not even unpaid parking tickets—had no open complaints on him, and no indication of any illegal implications. He'd been an electrician and served on the Eternal Springs volunteer fire department. As Houston said, he was clean as a whistle.

Another dead end.

Maddox rested his head back on the chair. "We've already questioned the people connected to Second Chances and the site."

"Maybe that isn't the connection."

"What do you mean?" Maddox straightened and stared at his partner.

"Just that perhaps Second Chances has nothing to do with his murder."

Maddox pulled up his own notes. "Okay. So we go back to a connection with the site itself. I talked to Baxter. Don't see how he can be involved."

Houston turned to another page in his file. "So that leaves the electrician, Denny Keys. The plumber, Bob Johnson. The supplier, Y Building Supplies."

"And Layla Taylor." Just including her left a bad taste in Maddox's mouth, but he had to do his job.

"Do you really think she's connected?" Houston set down his papers and peered over the desk at Maddox.

"She was the contractor and the site foreman. She's the single connection to all these people. And she knew the victim."

"But as you mentioned, Baxter said it's a small community and industry. Of course they're all connected."

"She knew everything about the site, including when Ms. Caldwell would move in."

"So did everyone else on the site, right?"

"True." Maddox scratched his head. They were getting nowhere fast.

Houston rested his elbows on his desk. "Why do you want her to be involved in this so badly?"

"I don't." He really didn't, but he had to make sure he treated her like anyone else involved in the investigation. "It's just what makes sense. Especially since her office was broken into. I don't think she's personally involved. But I do think she's a key connection."

"Okay, we can keep that in mind. Check out that angle."

"In the meantime, let's go visit the electrician, plumber, and supplier."

Houston stood and led the way down the hall.

Maddox fell into step with his partner. "And I'm still not wild about Layla asking questions, sticking her nose in the investigation."

"She's probably just trying to help."

Maddox stopped and grabbed Houston's arm. "Why do you want her *not* to be involved so badly?"

"Because I think there's the possibility of something between you two." Houston had the decency to blush as he pulled his arm from Maddox's grip.

First George, now Houston? Were they scheming behind his back?

"I know you like to keep your love life personal, and for the most part, I think I do a good job of respecting that."

Maddox took hold of Houston's arm again, this time leading him out the back entrance. "But?"

Houston sighed and pulled his arm free again. "But there's something about Layla. And you. Together."

"Yeah, we fight like cats and dogs." Maddox managed to squeeze out a weak chuckle, despite the awareness sneaking up his throat.

"Funny you should say that."

Houston had gone off the deep end. "Why?"

"The boys' dog and Margie's cat have this thing. They take turns chasing each other around the house. They bat and snarl at one another pretty much all day."

"My point exactly."

"But then as it turns to night, they curl up together on the couch and fall asleep." Houston grinned and clapped Maddox's shoulder. "That, my friend, is what makes me so sure there's a future for you and Layla."

Maddox shook his head. "Man, I don't get it."

"You'll figure it out." Houston laughed and crossed the lot to the cruiser.

His partner had apparently been working too hard. He made not a lick of sense.

Maddox folded himself into the passenger seat, fastened his seat belt, and tried to organize his thoughts to ask Houston what he meant.

His cell phone chirped on his hip. He grabbed it and flipped it open. "Hello."

"Hey, Maddox. How ya doing?" George wouldn't use his regular greeting if something was wrong with Pop.

"Hiya, George. What's up?"

"They're releasing your father."

"Already?" But he'd had a heart attack. Suffered damage.

"They've run all the tests they can for now. Doctor says results will be in later, and they'll call Tyson. He's doing well, so they're processing his paperwork now."

Maddox sighed. "Do I need to come get him?"

"Nah. I'll take him home and get him settled in."

"Thanks, George. He doesn't deserve you."

"You'll stop by tonight to see him?"

Apprehension flooded his senses. "That might not be such a good idea, Uncle George."

"Don't be bullheaded, son. Just drop by and check on him. I can't stay with him 24-7."

Guilt shoved the apprehension out of the way. Pop wasn't George's responsibility. "I'll come by after my shift."

"Good boy. I'll let Tyson know."

The disconnection buzzed against his ear. Maddox replaced his phone in silence.

So many conflictions—over Layla and Pop—washed over him that he couldn't filter them all. He needed guidance. Wisdom. Peace.

But all three seemed lost in the swirl of emotions.

Houston lifted a piece of paper. "Did you see the memo?"

Maddox's heart seized. "*The* memo?"

Houston nodded.

"No. What's the news?"

His partner dropped his head. "I'm sorry, Maddox. He's staying on as commander."

Maddox's tongue doubled in size. He swallowed. Again. "Man, it's okay. I probably wouldn't have gotten the promotion anyway." Great. One more thing his father would fault him for—not even being able to snag a promotion.

What was he going to do? Did he want to stay as an investigator with no promotions in sight?

"THIS IS ALL SO scary." Alana fluffed her bangs in the emergency room waiting area.

Layla looked around the room filled with members of Eternal Springs Christian church. She was becoming sick of the place. But this time she wasn't alone in her worry. After Layla had made a few calls, most of the congregation rushed to the hospital. Everyone was worried about Pastor.

Especially in light of Ms. Ethel's passing. And Mr. James still in ICU with no hint of a diagnosis.

"I've been praying."

"Everyone has. It's terrible." Alana laid her hand on her sister's. "Thank God you were there when he collapsed."

Layla nodded, but she didn't feel lucky. She felt sick. All the blood from his nose. His gasping for air. She'd been terrified the ambulance wouldn't arrive in time. Pastor had been so pale. And cold. She shivered at the memory.

"Wonder when someone will come out and talk to us?" Alana peered at the nurse sitting behind the triage desk.

"As soon as they can. They'd probably like us to leave."

"We can't. Not until we know about Pastor."

"I know." Layla stood, unable to be idle any longer. It'd been hours since she followed the ambulance here. Hours since she called everyone. Hours since they heard anything. All she knew for certain was that Pastor had still been breathing, albeit laboriously, when he arrived.

Alana stood as well. "What?"

"Nothing. I'm just tired of sitting is all." And tired of waiting in this same room to hear if someone she cared about was going to make it.

"I checked on Ms. Betty a bit ago."

Layla stretched. "Any change?"

"No. Still no idea what's making Mr. James sick."

This was a hospital, for crying out loud. Doctors were supposed to be able to tell patients what was wrong with them. They hadn't for Ms. Ethel. Not for Mr. James. And now Pastor.

"I called Ms. Ethel's grandson to let him know what's happened. He said they'd planned for her funeral to be Saturday, but now, with Pastor sick . . . He's waiting for an update before he makes any announcements."

"Aren't we all?"

"Have you talked to Jeffery?"

Layla spun to stare at her sister. "No. What's wrong?"

"Nothing." Alana smiled. "I just heard this morning that Jeffery and his wife are expecting."

"Oh, that's wonderful. They've been trying." But inside she ached a bit that Jeffery hadn't told her. She'd had to hear the news through the grapevine. She pushed away the hurt. He probably intended to tell her tonight at practice.

Practice! Oh no. She glanced at her watch. Only thirty more minutes before she'd have to rush home and get changed to meet him at the studio.

"May I have your attention please?" A doctor stood at the entrance of the waiting room.

Everyone gave the man in scrubs and white jacket their full attention.

"Pastor Chaney is stable. We're admitting him to ICU."

The room exploded with everyone talking at once.

"What's wrong with him?"

"Is it the same thing as James Page?"

"Is this contagious?"

The doctor held up his hands, and silence

ensued. “We don’t know what this is. Because this is the fourth admission with the same symptoms, we’ve called in a specialist from the CDC.”

The Center for Disease Control was being called in? Layla hugged herself. *Lord, what’s happening here?* Wait a minute . . . fourth? Who was the other person?

“That’s all I can tell you at this time. No one will be allowed to visit in ICU unless you’re Mr. Chaney’s next of kin.” The doctor spun on his heel and took off down the hall, ignoring the questions some people asked.

The noise level in the room hummed as people began talking again. Layla grabbed Alana’s hand and led her outside where she could think.

“This just got even scarier.” Alana’s bottom lip trembled, just as it’d done when she was a child and frightened.

Layla squeezed her sister’s hand. “At least they’ve called in someone who’ll figure it out.”

“You think the CDC will?”

“That’s what they do.” At least, she prayed they’d make sense of everything.

Alana nodded. “I guess there’s nothing else for us to do here.”

“I’ve got to meet Jeffery at the studio.” She glanced at her watch again. “I’m already cutting it close.”

Alana gave her a hug. “I’m going to go update

Ms. Betty and see if I can get her to go to the cafeteria with me for supper."

"Good idea." Layla planted a kiss on her sister's cheek. "I'll call you tonight. Call me if you hear anything."

"I will."

Layla rushed toward her truck, her nerves in even tighter knots. The CDC. Had they all been exposed to something toxic? Would she get sick? Alana?

Who was next?

TWENTY-ONE

"Freedom prospers when religion is vibrant and the rule of law under God is acknowledged."
—RONALD REAGAN

THE TABLE HUMMED. LOUDLY. He must be dreaming.

It hummed again, even louder it seemed.

Maddox rolled over and grabbed his cell from the coffee table. "Bishop."

"Detective Bishop, this is dispatch. Emergency call at Second Chances. Report of an explosion. Fire and emergency medical personnel are en route. Eternal Springs PD has requested law enforcement backup. Specifically asked for you and Detective Wallace."

Maddox shot upright. He raked a hand down his face. "Yeah. I'm there."

"Detective Wallace is on his way. Requested you meet him at the scene."

"Got it." Maddox shut his phone and stood, stretching. Sleeping on his father's couch wasn't much better than the hospital chair.

He reached for his shirt and tugged it over his head, then checked the time. Three a.m. Jeans would have to suffice. He'd come over to his father's after his shift and running by his place to shower. Where had he put his shoes?

The bedroom door creaked open. "Maddox?"

He didn't have time to deal with his father. "Go back to bed, Pop. I've got a call." By the front door—that's where he'd left his shoes.

"A murder?" His father swayed on his feet.

Maddox moved fast to steady him. George had warned the medications made Pop light-headed. He'd been sleeping soundly from the time Maddox had arrived last night. "No. I don't know." He turned his father toward his bedroom.

"Are you coming back? We need to have a serious talk, Maddox."

Tension tugged at him as he helped his father into bed. "I don't know how long I'll be gone." He pulled the comforter over his father, turning it down under the shoulder. Just like his mom had tucked him in every night as a child.

Pop looked up at him, his face serene. "Be

careful, son. I love you." His eyes fluttered closed, then his breathing evened out. A loud snore followed.

Maddox froze, but his heart raced. His father had never—No, it had to be the medication they had Pop on.

He didn't have time to think about this. He carefully closed his father's bedroom door, slipped on his shoes, then rushed for his car.

The early morning temperatures had dipped below forty. Maddox shivered, wishing he had a thicker jacket. No time to go in and borrow one of Pop's.

As he drove, he sorted out what the dispatcher had said. An explosion? From what? They didn't keep explosive materials at Second Chances. Not that he knew of anyway, and he couldn't think of a reason why they would.

His body chilled as his thinking process continued. Explosions happened because of illegal drug manufacturing. Was that why local PD had requested Houston's and his presence? He punched harder on the accelerator.

Traffic was minimal. He even managed to drive over the bridge without getting nauseated.

Well before he'd passed through Westlake and hit Eternal Springs city limits, he could see the orange hue of the dark sky. The closer he drew to the scene, the heavier the fog. No, it wasn't fog—it was smoke. Dense and unforgiving.

He turned onto the street that housed Second Chances, red and blue flashing lights were beacons guiding him. He parked beside Houston's cruiser and stepped into the cold air, now heavy with smoke, ash, and chaos.

Stepping from the car, he spied Houston's bright orange sweatshirt. His partner didn't know the meaning of dressing subtly. Right now, it worked for Maddox.

"Houston!" His voice was lost in the commotion.

Maddox stepped over extended hoses, around firemen and EMTs. He grabbed his partner's arm. "What's happened?"

"From what the fire department can determine, a device was detonated in the main building. None of the housing halls were directly hit, although some of those sleeping in them are being treated for smoke inhalation and cuts from the glass blown from the blast."

"A bomb?" He tried to wrap his mind around the implication. Somebody had set a bomb at Second Chances? Why?

Houston nodded. "That's what the fire department says. They've called in their specialists for confirmation."

Maddox glanced over the pandemonium, his chest constricting. "Where's Alana? She lives on the second floor of the main building."

"She wasn't there when it went off."

He let out a sigh. "She's okay?"

"They took her to the hospital to check her out, but they said she's physically fine." Houston tossed him a look that told him there was more. "She was in the back part of the main building, in a storeroom. She and her fiancé had been putting some of her things in storage." Houston shook his head. "Her fiancé was carrying a box down the stairs when the detonation hit."

Maddox's muscles tensed. "And?"

"He was hit pretty bad. He was the first one the ambulance rushed off. Alana's second in command and the doctors are with the residents right now. Everyone is accounted for."

"Has anyone called Layla?"

"I thought you would want to." Houston gave him a pointed stare. "And maybe this should be in person, Maddox."

What felt like infinity passed. Yeah, Layla needed to be told in person. She'd probably need someone to drive her to the hospital. "I'll go now."

Houston clapped his shoulder. "Good man. Keep in touch."

Maddox rushed back to his car, letting the words he'd say firm up in his mind. How, exactly, did you tell someone about such a tragedy?

If only he knew something that would soften the blow.

Knowing Layla, he'd better have facts. He whipped out his cell phone and dialed the direct line for the dispatcher. He'd have them patch him through to the hospital. No way would he deliver bad news to Layla without knowing the current status of her sister and Alana's fiancé.

It was bad enough that he'd have to be the bearer of such devastating news.

BAM! BAM! BAM!

Layla buried her head under the pillow. It could *not* be time to get up yet.

Bam! Bam!

"Layla!"

That was no alarm clock. She bolted from her bed. Her feet got tangled in the sheet and she fell. Her recently scabbed-over knees took the brunt of her weight. Pain made her cry out. Loudly.

"Layla, are you okay?"

She growled under her breath and grabbed the side of the bed, pulling herself upright. Great, the scabs were bleeding under her flannel pajama bottoms. She hobbled down the hall.

Bam! Bam! Bam!

"Layla!"

She jerked open the door. "What?" Her breath caught in her lungs.

Maddox stood on her porch. In jeans and a sweater, he looked like a vision straight from her dreams. His bluer-than-blue eyes glistened under the motion detector lights. His face boasted a five o'clock shadow on its strong lines. The total package of Maddox Bishop tied her stomach into knots. Tight knots.

"Are you okay? I heard a thump." His lids were at half mast.

Her heart skidded to a stop. She must look like a swamp witch or something. She smoothed down her oversized pajama top. "Uh, yeah." And then the oddness of it all smacked her. "What time is it?"

He glanced at his watch. "Four."

The sleep and fuzziness evaporated as adrenaline surged through her. Even her knees stopped hurting. "What's wrong?" Her office again?

"First off, you need to know that Alana's okay."

She sagged against the door frame. "What happened?"

He hesitated, then wrapped an arm around her waist and stepped over the threshold with her. He pushed the door closed with his foot, then led her to the couch and sat her down. He sat beside her, keeping his arm around her. "It's Second Chances."

She was going to be sick. "W-What?"

"Best they can figure out at this point, there was a bomb in the main building."

"A bomb?" *Oh, dear Lord . . .* "Alana?"

"Is fine. She's at the hospital getting treated for minor cuts and smoke inhalation."

A bomb. Second Chances. Her childhood home. Tears burned her eyes. "The retreat?"

White circled his lips. "The main building's pretty much gone."

She couldn't have stopped the tears from falling if she'd wanted to. All the memories . . . Alana and her growing up . . . Daddy. She buried her face in her hands.

Maddox pulled her to him, holding her. Warmth seeped from him deep into her. Soul-deep her daddy would've said.

Layla let the sobs have their way, then sniffed and pushed away from Maddox. "I need to go see Alana. She'll be beside herself."

He tightened his hold on her. "Layla, there's something else."

Oh, God, give me strength. "What?"

"Alana's fiancé was closer to the blast than anyone. He received some severe burns."

"Cameron?" *Sweet Jesus, help him. Help Alana. Help us all.*

"It's pretty bad." Maddox's expression was graver than she'd ever imagined.

She took a moment to register the information. Then eased out of Maddox's hold. "I'll get dressed. I need to be there for Alana. And Cameron."

He nodded. "I'll drive you."

Layla stumbled down the hall to her bedroom. She threw on the first thing she grabbed from her drawer—a pair of sweats. She brushed her teeth and hair, then slipped her feet into tennis shoes. In less than ten minutes, she returned to her living room to find Maddox waiting on her couch. "I'm ready."

He stood and took her elbow. While she didn't need someone guiding her, it sure was nice and comforting to feel his hold on her. He opened the passenger door of a cobalt blue Mustang for her.

She waited until he'd started the engine to speak. "This doesn't look like a sheriff's department–issued vehicle." Talk about anything to stop worrying. About Alana. About Cameron. Mourning the loss of her childhood home of memories.

"It's my personal car." Maddox whipped the car out of the driveway and onto the road. He punched the gas, flying toward Lake Charles.

Back pressed into the seat, she could see how the car fit the man. Even the color . . . it made his eyes seem that much bluer.

She glanced out the window and noticed an orangish glow to the predawn sky. "Is that . . . ?" *Oh, Lord, please watch over Cameron and Alana.*

His gaze followed hers. "Yeah." He punched the gas harder. "Look, the housing parts of the retreat were barely damaged."

She gave a grunt. "That you can see." But as a contractor, she knew what the damage could be. Had seen way too many times people thinking they had minor damage, only to learn they had to do some heavy repairs. Heavy and pricey.

"Was anybody else hurt?"

"As far as we can tell, everyone else was like Alana—minor cuts and smoke inhalation."

"Except for Cameron."

"Yes." His jawline was firm as he concentrated on the road.

Thank You, Jesus, that no one else was badly injured. God, please put Your hand of healing over Cameron. If something happened to him, there was no telling how Alana would fall apart.

Layla had to be strong. For Alana. For Cameron. For everybody at Second Chances. She already sensed the suffocating pressure of responsibility cloaking her shoulders.

Maddox laid his hand over hers. "Layla, I know you've got to be scared and upset, that's only natural. If you need to talk, I'm here."

The gentleness of his tone almost made her cry again. But she couldn't afford to be weak and break down. Alana would be a mess. Layla had to be tough. Then again, she'd always had to. It was her lot in life. Nothing would change.

"Thanks, but I'm fine."

"Okay." He patted her hand, then gripped the steering wheel with both hands.

She watched him from the corner of her eye. What an enigma. Relentless and intimidating cop, yet sweet and sensitive when it came to his father—and with her this morning in the midst of a personal tragedy.

He slowed down as they ascended the I-210 bridge. His lips pinched closed. She could barely make out the sweat beads on his upper lip under the streetlights of the high bridge. His knuckles were white against the steering wheel.

What was making him so nervous? She glanced out the window, looking out across the west fork of the Calcasieu River. Nothing seemed amiss, save the bright orange behind them. The remains of what had once been a building very near and dear to her heart.

Layla denied the tears as Maddox topped the curve at the apex of the bridge. He kept his speed under the limit as they descended. When they reached level road, he gunned the engine and they sped off the exit.

Maybe she was just imagining things. Wouldn't be surprised—so much had hit her so quickly. *God, what am I supposed to do?*

Only the hum of Maddox's Mustang as he spun into the hospital parking lot answered her.

He kept his hand on the small of her back as they entered. They checked the packed emergency room waiting area but didn't find Alana. So many people she recognized from

Second Chances. Some had bandages on them, some cried, and some paced. It was standing room only.

Maddox flashed his badge at the triage nurse. "Alana Taylor?"

The nurse checked the computer, then pointed down the hallway. "Exam room 2."

Maddox guided her down the corridor amid all the hustling of doctors and nurses. It was nice to have him there to handle issues. She was pretty certain she'd never have gotten this far without him and his badge.

He stopped outside the room with a big number 2 plastered on the outside. "Would you like me to wait here?"

She didn't know. Without answering, she pushed open the door to find Alana sitting on the examining bed, crying. Two large bandages were on her face—the biggest on her forehead and a smaller one on her right cheek.

She looked up as they entered, her tear-streaked face reminding Layla of when they were little and Alana would get hurt. "Oh, Layla." Alana held out her arms.

Layla crawled up on the bed beside Alana and gathered her younger sister in her arms. She rocked her, petting her hair and making shushing noises. "It's going to be okay."

"C-Cameron," Alana wailed. "They won't tell me anything."

Layla turned her head and made eye contact with Maddox. She silently pleaded with him to use his police magic again and get an update on Cameron. He nodded, then left the room.

"Shh. We'll find out. It'll be okay."

Alana clung to her, sobbing for all she was worth. It nearly ripped Layla's heart from her chest. She held her sister tighter, trying to provide as much comfort as she could.

Finally Alana's sobs lessened to sniffles. Layla released her and studied her sister's face. "How bad is yours?"

"Stitches where glass got me. Nothing serious. Not like Cameron." Her eyes filled with tears again.

Layla took Alana's hand and squeezed. "Whatever it is, we'll get through it."

"The house. It's gone." Tears streamed down Alana's cheeks.

Swallowing, Layla forced her own pain from her expression. "It was just a building. It can be replaced." She smoothed back Alana's bangs and pasted on a smile. "I happen to know a really good contractor who can build a new one."

Even though it wouldn't be the same. Not ever again.

TWENTY-TWO

"The future belongs to those who believe in the beauty of their dreams."
—ELEANOR ROOSEVELT

ONCE AGAIN HE WAS cast into the character of the bearer of bad news. And he didn't like it one bit.

Maddox dragged his feet down the emergency room hall as he headed back to Layla and Alana, having gotten the report on Cameron Stone. It wasn't good. The young software designer might not live to see tomorrow. The doctors weren't hopeful.

He hesitated outside the exam room, sucking in air and strength. The stench of disinfectant wasn't as strong as before. Or maybe his senses were adjusting to the smell. He tapped on the door left ajar.

"Come in." Layla's voice sounded strong. Good, because what he'd tell them would crush Alana.

He inched into the room and shut the door behind him.

Hope flickered in Layla's eyes. He hated to let her down.

"Well?"

He moved to the edge of the bed, standing

before the Taylor sisters. He felt like the Grim Reaper. "They were able to stabilize Cameron enough to take him up to ICU."

"Praise God," Alana whispered. "At least they were able to stabilize him. That's good news."

Praise God? The man probably wouldn't live throughout the day, and she praised the God who had allowed this to happen? She was in shock, had to be.

"It's not good, Alana. He's got severe burns over 30 percent of his body. His organs have sustained a lot of trauma." Good thing he'd memorized what the doctor had said.

She gasped and trembled.

Layla wrapped an arm around her sister and pulled her close. She squared her shoulders. "What else?"

He let out a quiet breath, wishing they'd go find the doctor and talk to him themselves. "They'll be able to tell you more once he's settled and evaluated in the ICU."

Alana jumped off the bed. "Let's go."

Layla grabbed her arm. "Whoa there. Have you been released?"

"I was never admitted. They just gave me oxygen and stitched me up." Alana jerked her arm free of Layla's grasp. "I need to be with Cameron. He needs me." Her eyes glistened as they filled with tears.

Slipping to her feet, Layla looked at Maddox.

"We're going up to ICU. Could you please make sure the nurses know where Alana is in the event they need her?"

Normally he'd balk at being an errand boy, but this was an emergency.

And it was Layla.

He ignored *that* implication. "Sure."

She smiled and his heart stalled. "Thanks." She followed her sister from the examining room, heading toward the elevators.

Maddox relayed information to the busy nurses' station, then moved to follow the sisters. His cell phone vibrated on his hip. He snatched it open. "Hello."

"Hey, partner. How's it going there?"

"It's crazy here. Lots of people everywhere." Maddox ducked out the ER entrance for a little privacy. And some quiet. Dawn crested, but the air still carried a cold edge.

"And Alana?"

"She's fine. Just went to find out about her fiancé. Doctors have admitted him into ICU, but his prognosis isn't good." He moved out of the walkway into the parking lot. "What's the story there?"

"Fire investigator confirmed it was a bomb. The forensics team has it, trying to trace the compounds back to its maker."

"What else?"

"Initial thought is we're dealing with an

amateur. Investigator said it's a rough unit, shoddily made. Probably put together on the fly."

"That's so helpful." He glanced up as the med-helicopter took off—someone else who might not make it through the night.

"They're cross-checking the method, means, and compounds with known bomb makers to see if they get a match."

"How long will that take?" People went in and out of the emergency room entrance like ants to a picnic.

"Said a day or so. I asked them to rush whatever they could."

Cars started. Engines revved. "That's something."

"I'm about to head from the scene. Thought I'd run by and interview Denny Keys, the electrician. Want me to swing by and pick you up?"

It was his job . . . but it was Layla. "Nah, I have my car here. And Layla doesn't have a ride. I'll stick around here for a few. See what I can learn. Call me when you finish up, and I'll meet you at the station."

"Sounds like a plan."

Maddox shoved his phone back into its clip, then rushed into the hospital. The chill followed him as he waited for the elevators.

None of this made sense. He could understand burning the Hope-for-Homes site—it destroyed evidence of the murder. But why was LeJeune murdered in the first place? Then the break-in at

Taylor Construction? And just when he'd begun to think the connection wasn't Second Chances, there's a bomb?

He stepped onto the floor housing ICU and almost passed the waiting room, but he caught a glimpse of Layla and Alana with their elderly friend Betty Page and several others. He paused in the doorway, not wanting to intrude on what had to be a very private moment.

Layla and Alana, along with three or four others, knelt in front of Mrs. Page. All were crying. All had their eyes closed but were whispering.

Had something happened to Stone? No, that couldn't be it. Alana appeared too together for it to be her fiancé.

Suddenly those kneeling stood and helped Mrs. Page to her feet. Two young men flanked her as they shuffled from the waiting room.

Mrs. Page paused in front of Maddox. Her eyes were red and puffy. Tears still glistened in them. "How's your father?"

"They released him." He smiled, remembering his father's words this morning. Even if it was the medication that caused Pop to speak as he did, Maddox would carry the memory in his heart.

"I'll keep praying for him." She nodded and allowed the young men to guide her to the elevator.

Maddox's gaze drifted to Layla, who stood and joined him just inside the waiting room. "Her husband died a few moments ago."

She'd just lost her husband, but the lady had taken the time to inquire about his father's health. "That's awful."

"It is. But she'll be okay. She's strong in her faith, and her two grandsons arrived this morning to stay with her."

What did faith have to do with losing someone? Someone you loved with all your heart? Did faith comfort you when you missed the person with every ounce of your being? Did faith stop the guilt or regret?

Layla took his hand and pulled him into the hallway. "It's not looking good for Cameron. The doctors are talking about getting him stable enough to transport him to Baton Rouge's hospital. It has a specialized burn unit."

He glanced through the window at Alana talking with some of the others. She was still crying. He couldn't imagine what she was going through.

"About Mr. James's illness . . . the hospital called in a specialist from the CDC. Not that it'll do Ms. Ethel or Mr. James any good, but maybe they can help Pastor."

"Who? What?" The CDC?

"Our pastor. He was admitted yesterday afternoon. Same symptoms—nose bleeding, not being able to breathe, coughing uncontrollably, then loss of consciousness." Layla kept her voice low, so he had to bend closer to hear her clearly. "The doctors called in a specialist from the CDC. He got here this morning. He's running some tests on Pastor—a gas chromatography, carboxyhemoglobin test, whatever those are."

If the pastor was admitted, then the connection *had* to be the church. Layla had been right. "Maybe the specialist will figure everything out."

"I hope so. We've been praying." She glanced over her shoulder. "Having the church members around praying for Cameron has helped Alana tremendously. She's holding up really well."

He studied Alana through the window and had to admit Layla was right. Alana looked poised and . . . peaceful.

How was that? Her fiancé was going to be transported to a special hospital, might not even make it, and she looked at peace. Was that faith? Prayers? What if all this—?

Alana rushed from the waiting room, holding out her cell phone as if it were a dead rat. Her eyes were wide and her face pale. "Layla, Maddox. You have to see this text message!"

WHAT IN THE WORLD?

Layla reached out for Alana and drew her into a sideways hug. "What is it, honey?"

Her sister trembled in her arms as she handed her a cell phone. "Here. Read. For. Yourself."

Keeping her arm around Alana, Layla hit a button to bring the backlight up. Her heart thudded as she read:

tell UR sister 2 stop with the ?s
R next time it wont B a bldg blown

Layla's world tilted as her knees went weak. She tightened her grip on her sister, more to keep herself upright. "M-M—"

Maddox took the phone from her and repeated her actions. His brows shot into his forehead, and he lifted his gaze to meet hers, then looked at Alana. "Do you know this number? The one that sent the text?"

She shook her head. "I've never seen it before."

He looked at Layla. "Do you?"

"No."

He pocketed the phone in the front hip pocket of his jeans. "I need to take this for evidence."

Alana nodded and wrapped her arms around her stomach. Layla could relate—she felt sick to her stomach herself.

"Who's your service through?" he asked Alana.

She rattled off the name although she continued to shake against Layla.

His stare penetrated Layla. "I'll get Houston on this immediately." He reached out and squeezed her hand, providing her a moment's comfort. "I'll be right back. Don't go anywhere." Maddox ran to the elevator.

Layla tightened her hold on Alana as she led her to the waiting room and eased them both to a couch. The enormity of it all slapped against her.

The bomb at Second Chances was *her* fault. She'd been asking questions that made someone angry enough to blow up a building.

With her sister inside.

Layla's body stiffened and she bit her bottom lip. Tears burned her eyes, and sobs tore inside her. She jumped to her feet, mumbled about having to go to the restroom, then made a quick getaway.

Once inside the bathroom, she shut herself in a stall and hugged herself, rocking.

Oh, God . . . oh, God . . . oh, God. Cameron could die, and it'd be all her fault. Because she'd asked the wrong questions. Or too many questions. Or questions period.

The home she'd grown up in was no more, and she was to blame. Her sister was injured and could lose the man she loved, and Layla was solely responsible.

Sobs exploded from her, destroying her control like the bomb had destroyed their lives. She continued rocking herself, pushing her fist against her mouth. *Oh, God, what have I done? Please forgive me. Help Alana to forgive me.* She doubled over. *God, help Cameron forgive me.*

TWENTY-THREE

"For time and the world do not stand still.
Change is the law of life. And those
who look only to the past or the
present are certain to miss the future."
—JOHN F. KENNEDY

"I'LL GET RIGHT ON this. Keep her cell until I can get copies of the records." Houston's excitement came through the phone.

Maddox stepped outside the hospital's main entrance. The wind was still cold, cutting through him. "Planned on it."

"This could be our break. Aren't you glad you're still gonna be in the thick of things and not behind some stupid desk?"

Maddox stared at the people rushing to and from the parking lot and considered his partner's words. He wouldn't turn this case over to anyone. If he were commander, he wouldn't be tracking down leads, catching the bad guys. Speaking of bad guys . . . "Houston, we have to provide protection for Layla and Alana." If something happened to her . . . or Alana . . . "This message is a warning."

"I'll run protection detail by the commander, but you know how that is. There hasn't been a threat made to them personally. Not by name."

Maddox's muscles knotted. "Come on, you know that message is a threat against them. The bomb was a clear threat that this person means business. Layla was digging around—"

"Interfering in a murder investigation."

"Yeah, but she was just trying to get answers. She didn't—"

"I know all that, Maddox. I'm just giving the argument the commander will. You know how he feels about a *wasted use of police officers*."

Maddox steeled his grip on his cell. "I get that. But we can't leave them out there without protection. Even if the commander doesn't approve it."

Houston's chuckle was barely audible.

"What?" This wasn't funny. This was Layla's life.

"That cat-and-dog thing again."

Maddox leaned against the cold brick wall, not even slightly amused. "While I appreciate you trying to develop a sense of humor, isn't our motto *to serve and protect?* Did you miss the *protect* part, Houston?"

"No. I'm laughing at you, not the situation."

"Well, why don't you get busy getting those phone records so we can find out who sent the message?"

"Aye, aye, captain." The amusement was back in Houston's voice.

Maddox shut the phone and headed back into

the hospital. Houston didn't mean anything. He'd used his warped sense of humor many times over the years to lessen the tension they felt when working a murder case. But this was Layla.

He didn't have to wait for an elevator. He stepped inside and punched the floor for the ICU. He couldn't explain what his deal was about Layla. Didn't even want to try. There was just some feeling—not a stupid cat-and-dog analogy that made no sense, but . . . something. The way she was so strong when she needed to be, yet so soft and caring at the same time. He'd never met a woman like her.

He strode off the elevator and paused outside the ICU waiting room. Layla sat with Alana, who looked different . . . off . . . broken. Her body language screamed defeat—from the slouched posture to the way she kept her head ducked.

Chills fused his spine. Had they gotten another threat?

He entered the waiting room in clipped steps. "Have you heard anything else?"

Alana looked up first. She had tear tracks down her face. "They're preparing Cameron for transport. They'll airlift him as soon as they can."

But she didn't look as peaceful as she had before. "That's good, right?"

"Yes, it's very good for him to get specialized care."

Layla jerked to her feet. "Tell her she's free to go to Baton Rouge to be with Cameron. She thinks because of that text message, she has to stay."

Normally she'd be correct. But these were extenuating circumstances if Maddox had ever seen any. Her fiancé could die—of course, she should be with him. "Alana, you can go. I just need to keep your cell phone." And if she was out of town, she'd be safer. Out of reach from the bomber.

"See, I told you." Layla nodded, becoming animated again. "You can get a flight and be on a plane this afternoon."

"Cheaper to drive, and I'd get there just as fast."

Layla frowned. "I don't think you're in any shape to drive. Especially alone."

"Then come with me."

Looking at him, Layla shook her head. "I don't think I can."

Conflict warred in his mind. On one hand, she'd be out of town, away from the threat and where she couldn't probe. On the other hand, she'd be out of town, where he couldn't protect her. And she was the strongest lead they had. The bomb was a message to her. A very deadly threat.

Before he could answer, Layla sighed. "Alana, I can't go. Not right now."

Alana had fresh tears. "I shouldn't either. There's so much that needs to be done at the retreat."

Layla wrapped an arm around her sister's shoulders. "You go and be with Cameron. Fred will take care of Second Chances."

"I can't let him take the responsibility."

"Yes, you can, and you will. That's why you hired him. It's his job." She squeezed Alana and then released her. "It's the most logical choice." Layla took a step back. "But I still don't want you driving."

Alana crossed her arms over her chest. "It's the most logical choice."

Maddox swallowed the grin tingling his lips. Alana had gotten her sister with her own words. Much like George often got Maddox.

Layla looked to Maddox. "What's your thought?"

Did she really just ask his opinion? He threw his hands up in mock surrender. "Hey, I have no dogs in this fight."

She narrowed her eyes at him but smiled.

"I'm going to go." Alana widened her stance, cocking out her hip. "And I'm going to drive."

"Alana—"

"No. This is what I'm going to do." She grabbed her purse from the waiting room couch. "I'll call you tonight with my hotel information." She snapped her fingers. "I don't want to take the time to get a new cell phone, so I'll just call from the hotel."

Layla shook her head and yanked her cell off

her hip and handed it to her sister. "I don't want you traveling without a cell. Take mine. I'll be fine without it."

"But you use your cell for business."

"Take it." Layla shoved the flip phone toward her sister. "I'll check the office voice mail every couple of hours."

Alana took the cell, then leaned over and kissed Layla's cheek. "Thanks. I love you."

"Drive carefully. Call me as soon as you get to the hotel so I'll know you made it okay." Layla's face was laced with concern, almost parental in appearance.

Like his mom had looked at him every time he'd taken the car and left the house.

His chest constricted. Why did he have to think about that now?

"I will." Alana smiled at him. "Thanks, Maddox." She glanced back at her sister. "You were right—he's not as bad as I'd thought." Then she stepped into the elevator.

What had Layla said about him? He cut his gaze to Layla only to find she avoided eye contact. And she was blushing!

Cats and dogs?

HOW COULD ALANA HAVE said that? Talk about embarrassing. Heat coated her from head to toe—she could only imagine what Maddox thought.

His blue eyes deepened as he grinned at her. “Alana thought I was bad?”

“When you questioned her about where she was at the time of the murder.”

“Ah, so I was bad cop to Houston’s good, right?”

“Don’t tell me you two actually do that on purpose.”

It was his turn to blush. She didn’t feel so bad now. “I thought that was only for television dramas.”

“Nah. Houston and I perfected it years ago.” He scowled. “Does it work? Is it intimidating?”

She burst out laughing, then almost choked on a breath. Layla covered her mouth with her hand, horrified. How could she be standing here laughing when Cameron was being prepped to be airlifted to another hospital? How could she flirt while her sister’s life was in such shambles?

Maddox touched her shoulder. “It’s okay to be alive, you know.”

Did she chastise herself out loud?

“Laughing is nothing to feel guilty about.”

Or had he read her mind?

“Come on, let’s get out of here.” He slipped his hand to the small of her back.

She let him lead her to the elevator, not trusting herself to speak. Either she’d spoken aloud, or her emotions marched across her face. Didn’t matter—both options mortified her.

The elevator doors slid closed. Silence hung heavy between them.

"So, does that mean you didn't think I was all that intimidating?"

Her heart slipped sideways in her chest. "Huh?"

"If you told Alana I wasn't as bad as she thought, does that mean you don't find me intimidating?"

Ding! The elevator grinded to a stop.

Saved by the bell . . . kinda.

Layla pushed from the elevator as soon as the doors opened. Maddox's low chuckle dogged her heels, finding amusement at her embarrassment, the cad. She needed to get away to save what was left of her dignity. Her composure. Her—

Oh, splinters! She didn't have her truck here. She'd ridden with Maddox. Stuck. Keeping her head down, she stopped at the entrance.

Maddox's warm hand found the small of her back again. It felt comforting. Familiar. "Come on. I'll take you home. I imagine you're beat."

The sun making strides to the center of the sky did nothing to warm the chilly air. The wind cut through Layla's sweats. She shivered as they made their way to his Mustang.

He turned the defrost to high as soon as he started the vehicle. "As soon as it warms up, I'll flip it to heat."

She nodded and shoved her hands under her

thighs for warmth. She prayed he wouldn't continue the humiliating conversation because she honestly didn't know what she'd say. She'd been on full-speed-ahead for so many days, she couldn't think properly, much less figure out her emotions.

But one thing was certain—she was drawn to Maddox Bishop in a way she'd never been drawn to Randy.

What did that say about her? She didn't have the energy to analyze what she was feeling.

Maddox switched the blower to heat. As warmth seeped through her, the exhaustion caught up with her. She yawned. And again. Closing her eyes, she leaned her head back on the headrest. She had to rest her eyes. Just for a moment.

From a distance she heard Maddox talking on a phone. She could barely pick out some of the words. *Commander. Stupid. Needs protection. Ourselves. Thanks.*

As much as she wanted to know what he was talking about, she couldn't move. Her head was so heavy all of a sudden. She was so warm. Comfortable. Secure.

"Layla." Maddox's soft voice sounded so far away, like from the dark recesses of her mind.

She didn't want to think about him right now. She just wanted to stay as she was.

"Layla." This time, Maddox's voice was

accompanied by a warm hand on her shoulder. So realistic. What a dream.

And then she was shaken. "You're home."

She bolted upright in the front seat of his Mustang. Oh, splinters, she'd fallen asleep. She ran the back of her hand across her mouth. Had she drooled? Had she spoken in her sleep? Talk about mortification.

Blinking rapidly, she grabbed her purse. "Right. Thanks for the ride." She reached for the door handle.

"Actually, can I come inside? I have something to discuss with you."

That brought her fully awake. What now? "S-sure." She led the way up the stairs, unlocked the door, and gestured for him to follow her inside. Layla flipped on the lights, tossed her purse on the entry table, then sat in her cushiony recliner.

Maddox lowered himself to the couch. "It's a really nice place you have here."

"Thanks." The reply was automatic. Fatigue tugged at her. She yawned. "But I'm sure that's not what you wanted to discuss with me."

"No, it isn't." He ran a hand over the top of his hair.

Did he realize he did that a lot, normally when he was frustrated? It was kinda cute, actually. That a big, strong cop would—

"We need to talk about the threat. To you."

Butterflies erupted in her stomach. “Okay.”

“Do you have any clue who would have sent that text to Alana?”

Was he for real? That was the stupidest question he’d asked yet. Even more stupid than asking for an alibi. “Now, if I did, don’t you think I would’ve said something to you?”

His blue eyes clouded. “We’re tracing the number the text came from right now, so we should have a definite answer soon. I’m just trying to figure out who you questioned.”

She ducked her head. “I was only trying to get some idea of who killed Dennis.”

“I know. But now I need you to tell me who all you talked with about it.”

“Everyone I contracted for the project—carpenters, suppliers, electrician, and plumber. I talked to all of them.”

“Then that narrows down the list of people who could’ve threatened you.”

She gripped her hands together in her lap. “Trust me, I want to help you find out who’s responsible.”

“We will, that’s our job. But you need to leave the investigating to us. Okay?”

“Yeah.” Because of her questions, Cameron might die. Alana would never forgive her.

She’d never forgive herself.

“Something else.”

She lifted her head to stare at him. “What?”

"There's danger of another threat. I need to make sure you're safe."

Her tired body went stiff. "What do you mean?"

His face reddened, and his gaze dropped to the floor. "Our commander doesn't think there's enough evidence to put you under police protection."

Oh-kay. "But?"

"But Houston and I do." His lifted his gaze to hers.

"So?" Maybe she was just utterly beat, but she wasn't following.

"I'd like permission for Houston and me to protect you in the evenings on our own time. To stay here, maybe on your couch. Just to make sure you're safe."

Here? Sleeping? In her house? Just down the hall from her?

She blinked, trying to imagine that. Trying to figure out how she'd be able to do anything with Maddox in proximity to her.

He stared at her with those hypnotic blue eyes of his. They yanked on her heart.

Oh, splinters.

TWENTY-FOUR

"All men profess honesty as long as they can.
To believe all men honest would be folly.
To believe none so is something worse."
—JOHN QUINCY ADAMS

THE BUILDING WAS SUPPOSED to have been empty.

He stared at the television screen, bile burning the back of his throat. Alana's fiancé would be airlifted to Baton Rouge for care in the burn-specialty unit.

They weren't supposed to be there. They'd had dinner reservations. He'd timed the bomb perfectly so no one would be there. No one was supposed to have gotten hurt.

But Cameron Stone had. Critically so.

Acid rebelled in his stomach. He stood, pacing, a drink in his hand. How had this gotten so out of control? He wasn't a murderer . . . an arsonist . . . a bomber. He was just a man trying his best to go straight and take care of his kids.

He was a good person. Sensitive. Caring, despite what Andrea claimed. He was loyal. Dependable. All his colleagues said so.

Why weren't Alana and Cameron at the restaurant in Lake Charles when the bomb went off? He'd double-checked the timer—no way it detonated early.

The news flashed to the hospital where a representative from the Center for Disease Control was interviewed. He turned up the volume, paying careful attention to the suit's words.

"We've established the common denominator in this illness. At this time, the CDC has temporarily closed the doors to the Eternal Springs Christian Church. As soon as we have more details, we'll alert the public. That's all. Thank you."

He threw his glass at the television. It crashed against the screen, glass tinkling to the floor. The flatscreen was ruined, shattered. Amber liquid oozed down the front, dripping onto the entertainment center and floor.

His carefully detailed plans were imploding. His body went limp, and he crumbled to the hard, cold floor. He lowered his head into his hands.

What had he done?

How could he save himself?

WHAT IF SHE REFUSED?

Maddox tried to read Layla's expression, but her facial features were set in stone. Maybe he should've had Houston broach the subject with her. She didn't move, didn't even flinch. He knew she'd heard him. Why wasn't she saying anything?

He cleared the unease from his throat. "Layla?"

She gave a little shake, as if mentally focusing. “What?”

Had she totally zoned out? “Permission for me and Houston to stay here and protect you at night?”

She stared at him, totally attentive. “Do you really think that’s necessary?”

Man, did he ever. But he didn’t want to scare her either. “I do.” And if she refused, he and Houston would just monitor her house from the drive. That would be less than ideal—not being able to see threats coming from the bayou behind her house—but he would not sit by and do nothing. Anything was better than that.

“Okay.”

Just that one word from her sent all sorts of emotions racing through him. Of course, the way her eyes stared at him with such trust in their green irises might have something to do with it too.

What was happening to him? After his resolve to never get seriously involved with a woman . . . traitorous emotions.

Responsibility sat heavy in his gut. “All right.” He stood. “I’ve got to run and check on my dad, pick up some clothes, touch base with Houston, and then we’ll be back.”

She stood as well, a little wobbly. “I’ll get some blankets for whoever has the couch. There are fresh linens on the guest-room bed already.”

He already knew he'd get stuck with the couch. Houston was all for doing his job, but he liked comfort too.

Maddox smiled as he fished his keys from his pocket. "We should be back in a couple of hours or so. Until then, keep your door locked."

She grinned back at him. "Yes, sir."

"I'm serious."

"I'm going to take a hot shower, then take a little nap."

"I'll see you soon, then." He waited until she nodded, then left.

As he raced down the bayou road back to town, a sick feeling came over him. What if someone was watching her house right now? Waiting until he left? Maddox gripped the gearshift tightly. *Don't be silly. There's no one watching. No one waiting to attack her.*

But he still drove a little faster.

He grabbed his cell phone, pressed the speed-dial button for his partner, and waited while the connection went through.

"What now?" Houston loved caller ID.

"She gave us permission to stake out her place."

Houston chuckled. "Sounds like you had to argue it."

"No. Just had to be convincing."

"I've finished my report on my interview with Denny Keys—nothing of any importance there.

Thought I'd swing by and do a quick interview with Bob Johnson and Ed Young. Care to join me?"

Maddox glanced at the clock on the dash—3:20. Plenty of time to knock out those two interviews, check on Pop, get some clothes, then be back at Layla's before it got really dark. "Which one is up first?"

"Y Building Supplies is closer to the office, so let's hit that one." Houston gave the address.

"Meet you there in fifteen." Maddox disconnected the call but didn't shut his phone. He pressed the preset number for Uncle George as he zoomed out of Westlake's city limits, heading to Lake Charles.

George picked up on the first ring. "Hey, Maddox. How ya doing?"

"Good. How's Pop?"

George chuckled. "Cheating. We're playing Texas Hold 'Em."

Maddox could make out Pop's objections to being called a cheater. Sounded like he was his old self. Would he even remember his sleepy words to his son this morning? That seemed like an eternity ago.

"Don't let him cheat. Look, this case I'm working is gonna have me out the next couple of nights. I hate to impose on you, but would you mind terribly staying with Pop?"

"Don't mind at all, son. As long as he stops

cheating." George chuckled amid Pop's protests again.

"Thanks, Uncle George. I really appreciate it."

"This the case involving that girl, Layla?"

He checked his rearview mirror before he got on the bridge. "Yeah. And it's connected to the bomb over at Second Chances."

"Horrible thing, son. You take care. Take care of that girl too."

"Thanks." Maddox paused. "Tell Pop I'll run by and see y'all in a little bit."

"Sure will." George's voice carried a hint of enthusiasm.

Maybe it was a start.

"See you soon." He snapped the phone shut and dropped it in the console, needing both hands as he drove over the bridge.

His pulse spiked. His stomach turned. He tensed to the point of aching.

This had to be the highest bridge in Louisiana. He knew it wasn't, but it sure felt like it. And the curve . . .

He gripped the steering wheel tighter. Very few people knew about his fear of heights. Stupid to have a hang-up over something that happened when he was sixteen. Falling off the balcony had landed him in a leg cast and benched him from football for a whole season. His friends had made fun of him for falling, and the healing had taken its toll. He'd never been able to breathe normally when not on solid ground since. The irony never failed to miss him—his father had been Special Forces and jumped out of airplanes while Maddox was terrified of heights.

Finally he descended the bridge and sped to his exit. Maddox let out a long breath before turning toward Y Building Supplies.

He pulled into the parking lot beside Houston's cruiser. His partner waited for him, leaning against the hood of his car. The man never ran out of obnoxiously loud print shirts. He smiled and straightened as Maddox stepped to the pavement. "About time, man."

"I was in Eternal Springs. Didn't want to speed, ya know. Setting a good example and all that."

Houston laughed. "Right." He pulled out his notebook and headed into the building.

They went to the customer-service area and requested to see the owner, Ed Young. They were asked to wait, and moments later Mr. Young appeared.

Houston showed his badge. "Mr. Young, I'm Detective Wallace and this is Detective Bishop. We need to ask you a few questions."

"Certainly. Let's go to my office." The silver infiltrating the man's light brown hair sparkled under the overhead lights of the hall. He was probably in his midfifties but walked with a youthful gait. He waved them into a closet of an office. “Sorry for the mess. It’s inventory time.” He shoved boxes and stacks of catalogs from the threadbare couch.

“This won’t take but a moment.” Houston took a seat on the edge of the couch. Maddox leaned against the wall.

Young sat in the ripped leather chair behind his desk and lifted a silver lighter. “What can I help you gentlemen with?” He flipped the top of the lighter open, then closed it. *Click. Click.*

“We understand you were the supplier for the Hope-for-Homes site.”

“Yes, I was.” *Click. Click. Click.*

“Did you happen to notice anything amiss with the site?”

Young shook his head. “No, but I wasn’t actually on the site much. I think I was only there twice. Once when the plans were laid out and then again when it was nearly complete.”

“I see.” Houston wrote in his notebook.

“I can get you the names of the truck drivers who delivered materials to the site, if that will help.”

“We’d appreciate that.”

Young set down the lighter and lifted his receiver. He asked someone on the other end to pull the file and bring him the information. He replaced the receiver and looked up at Maddox. “What else can I do to help?”

“How well did you know Dennis LeJeune?”

"Not very well. I know who all the building inspectors in the parish are, of course, but I knew Dennis no better than anyone else."

"Do you know anyone who'd want to hurt him?"

"Of course not. But as I said, I didn't really know him personally."

Maddox pushed off the wall and moved toward the desk. "What about Layla Taylor?"

"Layla?" Young blinked several times.

"How well do you know her?"

Young sat back in his chair. "I feel like I watched her grow up. Knew her dad pretty well. She's a fine contractor. I like her, and I like working with her." He sat forward. "But I'm sure you already knew all that."

Maddox ignored the inference. "Can you think of anyone who'd want to hurt her or her business?"

"Well, now . . . I can't think of anyone in particular, but I will tell you that a lot of men in the industry just don't like a woman contractor."

Maddox could understand. At one time he'd thought the same thing. But now . . . "Like who?"

"No one in particular. Just common knowledge. Of course, no one would say anything derogatory about Layla in front of me because I've let it be known that I like and respect her as a contractor."

Maddox had no response.

Houston jumped in. "How about her sister, Alana? What's been your experience with Second Chances?"

Young flipped his gaze to Maddox's partner. "None. I don't have apprentices in the building supply business. I hire manual laborers and drivers and salesmen. That's pretty much it."

Maddox moved to the edge of the desk. "What about the materials to make a bomb?"

"Excuse me?" Young's eyes widened as he stared at Maddox. "A bomb?"

"Yeah. Do you sell the stuff to make a bomb?"

Young shook his head. "I wouldn't know. What do you need to make a bomb?"

Houston met Maddox's look and gave a slight tilt of his head. "Just one last question, Mr. Young."

"Yes?"

"Where were you last Friday night between eleven thirty and midnight?"

"Let's see, Friday night is my bowling night. We were at the lanes until well after ten thirty. I left there, went through the drive-thru at Wendy's, then headed home. I got there around eleven or so, ate my dinner, took a shower, and went to bed."

"Was anybody with you?"

Young laughed. "Unfortunately no."

"Did you talk with anybody on your cell phone during that time? See a neighbor or someone when you arrived home?"

"I didn't talk on my phone that I can recall, and I don't think any of my neighbors saw me. You'd have to ask around."

Maddox took over the questioning. "Do you have any verification of what you've just told us?"

"Wait a second." Young leaned forward, reached into his back pocket, and pulled out his wallet. He flipped through it, then passed a thin piece of paper to Maddox. "Here's my receipt from Wendy's. Does that help?"

Maddox glanced at the time stamp of the receipt. Ten fifty-one. He handed it to Houston. "Thanks." He turned to the door.

Young stood. "Anything to help. It's horrible what's happened to the Hope-for-Homes site. And Mr. LeJeune. And the break-in at Taylor Construction. And now that mess over at Second Chances."

Maddox spun around to face Young. "How did you know about the break-in? It wasn't in the news."

Young smiled. "Where do you think Layla ordered the replacement glass for the window from?"

Right. Made sense.

Maddox thanked Young again, then left the office.

Another dead end. Maybe they'd get a hit with the plumber. Any kind of lead.

And the sooner, the better.

TWENTY-FIVE

"The difference between stupidity and genius is that genius has its limits."
—ALBERT EINSTEIN

WHY WOULDN'T SLEEP COME?

Layla flipped over to her stomach and glared at the clock on her bedside table. The hot shower had felt wonderful and relaxed her fatigued limbs. Her bed had been welcome and comforting . . . an hour ago. Now it was like a bad foldout cot on a construction site. She groaned and buried her face in the pillow.

The room was dark, thanks to heavy curtains and shades. No lights burned in the entire house. The temperature was on the chilly side so she could snuggle under the down comforter. Silence prevailed—no radio or television to distract her.

Yet sleep teased her, flitting just out of reach.

Maybe she was too tired. Maybe with all that had happened, her mind couldn't shut down enough to fall asleep.

She rolled to her back, snuggling the pillow against her chest. So much to do. Check on Pastor. Hopefully, the specialist from the CDC would have a clue what was making everyone so sick. She needed to call the insurance agent for Second Chances and file a claim for Alana. She should call Ms. Betty and see how she was faring. And find out about Ms. Ethel's funeral arrangements.

Tossing the pillow beside her, she sat and stared at the clock. Alana should be calling soon, letting her know she'd made it to Baton Rouge okay. Layla whispered another prayer for Cameron and Alana.

She threw back the comforter and padded to the kitchen. If sleep wanted to remain elusive, she could at least be productive. She set the coffeemaker and turned it on, then leaned against the counter and looked out the back window.

The bayou was so peaceful. Quiet. Calming in the way the wind lifted the curtains of Spanish moss off the cypress trees. Ripples cut over the water. Tranquil.

The phone rang, causing her to jump. Silly to be so nervous. Maddox's talk about needing protection made her jittery. She was perfectly safe, locked tight in her house. Her haven.

A second ring shattered her thoughts. Probably Alana checking in. She grabbed the cordless. "Hello."

"Layla Taylor, please." An unfamiliar lady's voice. Very curt and businesslike.

"This is she."

"Hello, Ms. Taylor. This is Monica Hermitage with NARI. I'm the liaison for the CotY awards committee."

Layla slid onto a kitchen chair. "Yes?" Her heartbeat echoed inside her head. *Thump-thump-thump.*

Thump-thump-thump.

"First off, congratulations again on winning the regional award. We had many wonderful entries so it's quite the honor."

"Yes, ma'am. I'm very excited."

"What I'm calling about is your entry."

She wanted to vomit, could feel the bile burning the back of her throat. "Yes?" *Lord, give me the strength to keep my dignity, no matter what.*

"Sometimes committee members like to visit the location and inspect in person. The address you listed doesn't have a specific owner's name. Could you please give me that information?"

Here it was . . . the other shoe dropping. "Unfortunately, Ms. Hermitage, the building burned down last week."

"Really? How awful."

"Yes. The authorities have determined it was arson, so there is a full investigation ongoing."

"I see."

The long pause was palpable over the phone. Layla could picture the expression on the woman's face. The narrowed eyes. The creased brow. The frown.

"Well, I'll report this back to the committee members." Was that a haughty tone?

Layla's hopes free-fell to the floor. "I do have other photographs and specs on the house I could send."

"I'll see if the committee would be interested in such." Definitely a snooty tone.

"Well, let me know if you'd like me to send the additional photographs and information."

"I will. Thank you, Ms. Taylor. Good day."

Layla punched off the phone, resisting the urge to fling it across the kitchen. Her dreams of winning a national CotY had just died. She wanted to hit something. The person who'd done all this was her preferred target. In lieu of that, she fisted her hands and concentrated on breathing slowly. Pulling in clean air, pushing out anger.

No one could understand her anguish, not even Alana. The loss of her father came over her just as strong as when he'd died. She laid her head on the table and allowed herself to cry. To release all the pent-up feelings she'd been pushing down—fear, anger, expectation, disappointment . . . grief. The tears flowed as did the yearning in her heart. *How much, God? I can't take much more. Help me to understand. To accept. To move on.*

"AFTER WE LEAVE HERE, I'm running by the apartment to get some clothes, then I'll swing by Pop's on the way to Layla's." Maddox followed Houston up the stairs to Bob Johnson's plumbing business.

"I've got to run home myself. Make sure the boys haven't destroyed the house before Margie gets home from work. She's pulling another double shift."

"What's going on?"

"That CDC specialist is running all kinds of tests on that pastor. Margie says the initial results show a poisoning of some sort. They're working to figure it out, and she wants to be around when all the tests come back."

Maddox nodded. He'd like it to be figured out too, especially if Pop was attending that church.

Houston opened the door to the office. "Let's do this."

They had to flash their badge at the counter to be allowed to speak to Bob Johnson. Moments later they were seated in his office. The air reeked of stale smoke.

Maddox took note of Johnson's appearance and demeanor. Stocky, maybe late forties to early fifties. Rough. And the way he crossed his arms? Totally on the defensive.

Houston opened his notebook. "We understand you were the plumber for the Hope-for-Homes site."

"Yes, I was."

"And you employed three residents of Second Chances on the site?"

"Yes. Darren Watkins, Sam Roberson, and Kenny Lindsay."

Houston looked up from his notes. "You rattled those names off mighty quick. You can do that with all your jobs?"

"No, but Layla had called me earlier this week and asked me about them and the site."

And because of those questions, Second Chances lay in ruins and Layla had death threats zinged at her. Maddox inched to the edge of his chair. "And how did you feel about that? Her asking you questions?"

Johnson's face reddened. "Well, I wasn't too happy, but she was just trying to help with the investigation."

"I see." Maddox glanced at Houston, who picked up the questioning. "Did you happen to notice anything amiss with the site?"

"As I told Layla, no, I didn't notice anything out of the ordinary."

"I see." Houston wrote in his notebook.

"And, no, I didn't know anything about any drugs being used on any of my sites." Johnson's arms over his chest were tighter . . . rigid. He'd locked his jaw, the muscle popping in his cheek.

Maddox leaned forward. "What drugs?"

"Look, I don't know what all Layla told you, but I've never seen anybody using, buying, or selling drugs on any construction site I've been on. Definitely not on the Hope-for-Homes site."

Layla thought drugs had been involved on the site? This could take the investigation into a new direction. Why hadn't she said anything to them?

Houston tapped his pencil against his notebook. "Layla thought there were drugs on a site you were on? On the Hope-for-Homes site?"

Johnson's Adam's apple bobbed once. "Look, she just asked questions. One of the other Second Chancers I had on a site got high. Layla said the only time he'd been off the grounds was when he was working with me on another job." He uncrossed his arms and sat straight, poking a finger through the air. "But I assure you, there were never any drugs on any of the sites I worked. Ever."

"Who was that Second Chancer? Was it Roberson, Watkins, or Lindsay?"

Johnson shook his head. "It was a newer one on the program. Gavin somebody." He shoved his arms back across his chest. "And he was never on the Hope-for-Homes site."

Houston scribbled.

"What did you think of Dennis LeJeune?"

Johnson twisted his gaze to meet Maddox's. "The inspector?"

"Yeah. You heard he was the one murdered, right?" Everyone else in town knew—it'd been in the news and in the paper. If this guy wanted to pretend he didn't know . . .

"I did hear that. Dennis will be sorely missed. What did I think of him? He was a good inspector, I can tell you that."

Maddox didn't miss how Johnson had referred to the deceased by his first name. "How well did you know him?"

Johnson shrugged. "I knew him from the business, of course, but he also was a bowler. Not on my specific team, but I saw him at the alley a lot. Was a pretty good bowler too. Played against him several times."

Finally . . . a personal connection.

Houston tapped his pencil again. "And what do you think of Layla Taylor?"

Maddox studied Johnson carefully. The man's face reddened again. "She's a good contractor. A little intense, but so was her daddy."

Intense? Yeah, Maddox could see that. "And as a person?"

"She's straightforward. Blunt. Sometimes guys don't take too kindly to that. Some have resented her."

"Like who?" Houston asked.

Johnson shrugged. "Nobody in particular. Just sayin' . . ."

Again, no particulars. The industry. The guys. Maddox was sick of the generalities. "Do you know anyone who'd want to hurt Layla or her business?"

"Like I said, I ain't heard anybody say anything bad about her. But guys talk amongst themselves."

"But you're a guy . . . you haven't heard

anything?" Maddox jammed his hands in his jacket pockets. Anything to curb the urge to take Johnson by his collar and ram him against the wall until he told the truth. And the stale smoke smell was giving him a headache.

Johnson stiffened. "I'm a boss. I overhear things, but water-cooler talk doesn't come to bosses."

This was going nowhere. "As a plumber, you know how to fit together pipes and things."

Johnson shot him a quizzical look. "Y-yes."

"Do you know how to make a bomb?"

Johnson's expression went slack for just a moment, then he scowled. "What kind of question is that? No, I don't know how to make a bomb. That's a stupid question to ask a plumber. What does plumbing have to do with bomb making?"

Quite the protest. Maddox leaned back and gave Houston a brief nod.

"Only one question left, Mr. Johnson." Houston rapped his pencil rapidly against the notebook. The tapping echoed off the walls holding only business licenses. "Where were you last Friday night between eleven thirty and midnight?"

"Bowling. It was a tournament. All the leagues were there."

Maddox stood and crossed his arms over his chest. Sometimes intentional intimidation worked wonders. "Was Dennis LeJeune there?"

Johnson looked up. "Yes, I believe he was. But his team was knocked out early. They didn't make it to the final cuts."

"Did yours?"

Johnson puffed out his chest. "We won first."

Houston shifted in his chair. "What time did you leave the bowling alley?"

"Right around midnight."

Houston scribbled. "There are people who can verify this?"

"My team. The workers at the bowling alley. Oh, and the unofficial photographer for all the leagues. After we won, we took group pictures."

Houston took down the names, then closed his notebook. "Thank you for your cooperation."

Maddox headed out of the office, his mind scrambling. He'd got a sense from the guy—there was something he hadn't volunteered. Information that would help break this case wide open. But with such an alibi . . .

Houston followed Maddox outside. "What do you make of him?"

"I think he's hiding something. His body language was all defensive. Remember that butt I found at the scene? Well, Johnson reeks of cigarettes."

"Yeah, I picked up on that. And what's this about drugs? Has Layla mentioned anything to you about drugs on the site?"

"No." And he was sorely disappointed she hadn't. If drugs were involved, they could be spinning their wheels. "But I intend to ask her tonight."

Houston's phone rang. He grabbed it from his belt and held up a finger to Maddox. "Wallace here." He paused. "Yeah. Are you sure?"

Maddox leaned against his Mustang GT and glanced at the late-afternoon sky. Dark clouds swirled. The forecast called for another stormy night, followed by yet another cold front. A brewing storm to match his mood—lovely.

"Well, thanks. Appreciate you rushing." Houston shut the phone and returned it to his belt. "That was about the text message."

Maddox stood straight. "Yeah?"

"Traced it back to a throwaway. Was bought two days ago at the local Wal-Mart. Looks like whoever sent the text message paid cash for the phone and minutes."

Those throwaway cell phones were a menace to law-enforcement investigations everywhere. Maddox wished they'd outlaw them. He spun his key chain around his finger. "So that's another dead end."

"Yep." Houston unlocked the cruiser and stared at his partner over the hood. "Maybe we'll get a break soon."

"I hope so."

"I'm heading to the house to check on the

boys. I'll meet you at Layla's in an hour or so."

Maddox nodded and got behind the wheel of his car.

They needed a break on this case. Something was there . . . a clue, a connection they had missed.

He needed to find out what it was.

Before someone came after Layla.

TWENTY-SIX

"All progress is precarious, and the solution of one problem brings us face to face with another problem."
—DR. MARTIN LUTHER KING JR.

BRRING!

Layla bolted upright in the kitchen chair, nearly knocking it over. What? She'd just closed her eyes for a moment. How long had she dozed? Darkness crept over the bayou. Thunder rumbled off in the distance.

Brring!

She snatched up the phone and glanced at the caller ID. Out of area? She pressed the TALK button. "Hello." Layla covered her yawn with her hand.

"Layla, it's me." Alana sounded farther away than ever.

And was that panic in her voice? Oh no . . . not

Cameron. "You made it okay? How's Cameron?"

"They're getting him settled in the burn unit. Listen, you got a text message."

Definitely panic. Layla yawned again. "From who?"

"That same number. Were you asleep? Wake up, this is important."

As soon as Alana said it was the same number, Layla had come fully awake. "What was the message?"

"Let me read it to you. I didn't want to use your phone, so I'm calling from the hotel." Muffling sounds came over the line. "Okay, here's the message:

Stop looking for answers or someone closer to you will be hurt."

Alana's breathing was so fast, she'd hyperventilate if she didn't slow it down. "Layla, what are you doing?"

Guilt held Layla's stomach in a vise, tightening with every breath. "I haven't done anything." Not in the last day or so anyway. But to know her sister was in another town, unprotected and alone . . . "I don't have a clue who's doing this. Or why."

"Neither do I. You need to let the detectives know about this message. If they need your phone, I can always overnight it to you."

"Wait. They might have an agency there that can come and get it or something." The message was clear. The only person she loved was her sister, so the threat had to be against Alana. But she didn't want to scare her sister.

"I want you to do something for me." Alana's voice was steady.

"I'll ask Maddox if I can come. Considering the circumstances, I'm sure he'll let me leave—"

"No, I'm fine. No one knows where I am."

Unless someone was watching. Following. Fear slithered through Layla, paralyzing her. "But you're the only one I'm—"

"For once, Layla, just listen to me. Do me one favor."

She'd never heard her sister be so . . . forceful and aggressive. Demanding. In charge. "I'm listening."

"Don't worry about me. Trust me, no one knows I'm here."

"Oh-kay."

"But I want you to go check on Mom."

Layla felt dizzy and nauseous all at once. "I don't think—"

"Stop interrupting me. You said you were going to listen."

"Sorry." But the pit of her stomach roiled with acid.

"If this person doesn't know you well, he or she doesn't know you haven't seen Mom. He doesn't know you refuse to go visit your own mother because you can't forgive and move on from the past. He doesn't know you're a stubborn, hardheaded mule."

"Is there a point to the insults?"

"Yes. If he doesn't know you well, he might think you do have a relationship with Mom. She's your mother, after all. Most people do have relationships with their mothers."

The harsh words stung. Yeah, most people did have relationships with their mothers, but most mothers hadn't been drug addicts who neglected their children. Most mothers weren't so desperate to numb their emotions that they overdosed on downers and caused respiratory depression resulting in an anoxic brain injury. Most mothers didn't cause damage to themselves that rendered them helpless and caused them to have to go into a full-care nursing home.

"Layla? Are you listening to me?"

"I hear you, Alana." But she couldn't do it. Not yet. "I'll call and check on her. Maybe Maddox will get a car there or something. Or, hey, I can call Lincoln Vailes and see if the Eternal Springs police could do that."

"You aren't listening to me."

"I heard you. And I said I'd check on her."

"No, you said you'd call and check on her. I'm asking you to go. Get in your truck and drive to the nursing home. See that she's okay."

“I c-can’t.”

“Yes, you can. And you will. For me.”

Oh, her sister knew how to play dirty. When had she become such an independent force?

“Layla, I love you dearly, but I’m sick of this.”

“You don’t understand. You were younger. I took care of you when she’d forget about us. When she’d be so desperate for drugs that she’d get so agitated and try to take it out on us.” And Alana wasn’t the one who’d found their mother out cold on the floor. She wasn’t the one who had to call 911, holding her breath in fear that their mother was dead.

“I know that. I’m not stupid. I know the truth.”

“Then how can you ask me to go before I’m ready?”

Alana’s sigh whooshed through the phone where Layla could almost feel her sister’s breath against her ear. “I’ve never asked you for one thing before. Have I?”

“That’s not fair. I—”

“No. I’ve never asked you for anything. The land, you volunteered it before I even thought of it. The loan, you came up with that and didn’t even ask for my input. You take charge . . . that’s what you do. I love you for it, but I’ve never asked for a single thing. I’m asking you now. Do this for me. Go see Mom and check on her.”

Maybe Layla could just duck her head into the room. See that their mother was the same as usual.

That would be checking on her in person, right?

"I have to be here with Cameron, or I'd go myself." The tears were evident in Alana's voice. "Please, Layla. Go. For me."

Guilt tightened her vocal chords. "Fine."

"You'll go?"

"I said I would." Now that she was committed, she didn't have a choice. But she'd just stick her head in the room. She wouldn't have to stay. Wouldn't have to sit there and see the damage their mother had done to herself, not caring about her family enough to break free of her addiction. "I'll go. Tonight."

"Promise?"

"Yes." Layla ground out her answer from behind clenched teeth.

"Call me when you get back. Let me know that she's okay, otherwise I'll worry all night. I mean, I'll be up anyway. I get to see Cameron for ten minutes every hour."

"That's good. I'll call you."

"Thank you, Layla. It means a lot to me."

"I'll let you know what Maddox says about the phone too."

"Okay. Well, I'm heading back to the hospital. Oh, I need to tell you where I'm staying." Alana gave her the information. "Thank you again. I love you."

"Love you too." Layla turned off the phone and set it on the kitchen table.

She stared out into the bayou, her insides churning. Lightning split the darkening skies. What had she agreed to do?

Lord, help me. Please. Help me get over the anger. Help me let go of the pain. Help me forgive as You forgive.

But she was human . . . and didn't know if she could truly forgive her mother. No matter how much she wanted.

"HEY, POP. WHERE'S GEORGE?"

His father looked up from the paper. Sitting in his recliner, he didn't seem sick at all. Nothing to indicate he'd had a heart attack and had been in the hospital.

"He went to pick up some dinner and grab some clothes." Pop lowered the paper to his lap. "I appreciate all the attention, but I don't need someone to babysit me."

Maddox denied the sigh. So much for his father's words of this morning. The I'm-a-big-military-man-and-I-am-invincible attitude had returned. He sunk to the couch, determined to be the bigger man this time. "Why don't you just enjoy being taken care of for a change?"

Pop smiled. "I guess it is kinda nice. George is even getting me apple pie."

"Is that allowed? On the diet the doctor gave you?"

"I'm not a child. I think I can figure out what

to eat." But he snorted. "Yes, George made sure that what I wanted was on the stupid diet plan."

Wow, ten whole minutes alone together and Maddox didn't feel belittled. Had to be a record. "How're you feeling?"

"Same as always. I think those doctors are wrong about me having a heart attack."

"Pop—"

His father held up his hand. "I know what you're gonna say, but even George thinks it's a good idea to get a second opinion."

Second opinions were good. As long as he got medical care. "I think that's a smart move."

Pop looked happier than Maddox could remember in a long time.

An unfamiliar feeling crept up his back. Maybe he couldn't remember because he'd avoided being around his father for quite some time. He blinked back the emotions, concentrating on anything else. "Can I get you something?" He glanced at the table beside his father's chair. It held a lamp, a bottle of pills, a glass of water, and a . . . a *Bible?*

"I'm good."

"Would you like some fresh water?" Maddox shot to his feet. "That doesn't even have ice anymore."

Pop laughed. "It's fine. I'm all set. Sit back down. Tell me about this case you've got."

Maddox dropped to the couch. Good thing because his knees were a bit weak. He couldn't remember his father asking about his work before. Ever. "Houston and I interviewed two suspects today."

"Close to solving the case?"

"I wish." He leaned back against the leather couch.

"Don't let it get you down. You're a good detective. You'll solve it."

The praise lit something in Maddox's chest. His father had never expressed pride in Maddox's job. Had never really praised him period. It was . . . strangely nice. Maybe George was right. Maybe he should try to form a relationship with his father. It'd been months since he'd visited his father's house. He'd kept their communication limited to phone calls.

"Son, I don't want to upset you, but I need to talk to you about something."

All the energy sapped right out of him. His father had softened Maddox up, only to hit him with a blow. Why had he allowed himself to hope?

"I owe you an apology, and hope you'll be able to forgive me."

His father—what? He leaned forward. "Uh, what're you talking about?"

"I made you feel like I blamed you for your mother's death. In truth, I did blame you. But it was only to cover my own guilt." Pop's eyes were moist.

What was he supposed to say to that? "It's okay."

"No, it's not. You were a kid. Supposed to miss curfew." He shook his head. "What you said at the hospital . . . you were right. I should've retired long before your mother was killed. I should've been home."

"Pop, I was just angry. I didn't mean that." Or did he?

His father smiled, but it was a sad smile. "We've gone on too long blaming one another. I never should have blamed you, but I was hurt. More than anything I've ever felt in my life. Your mother was like a part of me. When we lost her, a part of me died with her. The best part of me." Pop wiped his eyes.

Maddox felt his own eyes burning.

"That's no excuse. You had lost your mother, the one parent who actually acted like a parent. I should've been there for you, but I wasn't. I was too wrapped up in my own pain and anger. I lashed out at you." His voice hitched. "I can't tell you how sorry I am."

Tears filled Maddox's eyes, blurring his vision of his father. "I blamed you, Pop. I thought if you'd been home, nothing like that would happen. But that wasn't fair. It wasn't your fault. I needed someone to blame. Someone to be angry with. You were the easiest target." The words were so much easier to say than he'd ever imagined. And he wanted to say them. Wanted to move past this hurdle keeping him from his father. "I'm sorry, Pop. And sorry I haven't ever been able to find her killer."

Pop spread open his arms. Maddox found his legs under him and rushed to his father. He leaned into the embrace. Feeling the warmth. Smelling the familiar scent of his father's soap. Holding his father as Pop clung to him. His father shook as he sobbed. Maddox couldn't hold back his own emotions. It was as if a dam had burst and all the pain he'd felt as a little boy gushed through.

He gave his father a final squeeze, then pushed back. Maddox smiled as he sat in the chair beside Pop's recliner.

"You don't need to solve her case, son. Not for me."

"But wouldn't you like to know why? Why her? Why not the woman next door? Why not the woman down the street? Why was Mom singled out?"

"Sometimes we aren't meant to know. We just have to accept."

This wasn't his father at all. Maybe the medications really were causing emotional side effects. "How can you say that?"

His father reached for his Bible and opened it.

He turned to a place marked by a ribbon. "It says here in the book of Job: 'How great is God—beyond our understanding.' "

Unbelievable. "You're . . . quoting Scripture to me?"

"I can't tell you how much becoming saved has changed me. My entire life. I love reading the Bible, digging into God's Word." He shook his head. "I owe you another apology. I should have made sure you continued to go to church after your mother died. She'd started a great thing in you, and I let it fall away just as I did so many things."

"I didn't want to go, Pop. And I don't buy all that Bible garbage."

"Don't say that. God loves you. He's been waiting for you to come back to Him."

"Where was God when Mom was murdered? Why didn't He stop someone from breaking in and killing her?" The old, familiar anger swelled inside of Maddox.

"Son, you're still so angry. You have to let go. God can't heal your heart until you let go of the anger."

"Heal my heart? Mom died in my arms. I don't think God or anybody is going to heal me from that." The memory haunted him in his dreams. Sometimes seeping over into his waking hours.

"God can. And He will. If you ask Him. Psalm 18:2 promises that. It says, 'The LORD is my rock, my fortress and my deliverer; my God is my rock, in whom I take refuge. He is my shield and the horn of my salvation, my stronghold.' "

His father had become one of those religious nuts. Maddox shook his head. "I'm glad you've found something that gives you peace. Makes you okay with Mom's murder. I really am." He scooted back in the chair. "But I can't buy into all that. I deal with real people every day. People who kill for a reason, and some who kill just because they can."

"Oh, Maddox." Pop's eyes filled with tears again. "You have to forgive whoever killed your mother. Forgive him, so God can forgive you. He will. And He can help you forgive too. Just ask."

Tears again? Twice in one day? He'd never seen his father cry. Ever. Even at Mom's funeral Pop had sat there like a stone statue.

His cell phone vibrated. Maddox yanked it off his belt. "Hello."

"Maddox? It's Layla."

Her voice brought her image to the forefront of his mind. "Is something wrong?" What if someone was trying to break in? He stood, pacing the small living room of his father's house.

"Alana got a text message on my phone. From the same number."

His body went stiff. His feet took root in the carpet. The blood clogged in his veins.

Layla was in trouble.

TWENTY-SEVEN

"We must be our own
before we can be another's."
—RALPH WALDO EMERSON

KNOTS BUNCHED IN HER body, threatening to sink her in an ocean of misery.

Layla could do this. It was in and out—go there, stick her head in and make sure no one had tried to bomb the nursing home, then head back home. She could tell Alana that she'd kept her promise.

Layla had dressed in jeans and a sweater and now paced the living room in front of the windows. Maddox had told her not to move until he arrived. But she was losing her nerve with every minute that fell off the clock.

Car headlights shone through the window.

She moved to the front door. The quicker she could get this over with, the better she'd feel.

He only knocked once before she opened the door wide. And froze. "Detective Wallace."

He grinned in his red shirt with yellow flowers. "Ms. Taylor." He lifted a duffel bag. "I understand the slumber party's at your house."

Stepping aside, Layla waved him in. "I'm sorry. Come in. I thought you were Maddox." She shut and locked the door behind him.

"I figured if I got here first, I could call the guest bed. Leave the couch for Maddox."

She grinned and led him to the spare bedroom. "Here it is."

He tossed the duffel on the bed, then followed her down the hall to the living room. "Actually, Maddox should be here any minute."

"Oh, so he did call you about the text? I have to tell you, it's really got Alana tied up in knots."

"Text? What're you talking about?"

"He didn't call you?"

"No. Maybe you'd better tell me what's going on."

She told him the story, leaving nothing out. His face grew more somber with each sentence. When she finished, he grabbed his cell from his belt. "I'm going to call our commander and have him get in touch with the sheriff's office in Baton Rouge parish. We'll get a detective over to the hospital to pick up the phone tonight." He pressed a button and stepped into the hallway.

Layla's phone rang. She sprinted to the kitchen to answer it. "Hello."

"Are you standing me up for practice?"

"Jeffery!" She'd totally forgot. How could she forget dance rehearsal?

"I'm hurt. You forgot, didn't you?"

"I did. And I'm sorry. There's a lot going on right now. I have to deal with some personal things."

He chuckled. "No problem. My bride will be happy to have me help her out at the house." He paused. "Are you okay?"

"Yeah." She spied Detective Wallace closing his phone and moving back into the living room. "I just have to get some stuff handled. Again, I'm sorry."

"You know where to find us if you need us."

"Thanks." She turned off the phone just as another set of headlights punctured the night's darkness.

Detective Wallace opened the door for his partner. The two talked in hushed tones before Maddox stepped inside and set a gym bag next to the couch. He came to her and took her hands in his. "Houston's got someone on the way to the hospital. They'll get the phone, and we've requested an escort for Alana back to the hotel."

Gratitude warmed her more than his touch. "Thank you."

"Now, you want to go to the nursing home, right?"

Want wasn't the word she'd choose, but it was better to let it go than explain. She nodded.

"Get your coat, then. I'll drive." He looked over her shoulder to his partner. "You'll hold down the fort?"

Detective Wallace made a big show of sighing heavy and dropping onto her recliner. "It's a hardship, but I'll manage." He grinned, waggling his eyebrows at her.

She couldn't help but smile in return. The man had to be terminally sweet.

Layla grabbed her coat, then followed Maddox out into an angry wind. She snuggled deeper into the lining of her leather duster.

Thunder cracked.

She jumped. Maddox slipped an arm around her waist. "It's okay. I'm right here. Nothing's going to happen to you." He opened the passenger door for her.

His words and presence did give her a sense of security. Of calmness. But she wasn't worried about the person threatening her right now. She was terrified of visiting her mother.

She watched him walk around the car. When he was around, she wanted to smile all the time. Felt almost giddy inside.

And then she went cold as realization hit—she was falling for Maddox Bishop.

No, that couldn't happen. He was rough around the edges. And he was mad at God. She couldn't fall for a man who didn't love God. She'd gone that route once before, and look how it turned out.

Randy broke her heart.

Oh, Lord, help me.

Maddox started the car, the heater blowing, and backed out of her drive. Good thing it was dark because she needed to concentrate. Needed to think. Needed to pray.

Westneath Nursing Home was less than twenty minutes away, just on the other side of Eternal Springs. Not a lot of time.

"I don't think I know why your mom's in the nursing home." Maddox's voice shattered her reprieve.

He must have caught her expression by the dashboard lights because he was very quick to continue. "I shouldn't have pried. It's none of my business."

She couldn't even find the words to tell him. It was embarrassing. And painful. The truth about her mother was too awful to discuss. "She had a brain injury, leaving her mentally incapacitated."

"I'm so sorry."

The pity in his words undid her. Everyone always apologized, as if this horrible tragedy had befallen their family. That was so far from the truth. Her mother's condition was self-inflicted. Roseanna Taylor had made a conscious choice to continue taking depressants. She put herself in the nursing home, all because of her selfish wants with no thought to her family.

"It's okay." And it was. Her mother had gotten what she deserved.

Maddox drove the rest of the way in silence. She didn't offer any conversation on her end. What could she say?

He parked the car near the wing she motioned to. She reached for the handle, but her muscles protested. He came around and opened the door for her, giving her a hand to help her out.

Why was this so hard?

"Are you okay?" He stopped at the stairs to the hallway door.

She stared at the keypad beside the door. She'd never been here but knew the code. Alana always told her when they changed it. Funny how that was embedded in her mind. If only it weren't, she'd have the perfect excuse to give Alana.

"Layla?"

She nodded. No way was she going to explain why her feet were reluctant to move. Why her fingers trembled as she punched in the four numbers. Why she thought she'd vomit as she reached for the cold metal door handle.

Stepping onto the checkered-pattern tile floor, the smell of Lysol and bleach accosted her. Her body went rigid.

"Layla, are you all right?" Maddox was right beside her, his hand under her elbow, giving more support than he realized.

"Yeah. I'm fine." She could do this. Just walk down to the fourth door on the right, crack it open, and peek inside. Her mother was probably asleep. Hadn't Alana told her they put her mother down on the first wave of those incapable of tucking themselves in for the night?

"Are you sure? You don't seem okay."

"I said I was fine," she snapped. Then felt guilty. "Sorry," she whispered.

She forced herself to move. One foot in front of the other. This was simple. She could do it. *Oh, Lord, give me strength. Help me do this.*

Emotions dragged on her legs—anger, guilt, frustration, regret. Each one weighted every step she took. Her hands trembled.

Finally she stood before her mother's door. Then she glanced at the floor. Great, light shone from the crack under the door. They hadn't tucked her mother in for the night. She faced Maddox. "Could you please talk to the nurses? Let them know what's going on so they'll be alert?" If someone else got hurt because of her probing . . .

Maddox nodded. He gave her elbow a little squeeze, then headed down the hall.

She took in a deep breath, uncertainty clawing away any chance of peace. She hadn't seen her mother once since she'd entered the nursing home. The last image Layla had of her mother was on the floor of the house, seizing and unconscious, almost eight years ago. *God, please help me get through this.* She pushed open the door.

Mom sat in a high-back wheelchair by the window, facing the door. Her arms and legs were in awkward positions, curled and gnarled. Her head tilted to the side as if her neck couldn't support it.

Layla froze. Seeing her mother like this—helpless and distorted—snatched her breath. The vibrant woman she'd once been was gone. A catheter bag hung to the wheelchair. A strap held her in.

Tears streamed from Layla. Her mother . . . Mom . . . horrible. Being stuck in such a body had to be a living hell. Layla didn't even know if her mother recognized her or was aware of anything. But she couldn't just stand there staring.

She stepped next to the bed separating her from her mother. "Alana asked me to come check on you. There are some things happening that made her think you might be in danger."

"AAAAlllaaaannnnnaaaa." A bit of drool pooled as Mom struggled with the one word.

"Yes, Alana. She was worried about you."

"LLLLLaaaayyyyllllaaa." More drool.

Layla didn't move. Her spine straightened. "Yes, Mom, I'm Layla." Her mother recognized her! Remembered her!

"SSSSooooo sssoooorrrryyyy."

Her heart thumped faster as she moved closer to her mother. She bent to get at eye level. "Mom, did you mean to say you were sorry? Do you realize what you're saying?"

"GGGoooodddd."

Even in the slurred words, Layla could make out she said God. *Oh, Lord. Have mercy on Mom. She's trapped inside this . . . this farce of a body.*

She moved in front of her mother.

"Do not judge, and you will not be judged. Do not condemn, and you will not be condemned. Forgive, and you will be forgiven."

Tears washed unabashedly down her face. *Father, forgive me for not forgiving. Open my heart to Your will.*

HE'D HAD NO IDEA.

Maddox stood at the cracked door to Mrs. Taylor's room. Layla stood over her mother with her back to the door. Her mother's arms and legs were pulled into strange positions by contractures, her head lolled to the side. But her eyes were focused on her daughter.

He felt like an intruder. An eavesdropper. And he was. He'd had no idea her mother was in such a horrible condition.

Maddox swallowed hard. He couldn't conceive how he'd feel if his mother were in that wheelchair totally incapacitated. Maybe it had been a blessing in disguise that she'd died. He swallowed again, never imagining he'd think such a thing.

Layla's shoulders hunched. Her body shook as she ducked her head. The quiet sobs echoed off the bare walls.

Maddox balled his hands to stay in place. This was a private moment between Layla and her mother. He had no right to intrude. But he couldn't turn away.

She dropped to her knees and laid her head in her mother's lap. Sobs ripped from her, nearly ripping his own heart from his chest.

"Oh, Mom . . . I'm the one who's sorry." Layla wrapped her arms around her mother, wheelchair and all. "I'm sorry for not coming to visit you. I'm sorry for blaming you for all my troubles. I'm so sorry for not forgiving you for doing this to yourself."

Her cries stirred something primitive inside him. Something that made him want to scoop her up and hold her, shielding her and protecting her from all pain.

"I forgive you, Mom, and hope you'll forgive me. I love you."

Maddox couldn't even swallow. He didn't know exactly what he was witnessing, but he knew something had changed for Layla.

He inched back from the door and moved down the hall, shocked to discover his vision blurred because of tears.

What was happening to him? This was crazy. He'd never wanted to protect a woman from emotional pain before. Even talking about emotional issues made him break out in a cold sweat. That wasn't who he was. No, he was more of the love-'em-and-leave-'em type.

So why did he feel so strongly about Layla Taylor? She wasn't even his type. She was strong. Independent. Didn't fawn at his feet. And then there was that whole religion thing.

" 'How great is God—beyond our understanding.' "

He leaned against the wall as the Scripture his father had quoted to him earlier wrapped around his mind. It seemed everywhere he turned lately, God was there. In his face. Not in a beat-you-over-the-head-with-a-Bible way, but just . . . there.

And funny thing was, it wasn't bothering him as much as it had in the past. Something had changed. Him?

He pictured Betty Page's kind face as she inquired about his father after losing her husband. Peace. Was that God?

His father, telling him that he loved him. Was that God?

Alana's calm expression in the hospital waiting room. Was that God?

Layla's compassion and kindness to him when he'd been waiting for word on his father. Was that God? The scene with her mother just now. Was that God?

His cell phone vibrated. He yanked it from his hip and checked the caller ID—dispatch. "Bishop."

"Sir, report of a fire in Eternal Springs. Fire department and emergency medical personnel have been dispatched. You and Wallace have been requested on scene."

"Copy that." He'd just order Layla to sit in the car while he checked it out. "Address?" He pulled out a notebook and pen.

The dispatcher read him the street address. "It's Eternal Springs Christian Church, sir."

TWENTY-EIGHT

"Nearly all men can stand adversity,
but if you want to test a man's character,
give him power."
—ABRAHAM LINCOLN

"LAYLA."

She wiped the tears from her face before standing and turning.

Maddox filled the doorway. "I'm sorry, but I've got a call I have to go to. Do you want me to come by later and pick you up? I don't know how long I'll be."

She smiled and kissed her mother's cheek. "No, Mom needs her rest." She squatted in front of the wheelchair. "Mom, I need to go. I'll come see you again soon." She straightened and ran a hand over her mother's hair. It was still as silky as she remembered. "I love you," she whispered.

With a heart lighter than it'd felt in years, Layla followed Maddox into the hall. "Another murder?"

"A fire."

She had to double her steps to keep up with his long stride. "A fire?" Her throat tightened. Not another one.

He opened the door for her.

Rain came down in sheets, blown by the cold, driving wind. Puddles already lined the parking lot. She pulled her coat tighter.

"Let's make a run for it." Maddox pressed a button on his remote key chain. The lights inside the Mustang illuminated, casting shadows around the car, and a beep sounded above the pounding of the rain. He ducked and ran.

She followed suit, keeping her head down. Didn't really matter—her hair and coat were soaked as she pulled the door shut behind her. The chill went all the way to her bones. "I'm soaking your seat."

"It's leather. It'll wipe." He turned the key and revved the engine, then stared at her. "Layla, you need to know—the fire is at the church."

"My church?" Images of the beautiful stained-glass windows—true works of art—danced in her mind. "My church is on fire?"

"Yes." He rammed the car in reverse. The tires spun on the wet asphalt.

Her brain refused to process the information.

No, the church couldn't be on fire. Not the church.

"I don't know any more than it's on fire and the fire department has been dispatched. I was asked to the scene."

It was late. No one should be in the church now except maybe Pastor, and he was in the hospital.

A fire. Unreal. She clasped and unclasped her hands. Wait a minute . . . Why would Maddox be called to a fire?

"Maddox?"

"Yeah?" He didn't take his eyes off the road as he sped toward the church.

She hated to ask. Hated to give voice to her fears, but she had to know. "Is there a body in the church? Another murder victim?"

He spared her a glance. "Don't know. They didn't say."

"Then why were you called?"

"I'm not sure."

Sirens filled the air.

Layla's chest tightened even more. "Oh, Lord, please have mercy."

Maddox threw her a quick look, then concentrated back on the road.

She hadn't meant to pray aloud—the words had just slipped out. She gripped her hands together as the familiar sights of Eternal Springs rushed by the window.

The smell of smoke filtered through the heater.

Her nose tickled, then burned. Her pulse rose with the speedometer. The steady drone of the windshield wipers on high pounded in her head.

He turned onto the church's road. "I need you to stay in the car, Layla. No matter how much you want to get out and look around, you have to stay in the car. Okay?"

No, that wasn't okay. She wanted to see how much damage had been done. Know if anyone was inside.

"Okay, Layla? I'm serious."

"Yes. Okay." But she widened her eyes as he pulled into the church's parking lot, trying to take it all in.

"Stay here." He jumped out of the car and headed toward Houston, who stood talking with a fireman and Lincoln Vailes under the canopy of a large live oak tree.

Fire trucks were parked sideways in the lot, one even up on the front lawn. The lawn where they'd had two garage sales to make money for the sod. Water hoses stretched from the hydrant at street side across the pavement. Despite the deluge of rain, orange and blue flames licked the steeple and bell tower.

Fire ate the building she'd renovated not even a year ago, months of work devoured in moments by a relentless enemy. Tears pooled in her eyes, marring her vision. So much destruction. The Hope-for-Homes site. Her office. Second

Chances. And now, the one place left not violated that gave her a measure of peace . . . disappearing in a cloud of smoke.

Lord, when will it all stop? Hasn't Eternal Springs suffered enough?

"THE CDC HAS DETERMINED sulfur poisoning is the cause of the illnesses and deaths?" Maddox tried to follow what Lincoln and Houston threw at him. Amid all the chaos of firefighting and rain, it was hard to hear, much less grasp. The large tree offered some protection from the beating rain, but the wind kept them soaked.

"Right. And they believe this church contains the contaminant." Lincoln crossed his arms over his chest, smoothing down his Windbreaker.

Houston nodded. "At this point, we think it's safe to assume someone knew the CDC had made the link and sent a team to check out the church. To cover evidence, he or she started this fire."

It made sense, but . . .

"Did a little checking while I waited for you." Houston's expression screamed that Maddox wouldn't like what he had to say.

"What?"

"There are too many common denominators linking the fire at the Hope-for-Homes site, the bomb at Second Chances, and now this church."

Maddox swiped at the rain on his face. "Such as?"

"The house and this church both had construction work done in the last year. Second Chances had some remodeling done a little over a year ago."

"Not so uncommon. After the hurricanes of the last few years, there's been a lot of construction in the area."

Houston shook his head. "On both, Layla Taylor was the contractor *and* the site foreman. She was also both on the renovations to Second Chances. On all three, Dennis LeJeune was the building inspector."

Maddox's argument of coincidence washed away. He glanced over his shoulder at his car. Layla's silhouette was highlighted by the strobing lights of the fire trucks and police cruisers. He turned back to his partner. "What about the independents she contracted for these three jobs?"

"Same on all three: Denny Keys, electrician; Bob Johnson, plumber; Y Building Supplies, supplier; and J. B. Carpentry."

Not just Layla. It could be any of them . . . or the Second Chancers. Not just her.

He cocked his head. "Are you thinking conspiracy?"

Houston shrugged. "Can't rule it out."

"Come on, you've got to be kidding me. What do they have to gain?"

"It's fishy, Bishop. You gotta admit that." Lincoln wiped rain from his face.

Okay, he'd give them that. But Layla wasn't involved. She couldn't be. He *knew* she wasn't. "There's a connection. We just haven't figured it all out yet."

"We're running out of time here. Three buildings destroyed. Three deaths so far due to this poisoning."

"Three?" Ms. Ethel. Mr. James Page. Had the pastor died?

Houston shifted closer to the tree's trunk. "Remember that baby I told you Margie was concerned with that died?"

Maddox nodded.

"Guess where the family went to church?" Houston shook his head. "They didn't correlate the same symptoms because the other three who'd gotten sick were elderly."

A baby. Dead.

Maddox's gut twisted. "And the threats Layla's received?"

"Could be everyone involved is turning on one another. Could be why LeJeune was murdered. Now the threats against Layla," Lincoln said.

No, that wasn't right. "But the messages to Layla tell her to stop asking questions. If she were involved in some big conspiracy and they were turning on one another, they wouldn't tell her to stop asking questions. They'd tell her to keep her mouth shut. Or whatever."

"True." Houston nodded. "Unless they were trying to throw us offtrack."

Why was his partner being such a jerk about this? He had to know Layla wasn't involved. That she was in danger. "If she were involved, do you think she'd have run to us with the message in the first place?"

"She didn't. Alana did. You just happened to be there." Houston held up his hand. "Look, I'm just trying to be objective and consider all possibilities."

Maddox crossed his arms over his chest. No way was Layla involved in this mess. Not a conspiracy. "What about the break-in at her place? Surely you don't think she'd do that to herself?"

"What was really damaged, Bishop? Two computers gone and paperwork taken. The place trashed a bit. The only thing that was really broken was the window." Lincoln spread his hands. "All minor damage."

He glanced back at his car again. Layla's silhouette was still there, reminding him of her soft tones and willingness to pray over a stranger—his father. Her flawless support of her sister. The way she'd been with her mother.

No, she wasn't involved in any crimes. She was a victim.

He turned back to his partner and Lincoln. "I don't buy that. She's innocent."

Houston peered at him from under the branches of the tree. "Is that based on your detective instincts, or your feelings for her?"

Maddox's face heated. His entire body followed suit. "What is it with you, Houston? You go this whole route of cats and dogs and crazy talk, but then you accuse her of being part of some conspiracy of murder and arson?"

His partner shifted his weight to his other leg. "I'm just trying to look at the big picture. See what's what."

"Do you really think she's involved in some big plan to do . . . whatever?"

Houston glanced at the Mustang. A thick silence permeated the smoke-filled area. Finally he looked back at Maddox. "No, I don't. But we had to at least talk through the possibility."

Maddox glared at Lincoln. "What about you, Vailes? You know her. Do you think Layla's involved in a conspiracy?"

"No." He took a step back. "But your partner's right. We had to consider all options, no matter what our personal feelings are."

Yeah, he knew that. But to even consider her part of this mess was just . . . wrong.

"We need to figure out what the main connection is between these people." Houston waved toward the church. "These burnings."

Burnings—"Houston, we can run a check of all the buildings destroyed over the last year or so and see if there's a common denominator. That would also rule out some of the people involved." He was on to something . . .. he could feel it. "If we could find a link between several buildings destroyed over a longer period of time, it's possible we can eliminate some of the groups of people who are connected to these recent events."

That excitement sparkle glinted in his partner's eyes. "Yeah. Maybe we're on to the connection, but we just haven't searched far back enough to see the whole picture." He threw a mock punch at Maddox's arm. "Good work, partner. I'll put a call in to the office in the morning. Get them digging up some details."

Maddox nodded, his own instincts pumping adrenaline through him. "We also need to talk to this CDC specialist. See if we can figure out what we're dealing with on this poisoning issue. Maybe it'll give us another lead."

Lincoln looked at the church. "This is my church. Where Jade and I planned to get married." His words were nearly lost in the storm and noise surrounding the area. "It's destroyed."

Houston followed Lincoln's line of sight. "Maybe not. Won't be able to tell how much damage until the smoke clears. It was called in before it went up in flames, so it probably looks worse now than it really is."

"I hope so." Lincoln wiped his hands on his

pants. "Well, I better get back to work. I'll call you with a report as soon as the fire investigator lets me know."

"Thanks, man. Appreciate it." Maddox clapped Lincoln's shoulder before he walked away.

"Not much else for us to do here. Let's head back to Layla's. Maybe she'll have some ideas. We haven't really asked her what she thought."

Maddox nodded. "Meet you there." He turned and headed toward the car. He opened the door and his body went rigid.

Layla wasn't in the Mustang.

IT JUST *HAD* TO start storming after he set the fire.

He drove by the street, careful to keep the bill of his cap lowered so no one would recognize him. Not that anybody looked—everyone was focused on the church.

Why did it have to start raining? He'd used enough gasoline for the heat to build so the fire would destroy the church in a matter of minutes. Well before the fire department could arrive. He'd had no choice—he had to act. The letter awarding him the riverboat casino bid burned in his pocket.

With the rain's help, the church was still standing. Still holding his secrets for all to uncover.

He turned onto Eternal Springs' main street,

heading toward home. The rain had lessened over the last half hour. Just his luck.

At home, he stood under his carport and glared at the sky.

Was this a religion thing? God sending the rain to protect His house?

He didn't know—couldn't know—but it gave him enough of a shiver that he headed inside.

TWENTY-NINE

"Be not afraid of greatness:
some are born great, some achieve greatness,
and some have greatness thrust upon them."
—WILLIAM SHAKESPEARE

"WHAT ARE YOU DOING here?" Layla stood with hands on her hips. Anything so her trembling wouldn't be noticed. Not that it would with the clouds of smoke billowing over the bayou.

Randy turned, his eyes widening as he locked stares with her. "I could ask you the same thing."

"But I asked first." The rain had slacked to barely a misting, but it'd be enough to make her hair curl and frizz. She ran a hand over her strands.

"I'm fighting the fire." He spread out his arms, drawing her eyes to the coat, pants, and boots.

She should've registered his apparel but had just been so shocked to see him. Again. Here. "Oh."

"So, what are you doing here?"

"I was with Detective Bishop when he got the call." She jerked her head toward the big tree Maddox, Lincoln, and Houston stood under.

Randy's brows shot up. "What're you doing with a cop?"

Good thing it was dark because she was sure her face was beet red. "Long story, and I don't know that I'm at liberty to discuss it with anyone." Make him wonder.

He gave her that look that always said he wasn't buying what she was selling. "Why are the cops here anyway?"

"I would've thought you'd know, helping out the fire department and all." She ducked out of the way as two firemen headed back to the truck, tugging massive hoses.

"It was arson, that's for sure."

Her heart stumbled. "Really?"

"Yeah. The investigator's on his way." He frowned. "But maybe I'm not at liberty to discuss it with you."

Touché. She shifted out of the way of more firemen.

The unmistakable smell of burning wood drifted over the area. She glanced at the church and her stomach turned to lead. The entire stained-glass front was gone, reduced to shards on the ground. "This is so awful."

"Heard one of your sites burned down last week too. Your office got broken into. And Second Chances got hit by a bomb."

He always did know how to cut her to the core. "Guess you could say I'm having a bad week."

"Seriously, I'm sorry about Cameron. Alana must be beside herself." He'd been sweet to her sister, even when he was a jerk to her.

"She's hanging in there." Time to change the subject. "So, what're you doing back in town?" Great. How subtle.

"I'm moving back. They hired me back on at the department, obviously." He grinned. "Have you missed me?" He waggled his eyebrows, something that had once been endearing to her.

Now, it just made him look silly.

"Not really."

Randy laughed.

The heat marched across her face again. "But Natalie probably did." Why did she say that?

His cocky grin widened. "Jealous?"

She snorted. "Not hardly. Not worth getting jealous over."

"No, she's not. We're just good friends."

"I wasn't talking about her." As she said the words, she realized it was the truth. She didn't care enough about him or Natalie to be hurt. He no longer mattered to her.

She did a quick inventory of her emotions where Randy was concerned. No jealousy. No anger. No pain. Relief bubbled in her chest. It didn't even matter that he was back in town permanently.

He was nothing to her except a closed chapter in her life.

His grin faded. "I see you've kept your claws sharp."

"No, not really. I've just grown up. Learned my lessons the hard way."

His expression turned serious. "Look, Layla, I never meant to hurt you. I said some pretty ugly things to you—things I said in anger."

"Don't worry about it. No harm, no foul." She shrugged. Surprised that she meant what she said. "It's in the past."

"No, I'm sorry. I was a jerk."

"Well, you *were* a jerk." She smiled.

He grinned and shook his head. "So, we're cool?"

"We're cool."

"Good. I didn't like the way things were left between us." He leaned over and pulled her into a hug.

It felt . . . nice. Peaceful. Like she'd survived an ordeal and come out better on the other side.

"You take care," she whispered into his neck.

He straightened. "You too."

Layla pulled back, still smiling because she was really over the pain and anger. She turned back to the Mustang.

And met Maddox's smoldering stare.

SHE'D DEFIED HIS DIRECT order . . . to make out with her ex?

Maddox ground his teeth and concentrated on breathing instead of punching Randy Dean square in his smiling face.

Layla approached slowly, the smile wiped from her face.

And to think, his heart had stopped when he'd opened the door and realized she wasn't in the Mustang.

"Hi." She stopped at the passenger door and spoke over the roof.

"I thought I told you to stay in the car."

She glanced over her shoulder at Dean, then back to him. "I saw someone I knew."

"Your ex, right?"

"How'd you know Randy and I dated?" Her brows bunched. "Have you been checking up on me?"

"I'm a detective, remember? That's my job."

"To check up on me?" Her voice carried over the wind and ruckus.

"Just get in." He plopped behind the steering wheel and slammed his door.

She mimicked his actions. "You really checked

up on me. What's my past dating record have to do with anything?"

He started the car and slammed it in reverse. "Did it ever occur to you the coincidental timing of Dean's return? Showing up in town right about the time the Hope-for-Homes site was burned?"

"How do you know when he came back? I didn't even know until he just showed up at . . ." She lowered her head.

"Your dance performance last week, right?" Where she looked so beautiful she nearly took his breath away. He put the car in drive.

She jerked her focus to him. "How did you know?"

"As I said, I'm a detective." He punched the gas pedal harder.

Layla huffed.

He refused to say any more. Let her stew.

"To answer your implied question, no, I don't think Randy had anything to do with the house burning."

"Why's that?" Maddox clenched his teeth so hard his jaw ached. Hearing her take up for her ex . . . Well, he didn't like it. Not at all.

"Because Randy's a fireman. He puts *out* fires, not starts them."

"Who better to know how to start one than a fireman?"

Her mouth opened, then clamped shut.

Good. He didn't think he could take her making excuses for Dean. How could she? He'd seen her face that night at the performance. She'd been shocked and hurt. But they'd been hugging just moments ago. Smiling.

Had they kissed and made up?

His stomach turned. The thought of her kissing Dean made him nauseated.

"What would Randy have to gain by killing Dennis? He didn't even know him."

Maddox spared her a glance. She looked too good right now, with her hair all curly and messy. Had Dean run his fingers through it? Maddox strangled the smooth leather of the steering wheel and turned his attention back to the road. "Do you know that for certain?"

"I'm pretty positive. They didn't exactly run in the same circles."

"Maybe LeJeune showed up at the house for some strange reason—maybe to do a last check or something—and found Dean there about to set fire to it."

She snorted. "Like Dennis would be out on a site checking something at eleven thirty or later? And Randy just happened to have a gun on him, just in case someone showed up?"

Her sarcasm plowed across his heart. "Maybe he was setting you up. Did you ever think of that?" He turned onto her street. "Doing it to make you look guilty?"

She laughed. "Then he broke into my office—for what? And planted a bomb at Second Chances for no good reason. Oh, and then sent text messages to Alana's and my phones to threaten me to stop asking questions. Hmm. Wonder what questions I was asking that had anything to do with him."

Okay, so he hadn't worked out the plausibility of everything, but the guy was still a suspect in Maddox's book.

And forget the fact that he was so jealous it was all he could do not to turn the car around and go find Dean and pummel him into oblivion.

She pinched her lips together and stared out the window. He whipped the car into her driveway and killed the engine. He took several silent, deep breaths. "When I tell you to do something, I expect you to do it."

Layla flipped her hair out of her eyes. "Fine." She was out of the car like a bullet from his sidearm.

He rushed out to step in front of her before she could make it up the stairs. Darkness surrounded them as the midnight hour approached. "It was for your safety."

"I was fine."

"Do you have any idea what I thought when I opened the door and you weren't there? You've had threats against you." He hated the way his voice lifted on the last word.

Those cat eyes of hers widened. “I-I didn’t think about that. I’m sorry.” She gave a little shake of her head. “I didn’t mean to alarm you like that. I just saw . . . an old friend.”

Old friend? Who did she think she was fooling? “And you rushed out of the car to go talk to him, despite what I’d instructed you—for your own safety.” Was she that desperate to reconnect with Dean? How strong were her feelings for him?

Maddox stiffened. Why did he care?

Because he’d developed feelings for her. Real and deep feelings. And they were growing stronger.

“I’m sorry, Maddox. I didn’t mean to cause anyone to worry. Least of all you.” Her voice was so soft . . . so sweet.

He didn’t think. Didn’t want to. He needed to know how she felt about him. If there was a chance for something between them.

Never breaking eye contact, Maddox swept his hands on either side of her face, plunging his fingers deep into her silky hair. He hesitated for a heartbeat as he registered her quick intake of air. Then, as if in slow motion, he lowered his lips to hers. He could feel every pounding of his pulse. It echoed inside his head.

His lips grazed against hers. Soft. Supple. Warm. Inviting.

His head spun like the ground had just shifted. Her flowery scent surrounded him, filling his senses. He deepened the kiss, staggering a step closer, pulling her against his chest. Her response made him hold her tighter.

She jerked back, pressing her fingers to her mouth. Layla blinked several times. Without another word, she turned and sped up the stairs to her house.

He couldn't breathe. She'd stolen the air right from his lungs. He could only stare after her as she unlocked the door and pushed inside.

If Maddox had ever had any doubt that he was falling for her, that one kiss had cleared it up for him.

He'd never felt this way about any woman. Never *let* himself feel like this. But somehow, some way, she'd slipped past every one of his defense mechanisms.

Layla Taylor had him—hook, line, and sinker.

He was a goner.

THIRTY

"Faced with what is right, to leave it undone shows a lack of courage."
—CONFUCIUS

STUPID. JUST PLAIN STUPID.

How could she have kissed him?

Layla shuddered. She had no business kissing Maddox, or any man. Wasn't her life complicated enough right now without adding in the mess of a romantic entanglement? If only the kiss hadn't been so mind-numbing. Hadn't felt so . . . right.

And seeing Randy tonight, why had she ever thought she was in love with him? He'd made her feel less like a woman. Unlike Maddox. He made her feel safe. And very, *very* feminine.

No, she wouldn't consider the ramifications right now. Not while her knees still felt as gooey as the edges of the bayou.

She rushed inside, her hands trembling so bad she'd had to try to get the key in the lock four times before she'd got it right. Everything in her felt jumbled. Disjointed.

All because of one kiss.

But, wow, what a kiss!

She groaned and stormed to the kitchen. She yanked up the cordless and accessed her voice mail. Two messages from Alana. Cameron was stable and the doctors at the Baton Rouge hospital gave a more hopeful prognosis. The police had picked up the phone, and Alana asked about Mom.

Layla deleted the messages and moved to put on a pot of coffee. Anything to keep busy, or at least appear so, when Maddox entered. She'd pushed the door almost closed when she entered, but he hadn't followed yet.

Was he regretting kissing her? Why did he kiss

her? They were arguing about Randy and her not staying in the car, then the next thing she knew, she was in his arms.

And she'd never felt so comfortable in a man's embrace.

She let out a moan and bent, resting her elbows on the counter and shoving her forehead against her palms. What was she doing? *God, I'm so confused. A little help, please?*

The coffeemaker let out a shot of steam, then clicked to percolating. Another car sounded in her drive. Houston.

What would Maddox tell his partner? Things would definitely be odd between Maddox and her. Houston would notice. Would he say something? How would she answer?

She straightened. What if the kiss meant nothing to Maddox? What if he didn't bother mentioning it to Houston because it was no big deal to him? Was she making something out of nothing?

Kissing wasn't something she just went around doing. She didn't even kiss on a first date. Yet here she was, kissing Maddox in her front yard never having been on a date with him. Not really knowing him.

She was so messed up. Maybe she should forego the coffee and head straight to bed.

The door creaked as it opened, and Houston stepped inside. "Hey, Layla."

Turning, she pasted on a plastic smile. "Hi. I'm making coffee."

He slumped into a kitchen chair. "I need it." He stuck a piece of gum into his mouth.

Maddox hovered by the back door facing the bayou, his back to her. Good, because the heat already burned her face. If he looked at her, she'd turn beet red from embarrassment.

"Listen, I want to run something by you. See if you have any ideas." Houston motioned her to join him at the table.

She glanced at Maddox's straight back, then moved to sit across from Houston. "I'll try. Whatcha got?"

"The CDC specialist has diagnosed the mystery illnesses as sulfur poisoning."

What?

"He also believes the source of the contaminant is the church."

This was unbelieva—

"But since we can't get in there now to see, we were wondering if maybe you could think of anything that could cause sulfur poisoning. You oversaw the renovations just months ago, so maybe you can think of something."

Way out of her league. She wasn't a chemist or a scientist, just a contractor. She wouldn't kno—

"Anything at all. Even if it's out in left field."

"Hang on. Let me think for a minute."

The smell of rotten eggs. The corroded copper pipes and tubings. Something was there, something she knew, just outside the edges of her memory.

Maddox turned, facing her. He hovered over her, his expression unreadable. "Layla, if you know something, now's the time to tell—"

"Shh. I'm thinking. Give me a second to work it out."

Stink. Corrosion. *Think.* What was it? She knew something about this. She'd read an article—"The article." She jumped up, nearly knocking over the kitchen chair. "Hang on."

She raced to her desk in her bedroom and tugged on the bottom drawer where she kept all her back issues of magazines. Which one? She flipped through the indexes, scanning for the article.

"What are you doing?"

She started, then frowned at Maddox. "If I can just find the stupid article, I think I can figure it out."

"Article about what?" He moved to stand behind her. Where she could detect a hint of his cologne under the smoke stench of the fire.

Her heart raced into overdrive as soon as he'd entered her bedroom. Now, with his proximity and the smell of him so near, she couldn't concentrate. She took a step back, holding up a magazine like a shield. "Could you give me some space, please? I can't think with you hovering over me."

Maddox held up his hands and took a couple of steps backward. "Fine. Trust me, I got your message to back up loud and clear."

Was he talking about now or before . . . after their kiss?

No, she couldn't think about that right now. She had to find the article. She returned to scanning the indexes. Not this issue. She scanned the next. Not this one either. The third. No. The fourth. No.

"Can I help you?"

Layla shot him a look. "Yeah, go back into the kitchen. You're still too close to me. I can't think when you're around."

His eyes widened for a moment, then the edges of his mouth lifted. "Okay." He turned and strode from the room.

Good riddance. The man was sapping every strand of sanity from her.

SO, SHE COULDN'T THINK when he was around. Was that good or bad?

Maddox was going to run with it being good, which made him feel a lot better.

When she'd pushed him away and run inside, he felt as if something inside of him had died. All sorts of thoughts had slammed him. Did she wish it was Dean kissing her? Did he repulse her? Was she disgusted by his kiss?

But if she couldn't think when he was around, maybe that meant she was as attracted to him as he was to her.

Maddox raked a kitchen chair across the floor and plopped down. Not used to questioning where he stood with a woman, he stared across the table at Houston. "She's searching for some article."

"So she said." Houston looked at him funny.

"What?"

"You gonna tell me what's going on with you two?"

Maddox shrugged, hoping against hope he came across as casual. "I just let her know that if I tell her to do something or stay put, I mean for her to do that."

Houston grinned. "How'd that work out for you, buddy?"

"I think she gets my point now."

Houston narrowed his eyes. "Uh-oh. What'd you do?"

"What do you mean?"

"Come on. I'm your partner. I can read you like the latest best seller. You're turning all kinds of red, and she wouldn't even look you in the eye." He snapped his fingers and pointed at Maddox. "You made a play for her, didn't you?"

Heat nearly scalded Maddox's face.

Houston laughed. "You did." He continued to

chuckle, shaking his head. "How'd *that* work out?"

"I just kissed her. That's all."

"That's all?" Houston hooted.

"Shh." Maddox glanced at the doorway. "Keep it down, will ya? She'd probably blow a gasket if she knew I was telling you."

Houston put his hand over his mouth. At least he attempted to curb his amusement at Maddox's predicament. "So, what happened?"

"What happened? She kissed me back. Then all of a sudden, she pushes away and runs into the house." He kept an eye on the doorway. "Man, what's that supposed to mean?"

"That she likes you."

"Abruptly ending the kiss and running away means she likes me?" Maddox frowned. "That makes no sense."

"That, my friend, is a woman." Houston grinned. "Cats and dogs, buddy. Cats and dogs."

"I found it!" Layla rushed into the room with a magazine in her hand. Her eyes shone with excitement, lighting up her whole face. Maddox's insides quickened. "I knew I'd seen something that rang a bell."

"What?" Houston lost all signs of amusement.

"Chinese Sheetrock."

Maddox shook his head. "I'm lost."

She pulled out a chair and put her knee on it. "After all of the hurricanes and flooding, there was a construction boom to rebuild. Especially down here in the southern states. America couldn't keep up with the demand for construction materials. For several years suppliers imported Sheetrock from China."

"I'm with you so far."

"Okay. Well, apparently the process of collecting the gypsum that Sheetrock is made from isn't as refined in China as it is here in America. Several reports occurred in the past couple of years about the high toxicity and the complications arising from the Sheetrock from China. Here, let me read you this part." She lifted the magazine. " 'Toxic to copper, this Sheetrock emits sulfur gases that can damage air-conditioning coils, electrical and plumbing components, and other material. Data reports it has actually corroded air-conditioning coils, computer wiring, faucets, copper plumbing and tubing. Additionally, this Sheetrock emits a hydrogen sulfide, or "rotten eggs," odor when exposed to moist air.' "

She turned the page and continued. " 'Most disturbing, however, is the effects this Sheetrock can have on one's health. Prolonged exposure to the Sheetrock, especially those with high levels of carbon disulfide, can cause breathing problems, chest pains, and even death.' "

"Wow." Maddox couldn't think of anything else to say. He had to let this soak in.

“Pastor called me to look at the plumbing at the church because the copper pipes had corroded. Bob Johnson had replaced them twice already but couldn’t determine the cause. When I was there, the odor was atrocious. Now that I think about it, it did smell just like rotten eggs.” She slapped the magazine to the table.

Houston nodded. “This has to be it.”

“Where did you get your Sheetrock from? For both the church renovations and the Hope-for-Homes house?” Maddox asked.

“My normal supplier: Y Building Supplies.” Her eyes widened. “Oh, goodness. I bet Ed hasn’t a clue. I wonder if someone sold him a shipment of the Chinese Sheetrock and never told him. He’ll have a fit when he finds out.”

Or he’d bought this imported Sheetrock with full knowledge and sold it to Layla without *her* knowing. Maddox shifted in his chair. “We’ll look into that tomorrow.”

“As well as see what else we turn up on a couple of other angles we’re considering,” Houston said.

“You don’t understand.” Layla moved to the counter and poured herself a cup of coffee. “Ed is meticulous about his work and his reputation. He’ll literally come unglued if someone pulled the wool over his eyes about this.”

Maddox stood and moved beside her, grabbing one of the empty mugs she’d set out beside the coffeepot. "Don't worry, we'll get to the bottom of it. Tomorrow. Too late to look into anything tonight."

Houston stood and pushed his chair to the table.

"Want some coffee?" Layla held up a cup.

"Nah. I'm crawling into that inviting spare bed of yours." He nodded to her, then shot a pointed look at Maddox. "Night, kids."

Maddox took a sip. It nearly scalded his tongue, but he paid no attention.

All he could think about was that he was all alone with Layla.

THIRTY-ONE

"Any man worth his salt will stick up for what he believes right, but it takes a slightly better man to acknowledge instantly and without reservation that he is in error."
—ANDREW JACKSON

NO! HOUSTON COULDN'T GO to bed and leave her alone with Maddox.

But he showed no signs of turning back to the kitchen. His footsteps clattered on the wood floor down the hall.

The coffee she'd just drank soured in her stomach. Layla rinsed out her cup and set it in the draining rack. She turned to find Maddox too close . . . staring.

"What is it with him and that gum? He pops it constantly. Gets on my nerves." Anything to talk about except that kiss.

"He quit smoking about a year ago. Got addicted to gum." Maddox's eyes twinkled.

Made her stomach knot. "Well, I guess I'd better call it a night too." She feigned a yawn. "Been a long day."

He set down his own mug and took hold of her shoulders. "Aren't we going to talk about it?"

A swarm of butterflies swooped through her. She licked her lips with an arid tongue. "Um, about what?" As if she didn't know.

He smiled, then ran his hands down her arms to take her hands in his. "Come on, let's go sit in the living room and talk for a bit."

Splinters! What was she going to say? Maybe he wanted to tell her it was all a mistake, which it was. She let him tug her to the couch, then sat. She drew a throw pillow into her lap.

He sat entirely too close to her. Was he trying to deliberately rattle her? If so, it was working.

All too well.

"Layla, let's talk about what's going on between us." His eyes—those blue, blue eyes—they did really strange things to her.

"I should've never kissed you." The sentence barely made it past the knot in her throat.

Maddox frowned. "Why? And as I recall, I kissed you." He gave her a shaky smile.

Which made those butterflies in her stomach do cartwheels. "Either way, I don't go around kissing men I don't even know. Or allowing them to kiss me."

"But you do know me." He reached for her hand. "You know who I am."

She pulled her hand behind the pillow. "I don't know anything about you, other than you're a detective."

"You know I have a father who had a heart attack."

No fair, bringing that up—played too deeply on her emotions. "Yes, I know that. But I don't know anything about your childhood. Your family, other than your father."

His face fell. "My mother was murdered when I was seventeen."

"Oh, Maddox, I'm so sorry." She reached for his hand and squeezed. "I didn't know."

He lifted his gaze to hers. "I was late for curfew. Came in and found her." His Adam's apple flitted up and down. "She died in my arms."

She leaned over and gave him a hug. She could feel his heartbeat. Layla sat back. "I'm so sorry."

"Not exactly what you wanted to learn, huh?" His crooked smile touched her deeply.

"I understand. Kinda." She kept hold of his hand. Maybe it was time she took a chance with her heart. Now that Randy no longer had any power over her, could she trust another man?

Layla hauled in a deep breath. “Almost eight years ago, I came home to find my mother unconscious on the floor. I was so scared she’d die before the ambulance arrived.”

“If you don’t mind my asking, what does she have?”

A little snort snuck out. “An addiction.”

“Excuse me?”

“She overdosed on Valium. Gave her a brain injury that left her . . . well, you saw how she is.” For the first time in many years, anger didn’t gnaw at her as she remembered her mother.

He blinked several times, then pinned her to her seat on the couch with his stare. “I’m so sorry. That must’ve been awful for you.”

“No worse than what you had to go through.” What were the odds that both of them would have such traumatic events in their teens?

“That’s why I became a cop. I didn’t want anyone else to go through the pain of not knowing what really happened.”

Her heart ached for the young man he’d been. “You never found out?”

He shook his head. “I actually tried to work the case when I was first promoted to detective. Not enough leads.”

That had to be agony—not knowing. At least with her mother, she never had a doubt about what happened. “I’m sorry. This is going to sound trite, but I have to say it anyway. Sometimes faith is just accepting when you don't know. Even if you never know. It's the reassurance that God loves you no matter what. That He's always there with you, if you but accept His gift of salvation."

He relaxed back against the couch but still held her hand. "Your faith is really part of you, isn't it?"

She smiled. "Yeah, it is. It's who I am." And if he didn't have faith, she couldn't have him in her life. Not in the way she wanted him. "You said before that you didn't believe in God." She held her breath as she waited for his response.

He ran a thumb over her knuckles. "I did say that." His brows lowered.

"You don't believe in Him?"

"I don't know." He lowered his eyes to focus on their joined hands. "I've spent my entire adult life refuting God because of what happened with my mother."

"I can understand that." She flipped her hand over in his. His steady stroking was distracting her from the conversation. And this discussion needed to take precedent. "Sometimes a tragedy can cause people to question their faith."

He shook his head. "You don't understand, Layla. I didn't question my faith. I was angry . . . furious that a god my mother worshipped would let her die in my arms."

Tears burned her eyes. She squeezed his hand. "It's always your choice, Maddox. You can question or turn from faith, or you can let God use the tragedy to strengthen your faith. It's all up to you."

"I blamed my father, who I thought should've been home protecting her. He, in turn, blamed me because I was late for curfew and if I'd been home on time, she probably wouldn't have been murdered. We haven't gotten along since."

The parallel in their lives was remarkable.

"So not only did I lose my mother, but in a way, I also lost my father."

The tears seeped to the corners of her eyes. "I totally understand. My father died from a sudden heart attack. He was my whole world, and I loved him to distraction. My mother had always taken Valium, ever since I was a little kid. But because my dad was so perfect, I just ignored her failings." She let the tears fall as she remembered and relived the pain. "After Dad died, I begged her to get help. I yelled at her to straighten up. She just sunk deeper into depression, which fed her addiction."

Maddox moved closer, pulling her against him.

"That day I found her, I was so mad at her for doing that to herself." Layla hauled in a deep breath. "I secretly prayed that she'd just die."

Had she just said that out loud? She'd never told anyone about that. Had been terrified God would strike her dead because of it. Had spent serious time fasting and praying for forgiveness.

He held her tighter. His chest vibrated as he breathed deeply. "I know what you're saying. I thought if God was such a wonderful god, he'd have taken my father instead of my mother."

Sniffing, Layla pulled away from Maddox. "Today was the first day I've seen my mother since she went into the nursing home."

Shock marched across his face.

She let out a half laugh-half sob. "I know, right? Not what you'd think of a Christian, is it?"

"But at the nursing home . . ."

"Yes, it was okay. I'd been praying for God to take my anger for years, yet I wasn't doing my part. I wasn't stepping out in faith that He *would* deliver me from my own emotional traps. I was still acting, or reacting, to my own feelings."

"But that's understandable." He reached for her.

She kept out of his reach. "Holding on to my anger for almost eight years? And loving Christ as I do?" She shook her head. "No, it's not understandable and it's not acceptable."

"But you went."

Layla paused. "I did. And God blessed me because of it. But it makes me wonder—how many blessings have I missed out on because I'm too stubborn to be obedient all the time?"

"You know, my father said something similar to me recently."

That lightened her mood. "He did?"

"Yeah. I guess you know he started going to your church."

"Yeah."

"Well, I'm seeing a change in him. A good change."

Her heart pounded. "Becoming saved is like that."

"And I noticed how your friend Mrs. Page was. Even after her husband had just died, she asked about my father."

She smiled. "Ms. Betty's amazing."

"And you and your sister. Both praying with people, looking all peaceful when you do." His face reddened.

She was the one to take his hand this time.

"I just don't know if I fit into religion. I've done a lot of things in my time that I'm not exactly proud of." The blush deepened.

Her insides twisted. He was considering salvation? "And I just shared with you a great example of how imperfect I am."

"But I haven't even believed. I've made fun of Christians, calling them religious nuts." He lowered his head. "You included."

She laughed. "I've been called worse, I assure you."

"Maybe so." He leaned back and used a finger to push a lock of hair from her forehead.

The gesture was . . . intimate. It made her

shiver. "Well, I think I need to head to bed. I'm exhausted." She stood, hoping her knees would support her.

Maddox stood as well, capturing her hands in his. "So . . . we know a little bit more about each other now." He smiled.

She warmed. "We do." Did the foreshadowing of a faith to come give her permission to let her emotions go? *God, what do I do here?*

His stare bore into her. Deep into her.

He dipped his head and grazed his lips against hers. Soft. Gentle. Like a baby's whispering breath. And then he rested his forehead against hers, still staring into her eyes.

Layla's heart pounded so loudly, surely he could hear it. She dared not move.

Suddenly he straightened and let her go. "Sleep well, Layla."

"Er, you too." Splinters, she sounded like a moron. Forcing her feet to obey, she stumbled down the hall to her bedroom. She pushed the door closed with a resounding click.

She flung herself across her bed and stared up at the still ceiling fan.

Lord, I'm falling fast.

THE SUN SLIPPED PAST the curtains of the front window, streaming into the living room, right into Maddox's eyes.

He flopped to his side, almost falling off the

couch. He stood and stretched, his joints creaking in protest. Why didn't they make couches long and wide enough for a man of his stature to sleep on them comfortably?

"Coffee's ready."

Maddox jumped.

Houston grinned from the doorway, holding up a travel mug. "How'd you sleep?"

"Not as good as you, I'm sure."

"I slept like a baby." Houston grinned wider. "Get a move on, buddy. We have leads to follow."

"I need a shower." Maddox ran both hands over his head.

"Hop to it, but keep it quiet. Layla's still sleeping. I checked." Houston leaned against the doorway. "How late did you keep her up?"

"Mind your own business." He grabbed his duffel and headed to the bathroom down the hall, his partner's chuckles on his heels.

Fifteen minutes and a lot of hot water later, he returned to the kitchen.

Houston leaned against the counter, waiting. "Ready?"

"Layla still asleep?"

"Haven't seen her up and about yet. Which brings me back to my original question—how late did you keep her up?"

"Shut up. Let's go." Maddox grabbed his gun and badge from the coffee table and headed out the door, making sure he turned the knob's lock.

His partner chuckled as he followed him out. "I'm driving today." He headed for the driver's side of the cruiser.

"Fine."

Houston cranked the engine and slipped the gear into reverse. "Can you call your contact at the courthouse and see if she'd be willing to go in on another Saturday to get us some information?"

Megan's image screeched across Maddox's mind. She'd been less than thrilled with their last date. She claimed he'd been too preoccupied to pay her the attention she desired. She'd been right on one count—his mind had been elsewhere. But not with the case as she'd thought. No, with Layla.

"Maddox?"

"Yeah. I can try." He whipped out his cell and dialed Megan's number.

"Hallo." No mistaking the sleep in her voice.

"Megan. It's Maddox."

"What do you want at—are you seriously calling me at eight thirty on a Saturday morning? This had better be good."

He winced at her whining tone. "I need you to go into the courthouse and look up some records for me."

"You *are* kidding. Two Saturdays in a row? I don't think so."

"Please, Megan."

"Sorry, Maddox, the payment wasn't nearly what it should've been."

He glanced at Houston, who hung on every word he said. "It's really important. A murder investigation."

"If someone's already dead, it'll wait until Monday."

"Megan . . ."

"Don't *Megan* me." She yawned directly into the phone, nearly rattling Maddox's eardrum. "Since you already woke me up, what's in it for me if I go look up whatever you need?" The lilt to her voice was the invitation.

But it was Layla's face that remained in the forefront of his mind. "Satisfaction from knowing you helped solve a murder."

"If that's the best you can do, I'm hanging up."

He sighed. "What do you want?"

Her chuckle rumbled. "That's more like it. I want a romantic dinner alone with you. Here. At my place."

Once that would've been an offer he'd jump on. But now, with Layla . . . "I'm sorry, Megan. I can't."

"Then I'm hanging up and going back to sleep."

"I'll need the name of your supervisor, as well as his phone number."

"What?"

"I'll find a judge who'll sign a warrant today. If

you won't go in, I'll have to call your boss and get him out of bed and down to the courthouse to get the records for me."

"You wouldn't. *She's* not a morning person."

"Try me. This is important."

"Fine. I'll meet you there in thirty minutes."

Maddox shut his phone and smiled at Houston. "She'd be happy to help us. She'll meet us at the courthouse in half an hour."

"Then maybe we'll get some answers."

They couldn't come fast enough for Maddox.

But he had questions of his own. Personal ones. He'd stayed awake for hours after Layla had gone to bed last night, thinking about what they'd talked about. Religion. God. Accepting the unknown. Faith.

Was it possible God was using everyone to get His point across to Maddox? How long would he put off God?

THIRTY-TWO

"Compassion will cure more sins than condemnation."
—HENRY WARD BEECHER

LAYLA ROLLED OVER AND peeked at the clock on her bedside table. 9:22. She blinked, then looked at the clock again. Was it really that late?

She jumped out of bed and thudded to the

bathroom. It'd been years since she'd slept in like that. She turned on the shower, quickly brushed her teeth, and then grabbed clothes for the day.

What would her houseguests think of her laziness?

After a quick shower, Layla dressed and made her bed. She stared at her reflection in the mirror. What did Maddox see in her? She'd asked herself that question, along with many others, as sleep eluded her last night.

God, I could really use some answers. A little direction, please?

She opened her bedroom door. The welcoming aroma of her French roast engulfed her. Her mouth watered. Bless them for having made coffee.

Passing the guest bedroom, she noticed the bed was neatly made but no one in sight. No indication someone had been in the room last night. She grinned. Houston's wife must have taught him well.

The living room was vacant as well. The linens she'd left for Maddox were neatly folded in the chair. Wonder who taught him well? The jealous thought seared her brain. Layla shook her head and moved on, not willing to let the green-eyed monster out to play.

She headed into the kitchen, her body responding to the smell of coffee filling the house. Neither Maddox nor Houston was there. She poured herself a cup of Joe and took a sip. Wonderful. Looking out the windows, she spied Maddox's Mustang but Houston's car was absent from the drive.

They left already. If only she hadn't slept in, she'd know where they were and what they were doing. They must think her terribly languid.

Maybe she could do something to help. She knew everybody in the industry and could probably get a lot more information faster.

Chinese Sheetrock. She still couldn't imagine it'd happened here in Eternal Springs. But that was the only thing that made sense. Everything added up to the Chinese Sheetrock. The smell. The corrosion. The illness.

The industry had taken preventive measures back when the news first broke. Suppliers checked their origination shipment paperwork very carefully now. Cross-checked even. Bills of lading were inspected with a fine-tooth comb. Not one incident of substandard materials had come up in their parish. Had someone gotten slack in their diligence after time passed, thinking the danger was over?

Ed Young would have a fit. Heads would roll when he found who'd let it slip through. She couldn't even imagine the implications of what he would go through. Having to go back and make sure quality materials had been used.

Knowing Ed, if he found more of the imported Sheetrock had been supplied, he'd replace it at his cost. That could really hurt his business. Maybe she could help him. She could definitely offer to contract any replacement jobs at no charge.

Layla finished her coffee and grabbed the phone. If she could get Ed looking into his paperwork, it was possible he could determine who'd messed up, when, and how much damage could possibly be done. While no one said anything, there was always the possibility of getting sued. The quicker Ed could get the details, the sooner he could act proactively.

She dialed Ed's cell phone and turned off the coffeepot as she waited. She needed to run by the office and install the new phone system that had arrived yesterday.

"Ed Young."

"Hi, Ed. It's Layla."

"Hello there, young lady. How are you?"

"Pretty good. Listen, I need to tell you some bad news."

"What?" Fear came through in his voice.

"I'm sure you know several members of my church got sick. A couple have died."

"I did hear that. I'm sorry."

"Well, the hospital brought in a CDC specialist who determined they had sulfur poisoning."

"Sulfur poisoning? That's strange."

"It gets worse." She didn't like being the bearer of bad news, but being informed was the first step.

"How's that?" His tone was cautious.

"We've linked the source of the sulfur to the church."

"Is that why it burned down last night?"

"No, the fire investigator has ruled it was arson." Because Randy had been adamant. She should probably ask Maddox about that.

"Arson?"

"Yeah. But anyway, we think what caused the sulfur poisoning in the church was Sheetrock imported from China."

"What are you saying, Layla? What's going on?"

No mistaking the pure panic in his voice. She felt so bad for him. "I'm saying someone sold you some Chinese Sheetrock. I don't know how it happened, but it's the only thing that makes sense. Don't worry, we'll figure out what's going on. Listen, you should probably start pulling your bills of lading and see what other projects you used Sheetrock on that came from the same shipment you used on the church."

His breathing became ragged, labored.

Already thinking about the damage to his reputation. Layla could understand. Totally. "I know it's a lot to grasp at one time. How can I help?"

"I really want to discuss this some more. I don't want to impose, but . . . well, I wonder if you—"

"Whatever it is, I'm happy to do." This is what it was all about—helping each other out.

"I'm at a site right now and really can't leave. I'll be taking a break soon. If it's not too much trouble, could you meet me here so we can talk?"

"You're at a site?" That was odd.

He chuckled. "Persnickety customer who won't allow just regular deliveries to be dropped off. Special orders. And I'm double-checking some of the measurements."

Ahh, that made sense. "Sure. What's the address?" She wrote it down as he told her. "I can be there in about fifteen minutes. How's that?"

"Perfect. Thanks, Layla. I really appreciate it."

"No problem, Ed. You'd do it for me. See you in a few." She hung up the phone, called her sister's hotel, but Alana had already left for the hospital. She left a brief message about the cause of the illnesses, told Alana she was praying for Cameron, then hung up.

Layla grabbed her purse and keys, then paused. What if Maddox and Houston came back? They'd have no way to get in. She grabbed the phone again and dialed Maddox's cell. His voice mail picked up on the first ring. She left him a message of where she was headed, including the address in case he needed to run by and get the keys.

She locked up the house and rushed outside. A heavy wind pushed against her, nearly knocking her into her truck. She smiled as she passed Maddox's Mustang. The memory of their kiss still warmed her.

Maybe when this case was over, they could sit down and have a longer conversation about God and faith. Who knew how God was working on Maddox, even right now?

She smiled wider. *Thank You, Father.*

"IN THE LAST SIX months, counting the fire at the church, the Hope-for-Homes house, and Second Chances, seven buildings have burned down, all with suspicious causes." Maddox handed the report they'd picked up from the fire investigator on their way in to Megan. "I need to find out who was the contractor on these."

The empty office was cold. Janitors milled outside Megan's office, an occasional chuckle or such seeped under the closed door.

Megan took the paper and typed on her computer. She hadn't taken the time to put on makeup or even put in her contacts. Maddox hadn't realized how much makeup she wore. Without it, she wasn't as attractive as he'd thought. Not like Layla, who barely wore any makeup at all. Then again, she didn't need it.

"On four of them, Taylor Construction is listed as the contractor." Megan pushed her glasses up the bridge of her nose and stared at the computer screen. "Bayou Construction was the contractor on two of the others and there isn't one listed on the last."

"So the common denominator isn't Layla." Maddox stared at Houston, smiling. Try as he might, he couldn't hide his pleasure that he'd been right about her. His heart wouldn't have steered him wrong. Not like this.

"Can you tell who the building inspector was on all six of the sites?"

"Easy." She clicked the mouse a couple of times. "Dennis LeJeune."

Maddox's adrenaline level spiked. "On all six?"

"What the computer says." Megan let out a loud sigh. "Anything else?"

Houston leaned further over Megan's desk. "Can you tell who was contracted to work on the sites? Like the electrician, plumber, carpenters . . . ?"

"That's a little harder, but I think it's listed on the permit paperwork." Her nails tapped on the keyboard.

"Commander left a voice mail for me this morning," Houston said.

"And?"

"Just wants an update. He's read our reports."

"He wants some answers."

Houston nodded. "Yeah, I think he's getting some slack from above because the Hope-for-Homes site was so publicized. Now, a church."

"Hang on, I have to go split screen." More tapping as she typed. "Okay, the electrician on four of them was Denny Keys. The other two was Simon Roach."

Maddox shook his head. "What about the plumber?" He still had a bad feeling about Bob Johnson.

Megan cut her eyes at him, then typed on the keyboard again. "Five of them used Bob Johnson. One used a Milt Anderson from . . . Arkansas?"

Houston scribbled in his notebook. "Five of the six, and the sixth used an out-of-stater?"

"What about the carpenters?" Maddox asked Megan.

Once again her fingers tapped. "Three used J. B. Carpentry. The other three used John and Sons Carpenters."

Houston nodded as he wrote. "And the supplier?"

"Just a minute." She typed, clicked the mouse, then typed again. "Y Building Supplies."

Houston poised his pen over the notebook. "On how many?"

Megan leaned back in her chair. "All of them."

THIRTY-THREE

"To love someone deeply gives you strength. Being loved by someone deeply gives you courage."
—LAO TZU

THE MIST DRIFTED DOWN, coating Eternal Springs in a wet sheen.

Layla jumped from her truck onto the mushy ground of the construction site. The new high-rise apartments. She'd put a bid on the job, but the developer had gone with another contractor. A shame . . . this was a prime gig.

"Hey, Layla. Up here."

She glanced heavenward. Ed stood on a beam and waved. "Come on up. I want to show you something. I'm sending down the car."

"Okay." It'd been a long time since she'd been on the site of such a tall building. Always gave her a rush to stand high and look down at the building being constructed from the ground up.

Ducking, she crossed what would one day be the apartment clubhouse and headed toward the makeshift elevator. The car eased to the bottom with a squeak. She lifted the guard, stepped inside, shut the guard, and selected the top as her destination. A jerk made her grab hold of the side, then a smooth ascent.

The climb to the top of the building was slow, but Layla enjoyed seeing the construction. They'd made good progress despite the weather. Looked like they'd hit their projected completion date and be ready to open in late spring.

Higher up, the mist appeared as a foggy cloud. Heavy and dense. Almost like it was sitting right over Eternal Springs. Odd, yet beautiful. Very peaceful.

Maybe that's why she'd always loved to visit the tall construction sites on a Saturday. Most were quiet. She could be alone with her thoughts. She could see out farther and appreciate God's handiwork in nature.

The car vibrated to a stop on what would one day soon be the penthouse floor. Layla lifted the guard and stepped carefully onto the walking platform. She stood still for a moment, allowing her equilibrium to set before she moved.

"Over here." Ed stood in the corner area.

Was he crazy? He was a supplier, not at all used to being on a site. Especially one that had such potential for accidents. It was dangerous for him, and he should know better.

Layla picked her steps toward him. "What are you doing? You shouldn't be up here. Especially alone."

"I had to check this. The contractor says it's not

working, but I think they installed it incorrectly. Will you come have a look?"

"Yeah." Still didn't make sense why Ed was up here all alone. The contractor should be here checking this out. Even if it was Saturday. "What is it?"

Ed leaned against an interior support beam as she approached. "Hey, did you hear I got the bid for the riverboat casinos?"

"No. Congratulations." But if word about the Chinese Sheetrock got out . . .

"I'm pretty excited."

"I bet." The wind gusted. Layla instinctively widened her stance. "What do you want me to look at?" The sooner she got Ed down, the better she'd feel.

"Just a second. I want to talk to you first."

She grabbed on to a rafter. "What's gotten into you? You're acting all weird. We can talk once we get down to the ground." Where she wouldn't worry that he'd fall to his death.

"I just want to ask you something."

She let out a sigh. Fine. Play his game, then get him to safety. "What?"

"How's Cameron?"

"Alana said last night that he was stable. The doctors in Baton Rouge have given him a pretty good prognosis." Did he really want to have this discussion up here?

"Good. That's good. I hate that he got hurt."

"Me too." She glanced in the area around Ed but could find nothing he'd need her to look at. "What's going on?"

"Why weren't he and Alana at the restaurant? They had reservations. They should've been at the restaurant."

"I don't know. I think Alana said she was really tired and needed to get—" Wait a minute . . . how did Ed know?

He smiled, but there was something off. Something different about him.

"Ed, what's going on?"

"I never meant for Cameron or Alana to get hurt." He sighed and stuck his hand in his coat pocket. "You were just supposed to stop asking questions. Stop probing." He shook his head. "You couldn't do that, could you?"

A metallic taste sat on her tongue. Shock? Betrayal? A combination of both, but it made her stomach turn. "You. Why?"

"Because, my dear, I kept using the imported Sheetrock. After the news hit and the industry beefed up the standards, the prices of Chinese Sheetrock bottomed. I could get it for a fraction of what I charged. I made a tidy profit."

He'd sold out for money? Anger churned with disgust inside her as images of friends swarmed her mind. "You made a profit, but you also killed Ms. Ethel and Mr. James. Made Pastor Chaney so sick they don't know if he'll survive.

Cameron. And that newborn baby. All dead because of you." She'd trusted him. Believed in him.

He let out a dry chuckle that rode on the wings of the wind, surrounding her until chills crept down her spine. "You don't get it, do you? I'm going straight. I cancelled all orders from the Chinese. You just couldn't keep your mouth shut for a few more weeks."

"Mr. LeJeune?" Her heart hammered.

Ed shook his head. "How do you think all the buildings with the imported Sheetrock passed inspection after the industry cracked down?"

Dennis LeJeune in on it? "But he was such a stickler for going by the book."

"Yes, but he was also nearing retirement and the parish commission's plan wasn't as much as he'd thought."

Bile clogged in the back of her throat. She just couldn't believe it all, yet now so much made sense. She needed to tell Maddox.

"I did it for my family. But don't you see—I'm on the up-and-up now."

"You're a sick man." She pivoted on the walking platform.

"Whoa. Where do you think you're going?"

"Away from you." She glanced over her shoulder.

He pulled a gun from his pocket. "I don't think so. Stay right where you are."

She faced him and froze. At this close range, even if he was a horrible shot, he'd hit her. Her blood ran colder than the wind whipping around the beams. "What are you going to do? Shoot me? Add another murder to your growing list?" Panic pushed adrenaline through her veins. Her heartbeat echoed throughout her body. Every nerve was on end.

"No. I couldn't shoot you, Layla. I've always liked you." He kept the gun pointed at her. "These high-rise construction sites . . . they sure are dangerous, aren't they?"

Oh, God, he's going to push me and make it look like an accident. Like I fell. Sweet Jesus, help me.

MADDOX LED THE WAY back to the cruiser. "Wonder where we can find Young today?" The rain had slacked to a mist. A very cold mist.

"Building supply stores are retail, man. Open on Saturday. I bet we'll find Mr. Young in his office." Houston unlocked the car and climbed behind the steering wheel. He turned over the engine and pushed the heater/defroster to high.

Slipping into the passenger's seat, Maddox clicked on his seat belt. It hung on his cell holder. He pulled out the phone to untangle the belt and noticed he had a voice mail. Man, he'd forgotten to take his phone off silent this morning.

He held down the 1 button to enter his mailbox

as Houston turned toward Y Building Supplies. The automated voice requested his passcode. He entered it, then listened as the computer informed him he had one unheard message. Maddox pushed the button to play the message as Houston hit Ryan Street.

"Maddox, this is Layla. I just wanted to let you know I'm running by a construction site to meet Ed Young. He needs my opinion on something. In case you need to get into my house, the address to the site is 220 Helena Street in Eternal Springs. It's where the new high-rise apartments are being built. Anyway, you can find me there if you need a key. Uh, bye."

No! This couldn't be happening. Not Layla.

"Turn the car around." Maddox hit the button to activate the speakerphone, then pressed the button to replay the message.

Houston's knuckles whitened as he spun the car around. He activated the single strobe light of the unmarked vehicle.

Maddox tried to call her, but it rang four times, then went to voice mail. "Layla, it's Maddox. Call me immediately. It's urgent." He hung up and redialed. The call went straight to voice mail.

His heart crawled up into his throat, blocking his breath. His whole body went tense.

Houston swerved around a car. "It'll be okay. What time did she leave that message?"

He hadn't even paid attention. He scrolled through his menu, selected the Missed Calls option, and reviewed the time stamps. Maddox glanced at the dashboard's clock display. "Twenty-five minutes ago."

Houston punched the accelerator, the cruiser gunned past a truck moving into the right lane.

This couldn't be happening. Not now. Not when he'd finally lowered his defenses and allowed a woman to sneak into his heart. She couldn't be taken from him.

Her face floated before his mind's eye. So beautiful. Peaceful. The words she'd spoken to him just last night replayed in his head. "It's always your choice, Maddox. You can question or turn from faith, or you can let God use the tragedy to strengthen your faith. It's all up to you."

Was faith really a choice? Could it make a difference?

What was that Scripture his father had quoted? *"How great is God—beyond our understanding."*

Layla believed in the Bible. She had faith. Wouldn't God protect her?

God hadn't protected his mother.

But Layla told him God was always with you. Surely He'd be with her now.

Why hadn't God been with his mother?

Maddox swallowed. Layla also mentioned something about faith being acceptance of what we couldn't control. She lived this faith. Believed it with her whole heart. So did her sister and so many others.

He closed his eyes and swallowed again. *God, if You're really there and You're the God Layla says You are, please keep her safe.*

THIRTY-FOUR

"With the new day comes new strength and new thoughts."
—ELEANOR ROOSEVELT

"I HATE THIS, LAYLA. I truly do." Ed never took the gun off of her.

"Then put the gun down and let's talk about this." Maybe she could reason with him. Get him to let her go.

He grinned, but it was far from his usual smile. "We both know there's nothing to talk about. Not anymore." He shifted, using the nearest beam for support. "You wouldn't stop. I couldn't let you figure it out."

If she was going to make it out of this alive, she'd have to think fast. *Dear God, help me. Show me what to do.*

"What about your kids, Ed? How can you do this to them?" If she kept him talking, maybe he'd be distracted enough for—what? What was she going to do? Wrestle the gun from him at five stories high? Barely moving, she took a step backward.

The mist had dissipated, but the boards were still slick. She used the heel of her boot to guide herself as she slowly reversed.

"Do to them? Don't you see? I'm doing this for them. Everything I've done is for them. And once this mess is concluded, I have the casino deals. I'll make plenty of money and can get custody of the kids. Hey, Andrea might even want me back."

He was insane! "Maddox will find out. He'll know you killed me. He won't let you get away with this." She took another slow step back.

Ed snickered. "The only one who could piece it together was you. I bet you're the one who figured out it was Chinese Sheetrock. Right?"

She stuck out her chin, refusing to let him see how terrified she was. "Yes." Despite the fear sending shooting sensations throughout her, she took another half step backward. *Lord, help me do this.*

"I knew it. Knew it'd only be a matter of time. I'd hoped what happened at Second Chances would give you something else to focus on. But no. You're like a bulldog, you know that?"

Layla took another step back. She'd moved a total of about four feet, enough to reach the next support beam. "What did you expect me to do? I thought someone was targeting us. You, Ed. I wanted to solve this to protect all of us." She inched her foot back.

He didn't notice her movements. He kept the gun trained on her but apparently didn't notice her distance. "That's why I didn't want to hurt you." He shook his head, glancing at the ground a good five stories below them.

She took two quick steps back.

His gaze came back to her face. "I never wanted to hurt you."

"Then don't." She eased her foot back. Her heel slipped on the slick board. She grabbed a support beam.

He extended his arm, the gun trembling. "Stop right there. Don't move another inch or I'll shoot." His eyes narrowed. "Did you think I didn't see you taking steps back? Do you think I'm that stupid?"

Even with her mouth burning with the distaste of fear, Layla shot her gaze around. Maybe there was a spare board handy. A hammer. Anything that could be used as a weapon. Nothing.

"Always underestimating me. Andrea. Dennis. Everybody. Even you."

"Me? How'd I underestimate you?" A loose beam maybe? She leaned against the one closest to her. Steady.

"You called me today to tell me about the Sheetrock. It never crossed your mind that I could be the one switching them out."

"That's because I believed in you, Ed. Believed you to be the man my father said you were." Was she about to see her father again?

"Your daddy was a good man, Layla. Don't you ever forget he was a good man."

"Then how can you do this? He spoke so highly of you. He'd be so disappointed with what you're doing." Maybe she could play on his sense of conscience. If he had one left. *God, show me what to do to get out of this. There has to be a way.*

Ed's face twisted into an expression she didn't even recognize. "We all gotta do what we have to. Andrea took my kids. My *kids,* Layla. I needed the money to support them. It was never supposed to be for a long time. Just enough to get me past the slow business and slump in the economy."

"But people have died, Ed." The end didn't justify the means. How could the man her father had spoken of so highly lose sight of that truth?

"I never wanted someone to get hurt. I didn't know the Sheetrock could cause people to get sick. I swear."

He really thought that excused him? "What about Dennis LeJeune? You shot and killed him."

"He made me. Gave me no choice. I was going straight, and he wanted a cut. He was gonna blackmail me."

Dennis LeJeune, a blackmailer? She would never have believed that. Then again, she never would have believed Ed was behind all these deaths. "Listen to me, Ed. It's not too late. I can talk to Maddox, get him to listen to you. If you turn yourself in, they'll go lighter on you." At least, that's what they did on television.

A lone siren wailed in the distance.

God, please help me. Please. I don't want to die. Not like this. Alana . . .

Ed snickered. "Why would I turn myself in? Don't you see? I'm going to get away with it. You're the only one who could figure it all out. Once you're out of the picture, I'm home free."

Out of the picture? Her heart jackhammered, crushing her lungs. *Dear God, help me.* "But I've told Maddox and Houston. They know what I know. Matter-of-fact, they left early this morning to get warrants before they came to you." She didn't know that, but she could pray they had figured it out.

The siren screeched closer.

How could she have been so stupid? All the facts were right there in front of her, yet she'd missed it. All because she'd chosen to believe the best about someone. How many others were fooling her?

"You're lying. You haven't told them a thing. And even if they look into me after they find you, they won't have proof. All the buildings where the imported Sheetrock was used have been destroyed. Your records are destroyed too. There's nothing to link me to the Sheetrock."

Maybe if he thought she wasn't the only one who knew, he would run instead of killing her. "I had a copy of my records at the house, Ed. I gave them to Maddox." Not exactly the truth, but she would.

If she lived through this.

"Another lie, Layla. I can tell. You were never good at masking the truth." He took a step closer, the gun still pointed at her. "I don't want to shoot you. Just step off the platform."

Layla's lungs closed off. She looked down. Five stories up, and he wanted her just to step off?

"Come on, just step off."

"I'm not stepping off. I won't kill myself."

"You either step off, or I'll shoot."

The siren sounded close. Very close.

Fear yanked false bravado to front and center. "Then shoot me. It'll be impossible to say this was an accident with a bullet in my body. They'll trace it back to you. That'll be another murder on your head." Her hands trembled as she grabbed on to a support beam.

"Don't make this hard, Layla." He took another step closer. He aimed at the elevator control panel and fired.

Tsing!

Sparks flew as the bullet made contact with the panel. A hissing noise followed.

"There's no escape, Layla. Just step off."

"You're either going to have to shoot me or push me. I'm not budging." She wrapped her arms around the beam.

Ed wouldn't shoot her—as she'd pointed out, her death needed to look like an accident. He'd try to push her. Youth and fear and a longing to live would make her stronger. Already adrenaline surged inside her, giving her courage and strength.

The gun wobbled in his hand. "Layla—"

A car roared onto the site, a single flashing light atop.

She glanced down, as did Ed. Maddox jumped from the passenger's seat, gun drawn. "Layla!"

"Up here! He's got a gun!"

Ed moved faster than she'd thought.

Pop! Pop! Pop!

A sharp pain shot across her temple. She felt herself falling. A blinding, white light flashed before her eyes. She couldn't feel the beam with her hands anymore.

Oh, Jesus . . .

MADDOX DREW, AIMED, AND fired in less than three seconds, the fluid movements second nature. "Layla!"

Ed staggered . . . wobbled, then toppled over.

His body hit several floors before crashing to the ground with a sickening thud.

Maddox holstered his gun. He'd always been a crack shot—the department's best, but that was the luckiest shot he'd ever made.

"I've called it in," Houston said.

Layla lay crumpled in a heap. All the way at the top. Maddox couldn't tell if she was even alive. "Layla!"

No response.

"Fire department and ambulance are on their way." Houston strode to where Ed Young's broken body finally rested. "They'll have the equipment to get her."

Maddox stared up, only making out a hump where Layla had once stood. "If she moves, she'll fall." All. The. Way. Down. His throat tightened, and his lungs nearly exploded. "I have to go up."

Houston shot him a stern look. "Hey, I know you think you're a superhero, but let's not kid ourselves. You don't have to do this."

As much as he wanted to let his partner go, Maddox knew he had to be the one. He had to go see Layla for himself. "I'm going." Already his gut clenched.

"You're crazy. I can't let you do this. Procedure says to wait in situations like this."

Sirens sounded, but they were still too far away. If she was unconscious and moved just a little bit, she could fall as Ed had done. Maddox wouldn't be able to live with himself if he witnessed that. "Waiting could kill her. I'm going." He marched toward the elevator shaft. No car stood at the ready. His legs felt like they were made of Jell-O.

"Maddox—"

He glared at his partner. "What would you do if it was Margie, Houston? It's Layla!" His chest would collapse any minute. "I'm falling in love with her."

Houston just stared at him, then finally nodded.

Okay. He could do this. His palms were coated with sweat as he grabbed a two-by-six above him and pulled up. Just like climbing a ladder. He could do this.

Don't look down. He concentrated on his breathing.

She was so high up. So. High. Up.

Sirens screamed closer. But not close enough.

Another pull up. Steady. Find footing. Secure.

His heart pounded. His pulse throbbed in his ears.

Grab another board over his head. Pull up. Steady. Find footing. Secure.

The wind whipped through the wall-less structure, pushing him. He held tight to the support closest to him. His pant legs popped as the cold swirled around him.

He could taste his heartbeat. Pull up. Steady.

Find footing. Secure. Grab another board. Pull up.

His tensed muscles jumped. Tensed again.

Pull up. Steady. Find footing. Secure. Grab another board.

He glanced down. Big mistake. His mouth went dry. He closed his eyes, fought to breathe normally.

The wail of the sirens drew nearer.

Maddox clenched his jaw. He could do this. For Layla.

Pull up. Steady. Find footing. Secure. Reach. The boards were wet from the mist, making his grip tenuous. His chest ached from the pounding of his heart.

A gust shoved him, a vortex around him, pulling him, tugging him, yanking. He wrapped his arms around a two-by-six and held tight. He glanced down.

The ground was so far below.

So. Far. Below.

His body trembled. His mouth felt as if he'd just bit into foil. Sweat beaded on his upper lip. He forgot to breathe.

No, he would ignore the paralyzing fear. He'd save Layla. Had to.

Maddox closed his eyes and pressed his forehead against the wood plank. *God, if You're there, I really need Your help. Not for me, but for Layla. I can't do this by myself. Please . . .*

THIRTY-FIVE

"It is difficult to know at what moment love begins; it is less difficult to know that it has begun."
—HENRY WADSWORTH LONGFELLOW

FALLING. FALLING. FALLING.

Warmth.

Layla couldn't open her eyes. Didn't really want to.

So warm.

Was she dreaming? Awake? Didn't really matter. She just didn't want to move. Didn't want the warmth to fade.

Blessed darkness surrounded her. Comforting. Warming. Soothing.

She sighed, the breath teasing past her lips.

A flutter of cold kissed her cheek.

She fought to open her eyes. The lids were so, so heavy. Couldn't muster the strength. Sank back into the weighted depth.

But it wasn't there to envelope her again. Cold and hard replaced it.

And pain.

Shooting down from her left temple, across her cheek and head. Her ear ached. A ringing hummed in her head.

She reached up and touched the ache. A knot lay under her touch. She pressed.

Splinters, but that hurt!

Her mouth was coated with metallic. She ran her tongue against the roof of her mouth, but the coppery taste remained.

Her head felt like an entire construction crew had set up residence inside. Pounding. Grinding. Grating.

She rolled to her back, only to have something press against her spine.

Something below her clanged . . . once, twice . . . then she couldn't hear it anymore.

Below her?

"Layla!"

Maddox!

She forced her eyes open and tried to move again.

"Don't move. At all."

She lay perfectly still. Blinked. Tried to get her bearings.

The metallic taste increased in her mouth as she remembered. Ed. The gun. Had she been shot?

Her eyes opened wider. She lay on the edge of the walking platform. Her leg dangled with nothing below it.

Nothing but five stories of wood, steel beams, makeshift floors, and air.

"I'm coming. Just don't move." Maddox's voice was strained.

He was coming for her! She smiled. Pain shot through the left side of her face.

Splinters! Had she been shot in the head?

She reached up and touched the tenderest area, her temple. Her fingers came back wet. Blood.

Nausea roiled her stomach. Panic seized her lungs.

Layla pinched her lips together, forcing herself to breathe through her nose. How badly was she hurt?

Ed had moved so fast, coming straight at her. She'd heard the gunshot, then . . . nothing.

Ed! Where was he? Did he still have his gun? Would he finish her off?

"I'm almost there. Hold tight." Maddox . . . reassuring. Safe. Protection.

Sirens erupted below her. Her head pounded. She groaned and covered her ear.

Oh, God, I don't want to die.

WHEN LAYLA'S KEYS HAD passed him and crashed, Maddox's heart followed. All the way to the ground.

He increased his efforts, calling out to her. Closer to her, he could see the precarious position she was in. If she rolled forward, she'd fall off the narrow board keeping her safe. He tightened his grip and climbed faster.

Pull up. Steady. Find footing. Secure. Grab another board.

Again.

"I'm coming, Layla. Just don't move."

Pull up. Steady. Find footing. Secure. Grab another board.

Breathe.

The fire department and ambulance had arrived below him. Several floors below him. Maddox refused to look down.

Pull up. Steady. Find footing. Secure. Wipe off the moisture from his palms. Grab another board.

She groaned.

Every nerve in his body almost shot out of his skin.

She shifted. Dirt trickled down, hitting him in the face. Her leg hung off the board supporting her.

"Be still, Layla. I'm almost there."

He climbed higher . . . faster. Adrenaline pushed him.

"Maddox?" Houston's voice rose up to him.

"Yeah?"

"We've got a net-thing stretched out below y'all."

But if they fell, they'd still hit some of the floors on the way down.

Maddox held still. Layla was right above him. He needed to be very careful in his approach. If he moved her the wrong way, they'd both crash to their deaths. Despite the net-thing.

He steadied himself and pulled up a final time. Layla looked up at him with wide eyes. His grip tightened.

"Can you get to the elevator?" Houston yelled.

That's right. The elevator was at the top. Here.

Maddox eased himself beside her, then let go of the board.

She was in his arms in an instant.

He held her tight against his chest. A big knot stuck out on her left temple. A trickle of blood seeped from the gash there.

But she was alive. She was going to be okay. *They* were going to be okay.

"The elevator?" Houston yelled.

"Ed shot it. Won't work." Layla's breathing came in little pants.

"Young took it out," he screamed to his partner.

A heavy silence followed, save for Layla's and his labored breathing.

"Okay, they're sending a ladder up to you now."

Maddox glanced down to the activity below them. He held tighter to Layla. So. High. Up.

The ladder jerked upward.

"You came for me." Layla's words were a whisper against his neck.

It fed his pulse. He kissed her crown. "We'll talk later about your actions. Right now, I'm just thankful you're okay."

"Ed?"

He swallowed. "Not a threat anymore."

She snuggled against him. "Now that you're here, everything's perfect."

Even though he smiled, Maddox couldn't help

but wonder how hard she had hit her head.

The ladder thudded against the edge of the building frame.

"Okay, Maddox, y'all get to the ladder and come down. Slowly."

The ladder was a good fifty yards away. And the walking platform didn't run in that direction.

Maddox's muscles seized. "Uh, I don't know that we can."

"I can." Layla shifted and grabbed the beam behind her, pulling herself upright.

His blood froze. "Don't move too much."

"I'm okay. Guess I just had the wind knocked out of me." She pulled to standing.

"A fireman is coming up to get you," Houston hollered.

"No, we'll come down." Layla yelled before Maddox could protest. She pressed the pad of her palm against her forehead. "Splinters, that hurt my head."

"Maybe we should wait for the fireman. You might be hurt worse than you think."

"I can still get myself down from a construction site, Maddox. This *is* what I do for a living, you know."

"It's not what I do," he muttered.

She offered her hand. "Come on, let's get out of here. My head's killing me and I want to get it looked at."

He took her hand and let her help him up. He

grabbed a two-by-six and held on for all he was worth. And then he looked down.

Big mistake.

Layla turned and balanced on the edge of a plank. "Just put your feet where I do. We'll reach the ladder in no time." And she took off.

His legs wouldn't budge. He couldn't even loosen his grip on the board.

"Just slow and steady. Not so hard, huh?" She glanced over her shoulder and frowned. "What's wrong?"

He hadn't moved. Couldn't.

"Maddox?"

He couldn't stop staring at the ground. So. Far. Down.

"Maddox, look at me."

He yanked his gaze to meet hers.

"What's wrong?"

"Uh, I'm afraid of heights."

"You're afraid of—Maddox, you climbed all the way up here."

"Had to. Had to make sure you were okay."

She smiled, and heat nearly suffocated him. "Then you need to follow me."

"I don't know that I can." Now she'd think he was a wimp. But he couldn't help it—his body still refused to move.

"Yes, you can." She came back to him, standing right in front of him. "You *can* do this. Just follow me."

"I-I—"

She leaned forward and pressed her lips to his. The kiss wasn't nearly as soft and gentle as before. This one was urgent, hard, strong. And sent him reeling.

Layla grabbed him and held him to her. She ended the kiss and met his stare. "You will follow me. I'll turn around, and you just concentrate on stepping where I do. Don't look down, don't look up. Just look at my back and mimic my moves. Got it?"

He opened his mouth to protest.

She gave him a quick peck. "For once, Maddy, don't argue with me. Just do as I tell you."

Maddy. Only his mother had called him that.

His body stiffened.

Before he could respond, Layla turned and began making her way to the ladder again. "Just follow me and do what I do. Grab the beams for support, step. Support. Step. Easy."

He reached for the wood and held it tight. It was steady. Strong. He took a step.

"That's right, keep coming," Layla coaxed over her shoulder. She took three more steps over open space, gently setting her foot on the narrow board. "Grab, step. Grab, step. You're doing great."

His breaths came in pants, but he concentrated on where Layla stepped. What she grabbed.

Grab. Step. Grab.

Follow Layla.

"That's good. We're almost there."

Grab. Step.

And then he was right behind her.

"Okay, now we have to pivot and step down to the ladder. Just watch what I do. Okay?"

The edge of the building felt so . . . open . . . exposed . . . high.

"Maddy, look at me. Concentrate."

He trembled, but he managed to give a nod.

"Good, just watch. It's easy." Still holding a support beam, she put her back to the open air. With her right foot, she stepped to the rung. She put her left foot beside it, then let go of the beam and held each side of the ladder. "See? It's easy."

She was literally hanging off the side of nothing—five stories high!

"Maddy? Come on. I'm right here. You won't fall."

How did she know?

"Grab the beam and turn around. You can do this."

He reached for the wood. His hands were slick with sweat and his grip didn't hold. He wobbled.

"Maddox, hold that beam!"

He gripped it again, pushing splinters into his palm.

"Good, now turn around."

Using only his toes, he pivoted. He fought for control against the tremors traveling down his legs.

"Perfect. Now, take a step back."

His feet had grown roots.

"Take a step back. I'm right here. You aren't going to fall."

He inched his foot back.

"Now stop."

He froze.

"Good. Now use your toe to feel the edge of the plank. You can look, but don't look down past your feet. Feel for the rung."

He'd never vomited on the job before, but he just might do so now.

"Feel for the ladder's rung. It's right there."

He took in a deep breath and closed his eyes. *Okay, God, You kept her alive. You got me up here. If You're real, You're gonna have to help get me down.*

"Not even two inches down. Come on, feel for it with your foot."

Maybe it was Layla's assurance. Maybe it was feeling as if his prayer had been heard. Maybe it was realizing that God wasn't a crutch for the weak. Or maybe he'd just lost his mind. At any rate, Maddox found his body responding to his commands.

He used his toe and found the rung. Stepped down. Put his other foot down. Let go of the board and grabbed the sides of the ladder.

"Excellent. Let's get out of here."

He kept his eyes closed as he descended. Layla

continued to whisper encouragements to him, but he wasn't really hearing her.

There was something else running through his mind and rewinding, over and over again. The psalm his father had quoted to him:

> "The LORD is my rock, my fortress and my deliverer; my God is my rock, in whom I take refuge. He is my shield and the horn of my salvation, my stronghold."

THIRTY-SIX

"I believe that man will not merely endure.
He will prevail. He is immortal,
not because he alone among creatures
has an inexhaustible voice, but because
he has a soul, a spirit capable of
compassion and sacrifice and endurance."
—WILLIAM FAULKNER

LAYLA WAS TRULY SICK of the hospital's emergency room. Although this time, she wasn't in the waiting room. For the first time, she was in an examining room as a patient.

She touched the bandage on her temple again. Eighteen stitches, the doctor said. Would leave minimal scarring. They'd ruled out a concussion. The nurse should be in soon with her discharge papers.

Where was Maddox? He'd ridden to the hospital with her in the ambulance, holding her hand the whole way. As soon as she'd gotten into an examining room, Houston came for him. Maddox said he'd be back, but that was so long ago.

The door opened and Houston's wife, Margie, stepped inside, clipboard and paper bag in hand. "How're you feeling?"

"Fine. Ready to go."

Margie smiled. "I've got all your paperwork ready." She waved the little brown sack. "As well as your medications."

"What kind of medication?" She didn't like taking medicine. Did her best to avoid it if at all possible.

"Just some pain killers. Trust me, honey, you'll need some later tonight." Margie handed her the sack, then went over her discharge instructions. "Do you have any questions?"

"Do you know where Maddox is?" The heat skyrocketed to her face. "I mean, I don't have a ride home or anything."

Margie grinned. "He's with Houston talking to their commander. He should be done in a few minutes."

"Okay."

"Want me to get him for you?"

"Oh, no." Her tongue felt two sizes too big for her mouth. "It's not important. I don't want to interrupt a business thing. I'm fine."

Margie smiled wider. “Why don’t you head down to the cafeteria and get yourself a big cup of coffee?” She reached into her pocket and passed Layla a five-dollar bill.

“Thank you, but I’m fine.”

“I insist. I think you need the caffeine. And I’ll tell Maddox where to find you when he finishes up with the commander.”

Layla scooted off the examining bed. “Oh, okay. That sounds good. Thank you.”

“You go right on ahead, honey. Get you some coffee and get some color back into your pretty face.”

Like the blush wasn’t enough?

Layla mumbled another thanks, then headed out of the examining area, past the emergency room waiting space, and toward the main entrance. She pushed the button at the elevator bay and waited.

What was she going to do about Maddox? There was no denying something strong pulsed between them. She could pretend it wasn’t happening, or try to figure it out.

The elevator dinged and the doors slid open.

Ms. Betty stepped out. “Hello, Layla, dear.”

“How are you?” She grabbed a quick hug as the elevator shut.

“As well as can be expected.” The elderly lady frowned as she lifted Layla’s bangs over the bandage. “What happened to you?”

"Just a little incident. I'm fine." She didn't want to go into details. Her mind was whirring already without reliving the moments. "What are you doing here?"

"I was just up visiting with Pastor. He's doing so well, now that they know what's wrong with him and how to treat it. The doctors expect to release him this afternoon."

"That's wonderful." The image of the church burning smoked across her mind. "But the church . . ."

"It's awful, dear, but God will provide for us. He always does. Matter-of-fact, church services will be held at the high school tomorrow morning. Same time as normal. That principal, he's such a wonderful man." She laid her hand over Layla's. "You will attend, won't you, dear? We'll be having a special prayer for Cameron."

"I'll be there."

"Well, then, I'll see you tomorrow." Ms. Betty gave a final hug, then shuffled off toward the doors.

Layla pressed the button and waited for the elevator again. But this time, she said silent prayers of thanksgiving for God's provision. And protection.

"HOUSTON, HOW DID YOU know Margie was *the one?*" Maddox led the way down the corridor to the elevators.

His partner stopped in his tracks. “What?”

He hadn’t really meant to ask the question. He’d been thinking it and it just slipped out. Too late to retract it now. “I asked how you knew Margie was the one for you. Back when y’all were dating.”

Houston chuckled. “This about Layla?”

“Never mind. I shouldn’t have asked.” Maddox punched the button with more force than necessary.

The elevator doors opened. They stepped inside, and the doors shut, pitching the two of them into silence.

“I knew because she made it worth it to get up in the morning, just to see her smile. I could see myself having kids with her, growing old and enjoying grandchildren with her.” Houston stared at the floor of the car. “She made me a better person. Still does.”

Maddox could understand. Layla was the first thing that entered his mind when he woke up and the image that haunted his dreams. She made him want to be great. “How long after meeting her did you know? Did it take weeks or months?”

Houston lifted his head and met Maddox’s eyes. “I suppose it’s different for everybody, but with me and Margie, I knew the first day I met her that there was something special about her.” He grinned. “I was a little on the hardheaded side back then, so I didn't recognize the way I felt for a couple of weeks."

"*Was* hardheaded?" Maddox grinned.

"Hey, Margie wasn't as sweet back then either. She was quite the spunky lady."

The elevator stopped on the bottom floor, and they headed to the emergency room.

"Margie's always kept you on your toes."

"Shoulda seen her before we got married. Partner, that woman nearly drove me insane. She could be downright difficult."

"Because you're so easygoing, right?"

"But of course." Houston grinned as he approached the nurses' station.

Margie snuck up behind him and planted a kiss on the back of his neck.

Houston's face reddened, but he gave her a quick peck on her cheek. "Hi, honey. How's it going?"

"Pretty good." She smiled at Maddox. "We discharged Layla, so I sent her to the cafeteria to get some coffee. Poor thing looked like she needed a jolt of caffeine."

"So, she's okay?" Maddox's heart beat a little faster.

"Got about eighteen stitches. No concussion. She's fine."

"Did she mention Ed Young?" She'd yet to talk about what happened before they arrived on scene.

Margie frowned. "No. And that's got me a little

worried. Most victims of such a traumatic event rattle on and on about what happened. How scared they were. How they thought they were gonna die. But not Layla." Margie shook her head. "She didn't mention it at all."

"Is there any chance she's forgotten because of the knot on her head? We assume Young hit her with the gun when we arrived, but it was so high up, we can't be sure."

"I don't think she's forgotten anything, Maddox. I think she remembers all too well."

"Thanks, Margie. I'm glad you were here to be with her."

Margie grinned wide. "You've got a sweet spot for her, don't you?"

His face heated.

Margie laughed. "Oh, my. I never thought I'd see the day when Maddox Bishop fell head over heels."

Houston joined in.

"So glad I could give you both such entertainment." His face felt as hot as an ember.

"But Layla Taylor's quite the handful, Maddox." Margie sobered. "She's the type that'll keep you in line. Just what you need."

"Thanks." He nodded to Houston.

His partner gave his wife a quick kiss, then followed Maddox to the cafeteria.

"Margie's right, you know," Houston said from behind him.

“About what?” Maddox slowed enough for his partner to fall into step beside him.

“You and Layla. Y’all make a good pair.”

Maddox couldn’t stop the grin. He thought so too. Now if he could just convince Layla. “Cats and dogs, right, partner?”

LAYLA SAT ALONE IN the hospital cafeteria, sipping the strong coffee. People milled around her, their voices lifting into a cadence that penetrated her drug-induced fuzziness, but she ignored them. Ignored everything but what kept flipping about in her own mind.

She could have died today.

Ed was prepared to kill her. No, he was determined. And had it not been for Maddox and Houston showing up when they did, he probably would’ve succeeded.

Having such a close call really put things into perspective.

Like her family. She desperately wanted to hear Alana’s voice. Tell her that she loved her. But Layla didn’t have her cell phone anymore, so it would have to wait until she got home. And Layla had been praying earnestly for Cameron. His recovery would be a long haul for her sister, but Alana was up to it. She loved her fiancé deeply, and they’d overcome this.

And Layla’s job. She loved being a contractor. Loved building and remodeling. But she’d let her job become a high priority. She didn't spend enough time away from construction. She didn't enjoy life fully. Not like Jesus wanted. He paid a high price for her life—she should be doing more to enjoy it.

Which brought her to Maddox. After Randy, she'd built a wall around her heart, determined never to let anyone close enough again to hurt her that way. But Maddox . . . well, he'd chipped away at that wall until her heart stood ready for the picking. His picking.

But he wasn't a Christian, and that was the biggest obstacle. After the disaster with Randy, Layla had spent a lot of time in prayer, searching God's Word for direction. And the wisdom revealed to her was that she shouldn't even date someone who didn't share her faith.

So, how could she even contemplate a future with Maddox?

"Hi, there. Are these seats taken?" From out of her mind, Maddox stood before her.

She smiled at him and Houston. "Of course not. Sit down."

They did, their chairs grating against the tile floor. She tried not to shudder as the sound rattled against her sore head.

"How're you feeling?" Maddox laid his hand over hers.

Warmth spread throughout her body. *God, if I can't fall in love with him, why do I feel this way around him? Is this a test? Am I supposed to resist the temptations of my own heart?*

"My head aches a little, but the doctors say I'm fine."

"Our commander would really like to get your statement today." Maddox kept his voice low, which she greatly appreciated.

"Okay."

"If you aren't up to it, we can put him off until Monday."

Houston's kindness made her smile. "No, that's fine. I'd rather get it over with." She let out a little sigh. "So, can we do it here? Now?"

Maddox squeezed her hand. "Because I shot the suspect, we can't take your statement. We need you to give it to another detective. Down at the station."

Splinters, why not? "Okay." She stood.

Maddox and Houston stood as well. Maddox put his hand under her elbow. "Are you sure you're okay?"

"Tired now. I'll be fine."

Houston moved to her other side. "It shouldn't take long to give your statement, then we'll take you home so you can get some rest."

"And I can pick up my car," Maddox added.

Rest. Yes, she needed that something awful. And then she needed to spend some serious time in prayer.

To decide what to do about Maddox.

THIRTY-SEVEN

"Faith is taking the first step even when you don't see the whole staircase."
—DR. MARTIN LUTHER KING JR.

LEAVING WAS HARDER THAN he thought.

Maddox tightened his grip on the handle of his duffel and stood in Layla's foyer. She'd given her statement, Houston had left, and he knew Layla needed sleep. But somehow, the thought of leaving her left a void in his chest.

He hadn't been able to sit in with her as she gave her statement, but he'd read it later. She hadn't talked with Houston and him on the way home about Young and what had happened. She must really be hurting inside.

"Thanks again. For everything." Her eyes were heavy, as if gravity pulled them to a close.

As much as he wanted to stay, he had to leave. For her. For him.

He leaned over and planted a soft kiss on her forehead. "Call me if you need anything."

She smiled, but fatigue tugged at her facial features. "I will."

He gave her another kiss, this one on the cheek, then opened the front door. It took every ounce of his being to walk down the steps and get into his Mustang. His emotions fought to stay, but his mind made him start the engine and back out of her drive.

Layla gave a little wave, then shut the door.

He should probably go home and get some rest too, but his mind and emotions were too tightly wound. He needed something more. To talk. To get a grasp of what was happening to him. To get some semblance of peace.

Somewhere in the midst of it all, he realized he'd fallen for Layla Taylor. Even more, he realized that he loved being an in-the-action type of guy. Suddenly it didn't matter that he wouldn't get promoted anytime soon. Now that things were the way they were between Pop and him . . .

Without really considering where he was going, Maddox found himself heading to his father's house. Since their talk, Maddox burned to get to know his father better and really forge a relationship. That Pop had let go of all his bitterness about Mom's murder . . . well, the changes in him were amazing, and Maddox couldn't help but wonder if Layla was right—Christianity and faith were the reason.

After all, God seemed to answer when he'd prayed during his climb to get Layla.

He pulled into Pop's driveway, his mood already lighter. He tightened his jacket as he climbed up the stairs.

Pop opened the door before he could knock. "Hey, son."

"Hi, Pop."

"Come on in. I have coffee ready."

Maddox stepped into the house. He hung his jacket on the peg, then followed his father into the kitchen. While Pop poured him a cup of coffee, Maddox took a moment to notice his father's home.

After Mom had died, Pop sold the house and bought this one. He said they didn't need the memories. Maddox only lived there for a few months before he left home. He'd been so wrapped up in his own anger and guilt that he hadn't paid attention to the details of the house.

But now that he looked at the cheery yellow kitchen, he could see how Pop mimicked the décor of their house with Mom. Even the way the canisters were set out on the counter was Mom's way.

Maddox swallowed and took the cup from Pop. How horrible it must've been for his father—to leave the home he'd shared with the love of his life, only to not realize he'd copied so much.

"What's on your mind?" Pop leaned over the counter, studying Maddox.

"Hey, can't a son come by and visit his father?"

"Of course." Pop took a sip of coffee, still peering at Maddox over the rim. "But this isn't one of these times."

"No, I guess not." Maddox leaned on the opposite side of the counter.

"Well, are you gonna make me pry it out of you?"

Maddox grinned. "It'd probably be easier for me if you did."

Pop set down his cup. "Then it must be about a woman."

"How'd you know?"

"There are very few things a man doesn't willingly want to talk about. A woman's the main one." Pop chuckled.

"They are a touchy subject." Maddox took a sip of his coffee. Strong and black, the way Pop always drank his. Maddox welcomed its briskness.

Pop ran his finger around the lip of his mug. Not prying. Not asking. Letting Maddox gather his thoughts.

"We've never really talked about you and Mom, before I was born, I mean."

Pop smiled. "Ah, how I fell in love with her. Or rather, how she fell in love with someone like me."

"No, not that at all. Just wondering how you knew. How you knew she was the one for you."

"I first met Abigail in the spring. I was new to Louisiana, Dad having just transferred to the state. Starting a new school midyear wasn't fun, but my first day I saw Abigail. She was beautiful. Took my breath away." Pop's eyes took on a misty, faraway appearance.

"She was a senior, same as me, and I saw her that first time in the courtyard during lunch. Man, that woman's smile could bring a man to his knees something quick."

Maddox smiled.

Pop looked at him. "You have her smile, you know."

His knees weakened. He slipped into the bar stool next to the counter.

"Anyway, there she was with George, laughing and sharing a piece of cake."

"Wait a minute—Uncle George?"

"Yeah." Pop grinned. "Didn't realize we'd been friends so long, did you?"

"I always assumed you and Uncle George were friends, not Mom and him."

"Oh, they were more than friends. They dated. Nothing serious, they both assured me later, but they were going out that first day I saw her."

"Wow. What happened?"

Pop took another sip of coffee. "Well, I caught her eye from across the courtyard. I was a goner as soon as she turned those baby blues on me." He smiled again. "You have her eyes too."

He knew that. Had always been proud of his eyes. His mother's eyes.

"The way she told it, she knew the moment she saw me that I was trouble, but she couldn't resist." Pop chuckled. "I think it was the other way around."

Now Maddox laughed. “Mom? Trouble?”

“Son, you have no idea. Your mother was quite the independent woman. Wasn’t gonna take any suggestions from any man, much less an order.” Pop ran a hand down his face, grinning as he waded through memories. “She’d light into me if I so much as told her what movie I wanted to go see.”

“Not Mom.”

“Oh, yeah. She’d tell me where I was taking her for dinner, what movie we were gonna see, and where we were gonna go park.” Pop shook his head. “That woman knew her own mind, that’s for sure.”

He’d never seen that side of Mom.

“So that first day, after I looked at her and could tell she was interested, I marched right across the courtyard, introduced myself, and asked her out right on the spot.”

“What happened?”

“She smiled, nearly knocking me over, turned, and told George she was going out with me, then accepted.” Pop lifted his cup. “We were inseparable from that moment on.”

“What about Uncle George?”

“I think he knew me and Abigail were meant to be together. Everyone said it was obvious. He and I became best friends, and Abigail couldn’t have been happier. We were the Three Musketeers, you know.”

Maddox thought of Layla. "So, it was basically love at first sight for you and Mom?"

"No, more like infatuated at first sight. Love comes later." Pop set down his cup and stared at him. Hard. "She turned me inside out from the get-go, don't get me wrong, but love is something that grows over time. Deepens as you experience life together."

He could see himself with Layla. Building a life together. Having a family. Growing old together.

"If you think you've met the woman who will love you for the rest of your life, don't wait. Don't put off until later what needs to be done today." Moisture glistened in Pop's eyes. "We both know how precious life is. Don't waste a minute of it."

His insides tightened. "Pop, she's a really strong Christian. I know you're a new one and all . . ."

"If her faith is real, then she'll be looking for a man who'll share her faith with her." Pop stared at him with the focus of a sniper. "Is that man honestly you?"

His tongue expanded. "I-I think so."

"Son, accepting the free gift of salvation isn't something you think. You either do or you don't. God doesn't want you halfway." He pointed at Maddox, brows lowered almost into a straight line. "And you don't claim salvation just to get a woman. Salvation's between you and God."

And that's what he needed to make sure of. That if he chose to follow God, it was for him, not for Layla. He thought of the peace he'd seen in his father . . . the kindness and acceptance of Mrs. Page . . . the strength in disaster of Alana and Layla—all things he wanted. He'd gotten a glimpse of mercy and strength when he'd begged God to help him.

"Let me loan you my Bible and make a couple of suggestions of Scriptures to read. They're ones that helped me." His father left the room.

Maddox followed Pop into the living room. His father lifted his Bible and handed it to him. "If you're serious about salvation, you should read what is called the Roman Road to Salvation."

Maddox took the Bible from his father and ran his hand over the leather cover. "The what?"

"The Roman Road to Salvation. It lays out why and how to become saved. Romans 3:23 explains how we're all sinners. Romans 5:8 tells you how Christ died for all of us. Romans 6:23 explains how we can all have eternal life through Christ. And Romans 10:9–13 shows how we are saved through our belief in Jesus Christ." Pop grinned. "Don't worry, you don't have to remember them all. There's a bookmarker in the book of Romans that has it listed, and all those Scriptures are highlighted in my Bible."

Maddox held the Bible against his chest, not

even able to explain the myriad emotions swirling inside of him. “Thanks, Pop.”

His father pulled him into a hug. He could feel Pop trembling. Pop kissed his cheek and let him go with a clap on the back. “I’ll be praying for you, son. Call me if you have any questions while you’re reading.”

No way could any words get past the lump in his throat. He nodded, then ducked out of the house. He held the Bible tight as he tromped back to the Mustang.

His heart bammed so hard, and he didn’t know why. What he did know was that he was going home to read.

And see if God spoke to him through his father’s Bible.

THIRTY-EIGHT

“No man is excluded from calling upon God, the gate of salvation is set open unto all men: neither is there any other thing which keepeth us back from entering in, save only our own unbelief.”

—JOHN CALVIN

“THAT’S WONDERFUL ABOUT CAMERON, Alana. I’ll let everyone at church know this morning.” Layla dug in her closet for her black flats. Hadn’t she worn them last Sunday?

"I talked to Fred yesterday. They've got all the residents situated. He said you'd sent a crew over yesterday to start cleanup. Thanks."

"No problem. Once it's cleaned, I can get in to see where we stand for rebuilding." Had she stuffed the shoes under her bed again? Wedging the phone between her chin and shoulder, Layla dropped on a knee and reached for the bed skirt.

"I'll head back home sometime this week. Once Cameron's moved out of the burn unit's ICU." Alana sounded more hopeful than even the last time they'd spoken.

Yes! One shoe found. "Don't rush. We'll handle everything here that needs attention." The other shoe was farther under the bed. Layla lay on her stomach and stretched. "Oh, and I'm visiting Mom this afternoon after church. I'll give her your love."

Sniffles sounded over the connection. "You and Mom . . . it's such an answer to my prayers."

Layla sat and slipped on her flats. "I know. And thank you for being understanding all these years."

"Wasn't easy, I'll tell you that." Alana snickered.

"Yeah, I guess not." Layla grinned as she stood. "Mr. James's funeral is going to be Thursday, Ms. Betty said, and Ms. Ethel's grandson left a voice message yesterday. Ms. Ethel's funeral will be Wednesday evening."

"I'll definitely be back to attend those." Alana coughed into the phone. "So, are you going to give me the scoop on you and Detective Bishop?"

The blood rushed to her face. Layla sat on the edge of her bed. "Maddy? There's not really anything to tell."

"Really? You go from Detective Bishop to Maddox and now to Maddy? And there's nothing to tell? Come on."

Layla smiled into the phone. "I'm working it out."

"Come on, Layla. I'm your sister. Who else are you gonna tell your deep, dark secrets to?"

"I have feelings for him—strong ones, but it's complicated."

"What, he doesn't have feelings for you? Get serious. I've seen the way the man looks at you. Well, when he isn't furious with you." Alana giggled.

"He's not a Christian."

"Oh." Alana sobered. "Well, I'll be praying."

"Thanks." She worried her bottom lip. "Alana, do you think it's selfish for me to want his salvation so I can let myself fall in love with him?"

"Yes. But that doesn't mean it's wrong. I think it's totally understandable."

"How do you think God sees it?"

There was a pause. "You know what, Layla? I

think God sometimes puts people in our paths to help us get a message from Him."

Layla frowned. "So, you think all of this was God's doing so Maddox would become a believer? I find that hard to believe."

"Who's to say? I mean, really. We know we can't understand God's ways. Maybe it was all His master plan. Maybe not, but we know He'll take what was meant for evil and turn it to the good."

That made more sense. Layla smiled. "Thanks, sis." She checked the time. "Now I gotta get or I'll be late for church."

"Give everyone my love."

Layla turned off the cordless, returned it to its base, and grabbed her purse. She stepped onto her porch and lifted her face heavenward. The sun shone brightly, warming Eternal Springs. Even the breeze was gentle, reassuring. The calm after the storm.

She climbed into her truck—not an easy feat in a dress—and drove toward the high school. She planned to check out the church's damage next week. God willing, it wouldn't be too bad.

Layla parked in one of the larger spaces in the school's lot, then made her way to the auditorium. Friends and church family members waved and hollered out greetings. Most inquired about Cameron, and she was thrilled to tell everyone of his recovery progress.

She took a seat next to Ms. Betty as the worship band began playing from the stage. They had plenty of room to set up all their instruments. Nice. Maybe when she rebuilt the sanctuary, she could work in a permanent stage.

Pastor Chaney took center stage. Applause erupted as the congregation stood.

Layla got chill-bumps.

The choir lifted their voices in the first stanza of "Amazing Grace." Layla got all warm inside as she sang the hymn that was like a balm to her spirit. As the last note carried across the room, tears filled her eyes.

Thank You, God, for sending Jesus to save us all. Your grace is amazing.

Pastor read passages of Scripture, his voice booming from the stage. Layla shared her Bible with Ms. Betty, reading together from the book of Romans, one of Layla's favorite books of the New Testament.

"But what does it say? 'The word is near you; it is in your mouth and in your heart,' that is, the word of faith we are proclaiming: That if you confess with your mouth, 'Jesus is Lord,' and believe in your heart that God raised him from the dead, you will be saved. For it is with your heart that you believe and are justified, and it is with your mouth that you confess and are saved."

The Scripture stayed in Layla's mind as Pastor

preached a sermon, led a special prayer for Cameron, and the choir led two more songs. After the benediction and final prayer, Layla led Ms. Betty out into the aisle. She couldn't wait to tell Pastor how much she'd enjoyed the service today.

The walkway to the exit was crowded as members of Eternal Springs Christian Church took their time talking to Pastor on their way out. Everyone was so pleased he'd made such a recovery.

Layla followed the crowd, but her mind was still on the Scripture. *Jesus is Lord.* She smiled as the line inched forward. Yes, He was indeed. Her heart truly believed that.

"Thank you for joining us. Your father tells me you have some questions about faith. Perhaps we could meet tomorrow and talk?" Pastor Chaney spoke to someone two places in front of Layla and Ms. Betty.

"I'd like that."

Her heart stuttered. *Maddox!*

Layla stood on tiptoe and leaned to see around the people in front of her. Sure enough, she caught the back of Maddox's head, standing alongside his father. He wanted to meet with Pastor? Her lungs nearly exploded as her insides turned to mush.

"Here's my card, son. Call me tonight, and we'll set up a place and time to meet."

"Thank you. And I really enjoyed the service today." Maddox's voice was clear and strong.

And laced with emotion.

Her own voice caught as the line moved forward and she stood before Pastor.

"I guess we have some rebuilding to do again, Layla."

She smiled and nodded, still not finding her voice.

"I'll call you later this week."

"Okay," she managed to squeak out before she moved out of the auditorium.

The sun's bright beams nearly blinded her. She blinked to focus, determined to find Maddox before he left. She rushed down the stairs.

She needn't have worried. Maddox stood off the sidewalk with his father, obviously waiting. "Layla."

Just the way he said her name made her melt. "Hi, Maddox." She affixed a smile that she hoped wasn't too bright. "Hello, Mr. Bishop. Nice to see you again."

"You too, Ms. Taylor."

"How're you feeling?"

Maddox's father smiled. "Right as rain."

She looked back at Maddox. "Fancy meeting you here."

He turned red. "I'm hoping it'll be a common occurrence."

Her breath hitched. "Really?"

He smiled, and its brightness competed with the sun's rays. "Really. Listen, Pop and I put on a venison roast this morning. We'd really like it if you'd join us. If you don't have plans, that is." Maddox ducked his head and toed a loose rock off the sidewalk.

Electricity zapped through her. "I'd like that." She met his stare as he lifted his head. "Very much."

STILL NO SIGN OF her.

"Stop staring out the window. She'll get here. A watched pot never boils." Pop opened the oven and stuck the pan of yeast rolls inside. "Get some glasses out for the tea."

Maddox moved away from the window and grabbed glasses from Pop's cabinet. One nearly slipped but he recovered. It wobbled.

"Boy, this girl must be the one because she's sure got you all tied up in knots."

A diesel engine sounded in the driveway before Maddox could respond. He rushed to the front door and opened it.

Layla hopped from her truck. She wore jeans and a button-down denim shirt. Her hair had the same flyaway appeal as it had this morning in church.

She'd never looked so good.

Once inside, they sat down to eat. Pop blessed the food, and for the first time, Maddox really paid attention. He looked forward to his talk with Pastor Chaney. Pop had told him to write down questions he had, and Pastor would be happy to help him find the answers.

After lunch Layla insisted on doing the dishes. Maddox helped, because just being around her made him happy. More than he'd ever thought possible.

"I'll be right back," Pop announced, leaving them alone in the kitchen.

"So," Layla handed him a sudsy plate to rinse, "I couldn't help but overhear you're meeting with Pastor tomorrow."

"Yeah. I'm pretty excited."

She handed him a glass. "What did you think of the service this morning?"

"Kinda funny that it was about the part of the Bible Pop had me read last night."

Layla wore that shy smile that nearly slammed his heart into his spine. "That's not funny, that's God."

Her saying that didn't bother him in the least. Matter-of-fact, it made him smile.

She pulled her hands from the soapy water. A bubble drifted up and landed on the tip of her nose. "I think that's all of the dishes." She looked so cute and happy. It felt so right that she be here with him, doing domestic things.

Maddox couldn't resist. He grabbed her by the waist, spun her to face him, and kissed her.

Soundly. Thoroughly. With all the emotion bottled inside of him.

"Excuse me." Pop's voice echoed through the kitchen.

Layla jumped away from him, her face brighter red than Houston's Hawaiian-print shirt.

"I, uh, have something for you, Maddox." Pop held a cardboard box.

"What?" He slipped his arm around Layla's waist again.

"Come on into the living room. Both of you." Pop turned and strolled out.

Maddox pulled Layla to him quickly and planted another kiss on her lips.

She kissed him back, then shoved him away. "Behave. Your father's waiting." She led the way into the living room.

Pop sat in his recliner, the box on the coffee table.

Maddox sat on the couch closest to his father while Layla sat beside him. "What's this?" He motioned to the box.

"Some of your mother's things. I thought you should have them."

He sat still for a moment, waiting for the anger and resentment to rise up. It didn't. He smiled at his father and reached for the box. "What's in here?"

"Some of her pictures. Mementos." Pop shook his head. "Some stuff she had in a box that I never went through."

Maddox opened the box and pulled out a picture of his parents, along with George. "How old were y'all here?" He handed the photo to his father.

"That was taken before our senior party." Pop grinned. "Good times." He handed the picture to Layla. "See what a handsome devil I was back in the day?"

She smiled at Pop. "Back in the day? You're still a handsome man."

His father laughed and slapped Maddox on the back. "Ah, this one's a charmer. But smart. Better keep her."

With a warm glow burning in his gut, Maddox nodded at his father but kept his gaze on Layla's blushing face. "Oh, I intend to."

THIRTY-NINE

"He that cannot forgive others breaks the bridge over which he must pass himself; for every man has need to be forgiven."
—THOMAS FULLER

IT HAD BEEN AS near a perfect day as could be.

Maddox leaned back on his couch, smiling to himself. Being with Layla at Pop's, he'd felt . . . complete. Like everything in his life was finally coming together and making sense.

The case was solved, making his commander

happy. Another notch in Houston's and his work-performance record.

Layla was safe, and they had a date tomorrow night. He didn't know where the future would take them, but he'd do his best to make sure wherever it went, they'd go together.

He'd talk with the pastor tomorrow. He'd reread the Scripture his father had shown him, and it resonated inside of him. Made him feel more hopeful than he ever had before.

And Pop. For the first time ever Maddox really felt like he could love his father freely, and that love was returned.

Maddox sighed. He spied the box sitting on the floor. He lifted it and pushed aside the weakened panels.

More pictures. Mom. Mom and Pop. Mom, Pop, and George. Mom holding a baby—him. She looked so happy. So alive.

He set down the pictures and pulled out a mini-album. The first page was her senior picture, with her swirly handwriting documenting important events. Several pages included familiar shots. Then a photo of her hugely pregnant. And her hopes for her baby written around the picture. Maddox's eyes filled with tears. He closed the album and set it on the coffee table.

The next item in the box was a stack of letters. He checked the address and return address. All the letters she and Pop had exchanged when he was away with the military. They were tied up in a red bow. With tightness in his stomach, Maddox set those beside the mini-album. It'd be too much a violation of Pop's and her privacy to read their personal letters.

Only one item remained in the box—a leather book. He took it out and held it, the pages were yellowed with age. Maddox flipped to the front page and scanned his mother's delicate handwriting.

It was her journal.

He started to put it back into the box, but something made him stop. He flipped to a random page and read.

> *Maddy is getting so big. So much like Tyson. The two men of my heart. What would my life be without them? And George too.*

He skipped several pages and scanned again.

> *Tyson is off again—I can never know exactly where. Now that he's in high school, Maddy needs his father. Thank goodness George is around. I'm a little concerned about him, though. I thought I smelled liquor on his breath last night when he came by to fix the leaky sink. I'm worried about him.*

Maddox waited for the bitterness to show its ugly head. Nothing. He smiled. Maybe he had been healed of the wounds of the past. He skipped ahead in the journal.

I cannot believe George! How dare he tell me he loves me? He knows my heart belongs to Tyson. He's ruined our friendship with his declaration. I wish Tyson were home.

What? Maddox sat upright on the couch, holding the journal in his trembling hands. Uncle George had loved Mom?

Pop had said George and Mom had dated. George had told him that he'd loved a woman and lost her.

Maddox's stomach turned. Had George been talking about Mom?

He turned the page, not skipping any.

George called today and asked if he could come by. I refused. He called tonight to apologize and asked if he could come by tomorrow night and explain. Tyson gets home next week, and I'd hate for their friendship to be awkward. I told George I'd see him tomorrow night at eight. Maddy has a date, so George and I can talk freely.

The next entry:

> *I had to kick George out of the house. He's still outside screaming. He told me he'd always loved me, that Tyson wasn't good enough for me, and that he'd be a better father to Maddy. He tried to kiss me! I could smell and taste the alcohol on him. He was drunk. He tried to do more, but I grabbed Maddy's baseball bat and hit him in the gut. He's screaming that if he can't have me, no one should. I don't know what to do. I wish Tyson were here. Should I call the police? Maddy will be home any minute now. George is scaring me. I should call the police.*

Maddox couldn't breathe. Couldn't think. His hands trembled as he turned the page.

Nothing.

The next page. Nothing.

The entire rest of the journal was empty.

Maddox went back to the last entry.

It was dated the day his mother had been murdered.

"ARE YOU SURE YOU want to play it this way?" Houston shot him a look that screamed his concern.

Maddox nodded. “It’s the only way. I owe it to her to find out the truth.”

“Your call.” Houston opened the door to Maddox’s spare bedroom. “I’ll be listening for the code.”

“Thanks, partner.” Maddox went back to the living room and paced.

Pop and George would be here any minute. He’d get one chance at this. One opportunity to learn the truth.

His only regret would be hurting Pop. He’d spent the better part of the night tossing and turning, going over his options. No matter what he did, Pop would get hurt. But this way, maybe, just maybe, Pop would get some closure. The truth would set them all free.

Layla had left not even half an hour ago. She had begged him to go another route or let Houston follow up. He’d declined, knowing he had to be the one to do this. Had to finish it once and for all. In the end, she’d prayed for him and his father. Was it those prayers that kept his nerves at bay?

A car door slammed. Then another one.

Maddox let out a slow breath. He lowered his head to his top button. “They’re here.”

A sharp rap on the door.

He crossed the room and opened the door. “Hey, guys.” He grabbed his father into a hug, then moved aside to let George and Pop enter. “Come in and sit down.”

"What's this big news you have for us?" Pop sat on the couch.

George sat in the chair. "Yeah, what's the news? Is it about Layla?"

"Or your meeting with Pastor?" Pop's eyes were bright with hope.

Maddox smiled down at his father. "I'll get to that in a minute."

"So it *is* about Layla." George slapped his knee. "Well, boy, don't keep us waiting."

"It is about love."

"I knew it." Pop grinned wide.

"You two getting hitched?"

"Actually, George, it's about Mom." Maddox planted his feet, holding his stance.

"Your mother?" Pop's brows bunched.

"About that box of her things you gave me yesterday. I went through them last night." He cut his eyes to George.

The man had the nerve to look as confused as Pop. "I don't understand."

"Me either," Pop said.

"Pop, you said there were things in there you never went through after Mom died."

"Right. Some of it . . . well, I just couldn't."

"I understand." Maddox hated seeing the pain on his father's face. Hated the pain he was about to inflict. But he had to know. Pop had to know. "One of the things in there was Mom's journal."

George's head jerked up. "Abigail kept a journal?"

"Yes, she did. And she wrote daily. Details." Maddox narrowed his eyes at the man he'd once loved more than his own father. "Explicit details."

Befuddlement marched across Pop's face. "I don't understand."

Maddox glared at George. "I'm sure you don't, Pop, but I think George knows what I'm talking about. Don't you?"

Pop looked at his friend. "George?"

"I don't know what you mean, son." But George's expression clearly said otherwise.

"I think you do. And don't call me *son*."

"Maddox, what are you talking about?" Pop's voice rose.

"Why don't we ask George?" Maddox let his full anger display in his scowl at George. "Why don't you tell us about the day before Mom died? The day you told her that you loved her."

Pop gasped. "What?" He turned to face George.

"It was a mistake. That's back when I was drinking. I don't even remember." George shifted in his seat, fidgeting.

"You did come back to apologize. The next day. The day she was murdered. You were drunk. You tried to force yourself on her."

"I did not!"

"George!" Pop stood.

Maddox laid a hand on his father's shoulder but glared at George. "Yes, you did. It's all in her journal. How you told her that if you couldn't have her, no one could." He swallowed the mix of anger and bile in the back of his throat.

George shot to his feet. "That's a lie."

Maddox pulled the journal from his back pocket. "It's all right here. You can't deny it. She ran you off with my baseball bat."

Pop looked shocked beyond belief. "How could you?"

"You took her from me to begin with. I had to sit back and watch her fall in love with you. Watch the woman I loved fall for another man." George spoke so fast spittle shot from his mouth. "And then you knocked her up and left her to further your career. She needed a man around. I had to step in for you. All those years, I was here for her when you weren't. She owed me."

"Owed you?" Pop tried to stand again, but Maddox kept his grip firm on his father's shoulder.

"So what, you killed her? She wrote that she was about to call the police because you were in a drunken rage outside."

George's face turned whiter than white as he collapsed back onto the chair. "I didn't mean to,

I swear." His eyes filled with tears. "I never meant to hurt Abigail. I loved her. She just said the most awful things." He hung his head. "I was drunk and didn't realize what I was doing."

"You killed Abigail?" Pop trembled under Maddox's touch.

"She wouldn't answer the door. Yelled that she was calling the cops. I don't know . . . I went to the back door, and the next thing I knew, I was inside. She was crying, backing up against the kitchen counter."

Maddox kept his body rigid. Still. Fought to control his own rage.

"She grabbed a knife from the drawer, held it up at me." Tears ran down George's face. "I don't remember what happened. Honestly, I don't. She ran to the bedroom for the phone. I followed. Somehow, I had the knife. She fell and . . . I don't know." George held his head in his hands.

"You murdered my wife." Pop shoved Maddox's hand aside.

Maddox wrapped an arm around his father's waist. "Houston, we have a problem."

His partner flew into the living room, gun drawn. He pulled cuffs from his belt. "George Vella, you're under arrest for the murder of Abigail Bishop. Turn around."

Pop turned and fell into Maddox's arms as Houston cuffed George and read him his Miranda rights.

Maddox held his father tight, crying along with him. “At least we know,” he whispered into his father’s neck. “At last, we know.”

Now Pop could have some closure. Peace.

And so could Maddox.

Finally.

EPILOGUE

Three Months Later

THE BANQUET ROOM WAS beautiful. Candles. Lights. NARI had outdone themselves this year on the Evening of Excellence.

Excitement zinged through the room. Everyone waiting for the big moment.

Layla reached for Maddox’s hand under the linen tablecloth. He squeezed it, then ran his thumb over her knuckles.

She sighed and smiled at him.

He sneaked a kiss on the back of her neck.

Chills shot down her spine. How could she love this man any more than she did right at this moment? After all he’d been through with George’s plea arrangements, Maddox had taken the time to come with her to the CotY Awards ceremony.

The emcee took the stage.

The room took a collective intake.

Layla’s palms coated with sweat. She dared not

wipe them on her designer cocktail dress. Alana would kill her.

"Now the Residential Exterior Specialty for region five, south central."

Layla held her breath.

"And the CotY goes to . . ." The emcee ripped open the envelope. "Bayou Construction."

Layla whooshed out air, pulled her slimy hand free from Maddox's hold, and clapped. Disappointment didn't mix well with the sweet iced tea.

After the rest of the awards and dinner, Maddox led Layla to his Mustang in silence. Once he'd tucked her safely into the passenger's seat, he slipped behind the wheel, then turned to face her. "I'm sorry you didn't win."

"You know, I'm disappointed, of course, but it's not upsetting me like I thought it would." Which surprised her. She'd been wanting a national CotY for as long as she'd been a contractor.

"Good, because you don't need some award to let you know how awesome you are." Maddox leaned over the console and wrapped an arm around her shoulders, pulling her toward him. "That's my job now."

His kiss was passionate and filled with love and tenderness, more than she'd ever dreamed.

He backed away, still close enough that his words blew across her face. "You're the most amazing woman I've ever met, Layla Taylor. God blessed me abundantly when He brought you into my life." He planted another kiss on her nose, then leaned back in his seat.

Yes, God had blessed her abundantly as well.

She leaned her head back against the leather seat as Maddox started the car. She closed her eyes, content with life.

She loved a man who loved her and loved God. She had a successful business that she loved. She had a sister who would be getting married in December, as soon as Cameron was ready to meet Alana at the altar. And she had her mother, who she'd not missed visiting every week in months.

Yes, God had blessed her.

She peeked at the love of her life driving. One day soon God would bless her with a father-in-law who reminded her of her own father. As soon as Maddox worked up the nerve to propose to her. And who knew—maybe one day she'd be blessed with a little baby, one born of love with Maddox's blue eyes and her sense of humor.

She smiled as the familiar Scripture of 1 Corinthians 1:9, her father's favorite, flooded her mind:

"God, who has called you into fellowship with his Son Jesus Christ our Lord, is faithful."

Yes, God was indeed faithful.

DEAR READER:

Thank you for journeying with me through the Louisiana bayou as I've shared with you the characters from Eternal Springs. Louisiana is near and dear to my heart, and I've loved sharing some of the culture with you.

The theme of this novel is forgiveness, as it's a topic I think we all deal with on some level quite a bit. I've laughed and cried as I've penned how Layla and Maddox struggle on their journeys to finding forgiveness . . . and acceptance. I hope their story has touched your heart in some small way.

The Roman Road to Salvation is such a laid-out plan from God. Just writing those scenes warmed my heart. After reading this book, if you've felt led to give your life to Christ, please contact me immediately so I may send you a special gift.

As a reader myself, I love hearing from other readers. Please visit me at www.robincaroll.com and drop me a line. I invite you to join my newsletter group and sign my guestbook. I look forward to hearing from you.

Blessings,

Robin Caroll

DISCUSSION QUESTIONS

1. Maddox turned from his faith during a personal trial. What does Scripture tell us about trials? See Psalm 66:10 and James 1:2–3. What major trials have you faced and how did you overcome them?
2. Layla wanted so badly to win a national award to prove her worth in her career. Describe a time in your life when you felt you needed justification from the world to prove yourself worthy in one way or another.
3. Forgiveness is something many of us have difficulty dealing with at times. Describe a time when you gave forgiveness. How did you feel? Now describe a time when you needed forgiveness. Were you given forgiveness or not? How did you feel?
4. What do the following verses state about forgiveness? Matthew 6:12–15; 18:21; and Luke 3:3.
5. Layla found it hard to reconcile with her mother because her mother caused her own condition. Describe a time when a loved one let you down. How did you reconcile your emotions over the disappointment?
6. Ed Young truly believed he was justified in doing bad things to provide for his children. Discuss a time when you've been tempted to

allow the "end to justify the means." What did you learn from the experience?

7. Guilt over his mother's murder plagued Maddox. What does Scripture say about guilt? See Isaiah 6:7; Ezekiel 18:19; and Hebrews 10:22. Have you ever let guilt influence your heart and actions?
8. At some point, we must all let go of the past—the hurts, the wrongs, the feelings. Describe what has been the hardest part of your past to let go. What did/are you doing to move forward?
9. A collection of verses in the book of Romans is referred to as the Roman Road to Salvation (3:23; 5:8; 6:23; and 10:9–13). Describe how these verses are applied to your life, past and present.
10. Layla wouldn't allow herself to fall in love with Maddox because he wasn't a Christian. What does Scripture say about romantic relationships with nonbelievers? See 2 Corinthians 6:14–15. Have you ever dated a nonbeliever? How did that affect your faith?
11. Maddox was ultimately betrayed by his Uncle George. Discuss a time when someone you loved and respected left you feeling betrayed. How did you deal with your emotions? What were you able to learn from the experience?
12. Maddox and Houston were friends as well as

partners. What does Scripture tell us about the importance of friendships? See Proverbs 17:17 and John 15:13. In what ways have your friends been a blessing to you?

13. Layla and her sister were very close. Describe how a loved one has enriched your life. How do you think you've touched theirs?
14. Scripture teaches that God is always faithful. Even during traumatic and tragic times. Yet Maddox didn't feel as if God was faithful to his mother and him. If there have been times when you've felt the same way, how did you overcome those doubts? Discuss how 1 Corinthians 1:9 applies to your life.
15. Everyone has faults. What did you think was Layla's biggest fault? Maddox's? What do you consider your biggest fault?
16. Maddox and his father pushed blame on one another for an instance over which neither really had control. Consider a time when you've been blamed for something that was beyond your control. How was the situation rectified? How did you feel? What insight did you gain from the instance?

Center Point Publishing
600 Brooks Road • PO Box 1
Thorndike ME 04986-0001 USA

(207) 568-3717

US & Canada:
1 800 929-9108
www.centerpointlargeprint.com